Praise for GAV THORPE

"*The Crown of the Conqueror* is an original, thundering bloody infantry-charge of a novel – George R R Martin, you'd better guard your Throne because a new usurper has arrived."

    Andy Remic

"*The Crown of the Blood* should really have a warning sticker on the front... it's one of those books that are almost impossible to put down."

    SFBook.com

"Gav Thorpe writes war as it should be written: brutal, dark, bloody, treacherous, confusing, and insane. The novel is well-written, with a complex plot that promises additional books, ruthless, fully developed characters, and a penchant for psychological realism that makes the book an adult read rather than a childish escape."

    Red Rook Reviews

"The setting and story are well thought out and are remarkably logical for a fantasy novel. If you enjoy military or historical fiction, you will enjoy *The Crown of the Blood*. Action, intrigue, conquest, and charismatic generals are waiting for you here!"

    James Atlantic Speaks

Also by Gav Thorpe

The Crown of the Blood

The Last Chancers
Angels of Darkness
Grudge Bearer
The Claws of Chaos
The Blades of Chaos
The Heart of Chaos
Malekith
Shadow King
Path of the Warrior
The Purging of Kadillus

GAV THORPE

The Crown of the Conqueror

THE CROWN OF THE BLOOD
Book II

**ANGRY
ROBOT**

ANGRY ROBOT
A member of the Osprey Group

Midland House, West Way
Botley, Oxford
OX2 0PH
UK

www.angryrobotbooks.com
The empire strikes back

Originally published in the UK by Angry Robot 2011
First American paperback printing 2011

Copyright © 2011 by Gav Thorpe
Cover art by Paul Young
Set in Meridien by THL Design

Distributed in the United States by Random House, Inc., New York.

ISBN 978-0-85766-121-0
eBook ISBN 978-0-85766-122-7

Printed in the United States of America

9 8 7 6 5 4 3 2 1

To Eric's wife Claudia
for putting up with all my books

ASKH
Spring, 210th year of Askh

I

The Crown lay in the pool of blood, glaring at Ullsaard like a golden eye. The new king wiped the sweat from his face and sat back on his haunches, casting about the throne room for another source of the voice.

He was alone.

He nervously looked at the Crown again. The gold glimmered in the last rays of dusk streaming through the window. Ullsaard noticed the smears, left by his fingers with the blood of Lutaar.

In the stillness he could hear the noises of the city beyond the palace. The coming night brought with it a last effort of looting from his legions before they would return to their camps. Even after three days it seemed that there were still doors left to be broken in, women to scream and defiant citizens to shout their protests.

The distant commotion served only to highlight the unreality of the throne room. A chill gripped Ullsaard as he stood. He backed away from the Crown, keeping one eye on it as if it were a serpent ready to strike. Trailing bloody footprints, Ullsaard crossed back to the throne and the slumped corpse of his predecessor. Lutaar's body had not moved, yet Ullsaard inspected it closely, fearful of some trick.

There was no mistake, Lutaar was most definitely dead. Most of his blood was on the floor, for a start.

With a growl, Ullsaard pulled the former king from the throne and pushed the body to the floor. Kneading his temples, Ullsaard sat down. He was tired, that was the obvious explanation for the voice he thought he had heard. Tired, not just from these past few days, but more than a year of fighting; such worry would take its toll on the hardiest constitution. Now that he was king, he could rest for a while to gather his spent strength.

The argument failed to convince Ullsaard. It was not a nagging inner voice that he had heard, not a vocalisation of his own thoughts. It had been as clear as another person in the room speaking to him, though not through his ears.

Ullsaard returned to his first thought: he was imagining things. While not a desirable development at this moment, it was more palatable than any other explanations; explanations that were half-formed in Ullsaard's mind and thankfully so. The voice had claimed to be Askhos, the first king, founder of the Askhan Empire, but that was impossible. That had been two hundred years ago.

It was far better to contemplate madness than the notion that somehow Askhos lived on two centuries after his death. And so Ullsaard's thoughts came full circle and he resolved to get some sorely needed sleep. The palace was deserted; he would return to his camp and tomorrow enter the city again as its rightful ruler.

"Just a piece of metal," Ullsaard muttered.

He pushed himself up, stalked a few paces from the throne to snatch up the Crown. He looked at it, turning it over and over in his hands. It was quite plain, the type of crown that could be fitted over a helmet. Ullsaard could tell by the weight that it was not even solid gold; more likely it was mostly made of bronze; iron had been even rarer two hundred years ago. It was nothing special. Ullsaard owned parade helms that were worth more in raw material. There was not even a gem or other decoration.

The value of the Crown is not in gold or jewels, Ullsaard.

He flung the crown away as if stung. Ullsaard staggered back, but this time there had been no pain. The king whirled around, convinced that there was another person with him, but the throne room was empty.

I am in the Crown and I am in you.

The voice was softly spoken, calm and assured.

"You are a trick of my mind," said Ullsaard. He strode to a window and took a deep lungful of evening air to calm himself. The smoke of cooking fires carried on the breeze, tinged with the reek of abadas from the legion camps beyond the walls.

I am real. I am Askhos.

Ullsaard shook his head and said nothing. He was not going to indulge this fantasy by speaking to it.

Ignoring me will not make me go away.

"Get out of my thoughts," said Ullsaard, eyes roving the city around the palace, seeking something real to latch on to.

He saw a group of soldiers pulling a heavily laden handcart across the Maarmes bloodfields. At first he thought it was piled with loot, but as they approached he saw more clearly that the cart was heaped with corpses, stripped of everything. There was a captain with them and as they reached the road circling the palace, the soldiers turned towards the street leading to the main gate of the city.

Legionnaires never change. There was a laugh in the voice. *Three days to loot the city and they spend the last night tidying up. You have led them well.*

Ullsaard could ignore the voice no longer; it clearly wasn't going to leave any time soon. Perhaps it was better to confront the voice, show it to be the madness it was.

"You cannot be Askhos," said Ullsaard, turning from the window. "Askhos died a long time ago."

My body died, but my spirit lives on. A body is nothing, just a collection of bones and fat, organs and muscle, nerves and veins. What makes a man is more than just flesh.

"How can that be?" said Ullsaard. "How can a spirit live on without the flesh to sustain it?"

It cannot. The Crown has been my temporary refuge, but I have lived again in each king that has worn it.

Ullsaard shook his head. The voice made no sense. He reverted to his earlier tactic of denial.

"You are just a trick of my mind, nothing more."

Could a trick of your mind tell you about the founding of this city? For instance, this hall took three years to build. The stone for the walls came from a quarry seventy miles to coldwards. The overseer was a short, fat man called Heraales. The marble of the floor came from even further away, in the mountains between Askhor and Maasra. A caravan of seven hundred abadas was needed to bring it to this place. Seventeen masons fashioned the dome above you. Three of them died during the construction, falling when the scaffolding collapsed. I can tell you their names as well, if you like.

"Stop it!" Ullsaard surprised himself, his shout ringing back from the walls. "This is nonsense. This cannot be."

Yes it can, and it is. Listen to me carefully, because you have done a very foolish thing and it is important that you believe me. I am Askhos. I am the spirit of the founding king, given immortal life through the bodies of my offspring. As each body died, I returned to the Crown, ready to take over the body of the next.

"The eldest heir of every generation. That is why Lutaar was adamant that Aalun could not become king."

Not Lutaar. Me. The Crown and the Blood are linked; are as one. The Blood holds the key to my immortality, and that bond is strongest in the eldest living son.

"I still cannot understand how such a thing is possible."

And you never will, Ullsaard. Think of it as sorcery, or perhaps the gift of the spirits the Salphors insist on worshipping. It is an alignment of many different things that enabled me to separate my being from the confines of a single mortal shell. It is not the only way that immortality can be attained, my brother took another, but it suited my purposes the best.

"Purposes? What purposes? And why would you keep such a thing secret?"

My purpose was to build this empire. Everything in the Book of Askhos is true. It is my grand plan, and it must be fulfilled. I could not risk the faltering of this great project, and so I took steps and made bargains to ensure that I would remain to guide it to completion. You have put that plan at risk and we must act to set things right.

Ullsaard picked up on something the voice – Askhos, if it was to be believed – had said.

"You said you made bargains. Bargains with whom?"

It does not matter, Ullsaard. It is ancient history, more ancient even than the two hundred years of this empire. I suppose I should thank you for one thing.

"What is that?"

Until now I did not know what would happen if another took the Crown. It seems that the Blood is strong enough in you to sustain me, yet not strong enough for me to take control.

"Is that what you did? You took control of your sons, ruled them from within?"

They were never really aware of it, simply shadows of themselves lurking at the back of my mind. I became them and they were simply put to one side.

Ullsaard dashed across the throne room and picked up the Crown. He pulled it down onto his head, congealed blood spreading, sticking to his forehead.

"Get out!" he snarled. "Go back to your Crown!"

Askhos laughed, touched with bitterness.

You have split me, Ullsaard. Part of me is still in the Crown, which I suspect is why I have not been able to push you aside. It is not like picking a tent to sleep in. I am here and in the Crown. This is as much uncharted territory for me as it is for you. There is only one who can unravel this tangle for us, but he is far away.

"Perhaps if I destroy the Crown? Then I will be free."

Askhos laughed again.

Destroy it? Melt it in a fire? Please do. And when you have, explain to the people of Askhor why you have done so. Some will believe you to be mad and have you slain; others will believe you tell the truth and will insist that I be allowed to rule. And there is no guarantee that breaking the Crown will remove me from your head.

Ullsaard groaned and pulled off the Crown, tempted for a moment to toss it out of a window. He stopped himself, knowing the truth of Askhos's words. To admit that something was amiss with the Crown, with himself, would be to invite doubt about his rightful rule.

Your civil war has brought the empire to the brink of ruin, Ullsaard. With my help, you must rebuild it. Firstly, you must lift your ban on the Brotherhood.

"Not a chance," said Ullsaard. "The Brotherhood were loyal to Lutaar. They will do everything they can to undermine me and restore Kalmud to the throne. Your oldest surviving heir still lives, and while he does there is the chance that you can trick him out of his body as you did your other sons. Don't take me for a fool."

From the moment Aalun brought you to my attention I never thought you a fool, Ullsaard. I should have recognised the Blood in you, but I thought it impossible. For two hundred years the succession, the intermarriages, the traditions served to keep me in power. All of that undone because Cosuas fell in love and allowed your mother to bear you. Still, I do not dwell on the past. The Brotherhood is the core of Greater Askhor. Without them there is no empire.

"We will do fine…" Ullsaard trailed off as he heard footsteps in the hallway beyond the throne chamber doors. He hurried across to the throne and sat down, holding the Crown in his lap.

The double doors opened a crack and a head poked round, a red crest hanging from the man's helm. Ullsaard recognised him immediately: it was Rondin, First Captain of the Fifth. The legion commander took a tentative step into the throne room, banged a fist to his breastplate and stood to attention.

"You told us to gather here at the start of Duskwatch, general," said Rondin. The other first captains – Donar, Anasind, Jutiil and Luamid – filed in behind him and offered their salutes.

"King," said Ullsaard. "I am not your general anymore, I am your king."

"Of course, king," said Rondin, nodding in apology. "Old habit."

Ullsaard smiled and waved them to approach.

"Time to develop a new habit," he said. He twisted and hung the Crown on the back of the throne, trying to appear dismissive. "At midnight the licence for the Legions to sack the city ends. Have your best companies on the streets to enforce the cessation of looting. We must send a strong signal to Askh and the rest of the empire that the turmoil has finished. From tomorrow, the labour continues under me as it did under Lutaar.

"Jutiil, I need you to search the city for any counsellors, treasurers, nobles and advisors from Lutaar's court. Bring

13

them to the palace. Nicely, if you can; forcefully, if you have to. With the Brotherhood disbanded, we have to set up a new administration."

You cannot replace the Brotherhood.

Ullsaard stopped at the interruption. He caught himself just about to reply and abruptly shut his mouth, earning himself odd looks from his First Captains. He waited for a moment to see if Askhos had anything else to say. The dead king stayed silent.

"The division, the anarchy of the past year is over. I am king and Greater Askhor will continue. Not only continue, it will grow, stronger than ever." He looked at his commanders and smiled. "We have fought hard for this day. We have earned it. Tomorrow will bring the rewards."

Dismissed by a nod from their new king, the First Captains saluted and filed out of the chamber, leaving Ullsaard alone with his thoughts.

Not alone, he remembered. Not alone at all.

II

The bloodfields, circuit and wrestling circles of Maarmes were filled with people. The babble of thousands died away as Ullsaard ascended the steps to the stage overlooking the crowd. On the stepped rows of benches behind him sat the noble families, the merchants rich enough to bribe their way onto the seats and the leaders of many other civic organisations, including lawyers, academics and master craftsmen.

All watched Ullsaard with wary eyes.

Glancing over the high society of Askh, he caught the eye of Etor Astaan, father to Ullsaard's friend Noran. The king had sought Noran's family that morning, to deliver the news that their son had almost died saving Ullsaard's life and was now in a coma, being tended to by the king's

14

family in Magilnada. Etor had taken the news placidly, and though he did not say as such his few comments implied he thought Noran an idiot for getting involved with Ullsaard's coup. Noran's mother had been equally stoic and displayed greater sorrow at the news of the death of her daughter-in-law and stillborn grandson.

Ullsaard had fled the awkward situation as soon as was polite, and the Astaans had been happy to see him leave. Now they looked at him with apathetic gazes. They were not alone. There were many on the benches of the nobles that had only attended this announcement through subtle and not-so-subtle coercion by Ullsaard's First Captains.

Regardless of how they had been brought here, every family was represented. It was important to conjure this display of support before the masses of Askh. Though they did not yet know it, it would also be important for the nobles; Ullsaard was about to make them all an offer they would find hard to refuse.

Several hundred legionnaires stood as a cordon around the outthrust of the stage. At a shout from their captains, they turned to face the king and lifted their spears in salute. This nicety attended to, they turned back to keep a watch on the restless crowd.

"This last year and more has been a trying time for all people of Greater Askhor," declared Ullsaard. From a life of parade grounds and battle orders he was able to pitch his voice to the furthest members of the crowd without much effort.

Thousands of pairs of eyes, men and women, children and elders, gazed up at him. There were some smiles, but not many. He could feel the fear of some in the crowd, worried what this change in rule meant for them. Most of all he saw anxiety, desperation. The people were eager for stability, for a return to their normal lives.

"I am your king now. Most of you will have heard of me. For those of you who have not, you can see for yourselves the manner of man that now rules this empire. I am of the Blood, a son of King Lutaar. I fought as a legionnaire, commanded a company, led a legion and became the most successful general of this generation. What I set my mind to, I achieve. Standing here before you is testament to that fact."

He approached the front of the stage and stretched out a hand, encompassing the crowd in its sweep.

"None of that matters. Greater Askhor is not the artifice of one man, though it was founded as such. All of us make this empire. You, the proud people of Askh; the noble and wealthy that sit behind me; and me. I have shown that no king rules without the consent of his people. I ask for your loyalty and your service. In return, I will give you safety and prosperity."

Ullsaard paused, allowing this to sink in. He hesitated, knowing the next part of his speech to be a lie. He readied himself for a complaint from Askhos, determined that he would not be distracted.

"The empire has not changed because another now wears the Crown of the Blood. Kings are born and kings die, just like any other men." He waited, expecting some comment from Askhos. The dead king said nothing. "The empire is all of us, and still bigger than all of us. And it is my intent that it will grow larger still."

Pulling out his sword, Ullsaard turned to duskwards and pointed the blade.

"Salphoria. Many of you will know of this place, beyond our borders. It was Askhos's will that the empire stretch from sea to sea. This summer, the legions of Askh will march on a great conquest, and bring the wilderness of Salphoria into civilisation. My soldiers cannot do this

16

alone. They will need the spears forged in your smithies. They will need the kilts tanned in your workshops. They will need the grain grown on your farms.

"And when Salphoria kneels before me, the rewards will be many. Gold and grain, jewels and livestock, bronze and stone, timber and iron. Salphoria is rich in all of these things. Prized farmlands await those with the knowledge to sow and till it properly. Vineyards and quarries, for those that can manage such concerns. These will become Askhan. These will become yours."

Now the moment had arrived. Ullsaard took a breath, full of pride. He turned to face the nobles, sheathing his sword.

"In the first days of the empire, Askhos bid his allies to form armies and conquer the world. He promised the spoils of victory to those that could take them. As your new king, I renew this pledge. The ancient rights of conquest are restored. Let the man with the strength and wealth, the courage and the ferocity, raise up a legion to claim what is rightfully his. Salphoria awaits us, and its many rewards. Stand by me, help me take this land, and it is yours."

He was confronted by a wall of disbelieving faces. The nobles exchanged glances with each other, some of them whispering to their neighbours. It was not the response Ullsaard had hoped for. Perhaps he had not made his offer clear enough?

"I am reinstating the rights of the noble families to raise and lead their own legions again. This summer, any of you can march to Salphoria and take what rightfully belongs to you." He rounded on the crowd. "Whoever here that marches with me will get their fair share as well. As it was in the time of Askhos, so it is again. Too long the power has been hoarded by the Brotherhood and the governors. I am setting free the shackles that have chained the beast that is Greater Askhor. This is a new time of glory. It is yours to seize!"

"These are different times." Ullsaard looked back at the nobles to see who had spoken. Laadir Irrin, head of one of the oldest and most powerful families, stood up. "Our forefathers were warlords and chieftains. What do we know of war?"

Ullsaard smiled, for he had expected this argument and already had a counter for it.

"There are many fine officers in the legions, and many that have retired who would consider again the opportunity to conquer for Askh. If you have not the stomach for the battle yourself, appoint another to lead in your place."

This provoked the reaction that Ullsaard had hoped for. There were shouts of protest and prideful boasts. No matter the pampered existence of many on the noble seats, they nevertheless shared the notion that they were brave and great leaders like their ancestors.

Surprisingly, it was Etor Astaan that stood next.

"I will raise a legion," he declared. "Though it has been generations since the Astaan's led an army in battle, I would not spurn the challenge."

This prompted more conspiratorial whispering. The nobles were finally realising the import of what Ullsaard was doing. If one amongst them raised a legion, not only would that shame the others, it would put them at a distinct commercial disadvantage. Ullsaard was right about the riches of Salphoria, and if he was forcing them to take their own share, they would have to act.

Others stood up and raised their fists, declaring their intent to lead a legion. Even a few of the merchants added their voices, earning themselves scornful laughter from the nobles. Ullsaard strode toward the mass of citizens spread across the field.

"Do not let these noble bastards have all the fun!" he roared. "Who here has the mettle to be a legionnaire? Which of you could be a First Captain?"

Claims and counter-claims were shouted up to Ullsaard. He unsheathed his sword again, rammed it into the planks of the stage and knelt beside it, looking at the crowd with wide eyes.

"Which of you wants a vine terrace in the Altes Hills? Who would like a mill on the Geinan River? How about running one of those salt mines?" He waved away his own suggestions. "Forget that! Who here would like a house in Carantathi? Perhaps you could live in the palaces of Aegenuis himself, with his hundreds of servants to attend you! Or perhaps the hot-blooded amongst you want to find out if those Salphorian girls are as feisty as some claim?"

He stood up and stretched his arms wide, fists clenched.

"It is in our blood to rule! Askhos decreed it, and we shall make it happen. Join me! Fight with me!"

The legionnaires led the cheers, all thought of watching the crowd forgotten. There was no more fear, there was no uncertainty. Every man and woman cheered, imagining the riches and comfort this campaign would bring.

Ullsaard ripped his sword from the stage and held it aloft.

"Askhor!" he bellowed. "Fight for Askhor!"

III

It was past midnight when Ullsaard finally slouched back to his chambers. He was surprised to find his chief servant waiting for him. With Ariid were two young, shaven-headed Maasrites, who Ullsaard assumed were also part of his household though he did not recall seeing them before.

"I believe all of the servants of the Blood left the palace, master," said Ariid. "If you still wish it, I will continue in your service."

Ullsaard slapped a hand to Ariid's arm.

"Why would I not want you? And who are these pair?"

"These are Keaila and Aminea, master," said Ariid. "The rest of the staff are on their way to Magilnada to attend to your family."

"Yes, of course they are," said Ullsaard, though it was news to him. Domestic arrangements had been the last thing on his mind since coming to Askh four days ago. "I am ready for bed."

"Everything is prepared, master. I was not sure whether you would stay here or in the king's chambers and so have made arrangements in both. Before you retire, there is someone who has been waiting to see you."

"I am too tired, Ariid. Tell him to come back tomorrow."

Ullsaard started towards the door to his bedroom but was stopped by a voice from the archway leading to the feasting rooms.

"That is an uncivil welcome for your son." Ullsaard span around to see his youngest, Ullnaar, leaning against the archway, a half-eaten apple in his hand. "And after I waited up for you…"

The king shook his son's hand, studying him intently. Ullnaar had changed so much since he had last seen him. There were patches of bristle on his chin and cheeks, and his face was harder-edged, no sign of the chubbiness that had filled his cheeks. His hair was close-cropped, the same golden blonde as his mother's.

The eyes showed the greatest difference. There were rings of fatigue under them.

"You look like you've had less sleep than me," said Ullsaard.

Ullnaar shrugged.

"When you came through the Wall, Lutaar tried to break the sanctuary of the colleges. I think he intended to take me hostage as last resort. Meemis and the other teachers hid me away until the soldiers had to leave to fight you. I was afraid, I admit. It was not until you came into the city yesterday that I realised I was safe."

"You are safe," said Ullsaard. "And tonight you will sleep here."

Ullnaar nodded and smiled. Beneath the cheery expression, Ullsaard detected the traces of the fear that had haunted his son. He had never thought Lutaar would breach the sanctity of the college grounds; sanctity laid down by Askhos himself.

Knowing what he now did, Ullsaard realised that Lutaar was Askhos, in some confusing fashion, and Askhos would have no qualms breaking his own rules if he needed to. It worried Ullsaard that he had heard nothing from the dead king all day; not a single insult, warning or unwanted piece of advice.

"Is something the matter, father?"

Ullsaard snapped out of his thoughts, realising he had been staring at Ullnaar. He returned his son's smile.

"I'm more tired than a whore after a legion's marched into town. I'm sorry, but we will have to talk properly in the morning. I'm in no fit state at the moment."

Ullnaar nodded and shook his father's hand again.

"Congratulations, *King* Ullsaard," he said. Ullsaard laughed, hung an arm over Ullnaar's shoulders and pulled him into a tight embrace, much to his son's embarrassment.

"Thank you, *Prince* Ullnaar."

Ullsaard let go and stepped away. He turned for the bedroom and almost stumbled through the door. He threw off his armour and clothes, while Ariid followed him around the room, picking them up. With a sigh, Ullsaard threw himself onto the bed.

Within moments he was snoring soundly. Almost as quickly, Ullsaard dreamt.

He imagined himself waking up in a cave. As he looked around he realised it was not so much a natural cave; the walls were smooth and hand-worked and a lintel of black granite topped the square door.

It was a mausoleum of some kind. At the far end of the long, low chamber sat a stone casket. A bearded man a little shorter than himself sat on the top of the stone box. He was middle-aged, with weatherworn features, dressed in a simple white kilt and a leather breastplate.

He looked very familiar.

"I've seen your face before," said Ullsaard

He approached the man, head stooped beneath a ceiling carved with spirals and shallow runes. He realised the floor and walls were decorated the same. The only light came through the door, a cold twilight that hid more in shadow than it revealed. The man gestured for Ullsaard to sit in front of him. Ullsaard stayed standing. He realised where he had seen the face before: on the golden icons of the legions.

"So this is what you really look like, Askhos? The banners bear a very good likeness."

Askhos smiled, but his eyes showed no mirth.

"They were fashioned from my death mask," said the first king of Askh. "I always thought they made me look fatter than I was."

Ullsaard looked around at the crypt and a thought occurred to him.

"This is where you are buried, isn't it?"

"Yes, this is my tomb," said Askhos.

"Nobody knows where it is."

"I do, and that is what is important."

Ullsaard walked towards to the open entrance, looking over his shoulder at Askhos.

"I can easily find out," he said. "I'm sure it's in Askhor somewhere, and I'll recognise a landmark or something."

"You are welcome to try," said Askhos, waving a hand towards the gleam of cold light.

Through the door, Ullsaard could see nothing but starry sky. Guessing that they were atop a hill, he ducked beneath the lintel stone and stepped out for a better view.

Ullsaard's panicked yelp echoed from the stones and he fell back into the tomb. Askhos's laughter rang around him. Ullsaard twisted to his hands and knees, eyes wide with horror.

"There was nothing," he said quietly, looking at Askhos. "Nothing but dust and the stars."

Askhos's laughter died away and he beckoned Ullsaard to come closer. The first king slapped a hand against the lid of the stone coffin.

"My bones are safer here than anywhere in the world," he said. "You see, I am a careful man and it would not do to let my remains fall into the hands of another."

Ullsaard's first thought was that if he could destroy Askhos's remains, he might rid himself of the dead king. He kept the revelation from his expression.

"I am in your head, Ullsaard. And in your dreams. Do you think you can keep your thoughts from me? Give up this idea. You do not know where this place is, no man does. Even if you were to find out where my body lies, you have not the means to reach it. There is no escape for you in that way."

Ullsaard growled, annoyed with himself, feeling betrayed by his own thoughts.

"So why have you brought me here? Why have you said nothing to me while I was awake?"

Askhos's face was marred by consternation.

"I did not bring you to this place. I have been speaking to you all day, have you not heard me?"

"Not a word, for which I am thankful," said Ullsaard. He walked up to Askhos and bent until his face was level with the first king's. "You don't have any more idea what's happening than I do."

Askhos did not flinch or lean away, but met Ullsaard's stare with his own.

"I do not know exactly what is happening, but I can make a far more informed guess than you. Tell me, back in the world where you sleep, where is the Crown?"

"I locked it in a vault," said Ullsaard. "I have no desire to wear it for the moment, but it needs to be kept safe."

Askhos said nothing, but there was a hint of a nod, as if he had an inkling of what was affecting him. Ullsaard spoke his reasoning aloud.

"You were in the Crown. I put on the Crown. Some of you passed into me, but some of you stayed in the Crown." He smiled triumphantly. "The further I am from the Crown, the weaker that part of you that is in my head."

"Not just your head, Ullsaard. I am in every part of you. I am you as much as you are. When you scratch your arse, I feel it. When you are hungry, I am hungry too. I see what you see, I hear what you hear."

"I am still in the palace. That is not so far away. Let us see what you hear and feel when I am scratching my arse in Salphoria, two thousand miles away."

"No!" Genuine horror clouded Askhos's face. "Do not leave the Crown behind!"

"Afraid of being lonely, old king?"

Askhos opened his mouth to protest, but closed it, utterly helpless. His shoulders sagged and he pinched the bridge of his nose as if he had a headache. When Askhos looked at Ullsaard again there was an imploring look in his eyes.

"Do not destroy the empire, Ullsaard. It is too valuable to risk."

"I have no intention of doing anything but make the empire stronger," Ullsaard replied, stepping back. He crossed his arms, annoyed by the accusation. "It is your plan that we rule all the lands between the seas. I will make that dream a reality."

"But you are going too fast, Ullsaard! It is not yet the time to take on Salphoria. And without the Brotherhood... Without the Brotherhood, you will fail. And when you fail, Greater Askhor will fail with you. You have Magilnada. That is a start. Cosuas has explored the Greenwater. Go hotwards and consolidate what he has taken, and push the Mekhani from their desert. There is no need to start a war with the Salphors yet."

"It is too late," said Ullsaard. "Not that I would change my course on your counsel. Already the nobles are raiding their treasuries to see how many legions they can raise."

"What have you done?" Askhos pushed himself from the casket and stalked towards Ullsaard. "What have you done?"

Ullsaard stood his ground.

"I thought you knew everything I did? Did you not hear my speech today?"

Askhos frowned and thrust an accusing finger at Ullsaard.

"Tell me what you have done? Why are the nobles paying for legions?"

"I am simply doing what you did, mighty Askhos. Rights of conquest have been given back to the noble families."

Askhos threw his hands up to his head and snarled.

"That is madness! They will fight you and each other, scrabbling over the spoils. There are reasons I withdrew those rights, curbed the power of the nobles and the legions. The empire does not need them now."

Ullsaard shrugged.

"By the end of the summer, it will be irrelevant. Salphoria will be part of Greater Askhor and the nobles will be so busy counting their new riches and measuring their new lands they won't even have a second thought to my taking of the Crown."

"A bribe? That's all this is? A bribe to the nobles to stop them arguing your claim to rule?"

Ullsaard shrugged.

"I was quite pleased with the idea. I came up with it myself. I will be going to Salphoria as well, to make sure things do not get out of hand."

Askhos shook his head and slumped back against the coffin.

"Take the Crown with you. Leave it in Magilnada if you have to, but do not be so far from it that I cannot see what is happening. You will need my help, Ullsaard. I have ruled this empire for more than two hundred years. What better advisor could you have?"

Ullsaard considered this proposal for a moment.

"One that isn't dead? One that doesn't want me dead so that he can reclaim his throne? Those would be a good start. I'm through with you. If I never hear from you again, it would be for the best."

"Don't…"

The whole scene shimmered and faded. Ullsaard felt his body disintegrating, flowing back into greyness.

And then he slept again, and had no more dreams.

MAGILNADA
Spring, 210th year of Askh

I

The stink of beer and sweat was strong in the drinking cellar, tinged with urine from the piss hole behind a curtain in the corner. Gelthius was leaning against the uneven stone wall, his chair rocked back on two legs, feet up on the stained wood of the table. A half-full cup rested on his chestplate, kept in place by his clasped fingers. His helmet was tipped forward over his eyes, but he wasn't asleep.

On the other side of the table, Loordin and Sergeant Muuril were indulging in some drunken finger-wrestling, hands entwined as each tried to twist the other man's wrist far enough to make him submit. Further down the table, Juruun was picking over the plates for scraps of food; he was always a hungry drunk.

Next to Gelthius, Gebriun was slumped in a puddle of red wine, one arm used as a pillow, the other dangling uselessly. Gelthius's first thought was how much of a pain it was going to be to get the stain out of Gebriun's tunic. They'd all have to help; otherwise the whole company would be punished.

But that was not an immediate issue; they had another day of leave before they had to head back to camp outside

Magilnada. For the last three days, the Thirteenth had whored, drank and eaten their way through everything the city had to offer. It was a last gasp of freedom before they marched on Salphoria proper.

Gelthius had mixed feelings about that. The advance duskwards would bring him closer to his family, but he was uncomfortable with the idea of Askhan legions tearing across Salphoria. There was no telling where they might end up and who they might kill.

"Smells even more like shit than normal."

Gelthius peered out from under the lip of his helm at a group of legionnaires staggering down the steps into the cellar. They had armfuls of cups and jugs with them, splashing wine and beer into the thin layer of straw covering the floor. He recognised them as members of the Fifteenth, survivors of the Greenwater campaign and the defence of Askh. As the twenty-or-so legionnaires fell along the benches and tables just across the cellar, one of them met Gelthius's gaze.

"And here's the reason it stinks," said the soldier. He nudged a few of his companions and pointed at Gelthius. "They let in fucking Salphor pigs."

There were sneers and jeers, but Gelthius ignored them. Muuril wasn't so forgiving. The sergeant pulled his hand free from the finger-wrestling and stood up. Loordin woke up Gebriun, who rose from his puddle with a snort.

"Didn't we just kick the shit out of you cunts already?" said Muuril.

There were scrapes of chairs as some of the other legionnaires in the drinking den turned to watch the inevitable fight. Most of them were from the Fifth, Donar's legion. If things got out of hand, they would weigh in with the Thirteenth, Gelthius hoped. After all, the two legions had fought side-by-side for two years during Ullsaard's grab for the throne.

"What did you say, pig fucker?" This was from the Fifteenth's sergeant, who emptied a goblet of wine into his mouth and tossed the cup to the floor in front of Muuril.

"What did you just call me?" Muuril cracked his knuckles, as much a part of the pre-fight ritual as the insults.

"Pig fucker."

Muuril looked around at his men, and then across to the soldiers from the Fifth.

"But I ain't never met your wife," said Muuril. Laughter filled the cellar for a moment while the Fifteenth's sergeant looked on impassively. "Tell you what, why don't you suck my cock for me instead?"

This brought a few gasps from the Fifth, spits and curses from the Fifteenth. This time it was their sergeant's turn to smile.

"But I don't want to know what your mother's shit tastes like," he said.

Gelthius didn't see who threw the first jug; it might have even been one of the Fifth. Within moments, the two groups of legionnaires were lunging at each other, fists ready.

A solid left hook caught Gelthius on the brow, knocking him back. A legionnaire backed away, shaking his hand painfully, knuckles likely broken against Gelthius's skull. Gelthius launched into the fray, kicking and punching, aiming for arms and legs.

It was a brawl, not a proper fight. No knives were drawn and in the close press of bodies it was hard to land a proper blow. Bodies grappled and rolled over the tables; bottles smashed. There were as many curses and insults as punches. Muuril and the other sergeant made for each other immediately. Gelthius's superior landed a good blow against his opponent's chin, rocking him back a step. He followed up by driving his knee into the man's gut. That was a mistake. His kneecap rang against armour. Muuril howled and fell back, clutching his leg.

The Fifteenth's sergeant raised a foot to stomp on Muuril but Gelthius dived into the gap, tackling the other sergeant to the ground. He smashed his elbow into the man's nose before being shoved to one side, rolling out of the way as a legionnaire from the Fifth lost his footing and almost fell on top of Gelthius.

Gebriun caught Gelthius in the eye with a flailing hand as he fended off a punch. The Salphor heaved himself to his feet, driving his shoulder into the chest of another man, legs pumping until the two of them tripped over a fallen chair and collapsed in a heap.

Untangling himself from man and furniture, Gelthius heard the tramping of more feet on the steps. He looked over his shoulder and saw armed legionnaires jogging down into the cellar. The designs on their shields marked them out as the Second Magilnadan, their officer calling for peace.

"This will not be tolerated!" the captain bellowed.

The struggling slowly ceased as the officer reached the bottom of the steps.

"Your names and companies will be taken. You will be punished for this ill-discipline."

There were glances between the legionnaires; nods of agreement between men who had been trying to batter each other unconscious just moments before. Gelthius helped up the man he had hurled to the floor and received a pat on the shoulder as thanks.

Muuril and the other sergeant seemed to lean against each other. As they broke apart, the man from the Fifteenth spun around to his men.

"Run for it!"

The legionnaires – Fifteenth, Thirteenth and Fifth – needed no further encouragement. As a solid mass, they swept pass the officer and plunged into the legionnaires on the stairs, sending them sprawling. Gelthius ran with the rest of them, shouting an apology over his shoulder as he stepped on the arm of a man who had fallen.

There were more soldiers from the Second Magilnadan upstairs; five of them between the erupting mob and the door to the street. Three had enough sense to jump out of the way; the other two were swept out of the tavern by the mass of legionnaires making a bid for freedom. Tumbling into the dirt street outside, shields and spears trampled underfoot, they were soon lost from view. Gelthius was one of the first to reach the door and broke left.

"Scatter! Back to the camp when you can!"

Gelthius didn't recognise the voice but took the advice anyway. With the others, he pounded down the cobbled road, the group growing smaller and smaller as others broke away into side streets and alleys. Laughing, Gelthius stumbled under an arched bridge linking two buildings.

He almost ran straight into another officer. Pulling himself back at the last moment, he twisted aside. The officer stopped and turned. With horror, Gelthius realised it was King Ullsaard. He straightened himself as best as he could, banging a fist to his chest in salute.

Ullsaard looked at him for a moment. The king cocked his head to one side, listening as the shouts of the hue and cry echoed through the archway.

"Are you running away from someone, legionnaire?" asked Ullsaard.

"Yes, your majesty," said Gelthius. There was no point denying it.

The king looked at him for a moment longer, and then his gaze moved past Gelthius and under the arch.

"Best keep running," said Ullsaard, gently but firmly pushing Gelthius to the left, back towards the centre of Magilnada.

With a grateful nod and a lop-sided smile, Gelthius set off, winking at the bodyguard of Thirteenth Legionnaires following their king. Just as the road took a sharp turn, he looked back and saw King Ullsaard haranguing the captain of the Second Magilnadan.

"Spirits bless you, general," Gelthius whispered to himself as he disappeared into the market crowds.

II

A second city as large as Magilnada stretched across the plains hotwards of the city gate. The gap between the Lidean and Minean mountain ranges was full of Askhans, nearly ninety thousand of them. More than ten thousand had already marched duskwards into Salphoria, led by impatient amateur commanders.

As he had done many times in the past days, Anglhan rubbed his hands with glee. All those men, who needed food, water, whores, abadas, rope, wine, sandals, and a hundred other things beside; all of them bringing chests full of askharins into his city. He had not hoarded it all to himself; he was greedy but not stupid. More than half the gold he had taken in taxes had been spent improving his two Magilnadan legions; recruiting and equipping three thousand more men, and ensuring both legions had plentiful armour, weapons and rations. He had invested in twenty of the Askhan spear-throwing machines, and had been disappointed to discover that with the Brotherhood prohibited by Ullsaard, lava-throwers were no longer available.

That was the money he considered his 'civic' fund, which he set aside for expenses concerning the city. From his personal fortune he had bribed quite a few Hillman chiefs to cease their raids from further into the mountains, persuading them that they could get more by staying at home than they could by harassing the caravans moving between Greater Askhor and the newly-conquered territories of the Free Country.

The rest he was spending as the mood took him. The palaces on the Hill of Chieftains at Magilnada's heart had never looked so grand, nor been filled with so many servants, administrators and general lackeys.

He huffed onto the gold and silver rings adorning his left hand and polished them on his woollen shirt, enjoying the lustre of gems and pearls. A clatter of feet on the gatehouse steps caused him to turn. Ullsaard was the first out of the tower. Seeing the Askhan king reminded Anglhan that he would need to despatch agents to procure him an ailur, purely for display; he had no intention of riding one of the fearsome war-cats.

"Hail King Ullsaard," Anglhan said with a grin. "I trust everything is to your satisfaction?"

"No, it isn't" said Ullsaard. "There's no decent road to march on beyond ten miles from the city and half of the legions haven't got campsites with fresh water."

"I have been sending water from our wells to help them," said Anglhan.

"Yes, and charging the First Captains for the pleasure," said Ullsaard.

"I have expenses," Anglhan said with a lugubrious shrug. "Wells don't dig themselves, and water doesn't leap into the buckets on its own, nor flow into barrels or drive abada carts."

Ullsaard answered only with a long, penetrating stare. Anglhan smiled.

"I promise that I have made no profit on the water, Ullsaard," said the governor. "My costs and charges are open to be examined."

"Yes, I'm sure they are," said Ullsaard. He sighed heavily. "What about the whores and merchants you keep sending into the camps?"

"I have not sent anybody, spirits strike me down if I lie!" said Anglhan. "It is not my place to tell proper tradesmen, and women, where they can and cannot go."

"You're a fucking governor, not a market stall holder," snapped Ullsaard. "I am issuing a general order tomorrow: any person found within half a mile of a legion camp without a token of passage will be killed. This whole area is full of mongrel bastards from all over the mountains and Salphoria. There's no telling what they've seen and who they're telling it to."

"And how does someone get a token of passage?" asked Anglhan.

"From me or a First Captain."

Anglhan pouted for a moment.

"Can a governor not issue them?"

Ullsaard's jaw twitched with irritation and his eyes narrowed.

"No, a governor can't," he said. "And if they could, I wouldn't let you near the things. You'd be selling them to the highest bidder quicker than they could be made."

Anglhan chose not to comment. He leaned his arms on the parapet and stared out over the assembling armies.

"This province needs a name," Ullsaard said, joining the governor. "Your patch is bigger than just Magilnada, and I'm not inclined to call it Free Country for long, it gives people the wrong idea."

"It used to be called the Faellina, or at least the tribes who used to live here were called that. That's how it works in Salphoria; the place is named after the people, not the other way around like you Askhans."

"I'm not Askhan, remember? I was born in Enair."

Anglhan waved away the quibble.

"The point still stands, Ullsaard. In Salphoria, the peoples and the areas are the same. There are no borders, none that you'd recognise. One chieftain says to another chieftain, 'The land this side of the forest is mine' and the other chieftain says that is fine with him or gets an axe in the head. That area gets named after the tribe, until the second chieftain gets brave enough to put an axe in the other man's head or his people grow numerous enough to gently shoulder the first tribe out of the way. You think Magilnada is a mongrel region? You're going to get even more confused the further duskwards you go."

Ullsaard cleared his throat, tapped his fingers on the top of the wall for a moment and then turned sideways to look at Anglhan.

"Faellina? Right. That's what we'll put on the maps."

The two of them said nothing for a while, both with their own thoughts. It was Anglhan that broke the quiet.

"Have you seen your family yet?"

Ullsaard shook his head.

"Haven't plucked up the courage for it yet. I'm going to get it in the neck because of the whole Meliu and Noran divorce... thing. I can't face my wives just yet. Ullnaar came with me; he headed to the house as soon as we arrived. I'll let him comfort his mother for a while before I show my face."

Anglhan said nothing. He had not delivered the letter from Ullsaard announcing his intent to divorce his youngest wife. Ullsaard must have seen something in Anglhan's face.

"Is there something else I should be worried about?" asked the king. "My wives are well? Noran is still alive?".

Anglhan couldn't meet Ullsaard's fierce stare.

"I didn't exactly hand over the letter…" said the governor. He continued before Ullsaard could say anything, the words spilling out. "Look, it didn't seem the right time when Noran was so bad, and you weren't king yet, and Allenya was heartbroken, and so was Meliu. They didn't need anything else to concern themselves with."

Ullsaard growled and stalked away. Anglhan watched the king until he had stepped into the tower. It was clear that not everything was going as well as Ullsaard had imagined. The governor would have to tread lightly while the king was around.

And that reminded him of another appointment. If he hurried back to the palace, he would have a bit of free time before Furlthia arrived.

III

It seemed as if every third person on the streets was a legionnaire. Furlthia weaved through the crowds, his hood drawn up as a gentle shower enveloped Magilnada. From the shadow, his eyes roved over everything. He noted the shield insignia of the different legions – at least five that he recognised, two others that were new to him. He watched the captains and victuallers haggling with craftsmen and armourers, while groups of soldiers emptied entire stalls of meat and vegetables into their sacks. The army had taken so much grain there was barely a sack or loaf of bread for the people of the city.

Furlthia grunted with annoyance. This was exactly what he had warned Anglhan would happen; the Askhans taking what they wanted and leaving nothing for anyone else. He knew any protests he might make would fall on deaf ears. Anglhan was involved in every part of the city, from the gate taxes to the bribes and contract levies. No doubt the governor was enjoying every moment of the boom.

And there was little likelihood of the situation changing. Magilnada was perfectly placed between Greater Askhor and Salphoria, and when the empire had conquered everything to duskward, the city would remain the pivotal centre of trade, dominating the road between the mountains.

As Furlthia cut through the Garden of Spirits, he dawdled for a while, paying his respects at the multitude of shrines. He looked at the decorated trees, the piles of pebbles on the chapelstones, the prayer-scripts and colourful ribbons hanging tattered from the flowering bushes. At least Anglhan had kept the Askhan Brotherhood out of the city. If he had not, these shrines would have been swept aside. Furlthia imagined one of the austere pyramids of the Brotherhood where he was standing, glowering down upon the city below.

As he heard bells ringing the time, he admitted to himself there were a few Askhan innovations that were preferable. The water clocks and watch candles were one example. Furlthia had learnt their Askhan measure of time when he had been among the pretend rebels who took Magilnada for Ullsaard. It was the second hour High Watch, halfway through the afternoon. He had another hour until he was due to meet Anglhan and left the gardens to find something to eat.

A plaza dawnwards of the gardens was filled with tables and benches, which in turn were filled with people eating and drinking. The majority of them seemed to be native Magilnadans, doubtlessly driven from their usual haunts by the mass of soldiers coming in and out of the city.

He found a space on a bench beside two older women, who were happy to ignore him and carry on their conversation in hushed voices. A serving girl, no more than eight or nine years old, came over with a steaming bowl and a cup of water.

"What is it?" Furlthia asked as she plonked the bowl in front of him. The contents were brownish-grey sludge with islands of unidentifiable meat poking from a gravy sea.

"Meat stew," she said.

"What sort of meat?"

The girl gave him an exasperated look and held out her hand.

"Best not to ask. Seven salts."

"Seven?" Furlthia was horrified at the price, almost double what he would have paid before the arrival of the Askhan legions. He glanced at the bad fare as he counted out the tin coins. There were pitifully few left; the loose group of anti-Askhan sentiment he represented gave him a stipend for each visit, but he could not afford to stay in the city any longer than necessary. Next time he would have to ask for more from the shadowy collection of Magilnadan chieftains, traders and ex-rebels who supported the cause for a free Magilnada.

Despite its grisly even gristly appearance, the stew was not unpleasant. The meat was probably rabbit, though it was impossible to tell for sure. It certainly didn't come from any animal raised on a farm. The water was also clean and refreshing, one of the other benefits of Askhan influence. In the short time they had been in control of the city, half a dozen more wells had been dug and improvements had been made to the sewers beneath the city.

Furlthia idled for a while, glad to surround himself with the normal folk of the city. He listened in to their conversations, detecting excitement about the Askhan invasion. He didn't hear a single word of dissent or anger, which irritated him considerably. He wanted to ask how they could be so careless about the future of their city, and point out just how hard times would be for them once they became just another Salphorian province of Greater Askhor.

He knew it would make no difference and held his tongue. He, and others who shared his allegiance, had tried hard to build a popular movement against Askhan rule, but they had failed to stir up any trouble at all. The Askhan system was clever, giving people the illusion of security and wealth, while at the same time it robbed them of dignity and freedom. It was no great thing to labour under the self-serving warlords of Salphoria, but at least the chieftains were a part of the society they ruled, raised in the same traditions and values. The Askhans obliterated people's identity; crushed their beliefs in everything but the glory of Askhor; imposed their laws and their customs.

Getting agitated, Furlthia left the plaza and headed up the Hill of Chieftains to the governor's palace. Anglhan's influence was clear to see. The plain white pillars of the great porch on its front were now covered with gilded pictures, and the steps up to them had been replaced with red and black marble. Colourful banners hung from newly constructed balconies, while a full company of legionnaires from the First Magilnadan stood guard to either side of the huge double doors.

The doors were open and a steady procession wound in and out; the palace did not just house the governor, but also his many treasurers, clerks, customs officers and sundry officials. Supervising this organised chaos was Lenorin, Anglhan's chamberlain, chief treasurer and overall civilian second-in-command. He was, luckily for

Furlthia, also a vehement opponent of the Askhans and one of the chief sponsors of Furlthia's anti-Askhan movement. The chancellor saw Furlthia enter the dim hallway and gestured for him to approach.

"Busier than usual," said Furlthia as the two of them sat down on a low bench along the wall.

"Ullsaard's army will be marching in a few days' time," said Lenorin. "Everybody's running around trying to sell their last stock, or secure a contract, or offer their services. It's embarrassing."

Furlthia raised an eyebrow.

"Embarrassing?"

Lenorin nodded, keeping his voice even but there was the faintest curl of sneer on his lip.

"Look at them all," he said, waving a hand to encompass the milling crowds of merchants, chieftains and craftsmen haggling, chatting and arguing. "Like dogs fighting for the scraps from the table of their master. Look at him, the tall one with the red hair. That's Gelthar, one of the Pretari chieftains. The moment he heard of the Askhan invasion, he deserted his tribe and came to the city to become a captain. His family has given blood and sweat for their lands for generations, but as soon as the Askhans show up he forgets all that and wants to sweep away his neighbours. He's not the only one. Half the men in this building are traitors and cowards."

"So, what's the plan to stop them?"

IV

The row of houses along the street was a testament to wealth and privilege. In a city where space was at a premium, the large gardens, high walls and multi-storey buildings were proof of the power of their owners. Each was built from white stone and dark red brick, with slate roofs and heavy wooden beams to support them. When a lot of Magilnadan families shared just one or two rooms, each small palace was a bold extravagance with half a dozen bedchambers, deep cellars, separate kitchens, feasting halls and multiple lounges and rooms of study and relaxation.

Originally they had been the homes of the city's founders and as Magilnada had fallen under the influence of the Salphorian tribes, the chieftains had taken residence. Some still showed evidence of this, with ancient flags hanging from the eaves and weather-beaten shields mounted beneath the upper windows.

The Magilnadan nobility had all been slain over the last couple of years and now the Hill of Chieftains was the select province of Anglhan's favourites; and Ullsaard, who had secured one of the properties for his family when he had taken the city for Askhor.

The king dismissed his bodyguard at the end of the street and walked alone past the fresco-covered walls and brightly painted gates. He came to the third house, its gate a vivid scarlet, the plastered walls adorned with paintings of the mountains, eagles flying above the peaks, golden lions prowling the valleys.

A smaller door opened in the gate as he approached, the servants within warned of his arrival. Stepping inside, the king found himself in a cobbled yard, an empty ailur pen to the right, a covered space for chariots and carriages to his left. A handful of servants greeted him, heads bowed respectfully. The man who had opened the door bowed and introduced himself as Irian. Ullsaard guessed him to be Anrairian or Ersuan by his stocky build and accent.

"Your family awaits your pleasure in the main reception hall, majesty," said Irian.

Ullsaard gestured for the servant to lead the way and dismissed the others back to their duties. He followed Irian across the courtyard and into the shadow of the wide porch. The doors to the house were already open and Irian stepped aside to allow the king to enter first.

Fresh flowers flanked the hall in tall vases and were hanging from the rafters overhead, filling the house with their strong perfume. The floor was lined with a deep red wood and the walls covered with patterned, abstract tapestries. Ullsaard advanced slowly, taking in every detail even as his thoughts were occupied by what he was going to say to his wives. He mentally cursed Anglhan for not delivering Ullsaard's letter, while at the same time he conceded that perhaps talk of divorce was best done in person. He just wished he was not the person who had to talk about it.

He passed several open archways and came to a set of double doors at the end. Irian slipped past at the last moment to fling them in.

"King Ullsaard!" the servant declared, stepping aside.

Ullsaard stopped level with Irian and stooped to whisper to him.

"This is my family, not a faceless rabble to be awed. They know who I am."

Irian shuffled nervously and bobbed his head in mute agreement. Ullsaard straightened and entered the hall with steady strides, unsure what to expect. In his mind, nothing had really changed, but he knew that he was king now and even his family would treat him differently.

The reception hall was about thirty paces long and twenty wide. It opened onto an internal garden at the far end and a long table ran almost the full length of the room. The floor was covered in a mosaic depicting a flock of red-feathered birds flying across a sky, the circle of the sun beneath the chair at the head of the table.

Ullsaard's family clustered around the chair, eyes fixed on the king; his wives, Allenya, Luia and Meliu; two of his sons, Ullnaar and Urikh; and his mother, Pretaa. A little further away stood another pair – two daughters-in-law, one of them holding Ullsaard's granddaughter Luissa.

The king saw none of them save for Allenya. His eldest wife looked at him with a mixture of relief and happiness and stepped forward to accept his long embrace when he crossed the room. Ullsaard buried his face in the thick curls of her hair and stroked the back of her head. The two of them held each other for some time, saying nothing, enjoying the moment of reuniting.

Eventually Ullsaard pulled himself back, planting a kiss on Allenya's lips. Meliu was the next to greet him, skipping up to receive his kiss on her forehead. She planted her own welcome on each bearded cheek. Luia nodded politely, but even her severe expression softened and a smile played on her lips when Ullsaard bowed his head to her. He shook hands with Urikh and Ullnaar, ruffled Luissa's hair and then waved for them to be seated at the table, which the servants were quickly lading with all manner of food.

He stood behind the head chair for a moment, hands on its back, and looked at his gathered family. Only Jutaar, his second son, was missing. Instated as First Captain of the First Magilnadan legion he was at the main camp overseeing his men's preparations for the invasion.

"It seems like an age since we've all been together," said Ullsaard. He shook his head, not quite believing himself. "Without all of you, I would have failed. Now I am king, and you are the most powerful family in Greater Askhor. It makes me so proud to be your husband, your father, and your king."

He sat down and grabbed a cup of wine. In one long draught, he emptied the cup and slapped it back onto the table. Smacking his lips, he grinned at Allenya.

"This may not be Askh, but it's good to be home!"

He was about to help himself to some chicken when he caught sight of Meliu gazing intently at him. Seeing her suddenly reminded him of something he had forgotten in the excitement of his homecoming. He rose to his feet so quickly that his chair toppled back to the floor.

"Where is Noran?" he asked, looking at Meliu. She flushed red, remembering her indiscretion with Ullsaard's friend.

"He is upstairs," said Allenya. She leaned across the table and laid a hand on Ullsaard's arm. "Please, eat with us. Enjoy your meal. You can see Noran when we are finished."

Ullsaard nodded. He waved away the pair of servants that stepped forward to help him right the chair. Sitting down again, Ullsaard leaned forwards, elbows on the table.

"Let's eat."

V

A bird chirped happily to itself in a gilded cage, answered by others of its kind from a tree in the gardens outside the window. Ullsaard barely noticed the bird as he entered. His attention was fixed on Noran. The former herald to King Lutaar lay on a low cot, sheets pulled back, his yellowish chest and shoulders catching the sun coming through the window. As well as its jaundiced tint, Noran's skin had a thin, weathered look to it. There was little fat and muscle left, his face gaunt, his limbs withered.

Meliu followed Ullsaard into the small bedroom, a bowl of broth on a tray. She placed the soup on a table beside the bed and knelt down next to Noran. Spoonful by spoonful, she fed him, dribbling the liquid between his parted lips.

"He breathes, and he swallows, but that's about it," Meliu said when she was done. She pulled a spindly hand from beneath the covers and held it, locking her fingers with those of Noran. "I have to let the servants clean him up and change the sheets."

Ullsaard looked at his youngest wife.

"Do you want to be with him?" he asked.

She did not stir from gazing at Noran's pinched face.

"I don't think he would want to be with me," she said. "After… After what we did, he would not have anything to do with me."

"I want to give you a divorce," Ullsaard said, blurting it out.

Meliu turned horrified eyes to the king, tears instantly reddening them.

"Why? I am sorry for what happened with Noran. You said you understood. Why would you do this to me? I know you don't love me like Allenya, but I've b–"

"Forget it," snapped Ullsaard. "I thought it would be something you wanted, so that if Noran recovers you could be together."

Meliu stood up, still holding Noran's hand.

"If you want to get rid of me, be honest about it. Do not pretend that it is for my benefit. You have always wanted Allenya alone, we know that."

Ullsaard backed towards the door.

"I made a mistake," he said. He looked at Noran again. "It's not going to matter anyway."

Meliu's face scrunched into the fiercest scowl she had ever mustered, taking Ullsaard by surprise. Fists clenched, his wife advanced across the room until she was right in front of him, the top of her head barely reaching up to his chin.

"You are a selfish bastard, Ullsaard," she snarled. "Would you prefer it if your friend died? Do you care about nothing except yourself?"

Ullsaard pushed her away, as gently as he could manage.

"I would prefer it if he died swiftly, not this lingering half-death. Maybe it was a mistake to keep him alive in the first place."

"Look at him!" shrieked Meliu. "He is alive. He just needs more time, to build his strength."

Ullsaard laughed and instantly regretted it.

"I am sorry. I don't find this funny, but you are lying to yourself if you think he will recover. You cannot keep him alive forever. I have never seen a man looking so ill." Ullsaard pulled the small knife from his belt and tossed it onto the bed at Noran's feet. "I would end his misery, but I leave it up to you."

Meliu looked with disgust at the knife. She snatched it up and for a moment Ullsaard thought she was going to attack him. Instead, she slapped it back into his hand, hilt-first.

"Murder whomever you like," she said. "Do not expect me to be as heartless. If you want him dead, do it by your own hand, not mine."

Ullsaard walked out, brushing aside the curtain of beads that covered the doorway. He heard Meliu's sobs as he continued along the landing. Servants were moving about the house lighting lamps. Ullsaard stopped at the top of the curving stairway, feeling awkward and out of place. This house already had its own life, its routines and small traditions, and he was not part of them. He was about to embark on the ruthless conquest of Salphoria, but it was in this quiet, domestic realm that he felt like a true invader.

Halfway down the stairs, he met Allenya coming the other way. She smiled, linked arms with him and turned him back towards the landing. Saying nothing, she gently guided him to a bedchamber at the back of the house.

"I have missed you," Allenya said as she drew the heavy curtain across the door. She pulled free two clasps and her long dress fell to the floor, revealing tanned skin. She lay sideways on the bed, pulling up one leg, stroking a hand down her thigh. "I hope being king has not tired you out."

Ullsaard looked down at his wife and grinned.

"Not a chance," he said.

He threw off his kilt and shirt and flopped on to the bed beside Allenya. Holding back his desire, Ullsaard ran his fingers across Allenya's breasts and down to her belly. He leaned forward to kiss her on the thigh, moving slowly down her leg towards her ankle. His hands moved beneath her, turning Allenya to her back as his lips moved on a return course up the inside of her leg.

A gentle but insistent tug pulled him alongside Allenya and she held his face in her hands, staring into his eyes. They shared a long kiss, tongues meeting tentatively at first. Ullsaard eased his leg over Allenya's, feeling the touch of the hair between her legs on his thigh. She wrapped her arms around his shoulders, pulling him closer, their kissing become fiercer.

Allenya broke away with a giggle, running clawed fingers through Ullsaard's chest hair, fingernails lightly scratching the skin.

"You are a great man," she said, barely breathing the words. "I loved you as a captain and I love you as a king."

"And as captain and king, I love you," said Ullsaard. "I would give up the empire for you."

"That will not be needed," Allenya said with a smile. "Though I must share you with Greater Askhor, there are some things which are mine alone. But you will never have to share me. This is for your eyes and no other."

Ullsaard straightened, allowing the evening sun to paint Allenya's body a golden brown. He looked at every part of her; her lips, her slender limbs, her firm breasts, her soft eyes. Ullsaard bent forwards to kiss her neck, but stopped as lips brushed skin.

Something Allenya had just said was percolating the fog of his desire.

"Is something the matter, my husband?" she asked, noticing his sudden hesitation.

Ullsaard could say nothing. What was he to tell her? That he had suddenly realised that perhaps they were not alone in the room? That the spirit of a dead king lived on in his mind, and perhaps was at that very moment ogling her naked body with Ullsaard's eyes?

Askhos had said he saw and heard everything that Ullsaard saw and heard. The Crown was more than a thousand miles away in Askh, but there was part of Ullsaard that was no longer him.

The thought revolted him. He imagined Askhos's face, twisted and leering as it shared Ullsaard's moment of intimacy. Did the dead king feel Allenya's nipples between his fingers, or smell the scent of the wetness between her legs? Would Askhos share the climax that was to come, experience the passion and release of that most personal of moments?

With a growl, Ullsaard flopped sideways onto the bed. His excitement had evaporated, his member flaccid at the thought of Askhos intruding upon this entirely personal situation.

Saying nothing, Allenya used her hands to work Ullsaard back to full manhood, but her attentions were in vain. The more Ullsaard looked at her, felt her grip on his shaft, the more the thought of the dead king lurking in his head sickened him. Even the lust that burned through Ullsaard was not enough to fight back the disgust welling up inside at the thought of sharing Allenya with another man, alive or dead.

"I am sorry," he told her. He pushed her hand away from his groin and held her close. She wrapped her arms around him and stroked his hair.

"It does not matter," said Allenya. "We are together. That is enough."

Ullsaard tried to keep the rage and frustration in check as he hugged Allenya tightly, but could not prevent hot tears from spilling down his cheeks, just for a moment. With a free hand, Allenya drew the sheets over them, Ullsaard nestled closer, head on her breast, drained in mind and body.

Sharing a cocoon of warmth and love, he drifted into a dreamless sleep.

VI

While a small band of legionnaires aggressively emptied the main hall of petitioners, Lenorin reappeared from the throng and told Furlthia to follow him. Furlthia found himself being led into a part of the palace he had not seen before; judging by the clean look of the stone blocks and the smell of fresh paint, the corridor he was walking along had not been built when he had last been in the city.

At the end, the corridor branched out into a circular vestibule, with steps leading around the wall to an open gallery above. Lenorin took the steps two at a time, his energy not diminished by his senior years. Furlthia was a little out of breath by the time he reached the top, having completed a full circuit of the domed chamber to access the gallery.

A small wooden door, almost hidden between two framed paintings of the city – from duskward and dawnward it appeared – opened at Lenorin's touch. The two of them had to duck a little to gain entry. Inside was a small room no bigger than a dozen paces across, filled with shelves holding stacks of clay tablets and piles of scrolls.

Anglhan sat behind a narrow desk, scribbling onto a wax tablet.

"Just making my notes for the day," the governor said without looking up.

Lenorin retrieved a canvas-seated stool from somewhere and invited Furlthia to sit down.

"I shall leave you two to your business," said the chancellor.

Furlthia watched him go. The room darkened measurably as the small door was shut; the only light was a candle lamp hanging from a chain in the centre of the ceiling. Furlthia cleared his throat but Anglhan held up a hand to quieten him before he could say anything.

"Just a couple more things…" Anglhan was so intent his brow was a deep frown, the governor regularly licking his lips with concentration.

Finally he placed his stylus onto the desktop and looked up.

"A while ago, you said that Aegenuis was calling a council of chieftains," said Anglhan. "Well, the Askhans are invading right now, so what's Aegenuis's plan?"

Furlthia dragged the stool closer to the desk and leaned forwards.

"To stop them," he said. "He knows that no single tribe is strong enough to hold against the Askhans. He wants to bring as many chieftains together as he can and form a single army."

Anglhan's shake of the head was doubtful. He scratched his nose, sorted through the pile of papers on his desk and brought one forth.

"Ullsaard has unleashed almost every legion in Greater Askhor," said the governor. "Nearly one hundred thousand soldiers by the last count. I'm in the process of raising a new legion at the moment. Aegenuis's only hope of survival is to accept the inevitable; he has to treat with the Askhans."

"Not a chance," said Furlthia. "You might be a spineless parasite, but true Salphors will fight the Askhans for every river, road and field."

"And they'll lose, and they'll die," said Anglhan.

"Ullsaard has made a mistake, and you know it." He jabbed a finger into the desktop to make his point. "Ullsaard is stretching the resources of the empire for this. He needs a decisive victory this summer, because when winter comes his people are going to starve without the grain trade from Salphoria. But his biggest mistake is to allow the nobles and army generals to claim what they can conquer. The legions will spend as much time in competition with each other as they will fighting us. If Aegenuis can meet this disorganised attack with stiff defence, Askhan hunger for the fight will drop."

The Magilnadan governor considered this, hand rubbing a flabby cheek. Furlthia was a little surprised, having expected Anglhan to dismiss Furlthia's arguments with his usual bluster. Instead, Anglhan leaned back, chair creaking loudly, and put his hands behind his head.

"Until the Askhans can establish themselves further duskwards, their position is fairly precarious," said the governor. "For now, all their supplies have to come through the Magilnadan Gap. Once they get their claws into the land further into Salphoria, you can kiss those farms and woods and fields goodbye. Whatever Aegenuis wants to do, he has to act quickly."

Studying Anglhan, Furlthia sensed that the governor's mind was working over some idea or other. He had a semi-vacant look that Furlthia associated with Anglhan's more outlandish schemes of the past. He decided to push the matter further.

"If I was able to get certain assurances from Aegenuis, would you be prepared to act against the Askhans?"

Still affecting an air of nonchalance, Anglhan regarded Furlthia with heavy-lidded eyes.

"What sort of assurances?" he asked, just failing to appear casual.

"What would you like?" said Furlthia. "What would you want out of a deal with the Salphorian king?"

Anglhan sat forward, suddenly brusque and focussed.

"Regained independence for Magilnada," he said, counting out the points with upraised fingers. "The lands that were called Free Country to become independent under the rule of Magilnada. Recognition of my position as ruler of Magilnada. Agreement to provide warriors for the defence of Magilnada against Askhan reprisals."

"Is that all?" said Furlthia with half a laugh. "Let me get this right. You want Magilnada and the Gap to be its own kingdom, with you as the king?"

"That would be the short version of it, yes," said Anglhan. "Look at it this way. At the moment, I am an Askhan governor, with tremendous powers and resources. Unless Aegenuis can offer me more than that, guarantee freedom for me to rule as I see fit, he has nothing to offer."

Taking a deep breath, Furlthia stood and paced back and forth across the small archive room. He weighed up Anglhan's proposal. It was not for Furlthia to decide, but he was not going to travel all the way to Carantathi with a deal that would earn him nothing but Aegenuis's anger.

"What are you offering in return?" he asked.

"If my considerations are met, and Aegenuis is willing to swear an oath to it, then I will do whatever I can to halt the Askhan advance before it starts. I will buy him the time he needs to be ready for the Askhans."

"How are you going to do that? You've seen how vulnerable Magilnada is, and you know that Ullsaard will crush you the moment he thinks you are betraying him."

"That's not Aegenuis's problem, is it? Or yours. If that happens, Aegenuis has lost nothing. I'm willing to stake my future, my life, on stopping the Askhans just as he is. The rewards have to match that risk."

"All right," said Furlthia, stepping towards the door. "I can't make promises for the king, but I will take your offer to him."

"That's all I ask, my friend," said Anglhan. He raised his stylus. "Are we finished here?"

Furlthia opened the door but stopped before stepping through. Once he left, he would be obliged to carry through his promise. When that happened, events would be set in motion that he knew he would not be able to control. Anglhan was a slippery creature, and no doubt there were plans and prizes in his mind beyond what he had asked for or offered. Could he be trusted? No. Could he inflict a lot of damage on the Askhans? Yes. For better or worse, and Furlthia really hoped it would be for the better, Anglhan would have a role to play in protecting Salphoria against the Askhan invasion.

"Was there anything else?" Anglhan asked, peering at Furlthia over the top of a parchment sheet.

Furlthia hated the smugness of the man. Every instinct was warning him that he had been lucky to escape his previous involvement with Anglhan and it was idiocy to get entangled with his schemes again. It wasn't just Furlthia's life that would be held in the balances, tens of thousands of Salphors would die in the coming war.

Furlthia ducked out onto the gallery and shut the door behind him. It was a huge risk, but one that he had to take.

SALPHORIA
Summer, 211th year of Askh

I

The Salphorian settlement was nothing more than forty or so round stone huts with straw roofs. A wooden palisade surrounded the village, but there were no towers or ramparts from which the wall could be defended. Several hundred warriors had drawn up outside the palisade, gathering in unruly groups each a few dozen strong. They wore patterned woollen trousers and jerkins, carried axes and spears and bore shields of stiffened leather painted with animal faces, crossed swords, lightning bolts and many other designs.

On the hillside meadows around the village cattle and sheep wandered untended, oblivious to the six thousand Askhan legionnaires poised at the top of the hill overlooking the scene.

Ullsaard flapped at the flies buzzing into his face as he looked down the river valley leading to the village. Black-fang twitched her ears and tail as the midges pestered her, but was otherwise placid enough.

Ullsaard felt good today. Atop his ailur, the Thirteenth behind him and an enemy in front, the world had become simple again. He had left Magilnada after only a few days. Not left, but fled. Fled from his family. The haunting presence of Askhos inside had driven Ullsaard to distraction, and it was clear that his reticence to spend time with his family was upsetting them, especially Allenya, Meliu and Ullnaar.

Thinking that he was doing more harm than good by staying, Ullsaard had quit the city, joined up with his favoured Thirteenth to march duskwards into Salphoria. He knew he was looking for a fight; he hoped some violence would expel the confusion and frustration that had dogged him since he had taken up the Crown.

The king glanced up at the morning sun, guessing that the time was roughly an hour before Noonwatch. His scouts had found the village during the night and at first light the legion had broken camp and marched downstream. A small group of men detached from the other fighters and started up the hill towards him, a small cloth banner held up by one of them.

"Here comes their leader," said Anasind, standing beside the king.

Ullsaard said nothing as he watched the deputation hurrying up the hill. The eldest looked younger than Ullsaard, perhaps forty years old at the most. He wore a wreath of red-veined leaves around a thick bush of greying black hair, and a drooping beard and moustaches covered most of his face. His eyes roamed along the lines of stern-faced legionnaires and fluttered around for a moment before they settled Ullsaard.

"We no fight," said the man, bending to one knee. His broken Askhan was hard to understand, guttural and slurred. "We no fight."

Ullsaard shrugged and dismounted, tossing Blackfang's reins to an orderly. He walked a few paces until he was within arm's reach of the Salphorian delegation.

"You have no choice," he said.

The Salphors gathered around their leader, all talking at the same time. Ullsaard understood very little of what was being said, and did not pay much attention.

"No fight, no burning, no kill," said the spokesman.

"Where are your elders?" said Anasind. "Who is your chieftain?"

"I chieftain," the man said.

"No, you're not," said Ullsaard. He grabbed the man's jerkin and hauled him to his chest. There was fear and confusion in the Salphor's eyes, and he looked to his companions for help.

"Give meat!" one of them cried out. He pointed to the livestock on the pasture. "No fight, give you meat."

"Women!" said another, looking at the legionnaires. "Nice women, yes? No fight."

"Did you just call my soldiers a bunch of women?" said Ullsaard.

"No, no, no!" The self-appointed leader vigorously waved his hands in answer to the accusation. "Take our women. Our women good. Fuck lots, cook good."

Anasind and Ullsaard looked at each other. The First Captain shrugged.

"Best offer I've had in a while," he said.

Ullsaard folded his arms and glowered down at the Salphors.

"I didn't come here for your women, or your meat," said the king. "I want your land. You are Askhans now. Swear loyalty to me."

The spokesman cringed at the suggestion and shrank back towards his companions.

"No, cannot do that," he said. "Not take our lands."

He stepped towards Ullsaard with a pleading hand outstretched, but the king slapped it away.

"Swear your oath to me!" Ullsaard snarled. "Where is your chieftain? Why is he not here?"

The group shook their heads and muttered to each other, but said nothing to Ullsaard.

"It's the same as the last town," said Anasind. "He must have answered Aegenuis's summons as well."

"Too bad for him," said Ullsaard. "He'll not have a home to come back to."

The king turned his back on the Salphors and strode back to Blackfang. Swinging into the saddle, he unhooked his shield and pulled out his sword. Roused by the familiar noise, the ailur grew restless, swishing her tail and baring her teeth, ears flatted against the bronze of her masked chamfron. Ullsaard sat there staring at the Salphors.

Realisation that Ullsaard did not want their surrender dawned on the delegation. To their credit, they responded by standing straighter, puffing out their chests and matching his stare. As he watched the men stride stiffly back towards their village, Ullsaard wondered how much their fawning had been an act, or if the courage they were showing now was bravado. Everything he had heard before had put in his mind the idea that the Salphorian tribes were fierce and proud, and unlikely to surrender meekly.

For a moment, he considered halting the attack. Slaughtering a few hundred Salphors would do little to speed his conquest.

"What are your orders, king?" asked Anasind. "Shall I signal the advance?"

Ullsaard looked at the First Captain and back at the Salphors. He swung a leg and dropped off the back of Blackfang, tossing the reins to Anasind.

"I'll do it myself," said the king. He sheathed his sword and pulled free his spear from behind the ailur's saddle. "I wouldn't want to get out of practice."

II

Much to Ullsaard's annoyance, the Salphors withdrew into their settlement, perhaps hoping the wooden walls would give them some protection. He ordered the legion to encircle the village, two companies ready to storm the gate, the rest closing in on the walls. As the Thirteenth marched closer, arrows sailed out from the walls. The first inaccurate volleys did little to discourage Ullsaard; firing blindly over the walls was a waste of arrows.

Coming closer, the fall of the arrows grew in intensity, concentrated on the companies approaching the gate. One of these was the first company, led by the king, and when he was less than two hundred paces from the village he saw that the wall was not as pointless as he had first thought. What had appeared at first to be haphazard gaps between staves poorly lashed together, were in fact murder holes for the defenders to shoot through. Though towers and rampart would have added to the range of the defenders' shots, with the Askhans determined to attack this proved no disadvantage.

"Cunning bastards," muttered Venuid. Bearing the golden icon of the Thirteenth, the veteran captain of the first company ducked sideways as an arrow sliced just above his head, clattering off a shield behind him.

"Raise shields!" bellowed Ullsaard, bringing up his own.

The clatter of bronze and wood surrounded the king for a moment as the front rank of soldiers levelled their spears and brought up their shields. Ullsaard peered past the golden rim of his shield at the gate, more arrows whistling towards him. He felt the shudder of shafts hitting his shield as he continued to advance, hearing the occasional cry of pain from behind him.

Ullsaard shouted the command to halt at fifty paces from the gate. Breaking the shield wall for a moment, he leaned forward and looked to his left and right. The other companies were almost at the walls and were being pelted by stones and other missiles from within. He heard the calls for axemen and rams to be brought to the fore.

The companies attacking the wall formed roofs with their shields while others pushed through the ranks with sharpened logs and heavy axes. The axemen started the work, hacking at the ropes binding the palisade together. When a few stakes had been loosened, the men with the ram began pounding upon the timbers. The shouts of the captains beat out a slow rhythm, each blow accompanied by loud splintering and a shout from the legionnaires. They were helped by other men in the company kicking at the wall and pushing forward with their shields.

"Advance! Double pace!"

Ullsaard waved his company on with his spear and broke into a trot, shoulder-to-shoulder with the men on each side, those coming behind almost on his heels. Leather slapped, bronze jingled and men panted in the hot sun. The volume of arrows descending on the first company increased, but at the cost of accuracy. Covering the ground with swift strides, the Askhans were at the gate without suffering any more casualties.

Through the gaps between the logs, Ullsaard could see the press of Salphorian archers. He rammed the point of his spear through one of the holes, heard a scream, and wrenched the spear back. The tip was slick with blood.

While the second rank jabbed their long pikes through the gaps, the front rank stabbed their spears into the ground and pulled out knives to saw at the binding ropes. Ullsaard slid his sword between two timbers and sliced quickly, parting the fibres of a tar-covered rope. Arrows thudded against the gate from inside the village, and now and then the king felt a shaft hitting his sword. With a final snap, the rope split.

"Brace for push!" shouted the king, taking up his spear again.

All the men of the front rank turned sideways and leaned their shoulders against the inside of their shields. Ullsaard felt the weight of the man behind him pushing against his back, the pressure growing steadily as more and more ranks added to their weight.

"Forwards!"

Having shouted the command, the king planted his feet and heaved. Teeth gritted, he took a step, feeling the gate buckling slightly. He reset himself and pushed again, aware of the fifteen men behind him all lending their weight. Ropes creaked and wood bent under the strain. Ullsaard found it hard to breathe in the tight press, nostrils flaring as he sought to fill his lungs for another surge.

A loud crack sounded to the left and the momentum of the phalanx shifted, the sudden lack of resistance dragging the men in that direction. Ullsaard almost stumbled, but was kept upright by the proximity of the men to either side.

Though the gate sagged, it did not break. Another glance confirmed to Ullsaard that a heavy timber had been dropped as a bar across the inside. More crashing and victorious shouts to his right announced the collapse of the first part of the wall.

"Use your spears, lever up that bar," he told his men, manoeuvring his own weapon into position. A dozen spears thrust through the gaps in the gate at Ullsaard's shout. At the next command Ullsaard and his men heaved upwards, using the shafts to raise the bar. It moved about the width of a hand and then stuck solid against the brackets holding it in place.

Though curses filled his thoughts at this obstacle, Ullsaard kept his swearing inside his head; it was not wise to show frustration in front of his men. He cursed himself most vehemently for his impatience. They could have waited and brought up ladders from the baggage train; he might have ordered a bombardment by the spear throwers and catapults. There had been a number of options, not least of which had been to use the lava-throwers to burn out the Salphors, but his hunger for immediate action had driven him to a direct assault. Now it looked like he'd be stuck at this damned gate until one of the other companies saw fit to let him in; a humiliation whatever way you looked at it.

"Perhaps we should have knocked?" he called out to his men, who laughed dutifully. He could hear shouts and sounds of fighting inside the village and knew he was missing the battle. "The lads in the other companies are taking all the loot. One more shove!"

Whether it was for their commander or fear of losing out on the spoils, the first company redoubled their efforts, lunging en masse at the gate. One hundred and sixty men threw their weight against the offending obstacle with a throaty roar.

"Come on!" Ullsaard could barely take a breath to call out.

It was a hinge that gave first, to Ullsaard's right. The bottom of the gate swung away, causing the Askhans to stagger for a moment. Seeing their efforts rewarded, they piled on, straining every muscle.

With a last screech of twisting metal, the gate collapsed inwards, falling to pieces as it crashed down onto the packed dirt. Some of the men lost their balance, tripping over and stumbling amongst the splintered logs. Ullsaard brought up his spear, ready to fight, wary of instant counter-attack.

He did not have anything to fear. The Salphors were battling ferociously in the middle of their village, forming a circle against three other companies that had broken through the wall. Here and there pockets of warriors fought against a handful of legionnaires, while some fought face to face with lone opponents. This was not a grand battle of sweep and manoeuvre; it was a simple fight to the death.

"Break ranks and charge!" bellowed Ullsaard, leaping over the remnants of the gate.

Dashing along the dirt street, Ullsaard saw a legionnaire of the fifth company backed up against the wall of a hut, fending away two Salphors with spear and shield. The king met them at a sprint, driving his spear into the back of the closest.

The other Salphor turned quickly, braided beard whipping through the air. Ullsaard's shield caught the man's axe as the king pulled his spear out of the dead man. He jabbed towards the Salphor's face, forcing him back a step, only to be met by the point of the legionnaire's weapon in the side. Twisting awkwardly, the Salphor staggered away from the legionnaire, blood spilling from the wound. Ullsaard followed up, ramming his shield into that of his foe, knocking him to one knee. He kicked the man in the face, booted foot connecting squarely with his chin. A heartbeat later, Ullsaard rammed his spear through the man's leather jerkin, plunging the tip into his ribcage.

"Come with me," he told the legionnaire, heading further up the street to open space between the ring of buildings. More of the first company were streaming towards the battle to his left and right.

Unable to form the phalanx through the breaks in the wall and the narrow spaces between the huts, the Askhans could not bring their numbers to bear for a decisive onslaught. All across the village, a swirling melee was being fought; in some places it had devolved into a running fight with groups of Salphors chasing down legionnaires cut off from their companies and Askhans encircling isolated groups of defenders.

With a handful of other Askhans by his side, Ullsaard plunged into the fray. He bashed Salphors to the ground with his shield, stabbing at faces and guts with his spear, trampling and stumbling over the fallen. An axe caught the king a glancing blow on the right shoulder, opening up a long gash across his arm. Snarling with pain, he smashed his shield into the axe-wielding man, stunning him long enough for another legionnaire to drive his spear through the Salphor's groin.

His grip on his spear slick with blood, Ullsaard flexed his arm, hissing as the laceration parted with the movement. Though the wound was sore, it did not inhibit his movement. Still feeling confident, Ullsaard pitched into the fight, kicking away the shield of his next foe to expose the Salphor's chest to another spear thrust.

Splinters of wood from a snapping spear haft exploded into the king's face, blinding him for a moment. He ducked behind his shield out of instinct as tears, blood and sweat streamed into his beard. Something heavy hit the shield boss, jarring the king's arm. Blinking furiously, he stopped a sword blade with his spear's shaft, and whipped the tip into the man's face, cutting across cheek and lips.

The Salphor howled and swung his sword at Ullsaard's head. The king shuffled back a step and knocked the blow aside with the rim of his shield. Unbalanced, the Salphor stumbled face first into the blood-spattered earth. Ullsaard slammed a foot down onto the man's helmeted head and reversed his grip on his spear, driving the tip between the downed Salphor's shoulder blades, feeling it glancing from the man's spine.

His spear trapped, Ullsaard snatched out his sword and waded into the mass, his legionnaires around and behind him shouting the king's name. The Salphors fought with the desperation of doomed men, defending their homes and families with every last breath. Caught up in the frenzy of the fighting, Ullsaard had a grudging respect for his foes even as he cut them down and bellowed for his men to leave none alive.

Whether deliberate or accidental, at some point in the fighting, the thatched roof of a hut went up in flames, spilling smoked across the battle. Burning embers landed on other houses, setting them ablaze. The shrill screams of women, the wails of terrified children joined with angry shouts and cries of pain, the crackle of flames and ring of metal. Engulfed in the chaos, Ullsaard hacked and slashed, cuts on his face and arms, chestplate scored several times, his shield battered, the rim ragged with dozens of nicks.

Blood rushing, Ullsaard vented his frustration with every blow of his sword. He roared wordlessly as he fought, intoxicated by the sense of release and the thrill of fighting. In the smoke he felt alone, though shadows raged close at hand. Bearded faces loomed out of the gloom to be hacked at and cut down. The smoke burnt Ullsaard's throat and his lungs rasped with every heavy breath, but he laughed away such discomfort. Not for quite some time had he felt such feral joy, such vitality, only a spear thrust or sword swing away from death.

It was with a shock that he came up against two legionnaires racing through the smoke. He checked his sword just in time, even as they brought up their spears. He looked around, seeking the silhouettes of the enemy, but all he could see were the crested helms and spears of legionnaires.

The Salphors were all dead.

"Search the houses!" Ullsaard called out. "Kill any men. Take whatever else you find."

The crack of splintering wood drifted with the smoke as bands of soldiers kicked down doors. There were scattered, muffled yells as a cowardly few were found in their hiding places and swiftly despatched. Legionnaires emerged from the blanket of smoke dragging women and children behind them, or carrying bundles of loot, sacks of grain, haunches of meat, using their shields to bear piles of trinkets and jewellery.

His battle-rage subsiding, Ullsaard felt his strength leeching away as he circled the village, checking to see if there were any wounded Salphors to finish off. Amongst the looting, some of the legionnaires had organised themselves into casualty bearers, using spears and shields as stretchers to carry the badly wounded from the smoke.

After the cacophony of battle, the scene was strangely quiet; the noise of the flames, the sobs of the captives, groans of the wounded and casual conversations between legionnaires seemed muted and distant to the king. He heard the squeal of a pig somewhere, followed by laughter.

Ullsaard searched through the bodies until he found the gilded haft of his spear. He ripped it free from the back of the Salphor and took it in his shield hand; his right arm was now too sore to move, his fingers numb from the wound in his shoulder. Ullsaard did not look at the cut as he made his way back to the shattered gate.

Already the post-battle business was well underway, organised by Anasind and the second captains. Carts were coming down from the baggage train to carry the dead and the loot. Luaarit, chief surgeon of the Thirteenth, was directing his orderlies, attending to the wounded. The surgeon's arms were bloodstained up to the elbows, his leather smock splashed with smears and handprints. Ullsaard watched numbly as Luaarit knelt down beside a man with a long gash in his thigh. The king couldn't hear what was said, but the man was hauled to his feet between two orderlies and half-carried over to a table surrounded by buckets and bandages, the grass matted with blood beneath it.

Ullsaard turned away, raising his shield hand to catch the attention of Anasind. The First Captain jogged through the throng of Askhans streaming out of the village.

"How many?" Ullsaard asked.

"Seventy-eight dead on the field," said Anasind. "Perhaps add another hundred to that from those too injured to fight. Same again for walking wounded. It could have been better, but it could have been a lot worse. These Salphors are no pushover."

Ullsaard looked at the burning village, the column of smoke now piling high into the sky, a signal to those that could see that the Askhans had arrive.

"You should have Luaarit look at that cut," said Anasind, pointing to Ullsaard's shoulder. "Wouldn't want to get an infection."

"It's going to be a long summer," said the king, ignoring the First Captain's suggestion. He flexed his fingers, dried blood flaking from his knuckles. "A really long summer."

CARANTATHI
Autumn, 211th year of Askh

I

Smoke from lamps and the fire pit created a thin haze that wafted along the hall as arguing nobles shouted and gesticulated, creating eddies in the smog. The bleating goats in the yard outside made more sense to Aegenuis than the bleating of the chieftains in his hall.

The King of the Salphors leaned back in his throne, hands gripping the arms, and ignored the anarchy. He heard gnawing and looked down at his feet. One of his wolfhounds rasped teeth on a bone, head between the king's feet. He ruffled its ears affectionately, waiting for the storm of debate to blow itself out.

"Why do you just sit there and ignore us?"

Aegenuis glanced up to see his son, Medorian, standing in front of the throne. Twenty years old, Medorian had his father's dark red hair, rangy limbs and broad chest. He had the blue eyes of his mother and the down of hair on his cheeks was fairer than the greying bush that sprouted from the king's face. Most of all, it was the constant frown that marked Medorian out from his father.

The king sighed and returned his attention to the dog. The loudly exchanged growls and insults of the twenty chieftains washed over him, easily ignored. A bang of the main door and a sudden draft of air heralded a new arrival. Aegenuis looked up as the nobles parted, allowing Haegran to approach the king.

"The Askhans attacked the Vestil thirteen days ago," announced the chieftain. "Five tribes have fled into my lands since then. They cannot stay."

Aegenuis studied his cousin. There was no malice in his expression, only honest inquiry. Haegran genuinely believed that this was somehow not his problem.

"What am I going to do about it?" the king said quietly. The conversations subsided as the chieftains gathered around to hear their ruler. "Why do I need to do anything about it? I have told you what you have to do, but you will not listen."

The Salphorian king stood up, throwing off his cloak of dyed lion skin to reveal a vest of bronze mail and tautly muscled arms tattooed with red ink. Heavy gold bracelets hung on his wrists and silver rings adorned each of his remaining eight fingers. The clay bindings of beard braids clinked together as Aegenuis took a pace towards his subjects.

"I warned you that the Askhans were too many to fight," he said, patting a hand on Haegran's shoulder. "I warned this council that no tribe or people were strong enough to resist this onslaught alone."

"And the council voted against you," said Linghal, chief of the Hadril tribes. The youthful chieftain pushed his way through the crowd. "It would be an affront to the spirits of our ancestors to give our warriors to you. We were right. The Vatarti had pushed the Askhans back beyond the Laemin River, and the Menaeni defeated a legion only forty days ago."

"Only you would use a time like this to try to grab our lands, Aegenuis," said Liradin, ruler of the Cannin who had taken the first brunt of the Askhan attack. "Where were your warriors and promises when my hall was being burned?"

Aegenuis shrugged, walked to the table and picked up a jug of beer. He took a mouthful, drinking slowly.

"You should take that up with the Askhans," said the king.

Complaints broke out immediately, accusations hurled at Aegenuis from every direction. The shattering of the jug on the tiled floor silenced them all.

"I warned you!" roared Aegenuis. "I told you that Magilnada was just the start, but you said I was scared of noises in the night. When that bastard Ullsaard openly declared his occupation of the city, you gave me your excuses. 'He won't come to our lands', you said. You reminded me of the agreement with Lutaar, said the Askhans would respect the border of the Free Country. I told you that the Askhans were full of shit, and Ullsaard cares less about agreements than a cow cares about fly farts.

"Well, now Ullsaard is here and you still bicker like children about protecting your own lands, and keeping away from each other's towns. The Askhans don't care about your tribal boundaries, and I don't care either."

The king picked up another jug, took another swig and leaned back against the edge of the table.

"The Menaeni defeated a legion?" Aegenuis laughed, humour tinged with madness. He let a drop of ale drip from the spout of the jug onto the floor. "That's a legion. That's what we've beaten so far." He upended the jug, beer splashing the boots of the chieftains. The thump of the jug on the table was like the slamming of a tomb lid. "That's what's coming! Destroy a legion and they'll send two. Destroy two legions and Ullsaard will send four."

"So why do we fight at all?" said Medorian. He waved a

hand at the chieftains. "Do you want to just give our lands to the Askhans, maybe? Are you that much of a coward?"

Aegenuis lunged at Medorian, fingers grasping for his son's throat. Medorian twisted away and scurried into the nobles. The king righted himself and glared at them.

"We cannot defend our lands apart, each to his own," Aegenuis said. "We must bring our warriors together, enough to face ten legions, and crush the Askhans when they come."

"Where?" demanded Linghal. "Would you defend Asdargil's lands with this great army while the Askhans make sport of Hadril women and enslave Hadril children?"

"So you would sacrifice my people instead?" Asdargil shouted at Linghal. "Just like a Hadril whoreson to think like that."

"At least we tried to fight," Linghal snapped back. "We didn't come running to the king like kicked dogs, whimpering for help."

"It was your tribes that took half our stores last winter, you old bastard," said Asdargil. "The Askhans came before the harvest, what else are we going to do? Starve to death so you can build higher walls around your homes using timber stolen from our forests?"

Accusation and counter-accusations engulfed the chieftains as old alliances and enmities sprang forth again. Aegenuis found another jug of beer and pushed his way through the jostling chieftains. He slumped back into this throne.

We're all going to be killed, he thought, and took another drink.

TEMPLE

I

Dryness scratched at Erlaan's throat and crusted his eyes. He was lying on his back, on something hard, in a place with no light. He could smell nothing, nostrils blocked. He tried to lick his lips, but there was no moisture at all. He reached up to his face with a hand that felt like lead, fingers rubbing at his eyes.

Prising one eyelid open, Erlaan looked at a ceiling of yellow stone blocks. The air seemed yellow too; strange light ebbed from his right, like the glow of a lamp wick but more sickly, lacking any kind of warmth. Turning his head, Erlaan saw a slit-like window. He could see nothing outside, only a sliver of pulsating light.

Still lacking the strength to sit up, he turned his head in the other direction. On his left, someone else was lying on a slab of stone, level with him. He dully recognised his father, Prince Kalmud, a layer of white dust coating his skin. With much effort, Erlaan lifted his hand again and saw the same chalk-like substance covering him. It was like the powder used inside the moulds he had seen used to make slabs of wax for writing.

He tried to remember how he had arrived here. The last

72

thing he could recall was being called to the throne room by his grandfather, King Lutaar. Most of the palace staff had been there, along with Udaan, the Chief Brother. Lutaar had told them all that General Ullsaard had breached the Askhan Wall and was marching on the city.

Kalmud was very sick.

The memory came back in a flash. Erlaan's father could barely walk, and Udaan had helped him up from his bier as the guards and servants listened to the king's instructions. There was to be a calm and efficient evacuation. The throne chamber had emptied slowly, until only the king, his son, his grandson and Udaan had been left behind.

His father had said something that Erlaan had not heard. The king had smiled and shaken his head.

"The Brotherhood will take care of you both," he had said.

More Brothers had entered, silver-masked and cowled in black, and taken Kalmud away. Udaan had asked Erlaan to stand up and he had done so. Then the Chief Brother had done something with his hands, and Erlaan could remember nothing more.

Erlaan realised he was neither hot nor cold, though he lay naked without any sheet or blanket. Feeling was returning to his limbs, bringing strength. He sat up.

The room was square, no more than ten paces to a wall, and save for the tiny window the only other opening was an archway beyond which Erlaan could only see more of the same yellow stone receding into the distance. He tried to swing his feet to the floor but failed, his vigour not yet wholly returned.

He lay back and caught his breath, surprised by how much he had exerted himself. Every breath seemed to stick in his lungs and he coughed hard, tasting more of the dust in his mouth. Raising a hand to his cheek, he rubbed away some of the patina on his skin, feeling no stubble beneath his fingertips. He was as freshly shaven as he'd been in the throne room, but had the strangest sense that time had passed, as if waking from an unplanned sleep only to find the next watch had chimed even though it felt like only moments had passed.

With a grunt, he tried again to push himself upright. He managed to move himself to a sitting position on the edge of the slab. As sensation returned, it brought with it a dull ache, which reached down into his joints and bones.

On wobbling legs, Erlaan stood and tottered across the small chamber, his head almost brushing the ceiling despite his weak stoop. He steadied himself with a hand on the edge of his father's slab and bent closer. He could hear breath whistling through Kalmud's slightly parted lips and sighed with relief.

The chamber had all the appearance and feeling of a tomb; though the window was strange for a mausoleum. Confidence growing, Erlaan pushed himself up and took a step towards the window to see what was outside.

"That would not be advisable, prince."

The cracked voice caused Erlaan to turn towards the door. A short man stood in the archway. He was naked, devoid of all hair. His whole body was emaciated, bony joints sticking out through thin flesh. Eyes bulged in their sockets and glinted strangely in the light. Most remarkable was the covering of scars and tattoos that crawled across the man's skin; swirls and spirals that made Erlaan's eyes ache to follow them, connecting and broken by strange symbols.

Erlaan glanced back to the window and then focussed on the man, trying not to stare into those metallic-looking eyes.

"You have lots of questions," said the man before Erlaan could speak. "Let me answer some of them. My name is Asirkhyr. I am one of the chief acolytes of the temple where you now stand. You are safe."

Erlaan looked at Kalmud, and again Asirkhyr spoke before the prince could ask the question.

"Your father is no better and no worse than he was when you left Askh. The journey here has been a strain for both of you. I cannot explain how you came to be here in terms you will understand, but it takes a toll on the mind and body. You father's ill health means it will take longer for him to recover, and he may not recover at all."

Shaking his head, Erlaan sat down. He stared at Asirkhyr for a long time before opening his mouth to speak. Once more, the man cut him off.

"We are a priesthood, the founders of the organisation you know as the Brotherhood. The one you have known recently as Udaan will be here shortly to tell you more."

"I need water, and something to eat."

Asirkhyr looked startled by the question. He took a moment to compose himself before replying.

"There is no food and no water in the temple. We do not need these things to sustain ourselves. You will not need them either. Please, rest for a while longer prince, and do not look out of the window."

The man turned sharply on his heels and stalked away, disappearing down the corridor. Erlaan toyed with the idea of ignoring Asirkhyr's warning and glanced up at the window. The strange light that seemed to seep like oil through the gap in the stones put Erlaan on edge.

He decided it was better not to investigate and lay back on the slab, clasping his hands across his chest. As soon as he closed his eyes, he fell into a deep sleep, free from thought and dreams.

II

Sitting in his plain chair, Lakhyri was as immobile as a statue. Only the high priest's eyes moved as he watched his followers swaying and bowing around the Last Corpse, chanting their eternal chant, hoarse voices echoing from the chamber stones. The transference from the grand precinct to the temple had been arduous; Lakhyri had been forced to sustain the ailing Kalmud with his own vitality, draining his deepest reserves.

He had hoped to replenish his strength from the temple, but the ethereal energies that sustained him were at their lowest ebb, almost consumed. Drastic measures would be required. The loss of Askhos disturbed him greatly. He felt no loss or sadness at his brother's death, but the break in the line of the Blood verged on catastrophe for his plans concerning the Askhan Empire. The usurper's dissolution of the Brotherhood was another setback, cutting off another avenue for new life to be brought to the temple.

The grand precinct had been sealed, gateways and doors barred by ancient mechanisms and powerful wards. Its secrets were safe. Yet without Askhos, without the Brotherhood, the Askhan Empire had become a folly, just another frail kingdom without purpose. The saving grace was the rescue of Kalmud and his son. While the true heir to Lutaar still lived and the Crown remained intact, perhaps there was some small chance that the plan could be restored.

A disturbance in the air, a fluttering on the edge of consciousness, stirred Lakhyri's thoughts. One of the masters was close at hand. He felt the throbbing in his gut, the tremble along his nerves of an eulanui manifesting itself. He slowly turned his head to the black block of stone and bone that was the Last Corpse. No entreaty had been made, no ritual of audience performed. What was coming through, and for what purpose?

The sickly light of the temple churned as the master coalesced, the essence of the eulanui imbuing the Last Corpse with a semblance of life.

Awkwardly, the creature rearranged its spindly limbs, unfurling from the carcass-altar. Black flesh bubbled and writhed while multi-faceted, golden eyes swept the rings of supplicant worshippers. Tendril-fingers lashed in agitation.

HUNGER.

The force of the word-concept stunned Lakhyri, blinding him, making his ears rings, his heart shudder. The runes and patterns on his skin froze nerves and muscle, burning with their coldness as life force was leeched from his flesh. Worshippers fainted, collapsing outwards like a ripple in a pool. The youngest convulsed as they fell, heads hitting hard against the stone floor, limbs twitching.

Mandibles clattered and joints creaked as the eulanui stepped over the ranks of still worshippers, feeder tentacles swaying as they tasted the air. Regaining his senses, Lakhyri studied the creature, trying to recognise it. Its bearing was upright, lordly. More than that, there was an aura of shadow about the eulanui, which seemed to glitter like the night sky. Only once before had Lakhyri seen such a thing.

The high priest caught his breath. The apparition was *huayakaitoku*, leader of the eulanui. Not for more than a thousand years, as reckoned by the annals of the Askhans, had the ruler of the eulanui appeared. Fear gripped Lakhyri; a sensation he had not felt in all of that time. For the *huayakaitoku* to risk a fully material form was a grave matter indeed.

Lakhyri toppled out of his chair, falling to his knees.

"Greatest of the great, master of the masters," he moaned. "I am humbled by your presence."

The creature's head snapped around, its golden orbs fixing Lakhyri with their insectan stare. He saw his pinched face and dread-filled eyes reflected a thousand times back at him.

FEED.

The *huayakaitoku* slewed away from Lakhyri, clawed appendages dancing lightly over the bodies of the fallen worshippers, secondary tongues flicking out from slits in the flesh. It quickly passed the eldest, attracted to the vitality of the newest adepts. Banded tendrils lifted up three of the acolytes, wrapping around their chests, the tips plunging into their gawping mouths, jointed finger-stalks clasping limbs and heads.

Rearing up on its hind legs, the eulanui lifted the trapped youths towards gaping mouths. The sphincter-like openings had no teeth, but fronds of whisker-like hair erupted from ridged gullets, stroking the flesh of its victims. One tiny piece at a time, the acolytes disintegrated, the energy binding them together sucked from their bodies: skin, muscle, bones, nerves, arteries and veins, livers and hearts, teeth and brains, every part drained, falling to the ground as a haze of dead cells.

When nothing was left of the three, the *huayakaitoku* looked again at Lakhyri. Its flesh was slicker, the light in its eyes even brighter, gorged on the essence that sustained it.

DISTANT. SACRIFICE. SEEK. KING. CHILD. RESTORE.

Lakhyri nodded in understanding, remembering the same message from the last visitation.

"It shall be as you say, master of masters," gasped the high priest. "We will pave the way."

RETURN. IMMINENT.

Immortal bones slid while stone-like flesh slipped, as the *huayakaitoku* returned to the centre of the chamber and collapsed in on itself, folding back into the gap between dimensions, leaving the square block of the Last Corpse lifeless and dull.

Lakhyri swallowed hard, frightened by the encounter. With groans, the collapsed worshippers stirred from their unconsciousness. Lakhyri quickly pushed himself back into his chair and assumed an undisturbed pose. His mind raced. The eulanui were getting desperate, to feed directly on their followers. What did 'imminent' mean? The empire would not be ready for years unless Ullsaard could be stopped soon.

Lakhyri shuddered again at the conclusion he was forced to draw, the image of the dissipating acolytes at the front of his mind; what he had offered the eulanui by way of trade, they would take by force if necessary.

NALANOR
Autumn, 211th year of Askh

I

A dawnwards wind brought the chill of the mountains to the town of Geria. The Greenwater was ruffled with spray and square sails slapped against masts while the wind carried away the shouts and drums of the oarmasters on the galleys. Hair and cloak tousled, feeling the tinge of drizzle on his face, Urikh stood with hands on hips glaring at the docks, lip curled with anger.

"Why are three ships empty, still waiting to be loaded?" he asked the dockmaster cowering next to him. "You promised me four ships loaded or unloaded every hour."

The dockmaster fumbled with the armful of wax slates in his arms, each covered with manifests and work logs. Droplets of rain gathering on his bald head, eyes fixed on the cobbled ground, the dockmaster mumbled something Urikh could not hear.

"What did you say?" said the governor. "Do me the courtesy of making your pathetic excuses audible."

"The morning shift at dock three are not working because they haven't been paid, governor."

Urikh lifted the man's chin with a finger and stared into his narrowed eyes.

"You know what my next question is going to be, don't you, Liirat?"

The dockmaster nodded and shuffled his feet. A tablet dropped from his grasp and broke on the ground. Two more tumbled out of his arms as he stooped to retrieve the pieces.

Urikh's kick caught the man in the ribs, sending him sprawling, wax plates falling around him.

"They haven't been paid because you are an imbecile!" Urikh rasped. "Money comes out of my treasury and the payment coming in disappears somewhere between the docks and my vault. That is not just my fucking money; it is the empire's money!"

One hand nursing his side, Liirat crawled in a circle, gathering up the scattered slates. He piled them neatly and rose to his feet, a look of sudden defiance on his face.

"I ain't stealing your money, governor. It ain't my fault, honest. The Brothers used to work the payroll, taking out the taxes and such, but I don't know how they worked it out. There was twenty of them, used to run these docks, and now there's just me."

"Can you count?" said Urikh, calming himself.

Liirat nodded.

"Then count one tin to the taxes for every askharin in pay. It is not difficult. That means one whole askharin for every twenty the ship captains pay you for berthing. Do I need someone else to do this for me?"

"No, no, governor," said Liirat. "I can do that. But… Maybe I could have some help with the wages, someone who looks after the money going the other way?"

Urikh tapped his foot impatiently and folded his arms.

"I have sixteen wharfs and four harbour masters," he said slowly. "Three of those harbour masters are having no problem at all. Why should I spend more money hiring another person when I could replace you at no extra cost?"

"Please, governor…" The dockmaster wrung his hands and fidgeted with the belt of his robe. "I'll try harder. I need this work."

"The empire needs many types of men, Liirat. Perhaps you would be better suited to a hoe and plough than a tablet and stylus?"

"It's my back, governor. Can't work the fields, not with my back."

Urikh sighed, shook his head and considered what to do. It had been a lie that there were no problems with the other dockmasters. Across the whole river harbour a third less ships were being passed through each day. Now was the worst time to remove an official while he found another, with the harvest cargo and last surge before winter moving up and down the river.

"Go on, get back to it," he said, waving the dockmaster away. Liirat scurried along the quay, only to turn at a shout from the governor. Urikh pointed at the pile of wax tablets still on the wharf. "You will need these! Get the men paid and get them working."

Urikh heard laughter and turned to see three pilots leaning against the planks of a warehouse a short distance away. The men sheltered under the eaves of the roof as the rain fell harder, chewing strips of cured meat. They straightened up as Urikh stalked over to them.

"Enjoying an early lunch?" he asked. The men shrugged. Infuriated, Urikh grabbed the shirt collar of the closest and dragged him around the corner of the building and pointed out across the river. "See that? That's a berth at dock five empty. And you see that? That's a ship in mid-channel waiting for a pilot to bring it through the flats. Why are you here?"

"No boat, governor," the pilot replied sullenly. "Can't get out to a ship without a boat."

Urikh let go of the man and clenched his fists, causing the pilot to shrink back, fearing a punch.

"Why are there no boats?" Urikh barely stopped a scream of frustration.

"They're all up round docks ten and eleven, governor," came the reply from one of the others. "The rotation is all out of order, governor. Boats not coming back to where they started and leaving from docks where the ship ain't coming in. It's a mess, governor."

"Let me guess; the rotation was organised by the Brotherhood?"

There were nods of agreement. Urikh walked over to the pilot who had spoken and laid his arm across his shoulders, pulling him close. When he spoke, the governor kept his anger in check, his tone mild.

"Do you remember how the rotation worked when the Brothers were running it?" he asked gently.

"Yes, I do, governor," said the pilot, trying to edge out of Urikh's grasp, his discomfort clear.

"What is your name?"

"Kiraan Allin, governor."

"Tell me, Kiraan, could you run the rotation for me?"

Kiraan looked around nervously for a moment.

"But I'm a pilot, governor," he said.

Urikh smiled, adding to the man's unease.

"For an extra Askharin a week, I could make you chief pilot, in charge of the rotation. Would that suit you, Kiraan?"

The pilot smiled, eyes widening as he imagined his wages doubled.

"I think I could do that, governor, yes I could," said Kiraan.

Urikh fished into his pouch and brought out a golden coin.

"You best get started, chief pilot," said Urikh, pressing the askharin into the pilot's hand. Kiraan took a step away but was tugged back by Urikh's tight grip on his arm. "By tonight, I want every boat and every pilot working as fast as possible. If they are not, you answer to me. Is that understood?"

Kiraan nodded and swallowed hard.

"Yes, governor. Can I go now, governor?"

Urikh let the man go and watched all three of them hurry away along the quayside. He slumped against the wooden boards of the warehouse, kneading his forehead to ease the ache there that had plagued him since coming to Geria to take up office. Twenty days of misery, confusion and frustration.

Without the Brotherhood, nothing was working as it was meant to.

It had been more than two years since his father had removed the Brotherhood and though there had been problems before, it was not until now, with a province to govern, that Urikh realised how much had changed.

Without the Brotherhood's calendars, sowing and harvesting crops was haphazard, and the yield was perilously low; without the Brotherhood's records, taxes were not being collected and payments not being made; without the Brotherhood's courts, wrongdoers were left to old tribal justice, with mob beatings and executions increasing at an alarming rate; without the Brotherhood's communications, goods were sitting on wharfs and in warehouses, while ships pointlessly plied the Greenwater with empty holds or slowly rotted at their berths.

Without the Brotherhood, Greater Askhor was degenerating into isolated towns and villages, breaking apart from within.

Urikh was not given to despair, but when he contemplated the task of administrating Okhar with the people he had, he was unsettled. He had rounded up every man and woman in Geria that could write and count and pressed them into service as clerks, accountants and overseers. As many of these people came from the nobility, it had taken days of wrangling and concessions to have them leave their comfortable estates to take up office. Most of them were clearly serving their own interests as much as the empire's but they were his only option at present.

Leaving the riverside docks, he kicked at loose cobbles on the road and wondered whose job it was to fix them. Maintenance of public properties had been another area dealt with by the Brotherhood.

One sight lifted his heart slightly as he moved out of the shadows of the warehouses into the square behind the harbour; a company of his legionnaires stood in solid ranks waiting for his return. His father had been blunt in his advice, and had told Urikh that no matter what else his first priority was to keep the legions equipped, fed and paid; without them, his tenuous rule was worthless.

Urikh had done just that, and for the moment the officers and soldiers of the Seventeenth seemed content enough. Everything else was falling apart around the governor, but his legion was still at full strength and loyal.

The First Captain, Harrakil, was stood to one side of the troop, in animated conversation with another man. Urikh recognised him as one of the chief Gerian merchants, a man called Liitum; he waved his hands expressively and pointed hotwards while Harrakil continually shook his head in disagreement. The two of them broke off their talking at Urikh's approach.

"Why are you haranguing my First Captain, Liitum?" Urikh said. "I thought you were bound for Cosuan?"

It irked Urikh that his father had seen fit to name the new town at the mouth of the Greenwater after his dead mentor, but he had been wise enough not to argue the point. A large part of the task he faced as governor was sending men and supplies to the fledgling territory over two thousand miles to hotwards.

"I was due to leave this morning, governor," said Liitum. "Have you not heard the news?"

Urikh answered this with a hard stare.

"Three ships have been lost heading to Cosuan," the merchant explained. "Hotwards of Daasia, they were attacked."

"How do you know this?" asked Urikh.

"My nephew was one of the survivors. He arrived on a galley from Daasia last night and found me as I was readying to leave. He says that rumour has it two more ships were lost only five days earlier."

"Rumour can have all it wants, what has this to do with me? Besides, the Mekhani have no ships, so just make sure you don't put in on that stretch."

"That's the thing, governor," said Liitum. "My nephew says that the Mekhani did have ships, and they were further coldward than he's ever known."

Urikh looked at Harrakil.

"Have you heard anything about this Mekhani activity?" said the governor.

"Nothing like this," Harrakil replied. "A few accounts of bands moving out of the desert to raid the odd caravan, but they have never attacked on the river before."

"You have to give us protection," said Liitum, grabbing Urikh's sleeve.

The governor looked down at the man's hand until he slowly peeled his fingers away and mumbled an apology.

"Protection?" said Urikh. "You mean my legionnaires?"

"Yes, governor, yes," said Liitum. "Just a company on my ship would be all I need. I won't sail without them."

"If that is the case, perhaps I should give the contract to a man with more spine?"

"If you must," said Liitum. "I will happily sell you back the timber, ore and salted meat I have aboard."

Urikh looked at the merchant with narrowed eyes, trying to work out what advantage Liitum was hoping to gain. It made no sense for him to give back the goods at cost after paying for the berth and labour to load it. There was only one conclusion; Liitum was genuinely scared of sailing to Cosuan.

And if Liitum was scared – one of the greediest men Urikh had met – it would not be long before other traders and captains refused to travel hotwards. With winter coming it was vital that the settlement on the coast had enough stores to last out the season.

"Do we have any spare companies?" Urikh asked his First Captain.

"That depends on what you mean by 'spare'," said Harrakil. "I've got half the legion patrolling the border with Near-Mekha to protect against Mekhani brigands. The rest, well, they're here and spread out as garrisons along the river."

"How many?"

"Allowing for messengers and march time, I could have two thousand in Geria in ten days' time. What is it that you want to do, governor?"

"We have to make sure Cosuan is supplied for the winter," said Urikh, glancing between the two men. "It is impractical to send off a company here and there as needed, especially as there is no certainty that the Mekhani will attack again. I think we need to assemble a flotilla of ships and galleys and move everything Cosuan needs in one journey. A show of force to the Mekhani, and far easier to protect."

Harrakil nodded obediently while Liitum rubbed his chin, his expression one of calculation.

"Ten days is not a lot of time to organise such a thing," said the merchant. "And not with the docks working as poorly as they are. You could send out word to some of the ships meant to be unloading in the towns to cold-wards and have them carry on here with their cargoes. Yes, it could be done, but it won't be easy and it won't be cheap."

"It will have to be done," said Urikh. "The king would never forgive us if we allowed Cosuan to fail. We will sail hotwards in ten days' time, bolster the settlers and garrison, drop off all the supplies they need for the winter, and then we can worry about the Mekhani in the spring."

Liitum and Harrakil signalled their agreement but to Urikh's annoyance, they continued to loiter, perhaps expecting further instruction.

"Why are you still here?" Urikh snapped at the two of them. He shooed them away with a flick of the hand. "We all have lots of work to do."

II

Vapour swirled, moisture dappling the marble walls and pillars. Somewhere in the haze a servant splashed more water on hot coals to send a fresh cloud of steam billowing across the sunken bath. Black hair wetly plastered across her flushed face, Luia lay with her arms along the side, panting.

The water thrashed with bubbles and Huurit surfaced, gasping for breath. Muscles taut from years of wrestling, he paddled across to lounge beside Luia. With one hand he absently caressed her breast, massaging himself with the other. Luia glanced at him a flash of annoyance and took his hand from her chest.

"I'm not finished," she said.

"I'm a man, not a fish," Huurit protested.

"Prove it," said Luia, grabbing his hair to force him back down into the water. She lifted up her legs and thrust him beneath her, trapping his head between her thighs. Huurit flailed for a moment before dragging himself free, emerging with a splash at the other side of the pool.

"Trying to drown me," he spluttered, answered by Luia's laugh. The wrestler pulled himself out of the water while Luia ran an appreciative eye over his short, wiry body.

"Do not go too far!" she called out as Huurit stalked into the steam, bare feet slapping on the tiles.

She lounged for a while longer, eyes closed, until she heard someone entering the bath room.

"Back for more?" she said.

"Hardly, mother."

Luia opened her eyes to see Urikh pacing through the vapour, a thick robe wrapped around him. He pulled off the robe and used it to make a cushion on the bench alongside the bath. He lay down, arms behind his head.

"I will be leaving Geria in ten days," he said. "I trust you can keep the city from destroying itself while I am away."

Servants came forward with towels and a robe as Luia pulled herself from the pool. She stood with arms outstretched while they dried her.

"Why this sudden departure?" she asked.

Urikh sighed and rolled over to his side, head propped up on one hand.

"Something has happened with the Mekhani," he said. "They have been attacking ships between here and

Cosuan. I am assembling a fleet and taking the legion to teach them a lesson."

"Surely you have officers for that sort of thing," said Luia. A stool was put before her and she sat down, allowing one of her maids to comb her hair. "There is no need for you to leave."

"Not on the face of it, but I have to be seen to be a leader. You know, I am the only heir of the Blood who has never been a general? That sort of thing can be damaging. No, if I want to ensure the loyalty of the legions, I have to establish myself as a competent commander."

"And how will you do that, my dear? You know nothing about war. You were always bored by your father's stories, never listened to a word of them."

Urikh flopped to his back again, eyes fixed on the mosaic patterns on the ceiling.

"I learnt a thing or two from father when we took Magilnada. Besides, the whole point of going with the legion is to see how it all works, pick up a few things from Harrakil. Father chose him for me, so he must be good at what he does. I need to learn quickly."

There was an intensity in Urikh's expression that Luia knew well. It filled her with a mixture of pride and concern; pride because of his determination, concern that usually it heralded obsession.

"You have to be patient, dear. I know that already you are thinking up plots and schemes to become king. Do not deny it; I know you, I taught you! Do not be so hasty to replace your father. The empire is very fragile at the moment. Let your father establish his rule, and demonstrate your right to be his heir. If you do not, the Crown will be worthless when it passes to you."

"Ullsaard courts danger like a mistress," said Urikh. "I grew up half-expecting to hear of his death, and I have always known I have to be ready to take his place as head of the family. Now that he is king that is truer than ever."

Luia said nothing, uncomfortable with the thought of Ullsaard dying, especially now that he had achieved far more than she had ever hoped he would. The two of them sat in silence for a while until Luia chose to change the subject.

"What about Neerlima and Luissa? Will you take them with you to Cosuan?"

"Why would I?"

Her hair now bound in a long plait, Luia stood, allowing the servants to wrap a dark blue dress around her. She tightened the belt, adjusted the fall of the sleeves and sat at the end of the bench where her son lay. The servants disappeared through the curtain over the door.

"To show them the lands you now govern," said Luia. "Neerlima will be proud, and Luissa is nearly eight years old, it is time she started being seen."

"And by 'being seen' you mean on the market for a future husband? Who will ever meet your standards, mother? You once said that she would only marry a prince; now she is a princess."

"Another first," said Luia with a puzzled expression.

"What do you mean?"

"She is the first girl of the Blood to be born. Always the Blood have sired sons."

"Surely in two hundred years... Now that you say it, I realise you are right. Why do you think that is?"

A doubt crept in Luia's mind but she did not speak it; that perhaps Luissa was not the child of Urikh. There was no proof, of course, and such a thing would only harm Urikh. It was best not to speculate.

"Perhaps in previous generations, the daughters have been whisked away by the Brotherhood; like your grandmother was supposed to be."

"Pretaa was a court harlot, not a daughter of the Blood."

Urikh sat up and swung his feet to the floor so that he was sitting beside his mother. He leaned forward, elbow on knee, chin on fist, and stared into the still water of the bath. Luia feared for a moment that he was considering the possibility of Neerlima's infidelity.

"It is astounding to think about it," said Urikh. He shook his head in bemusement. "What a slender chance it is that we are here. Or that I am here, at least."

"What slender chance? You mean Ullsaard's defeat of Lutaar? No, that was not chance. For all that he annoys me with his crude ways, your father can be a great man. And do not forget, you played a large part in his success as well."

"No, not that," said Urikh. He scratched his chin, eyes narrowed. "Pretaa should have been taken by the Brotherhood because she carried the seed of one of the Blood but was not a wife. It was chance that Cosuas helped her to escape. Who can say what course would have been charted if not for that tiny thing?"

"Yes, dear, but to think of all the chance circumstance that brought us all here is to invite madness. My grandmother was rescued from Ersuan brigands by my grandfather. But for that, I might not exist. Last week it rained and I did not go to the market. The smallest thing, maybe, but who can say what might have happened had the sun shone? Maybe I would have overheard a conspiracy, or bought a dress that attracted the eye of a handsome man, or perhaps berated a jewelsmith for charging too much, leaving him annoyed so that he beats his wife when he gets home.

"Do not second-guess what has happened in the past, and do not think that chance has no part to play in the future. But chance and luck are not the same thing. The gambler relies on luck, and you are no gambler, dear. The man who plans, the man who thinks, a man like you, knows when chance favours him and seizes the opportunity."

Urikh sat up, a half-smile on his lips. He leaned over and planted a delicate kiss on Luia's cheek.

"What was that for?" she asked, startled by the uncharacteristic gesture.

"Thanking chance that I have your intelligence, and not father's," Urikh said. "Ullsaard undervalues you."

"You are wrong," said Luia. "How many other men would tolerate me? I openly defy him in front of others, and my appetite for other men is no secret. I was the same when he married Allenya, and he has had ample reason and opportunity to do away with me."

"It is only for Allenya's sake that he has not."

"In part. He loves Allenya, and lusts after Meliu like she is a bitch in heat. He keeps me around for a different reason."

Luia stopped herself. She did not want to say too much. She could not admit that in her heart she respected Ullsaard, even loved him for being the father of her son. How could she explain that it was not perversity that made her wayward, but a desire to see her husband strong, though on occasion she did get some delight from seeing him fume and splutter at her behaviour?

In the depths of the building a servant chimed the turn of Howling. Luia stood up briskly and patted Urikh on the cheek. He squirmed at the matronly gesture; he had done the same ever since coming of age, and Luia loved that it infuriated him.

"Dinner will be served shortly, get dressed," she said. "And think carefully about Neerlima and Luissa. You cannot keep either of them hidden in the palace forever. Just think on it."

Urikh nodded, lost in thought, brow creased with troubles.

He will make a fine king, Luia thought as she left him to his concerns.

SALPHORIA
Late Autumn, 211th year of Askh

I

The wind flapped at the fabric of Ullsaard's pavilion and brought a pattering of rain. The king sat in his campaign throne, brow knotted as he stared at the large map spread out on the rugs before him. To his right and left sat two of his First Captains, Anasind and Jutiil, and two others, self-appointed army commanders who had raised their own legions for the war; the first was Arrak Maalus, head of one of Askh's oldest noble families, a squat man in his fifties with a clean-shaven chin and head, but with jutting side whiskers that reached to his shoulders; the other was a Maasrite fleet captain, Lukha, who had arrived with three thousand legionnaires and twenty Nemurian mercenaries.

Ullsaard liked neither of the men, but suffered their amateur suggestions in silence, knowing it was the price he paid for having them help to finance his campaign. Of the five extra legions so far raised by the nobles, two had been all but destroyed, and the other three had achieved little except to spread fear and confusion amongst the Salphors. It did not matter; as long as the Salphors were under constant attack they would never have the time to gather their forces. In the wake of the ad-hoc invasions of the others, Ullsaard would sweep duskwards and tidy up, until he was camped at the walls of Carantathi. He felt some guilt at the legionnaires' lives being wasted in this way, but in the long run the campaign would prove to be less costly.

"Enough squabbling," said the king, stepping down from his chair. "Maalus, you will take your legion cold-wards of here, the Aaglios River. That secures these forested hills. There are likely to be tribes in the forest it-self, so don't try anything spectacular, you'll simply be ambushed. Lukha, you need to keep moving duskwards along the Aaglios, until you take this group of settlements here, at this fork in the river. I have it from my Salpho-rian allies that there is a town on the lake island. I figure with your expertise with ships that shouldn't be too much of a problem."

Lukha looked sourly at the map.

"So, Maalus gets hundreds of miles of the finest fir trees, while I have a lake and an island? What am I sup-posed to profit from? Fish?"

Ullsaard wanted to strangle the man, but fought the urge.

"We don't know where the Aaglios leads, but it is bound to be an important route duskwards to the sea," Ullsaard explained, not entirely hiding his irritation. "That island will be the perfect place for a dock. It'll be as large as Geria; maybe even as big as Narun if there's as much land to duskwards as I think there is. Maalus will be paying your port fees to ship that timber to the coast."

Maalus was about to object, but was stopped by Ull-saard's raised hand.

"And before you complain, Maalus, consider this," the king continued. "Docks mean wharfs and ships, and that means timber. This stretch of river could be the centre of

Askhan expansion in Salphoria, and there's going to be enough coin for everybody involved."

The two men exchanged a glance filled with suspicion. Maalus looked at the map again, rubbing a hand over his scalp.

"That is quite a way from Magilnada," he said. "I would not want to be sticking my neck to the block. Perhaps another legion or two would make the situation more secure?"

"No," said Ullsaard. "Winter's coming, and there's no time for you to raise any more legions. We need this advance to happen as soon as possible."

"I know I cannot raise a legion overnight, but you have five of them sitting here with nothing to do…"

"No."

Maalus frowned and stood up with a dismissive wave of his hand.

"I am not going to wander into the heart of Salphor territory with just one legion." The noble took two steps towards the tent door before Ullsaard grabbed his arm and hauled him around.

"You will march your legion tomorrow," said the king, speaking slowly and quietly. "If you do not, I will find someone who will."

Maalus tried to shrug off the king's grip but failed. He met Ullsaard's stare with a look of contempt.

"You cannot force me to do anything," said the noble. "If you want my men, you will allow me to choose where and when they march. I am not one of your captains, to be ordered around at your whim."

Ullsaard tightened his fingers until Maalus was squirming, knees buckling.

"This isn't Askh," hissed Ullsaard. "And I am still your king. I could cut your fucking head off right now and there is not a man in this camp would raise a word about it. I have offered you ample reward for your efforts. Do not test my patience."

The flush of anger drained from Maalus's face as he saw the look in Ullsaard's eyes. The king pulled Maalus back to his feet, let go of his arm and waved towards the door.

"Feel free to return to your legion now," said Ullsaard. He glanced over his shoulder to his First Captains. "Jutiil will accompany you back to your camp to help you make everything ready for your departure."

Jutiil stood up, one hand resting on the pommel of his sword. He smiled at Maalus and nodded for the noble to lead the way. Ullsaard watched the two of them until they had left and then turned to Lukha.

"Any questions or objections?" the king asked.

Lukha smiled hesitantly and shook his head.

"No, my king, that all seems to be perfectly clear."

II

The track was a ribbon of slurry, created by the constant drizzle and thousands of feet. The legionnaires sloped their shields above their heads to keep the rain from wetting their kit, giving the column the appearance of a snake three miles long, with round scales banded in sections of red, black, blue and bronze.

Ullsaard pulled Blackfang to one side of the winding track, heading up a shallow rise, the high grass leaving a wet swathe in the ailur's fur. For eight days he had marched, almost directly duskwards, following the muddy road alongside the Annillan River. From the Altes hills the waterway plunged down into the plains and then veered lazily through the grasslands, almost half a mile wide in places. The only evidence of people had been the clusters of abandoned huts clinging to the muddy flats around the river; the Salphors had fled before the advance of the Askhans.

Looking ahead, Ullsaard could see little through the gloom, but from his observations yesterday knew that there was a range of mountains somewhere to duskwards. How wide or high they were, he did not know, and whether they could be skirted to coldwards or hotwards remained a concern. From experience, he knew the Annillan would turn one way or the other as it reached the foothills, following the line of least resistance to the sea. Just how far that might be had been a subject of some debate in the camp for the past few days, with no clear decision. Much like the Greenwater campaign, this was a voyage into the unknown.

Staring at the expanse of wilderness, Ullsaard wondered if he had bitten off more than he could chew. Greater Askhor was vast, but it seemed that the loose conglomeration of lands and people the Askhans glibly called Salphoria might be almost as big.

It had taken two hundred years for Greater Askhor to be created, and he was looking to conquer a similar territory within a season. He had once said he would conquer Salphoria in a single summer if he had two hundred and fifty thousand men. He had less than half that, and yet had pressed on regardless. It seemed ridiculous when he thought of it like that.

His contemplation was broken by the approach of Anasind, accompanied by a leather-faced legionnaire. Ullsaard recognised the man as one of the ex-landship crew that had joined the Thirteenth for the attack on Magilnada. He had seen him again at the sacking of Askh, but for his life he couldn't remember the man's name.

"What's this?" asked Ullsaard.

"Someone who could be useful, king," said Anasind. "You wanted local knowledge. This is Gelthius, a Salphor in the Thirteenth."

"Gelthius, that was it," said Ullsaard. He smiled at the legionnaire, who had the expression of a small animal suddenly coming face to face with a hungry lion. Ullsaard was not sure whether this was due to his presence, or Blackfang's. The soldier was certainly keeping as far from the ailur as he could without actually hiding behind Anasind. "Glad to see you're still with us, Gelthius."

"So am I, right enough," said Gelthius. He glanced at Anasind before continuing. "I heard word that you was asking after people that might know these lands."

Anasind coughed pointedly and glared at Gelthius.

"King," the legionnaire quickly added with a bow of the head.

"So, you know these parts, do you?"

"Was born on the banks of this river, about three more days duskwards," said Gelthius. "Er, king. These are the lands of the Linghar."

There was a catch to the man's voice, and a slightly wistful cast to his expression, tinged with apprehension.

"You have family here?" the king asked.

"They was here when I got taken as a debtor, king," Gelthius said with a shrug. "I dunno if they still is. That were seven years ago and some."

Ullsaard regarded the legionnaire for some time, adding to Gelthius's discomfort. With a little nod to himself as he reached a decision, the king leaned over to the legionnaire and slapped a hand on his shoulder.

"Don't look so worried," said Ullsaard. "Do you think your company could spare you for a while?"

"Spare me?"

"You're joining my staff, Gelthius! I need someone like you to help me out."

"Me? Help you? I dunno about that, king. I don't know much."

"Neither do I," said Ullsaard with a wink. "But around here, you probably know more than most of us."

Gelthius looked uncertain, glancing at Anasind for guidance. The First Captain nodded encouragingly.

"I'll have to make you a third captain," said Anasind. "If you're going to be on the king's staff, that is."

The thought of the extra pay and privileges of rank seemed to ease Gelthius's concerns immediately and he smiled bashfully.

"If I can be of help, king, then I'll do what I can." His smile faded and doubt returned. Gelthius looked Ullsaard with pleading in his eyes. "You're not going to burn and kill everything are you?"

"Not unless I'm forced to," the king replied with a shrug. "Let's hope you can make your people see some sense."

III

Smoke drifted across the setting sun, the haze rising from nearly a hundred chimney holes and bonfires. Half-dug into the hillside, their turf roofs extending over stone walls, the houses of the Linghar were squat dwellings, with narrow doors and glassless, horizontal slit windows. There was no wall or palisade; the only obstacles were the animal pens fenced with woven reed taken from the river bank at the bottom of the long slope.

It was not the homecoming Gelthius had dreamed of; nor the one he had expected.

For this first time since becoming a legionnaire, he felt uncomfortable in his armour and uniform. Sat in the back of the abada cart, spear and shield stowed beside him, he was keenly aware of his tanned legs jutting from under his kilt, and the weight of his breastplate. He looked at the other three legionnaires in the wagon: Muuril, Gebriun and Loordin; Haeksin was up front steering the cart.

"How are you feeling, boss?" said Muuril. "Good to be home?"

Gelthius said nothing, still uncertain about his position with the others. They seemed to have taken his sudden promotion in their stride, but Gelthius was under no doubts that he was the least experienced of all the men. Muuril especially gave Gelthius problems; three days ago he had been Gelthius's sergeant, now it was Gelthius that was in charge. Muuril had been nothing but supportive, but Gelthius wondered whether the sergeant would really follow orders if it came down to it.

They were watchmates above everything else, and Gelthius hoped that counted for something; which was why he had brought them with him on this mission. On First Captain Anasind's suggestion, he had picked the men he trusted most. Gelthius hoped they trusted him just as much.

"Hey up, they've seen us," said Haeksin.

Families were coming out of the houses, women and children sheltering behind their menfolk as they gathered on the road. There were spears and shields in the crowd, but as the cart rumbled to a stop a few dozen yards away, Gelthius sensed curiosity rather than anger.

"Gear up," said Muuril, grabbing his spear.

"Not yet," said Gelthius, laying a hand on the sergeant's wrist. Muuril's expression conveyed his doubts on this course of action, but he let go of his weapon.

Gelthius hauled himself over the side of the cart, landing ankle-deep in a puddle. Cursing his Askhan sandals, he trudged up the hill, mud spattering his naked legs. He raised a hand in greeting.

"Is Naraghlin still in charge?" he called out. "Is he here?"

There was no reply from the sullen tribesmen, who had now formed a solid line from one edge of the road to the other, between the two outermost houses. Gelthius looked along the row of bearded faces, recognising most, though unable to recall many names.

He realised he had spoken in crude Askhan. He tried again with the Linghan tongue. The tribesmen exchanged looks and peered at Gelthius with renewed interest. One of them stopped forward, a young man not long out of his teens. Although much older than when he had last been here, Gelthius recognised him as Kalsaghan, Naraghlin's son.

"Who's asking?" said the youth. He stood with feet braced apart, shield held up to his left, a short spear in his right hand. His face was clean shaven, but his hair hung in long braids to his chest, bound with leather thongs. Older men closed protectively around him, spears ready.

"It's me, Gelthius." He pulled off his helmet so that they could better see his face. "Where's Naraghlin? I need to speak with him."

"Look at you, all dressed up in your Askhan costume," said Kalsaghan. "With your shaved head and your bare face, you look like a child."

"Rules," said Gelthius. "Come on, I need to speak with your father."

"He has nothing to say to you." This was from a red-headed warrior standing to Kalsaghan's left; a bear of a man Gelthius knew to be the chieftain's younger brother, Mannuis. "Go away."

"If I go away, the next time you see me, there'll be ten thousand Askhan arseholes with me," said Gelthius.

This was greeted with laughter.

"Really?" said Kalsaghan. "Ten thousand? They would be a long way from home if there were."

Gelthius tucked his helmet under his arm and strode up the track, stopping just a few paces from the line of warriors.

"It's true," he said. "Yes, they're a long way from home, and they're itching for a fight. Don't give them one. Stop playing around; tell me where I'll find Naraghlin. He's not gone to Carantathi with the others, has he?"

"I'm here, Gelthius."

The aging chieftain pushed his way through the crowd, wrapped in a thick cloak of a deep golden bear fur. He was about the same age as Gelthius, but his hair was a shock of white, his long beard the same. Bushy eyebrows stuck out from under the rim of his helmet and he used a staff for balance as he hobbled closer. There was suspicion in the chieftain's eyes.

"What are you doing here, Gelthius?"

"I come with a message from King Ullsaard of Greater Askhor," said Gelthius. He realised how grand that sounded as soon as he said it, and was not surprised to see several warriors curling their lips with derision. Naraghlin did not sneer. He simple nodded in a dejected way and waved for Gelthius to approach with a heavily veined hand.

"Couldn't make the council of chieftains," Naraghlin admitted with a sigh. He regarded Gelthius with rheumy eyes. "Too damned old for the journey."

"It's probably better that you didn't leave," said Gelthius. "It hasn't gone well for those tribes that had nobody to strike a deal with Ullsaard."

"So I've heard. Tell your friends that they can enter. Have them take the cart up to– "

The chieftain was interrupted by an astonished cry to Gelthius's left. A woman broke through the mass of warriors, greying hair fluttering as she ran across the road. She stopped short of Gelthius, staring at him with eyes wide in disbelief.

"Maredin?" Gelthius stared back at his wife, taken aback by her sudden appearance.

He had been so apprehensive about meeting Naraghlin, the thought of this reunion had been pushed from his mind; yet it had occupied his thoughts ever since the Thirteenth had marched duskwards from Magilnada at the start of the summer. Seeing her face, he had no idea what to say.

"What do you look like, Gelthius?" she snapped. "Dressed up like one of them Askhans and all."

Gelthius had to laugh. Ignoring her scowl, he threw his arms around Maredin and pulled her into a tight hug. Tears rolled down his cheeks.

"Never knew this day would come or not," he told her, burying his face in her hair, almost crushing her.

Maredin wriggled out of his grasp and glared at him, hands on hips. Gelthius recognised her scolding stance and stepped back out of instinct, one hand raised protectively.

"I suppose you'll be wanting something to eat, and a drink, no doubt," she said. "Is that right? Carted off by that debt warden, no word of explanation, and gone for more years than I can count. Now you're back, are you?"

"Don't start," Gelthius warned. "I will tell you everything, but I have to talk with Naraghlin first. Please, my love, wait for me at the house."

For a moment it looked like Maredin was going to argue. She contented herself with an angry huff and whirled away back into the amused crowd without saying another word.

"Wives, eh?" said Naraghlin, leaning on his staff as if the weight of the world bore down on his thin shoulders. "Still, you miss them when they're gone, don't you?"

Gelthius waved for the other legionnaires to drive the cart into the town. Muuril was the first to step down.

"What's happening, captain?" the sergeant asked, eyes narrowed at the Salphors. "Are we good?"

"Not sure yet," Gelthius replied in Askhan. "There's a lodging house up the next left fork in the road. Send the cart up there and tell the others to stay with it. I'm going to the chieftain's hall to speak with Naraghlin. Follow us."

"Yes, captain," Muuril said, smartly rapping his fist against his breastplate in salute. This elicited more laughter from the Salphors. The sergeant snapped a few orders to the men in the cart and fell in beside Gelthius.

The crowd parted as Naraghlin and Gelthius headed up the slope towards the summit, where the long hall of the elders stood. Two columns flanked the doorway, their tops carved in the likeness of a bear and a wolf. An embroidered banner hung between them, sodden with rain and tattered with age, depicting a youthful warrior facing a snarling wolf armed with nothing more than a knife. Beside the warrior reared a gigantic bear with a golden pelt. It was meant to be Naraghlin; an illustration of a remarkable feat of might from his childhood. Gelthius snorted, suppressing a laugh at seeing it.

He remembered that day, in the woods coldwards along the river. The wolf had been almost dead from its fight with a bear. Naraghlin had just finished off the wounded animal. Nobody had actually seen the bear. The omen of being rescued by a bear was good one though, and the group had agreed to spin a story to the elders when they returned with its ravaged corpse.

Gelthius hadn't known then that Naraghlin would later use the lie as proof that the spirit of the woods had blessed him; and killed the old chieftain to take his place as ruler of the Linghar. Gelthius had made the mistake of speaking out against this murder and had been left beaten close to death by Naraghlin's henchmen; he was warned never to speak the truth about what had happened in the woods that day, on pain of death.

That had been the start of Gelthius's woes, and as he followed Naraghlin into the gloomy hall, he wondered at the strange route that had brought him back to this place. One word from him to Ullsaard, and within a day, the town would be razed to the ground. Naraghlin and his cronies would be dead.

It was tempting, almost too tempting, but Gelthius reminded himself that it would not only be Naraghlin that would suffer. The legions were deadly efficient, but not very discriminating; there was no way to protect his friends without protecting those he disliked.

Naraghlin took off his cloak and spread it over the carved stump of wood that served as his throne. In the flickering of the fire pit, the chieftain's wrinkled face seemed animated, but there was little life in his eyes. Girls arrived with skins of mead, passing one to the chieftain and another to Gelthius. He sat down on the straw-strewn floor and signalled for Muuril to stand by the door.

Kalsaghan, Mannuis and half a dozen other local nobles entered, but Naraghlin dismissed them with a wave.

"Out! This is between the two of us," said the chieftain. He waited until the others had left before continuing. "What does your new chieftain want?"

"Swear loyalty to my king," said Gelthius. "Do not fight the Askhans."

"That's it?" Naraghlin swilled from the skin, mead glistening in his beard. "No tribute? No slaves?"

"That's not how the Askhans do things," said Gelthius. "Not if you agree."

"What then?"

"More Askhans will come here. They will show you how to build proper houses, sow fields of barley, improve the farms. They will bring boats and masons and many other men with crafts. They will offer the young men of the Linghar the chance to become legionnaires. They will teach you how to count in their way, and speak their tongue, and write, and read."

Naraghlin considered this as he took another mouthful of mead. He tossed the skin aside and wiped the back of his hand across his mouth.

"And?" said the chieftain. "If that was all, nobody would have fought the Askhans."

"The Askhans will remove the shrines in the wood and down by the river, and the wards over the doors, and will tell you never to talk about the spirits. An Askhan will come to the town and take over. You will renounce the title of chieftain, and your claim to rule. This Askhan will take taxes for the empire, and you will get nothing. If you behave yourself, you might get some land to keep for yourself."

"I'm almost dead, anyway, though I can't see Kalsaghan being too happy about that. So if nobody can talk about the spirits, who calls for the crow when I die?"

"Nobody does. Your body will be burnt and the ashes given to Kalsaghan to do with as he wants. That's how the Askhans do it."

Horror spread across Naraghlin's face.

"But if nobody calls the crow, I'll be trapped in my body when it gets burnt! Why would they do that to me?"

"It's the same for everyone," said Gelthius. "The Askhans say that there are no spirits, there is no crow to take us to Aleea. They say there is no Aleea to be taken to."

"But that's idiotic. If there was no Aleea, where do all the dead people go?"

Gelthius shrugged.

"They just laughed at me when I asked. They think people just stop when their body dies."

"No, no, I can't do this," said Naraghlin. "I'd be doom-ing the Linghar to torment and pain. If we do not make the tributes, the crow will not feed our fathers, and who will put the seed of the children in the belly of our women if there are no offerings to the dove? This Askhan madness has to be stopped."

"Nobody's done that for two hundred years," said Gelthius, standing up. "If you fight, our people will all be killed and the Askhans will grow crops and raise goats on the ruins of our homes."

"Then we will leave here, go towards the dusk and start over," said Naraghlin. "Our people have done it before, we can survive again."

"Maybe you're right," said Gelthius as he headed to the door. "But Ullsaard is a determined man. He wants all of Salphoria, one way or the other. Maybe you'll escape this year, but next year? The year after? The Askhans told me that they will rule all the lands between the seas. They're not going to stop."

"Unless we stop them," growled Naraghlin. "Aegenuis is uniting the tribes."

Gelthius stopped at the doorway and looked back, Naraghlin a huddled form in the glow of the fire, eyes staring into the flames. "It won't help. Think about it. I'll not be heading back until tomorrow. Don't throw our people's lives away."

Gelthius slapped Muuril on the shoulder and the two of them left the hall.

"Are they going to fight?" asked the sergeant, looking uneasily at the crowd of warriors waiting outside the long hall.

"I think they are," said Gelthius. "I'm going to get my family and then we'll leave. I think it won't be safe to stay here."

IV

Gelthius stood up against the reed fence around the small plot of land attached to his house. The night was cold and steam rose from the stream of his urine. He took a deep breath, glad to be out of the cramped confines of the burrow-like dwelling; and away from the constant questions of his family. Gelthius had told them everything; being a debtor on Anglhan's landship, the rebels in the mountains, the arrival of the Askhans and the fall of Magilnada.

He had seen disbelief in their eyes and had shown them the tattoo on his arm of the symbol of the Thirteenth; he had been drunk the night the others had persuaded him and it was a blessing of the spirits that his companions' crude technique had not left him with an infection.

He smirked to himself in the darkness, remembering fondly his time with the legion. It was not like that at all, here in Salphoria. Everyone was a rival in some way; everybody was trying to get ahead at the expense of someone else. Even brothers and sons were potential enemies. In the legions, success and failure was collective, with everybody living or dying by the efforts of others as well as their own. It was not perfect; many a freezing night spent patrolling a camp had taxed Gelthius's spirit.

As he walked back to the door, Gelthius noticed firelight further down the hill. He carried on to the main track and watched as the glow brightened, seeming to come from the long hall. In the quiet of the night he could hear raised voices, though he could not tell what they were saying.

Something was not right, and Gelthius's earlier suspicions returned. It had been a mistake to stay, but Muuril had convinced him that the Linghar would not dare tempt Ullsaard's wrath by harming his ambassador.

Gelthius should have insisted that such niceties were rarely observed between Salphors – hostages were taken all the time – never mind with an Askhan representative. Yet the temptation to stay with his family for a night had proved too much.

Ducking back into the house, Gelthius grabbed his knife belt and cloak.

"There's trouble," he said, looking at Maredin. "Grab what food and coin you have."

"What sort of trouble?" asked Gannuis, his eldest son, pulling a sheathed sword from a hook on the wall. Though barely turned sixteen, he was already taller than his father, with a crooked nose from drunken brawls. The younger, Minglhan, was asleep on a pile of blankets next to the fire hole. He stirred at a touch from his mother.

"Not the sort that we'll be able to fight our way out of," said Anglhan. He tapped Minglhan on the shoulder and pushed him towards the door. "Fetch your sister from her house. I'll head to the lodge and fetch my friends and the wagon. We'll leave duskwards and circle back to the army."

"Leave?" Maredin's voice broke. "Why would we leave? You go. We've been fine without you."

"Hush now," said Gannuis. "You think we'll be able to farm and hunt now that the others know about the Askhans? Just get your stuff."

Gelthius could not wait for the argument to be settled. Strapping on his belt, he jogged out into the darkness. There were more voices from around the long hall and he could see quite a gathering silhouetted against the light from the open doors.

Breaking into a run, he scrambled over the roof of another house and dropped down into the yard beside the lodging hall. Loordin was standing watch at the door.

"I think Kalsaghan and Mannuis are up to something," Gelthius said breathlessly.

"Not the chieftain?" asked Loordin.

"Maybe, but I don't think it's him, he seemed resigned to what was going to happen," replied Anglhan. "Get the cart ready and I'll fetch the others."

Loordin headed into the shadow of the stable without further comment while Gelthius stepped into the hall. It was one long chamber, a fire pit and hanging cauldron at one end, rough beds arranged along each wall with a scattering of tables and chairs in the middle of the room. The embers of the fire glowed dully and smoke drifted lazily through a vent in the thatched roof. There were only three men inside; the other Askhans. Gelthius put finger and thumb to his lips and gave a sharp whistle. Muuril was the first to rouse.

"What's happening?" he asked, snatching up his spear and shield, which he had left leaning against the wall next to his bed. "Is it a fight?"

"I hope not," said Haeksin, rubbing sleep from his eyes. "I've only just come off watch."

Gelthius quickly explained what was happening and left the legionnaires to get ready. He ran back to the stables to help Loordin, arriving to find that he already had the small cart on its traces and was hitching up a recalcitrant abada. Gelthius ducked under the yoke and grabbed the ring through the beast's horn, holding it still while Loordin looped the cart ropes through the harness around the abada's body. Heaving with all his weight, Gelthius dragged the abada's head towards the door and then leapt up onto the wagon seat.

Muuril, Gebriun and Haeksin were fully armed and armoured, waiting in the courtyard. They pulled themselves into the cart as it trundled past. Haeksin slid onto the driving board beside Gelthius and took the reins from him.

"Go get your family, we'll see you on the road," said Haeksin.

Gelthius needed no second invite and dropped down to the ground. He cut up the hill at a run, jumping over small stone walls and vaulting the woven reed fences separating the small plots of the families living between the lodging house and his home.

He found Gannuis standing outside the door, a burning torch in one hand, drawn sword in the other. Aranathi, Gelthius's daughter, stood beside her mother, sharing a woollen shawl; her husband, a stocky youth called Faeghun, hovered protectively close by, a cudgel gripped nervously in one fist.

"Come on," said Gelthius as he heard the rumble of cart wheels coming up the track. He snatched the torch from Gannuis and waved it over his head, until he could see the outline of the wagon in the starlight. "Make room there! Maredin, Aranathi, Minglhan; get on board. Everyone else, we're walking."

Gannuis and Faeghun watched the legionnaires with narrowed, suspicious eyes as the Askhan soldiers helped the women and child onto the back of the cart. Gelthius split the two Linghars, one to each side, Gannuis with Loordin, Faeghun with Gebriun; he positioned himself at the front while Muuril guarded the rear.

The abada plodded up the hill under the urging of Haeksin, while Gelthius forged ahead, searching for the fork in the road that would lead to the duskwards side of the hill. A few faces peered out of doors as they passed, but most of the Linghars were asleep already, weary from a day's toil and expecting to rise before dawn.

The houses gave way to the open hillside at the crest.

Here the rocks were too heavy and too close together for the Linghars to dig their homes. The track split, the main road continuing coldwards while a much less-travelled path switched back and forth down the steep duskward side of the mount.

"It's steep, be careful," Gelthius called back. Haeksin raised his hand in acknowledgement. "Watch out for rocks as well, this path don't get cleared too often."

"What are you saying?" Faeghun called back. "Who are you talking to?"

Gelthius ignored him, climbing down an embankment to cut out a loop of the path. As his sandaled feet scraped on the stone-filled dirt track, he froze.

There was torchlight at the bottom of the hill, about half a mile away as the Askhans measured it.

"Shit," Gelthius muttered.

It was too late to turn back into the village. They would have to deal with whatever was waiting for them. Gelthius carried on for a few hundred paces, stopping when he had a clearer view.

In the light of two torches, Gelthius saw a handful of Linghar warriors, perhaps a dozen at the most. He instantly recognised Kalsaghan amongst them. The tribesmen were sat on rocks beside the road, drinking and joking with each other, while Kalsaghan paced back and forth across the dirt road, hand on the hilt of a dagger at his hip.

Crouching in a bush, Gelthius listened but could hear nothing of what the men were saying. One or two seemed almost asleep. He glanced up the hill, hearing the creak of the cart axles and the crunch of the wheels. The hotwards face of the hill, above the waiting Linghars, was almost a cliff. The only way from the village to where Kalsaghan waited was down the track being followed by the wagon, or across the bridge over the river at the bottom of the dawnwards slope; neither was particularly quick.

Reaching a decision, Gelthius ran back up the hill to warn the others. He was panting hard by the time he saw the looming bulk of the wagon in the darkness. Gelthius hissed a caution as the abada almost lumbered into him, forcing him into a bush beside the narrow, steep track.

"There's men waiting for us at the bottom," said Gelthius as he pushed himself from a tangle of thorny branches, dried, dead leaves clinging to his hair and shirt. "They'll be able to hear the wagon, right enough."

At a word from Muuril, Haeksin hauled back on the reins and brought the abada to a halt.

"Let's not give them any warning, eh?" said the sergeant, advancing around the back of the cart.

Faeghun stepped up with Muuril, earning himself a glance of annoyance from the wiry legionnaire.

"Not sure we need you along, boy," said Muuril. Faeghun looked at Muuril with incomprehension, so the sergeant jabbed a finger into the Linghar warrior's chest and then pointed at the ground; a signal to stay put that crossed all language barriers. A stare from Gelthius silenced the youth's protest before he could give it voice.

"The others in the village might know we've left by now and come looking, so I need you and Gannuis to keep watch here and protect your family if they come," said Gelthius. He shared a glance with the other legionnaires, who nodded reassuringly; though they had no idea what he was saying, they could guess his intent. Gelthius patted Gannuis on the arm. "This ain't going to take too long, son. Holler if anything happens."

"What are you going to do?" asked Minglhan, head poking over the side of the cart. "You going to kill Kalsaghan?"

"Right enough," said Gelthius as he leaned past his son and grabbed his spear from the back of the wagon. "Don't worry, lad, I'll be back quicker than you know."

He nodded at Muuril to lead the way, and the group of legionnaires set off down the hill, padding quietly along the grass beside the stony track, shields and spears held ready.

"So, you gonna tell the king to attack or what?" Loordin whispered from behind Gelthius.

"The chieftain's thinking of heading duskwards, running away," replied Gelthius. "If he's clever, he'll head off first thing tomorrow and we won't see them for dust."

"Probably better that way," said Gebriun. "I remember my grandfather telling me about when the Askhans came to Ersua. Some joined up quick as a hawk, but some tried to hide in the mountains. Got short shrift from the Hillmen, and when winter came, thousands starved. I guess nobody learns, do they? We always try to fight what's going to happen."

Gelthius said nothing; he was far from happy about the whole situation. He had grown up in these hills, played in the river, hunted in the forests and even tried to raise a farm on the pastures to coldwards. He had no love for Naraghlin and his ilk, but it was another to condemn the whole of the tribe and the others of the Linghar people to brutal death and subjugation.

He silently cursed Aegenuis. If the Salphorian king had any love for his people he would tell them to lay down their arms and accept Askhan rule, just like the ancient Maasrites had done. That would never happen, Aegenuis was too proud, just like the rest of the chieftains; and too scared of what might happen to him if he showed weakness to his political enemies. Such men would rather have a glorious, bloody defeat than a peaceful, sensible surrender.

That was the problem with chieftains and kings, thought Gelthius. They always think they have more to lose than everybody else, but at the end of the day, they died with nothing just the same.

As the legionnaires sneaked through the bushes, the first fall of fresh rain pattered on the withering leaves around them. As the intensity of the rain increased, Gelthius hoped that the men standing guard at the bottom of the hill might be convinced to seek shelter. Peering through the dark, he saw that the flickering glow of the torches moved to one side of the track but not further. He adjusted his grip of his spear shaft, hand slick from the rain.

"How we going to do this?" he whispered to the others, who were nothing more than darker shapes in the downpour. "There's at least twice as many of them."

"We need to divide them if we can," said Muuril. "Loordin, work your way around to the right and attract their attention."

"How?" asked Loordin, face looming out of the night.

"I don't know," said Muuril. "Shake a bush, drop a stone, or something. We'll come up from behind them, from the left."

Loordin hesitated. From what Gelthius could see of the Loordin's face, the soldier was doubtful.

"I can't see my own feet," said Loordin. "What if I get lost?"

With a snarl, Muuril put his spear in his shield had to grab the collar of Loordin's breastplate and pull him close.

"I'm giving you an order, legionnaire," snapped the sergeant. "Stop whining like an unpaid whore and move your arse over there. Give us to a count of two hundred and then attract their attention, right?"

With a sigh of resignation, Loordin nodded. Muuril let go of the man's armour and slapped him on the shoulder to send him on his way.

"Follow me," said Gelthius, stepping to the left around rock outcrop. "We can come at them from the bottom of the cliff."

Water dripped from his helmet and soaked his shirt as he led the way, wet leaves slapping at his shins as he stalked through the grass and bushes at a crouch. Always keeping the glow of the torches in the corner of his right eye, Gelthius picked his way carefully down the slope, using the butt of his spear to test the ground for holes and rocks, knowing that any stumble now would be heard by the waiting tribesmen.

"One hundred," whispered Muuril, tapping Gelthius on the shoulder. "Try picking up the pace, will you?"

Gelthius eased himself across a stony hump and turned right, pausing for a moment to fix on the torches again before heading straight towards the flickering patches of light. The ground was levelling out and in the lee of the rock face the rain swirled about, blowing into his face with each sporadic gust of wind.

When he was about a hundred paces from the vague figures next to the trail, Gelthius found shelter behind the trunk of a tree. He dropped to his haunches and waited, eyes fixed on the Linghars. He counted eight of them moving around in the glow of the brands, but was sure there were two or three more that he couldn't see.

He took another step when the crack of a branch caused him to freeze on the spot. Ahead, the tribesmen had heard it was well. They looked to Kalsaghan, who picked out five warriors and sent them across the track to investigate

"He's fucking early," said Muuril. "He's counted too quick."

Haeksin rose up out of the grass but was stopped by Muuril's spear.

"Wait! Let them get a bit further away."

The tribal warriors that had stayed with Kalsaghan were focussed on Loordin's diversion; none of them spared a glance behind them to where the legionnaires lurked.

"That's it, let's go," Muuril told them when the flickering torch of the searching group was just a distant glow in the gloom.

The legionnaires stalked through the grass, almost shoulder to shoulder; Gelthius on the left, Muuril next to him, Haeksin on the sergeant's right, Gebriun on the other end of the group. They were less than fifty paces from the Linghars when Muuril snapped the order to charge.

In step, the four of them broke into a run, keeping pace with each other just as if they were not a group of four, but part of a phalanx one-hundred-and-sixty strong. The snap of branches and jingle of their armour warned the tribesmen, who turned around with astonished looks as the legionnaires burst onto the path.

Kalsaghan gave a warning shout as the legionnaires bore down on them, shields locked, spears jutting like the horns of a charging bull.

"At them!" roared the chieftain's son, breaking into a run. "Bring me the traitor's balls!"

Gelthius tightened his grip on the strap of his shield as the Linghars sprinted towards him. Kalsaghan and two others were the fastest and were a few paces ahead of their companions when the groups met.

"Take the hit!" roared Muuril.

The legionnaires skidded to a stop, sandaled feet sliding in the mud, a moment before the three Salphors reached them. Gelthius concentrated on raising his shield to block the two spear tips thrust at him, trusting Muuril to protect his right side. In coming for Gelthius, Kalsaghan and his two warriors had put themselves directly in front of the legionnaires, attacking the strongest part of the group. Their rush was met with the ineffectual crash of spears on shields.

"Strike!" bellowed Muuril.

As if guided by a single hand, the four of them jabbed forward their long spears. Gelthius aimed the point of his spear at the throat of the man directly in front of him. His aim was low, but the tip caught the Linghar warrior in the right side of his chest, easily punching through his leather jerkin. Muuril's spear took Kalsaghan in the gut, but the third Salphor managed to deflect Haeksin's blow. Shouts and curses accompanied the clatter of bronze and wood, a plaintive wail torn from Kalsaghan as he collapsed into the mud.

A sword bit into the rim of Gelthius's shield as the rest of the tribesmen arrived, the momentum of the warrior's charge knocking the legionnaire back a step. Without an order uttered, the small line broke. Muuril lunged into the Salphors, spearing one of the warriors in the side, while Gebriun tripped another with his shield before driving the point of his weapon into the man's back. Still regaining his balance, Gelthius stumbled again as a spear tip grazed across the cheek guard of his helmet and opened a bloody cut across his chin. He slashed at the warrior's legs with the edge of his shield, rearing up with his spear as the man jumped back.

Rain hammered on Gelthius's armour, the ground underfoot turning to slurry. The torch carried by one of the Linghars was lying next to the track, quickly guttering, plunging the fight into near-blackness. Gelthius swiped the point of his spear at the man in front, tearing through his arm. Dropping his weapon, the Linghar back-stepped, but not quickly enough. With an explosive breath, Gelthius lunged after him, stabbing his spear through the tribesman's thigh. The Linghar let go of his shield and splashed into the mud, cradling his wounded leg.

A startled cry on the right caused Gelthius to turn. He did not recognise who had shouted, but saw one of his fellow legionnaires dropping to his knees, red gushing from a gash in his throat. Gelthius had no time to wonder who was down; Kalsaghan was rising to his feet, one hand clamped to the wound in his midriff, a dagger in the other hand. With quick feet, the chieftain's son dodged the weaving tip of Gelthius's spear and closed with his knife, slashing at the legionnaire's chest. The blade rang against the bronze breastplate and scored across Gelthius's left arm. Gelthius kicked out, driving his foot into Kalsaghan's groin. Blood pouring down his arm, Gelthius rammed the rim of his shield into the fallen warrior's face, splitting open the youth's cheek with a crack of bone.

Another tribesman hurtled out of the gloom, tackling Gelthius to the ground in a spray of muddy water and flailing limbs, the legionnaire's spear spinning out of his grasp. The warrior punched Gelthius across the jaw, loosening several teeth. His hands tightened around Gelthius's throat. Stunned, the legionnaire swiped wildly with his shield, smashing the other man in the ribs, but the Linghar's grip did not weaken.

The helmet crest of a legionnaire appeared over the tribesman's shoulder a moment before a sword erupted from his shoulder. Kicking the man from him, Gelthius grabbed a proffered hand and allowed himself to be dragged to his feet.

"That's the last of this lot," said Muuril, wiping his bloodied sword on the dead tribesman's jerkin. The sergeant had lost his shield in the melee and held his spear on his left hand, the water washing blood across his kilt.

Muuril looked around as Gelthius recovered his spear. "Haeksin's dead."

Gelthius paused to take a deep breath, and could hear the shouts of the warriors that had been sent after Loordin. Gebriun was down on one knee, ripping the shirt of one of the dead Linghars to make bandages.

"Do you think they've caught him?" asked Gelthius.

"Not yet," said Gebriun. He drove the butt of his spear into the muck and gestured for Gelthius to hold out his wounded arm. Binding the cut with a strip of the ripped shirt, Gebriun then turned his attention to a ragged hole in Muuril's calf. "We'll just get ourselves straight and head after Loordin."

Feeling groggy, Gelthius spat out a mouthful of blood and tested his teeth with a probing finger. He winced as one came out with little effort; two others wobbled at his prodding.

"We'll get that sorted out back in camp," said Muuril. "Let's get going. Give the word to the others to come down the track. There's no point fighting here if they get caught by a band coming from the top of the hill."

Gelthius's shout was answered by Gannuis, his voice almost drummed out by the rain. Hefting his shield, Gelthius signalled to Muuril and Gebriun to move off.

The Linghars pursuing Loordin were shouting to each other in the darkness. It was hard to be exact about their whereabouts, but it was clear they had broken into at least two groups, one of which was coming closer, their cries echoing from the rock face not far behind the legionnaires.

"Can't see anything," muttered Gebriun.

"Stop a moment and listen," said Muuril.

All Gelthius could hear was the thudding of his heart and the splashing of rain. After a few moments, there came a clang of metal, followed by a cry of pain and the splash of something heavy falling.

"Off to the right," said Muuril. "Not far."

They broke into a trot, grass and ferns whipping at Gelthius's bare legs, the thorny branches of bushes scratching at him as he pushed through the tangle of vegetation clinging to the shallow slope.

A hazy figure appeared in the gloom, running full pelt. Gelthius brought up his spear out of instinct, teeth clenched despite the pain in his jaw.

The shape resolved into Loordin, without shield or helmet, the broken haft of his spear in one hand. He shouted in alarm and turned away before Gebriun's call halted him. Wide-eyed, the legionnaire approached, wiping the rain from his face with a bloodstained hand.

"Fuck me," said Loordin. "I thought you were all dead."

"No such luck for you," said Muuril. He pointed at the blood staining the soldier's fist. "Been having your own fun?"

"Got the drop on two of them," said Loordin, chest still heaving. "Ran away from the other three. One of them's got a bow. Almost winged me, the bastard."

"Where's your shield?" asked Gebriun.

"Too fucking heavy by far," Loordin replied with a smirk. "I didn't want those arseholes catching me, did I?"

A warning shout from behind caused the legionnaires to spin around, weapons at the ready. The three surviving tribesmen emerged from the dark, looking this way and that as they headed back to the road. They stopped in their tracks as they saw the four legionnaires, ready and waiting. The two groups stood about twenty paces apart, eyeing each other cautiously.

"What's your names?" Gelthius called out in Linghar.

"It doesn't matter," the tallest of the three called back. Water streamed from the unkempt braids of his beard, his thick hair plastered across a helmetless scalp. He held up an open hand. "Look, we didn't have to see you, right?"

"You were going to kill my family," Gelthius said. "What makes you think I'm gonna let you walk away?"

"Nah, we weren't going to kill nobody," replied another of the group. He glanced at his two companions. "We was just told to stop you leaving."

"You tell me what Naraghlin's planning to do, and I might persuade my friends to let you go. It better be quick, cos they're not happy about having to leave their nice, warm beds in the middle of the night."

"We're abandoning the town," the first warrior shouted. "Naraghlin's got no stomach for a fight. It was Kalsaghan's idea to stop you returning to your camp. Him and Mannuis was going to use your family as hostages; send you back to your new king with a false surrender."

Gelthius thought about this for a moment.

"Naraghlin's right, you have to leave," he told them. "We'll be back with the legion in two days at the most, and another two days before they get here. The tribe's got three days to get moving."

"You want us just to up and leave our homes?" This was from the third man, the youngest of the group, his blond hair tied back with a leather thong, his beard not long enough to plait. "Kalsaghan won't stand for it. He'll fight."

"He's fucking dead!" snarled Gelthius. "You'll all be dead unless you leave. That's the choice, right enough. Stay here and die, or go somewhere else."

"What are you talking about?" said Muuril, stepping next to Gelthius. "They're keeping us busy until the others arrive. Tell them to fuck off, or we're going to kill all three of them where they stand."

"My friend here isn't happy," Gelthius told the Linghars. "If I was you, I'd start running now."

The tribesmen gauged the legionnaires carefully. Not liking what they saw, they backed away until the darkness swallowed them. Gelthius heard the splashing of their feet as they broke into run, until even that noise was swallowed by the downpour.

"Let's get the cart and get going," said Gelthius. "It's a ways around the mound back to the town, but it won't take them long to bring back more warriors. We need to get out of here."

V

The rain stopped after midnight, some time around the turn of Gravewatch by Gelthius's guess. His wife, daughter and youngest son dozed in the back of the wagon while Faeghun drove the abada. The others walked beside the cart, sloshing across the muddy plains in silence. As the first glow of dawn smudged the horizon in front of them, Muuril had to concede to the pain in his wounded leg and ride on the wagon; a decision that provided shallow entertainment for the other legionnaires for the next few miles.

The sunrise ahead revealed low cloud, the whole sky tinged with foreboding grey. The wind kept the chill of the night and Gelthius marched on trembling legs, his face and arm sore. Though occasionally he looked back towards the place he had been born, he doubted the tribe would have pursued them any distance; the death of Kalsaghan would have dampened any spirit amongst the Linghar warriors. He hoped that Naraghlin would heed the warning and move the tribe away without a fight.

As the morning brightened, the legionnaires agreed to take it in turns to ride on the wagon and snatch some sleep. All of them had been awake for most of a whole day and the fight of the previous evening had taken its toll, despite their conditioning and determination. Although Gelthius was supposed to be in charge, he was happy to defer to Muuril's organisation and gratefully sank into the pile of blankets next to Maredin when the sergeant judged it to be the start of Low Watch.

Gelthius slept in snatches, woken frequently by the pain in his arm and the jolting of the wagon. Eventually fatigue won over discomfort and he fell into a deep slumber.

He was shaken awake by Gannuis. The early clouds were thinning and Gelthius blinked in the light, guessing it to be coming close to noon.

"It's Gebriun's turn, ain't it?" he mumbled, sitting up.

None of the others said anything. Gelthius pulled himself up using the side of the wagon and stood swaying in the back. The others were looking ahead, slightly to coldwards. Gelthius turned to see what had caught their attention.

A ribbon of glittering sunlight was snaking over the crest of a ridge a few miles away. It took a moment for Gelthius to work out what he was looking at: hundreds of spears and helmets. It was impossible to tell the individuals apart at this distance, but the smudge of red and black was unmistakeable. There was other movement ahead and around the main body of men; outriders moving on swift kolubrids. It was the Thirteenth in full column of march.

Never had Gelthius experienced such mixed emotions.

On the one hand, the sight of his legion filled him with relief. Within the hour he would be back amongst his comrades, wounds properly tended, food in his belly.

On the other hand, it was sight that filled him with dread. This was Askhor embodied, bearing down upon the lands of the Linghar with full force.

Not even on that strange day in Thunder Pass when he had watched the Thirteenth butchering Aroisius's rebels had Gelthius feared so much what those legionnaires represented. They were the end of the Linghars, his people. He had fought in the legion, shed blood for Ullsaard, and even helped put the new king on the throne in Askh; only now did Gelthius realise that he was a part of Greater Askhor. When the Thirteenth reached the town, his past, the history and traditions of the people that had raised him, would end.

Muuril laughed.

"Looks like the king couldn't be arsed waiting for a reply."

GREENWATER
Late Autumn, 211th year of Askh

A lush wall of green bordered the river – giving the waterway its name – but Urikh knew that less than half a mile from the banks the vegetation petered out into rock and desert. The Greenwater expanded to more than a mile in width, more a sluggishly moving lake than a river, eventually dividing into a broad delta some four hundred miles further hotwards.

The journey so far had been uneventful. The inhabitants of a few scattered fishing villages had been astounded by the appearance of the fleet and several times Urikh had played host to chattering local dignitaries whose people had been brought into the fold of Greater Askhor by the campaign of Prince Kalmud. Most of these brown-skinned men and women spoke hardly a word of Askhan, and instead made their feelings clear through elaborate presentations of fish and fruits, while boats jammed with screeching women and children carpeted the river with petals.

Two days ago, these isolated settlements had disappeared. The forest crowded close to the water, the unearthly howls and bellows of strange birds and monkeys splitting the air at night, while swarms of flesh-biting insects descended on the ships every dusk and dawn.

The reason for the absence of other people was obvious to Urikh; this was Far-Mekha, the heartland of the red-skinned savages, believed by most decent Askhans to eat their fallen enemies and infamous for the sacrifice of their babies to the beasts of the desert. The festival atmosphere that had accompanied the fleet in the earlier days waned, to be replaced by wariness and caution.

It was close to this place that the last expedition to Co-suan had been waylaid by a surprise attack, and the governor of Okhar was taking no chances. Smaller vessels in the fifty-strong fleet scoured the banks of the river, looking for shelters harbouring the waiting enemy, their lookouts searching the thick swathe of trees and bushes for hidden inlets that might conceal the Mekhani. Behind this screen, the main fleet followed, twenty galleys with full holds, protected by an assortment of biremes and triremes carrying two thousand men of the Seventeenth Legion.

Turning his gaze upon the tree-crowded shores, Urikh shielded his eyes from the sun rising almost directly to starboard, squinting at the light dappling from the water. At the heart of the fleet, he stood on the raised aft deck of the largest ship, the flagship of Narun given as a gift by the merchants of the city to the former governor, Nemtun. The ship was a monster of a vessel; more than a hundred paces long, built on three levels and carrying more than four thousand rowers, sailors, officers and le-gionnaires. The deck underfoot reverberated with the pounding of the oar-drums and the creaking of three hundred sweeps, while Urikh's ears were filled with the singing of the wind against the masts and rigging and the slap and splash of the oars. The crack of the flag atop the main masthead, the pattering of bare feet on wood and the shouts of the sailors as they trimmed the mainsail added to the noise.

"Excuse us, prince."

Urikh stepped aside as a gang of crewmen attended to the catapults mounted either side of the huge tiller arm. In the twelve days since setting off from Narun, he had become accustomed to the routine of the warship; at first light the two aft catapults and the one mounted on the low foredeck were untethered and loaded, ready to greet any dawn attack. Two spear throwers on each side of the ship were similarly armed, and the three hundred legionnaires aboard turned out in full kit.

Like the legions they often carried, the warship crews of Askhor prided themselves on their professionalism and discipline, and Urikh had noted the similarities of routine between the two armed forces. He also detected an undercurrent of rivalry, with the sailors and legionnaires never missing an opportunity to deride each other in a casual manner. On occasion these friendly exchanges spilled over into something more serious, and a couple of times Urikh had been forced to intervene in arguments between the ship's captain, Eroduus, and Harrakil, First Captain of the Seventeenth. In the end, the governor had threatened to have both of them thrown overboard as food for the giant crested reptiles that made this stretch of the river their home.

The men attending to the catapults worked quickly and with little comment, each knowing his task by rote. They removed the stones from the buckets and unwound the tension on the arms before securing the catapults' turntables with a maze of ropes and pins. Along the ship, fires were being re-lit and weapons stowed; the bulk of the legionnaires were dismissed, leaving a guard of fifty on watch.

All of this Urikh saw but did not notice, intent instead upon the green shores racing past. So effortless was the ship's passage through the water, and so well did the other warships maintain their stations, it felt as if they sat on a lake and the trees and bushes were moving aft.

Eroduus came up the aft steps two at a time, his long hair tied back, flapping behind him like a black and grey abada's tail. The captain's skin was the colour of aged wood, tanned and baked in the sun over many years, his face pocked and wrinkled, giving him an appearance much older than his forty years. The legend around Okhar held that he had not set foot on land for ten years, but Urikh had dismissed such tales as impossible.

Dressed in a simple white tunic and going about barefoot like his crew, Eroduus might have been mistaken for any one of the lesser officers. His only concession to rank was a cord around his throat on which he wore a gold medallion cast in the likeness of Askhos. Already sweating profusely in his woollen shirt and heavy kilt, Urikh envied the lighter clothes of his subordinate, but could not bring himself to dress like a commoner; he had an appearance to maintain as a governor and Prince of the Blood.

"Do you think they will attack today?" Urikh asked as Eroduus crossed the aft deck and stood next to him, legs braced slightly apart to effortlessly counter the regular swell and roll of the ship's movement.

"I do not think so, prince," Eroduus replied, his deep blue eyes showing disappointment. Despite his rough appearance, the captain spoke with the cultured accent of the Askhan nobility; for all his simple manners and common touch, Eroduus owned more than a dozen vessels and was one of the wealthiest men in the empire with estates in every province and a villa on the Royal Way in Askh. A powerful, influential man in Urikh's estimation, and one he had been careful to cultivate as an ally since becoming governor.

Urikh noticed that the captain was going to add something to his assessment, but had stopped himself.

"What is it?" said the governor. "Come on, speak up."

"I think you may have overdone things, prince," Eroduus replied with a wry smile. "Any Mekhani pirate who sees this fleet is going to shit himself and never come near the river again."

"Would that be such a bad thing?" asked Urikh, ignoring the nobleman's crude turns of phrase. There was no amount of good breeding that would stop a sailor swearing.

Eroduus shrugged, gnarled hands outspread.

"If you plan to send a fleet like this every summer, it would work," said the captain. "As soon as these bastards see ships coming down the river in ones and twos again, I would bet first use of my sister's fanny they will come out of hiding quicker than a sailor running to a whorehouse. It would be better to bring them to battle and destroy their ships for good."

"It worries me that these attacks have happened at all," said Urikh. "Nobody knew the Mekhani could build anything bigger than a rowboat. Are they using captured vessels, perhaps?"

"Not from what Liitum and the other captains told me," replied Eroduus. "These were new-built galleys, with a different rig to our ships. I do not know where they learnt how to construct such vessels, but I would say it was in response to seeing Prince Kalmud's expedition to the coast. That and the king's last efforts to hotwards have stirred them up, no doubt. Nobody had ever sailed these waters in such numbers before, so there had been nothing worthwhile for the Mekhani to prey upon."

Urikh wiped the sweat streaming down his face. Noticing this, the captain gestured to one of his officers and a few moments later a pair of crewmen appeared carrying a canvas-seated chair, which they set down in the shadow of the huge sail. Urikh sat down without word, stretching his long legs out in front of him, hands in his lap.

"Perhaps we should split the fleet," the governor said. "Send a ship or two ahead as bait to lure out the red-skinned savages."

"We could cram several hundred legionnaires into a couple of galleys and hold the rest of the fleet just out of sight upstream," said Eroduus with an appreciative nod. "All of the ships have beacons on their mastheads to signal warning. Once the Mekhani are committed, the captains would light the fires and we could sweep downriver and catch them without any problems."

"Then that is what we shall do," said Urikh. A breeze stirred over the side of the ship, bringing a brief but welcome moment of coolness. The young governor closed his eyes and folded his arms across his chest. "Talk it over with Harrakil and get a plan organised by Noonwatch. Make sure there are no arguments. The liodons look particularly hungry today."

Eroduus departed with a bow and a short laugh, leaving Urikh to contemplate the joys of authority. The prince allowed himself to relax, ignoring the prickling of heat on his flesh and drips of sweat down his back. It was good to have a plan, and it was even better when the plan was his.

II

Two columns of red smoke merged in the air downriver, dispersing swiftly across the trees to duskward, adding to the ruddy haze of the setting sun. The ships of the fleet were already moving at speed; the shouts and drums of the oarmasters had begun the first moment a smudge of crimson had been seen on the horizon.

Urikh paced slowly from one side of the aft deck to the other, keeping out of the way of the crewmen preparing the catapults. He clenched and unclenched his fists in nervous agitation, caught between the thrill of action and nervousness caused by the same. Warfare was a risky business and he had done his best to avoid being embroiled in its haphazard attentions; throughout his father's bid for the throne he had always counted on the protection of at least a full legion around him.

The Mekhani had made their move in a narrower stretch of the river, where the Greenwater divided into several channels as it passed through high banks of rock, the main flow no more than a quarter of a mile wide. Leaving behind the merchants, the warships raced along, foam spraying up around their rams, the rapid rise and fall of hundreds of oars turning the river to froth.

Irritated by his own restless behaviour, Urikh paced to the rail and stared down at the crew busying themselves on the main deck. He gripped the polished wood tight to hold steady and affected an air of unconcern, while inside his stomach lurched not just with the motion of the ship but the thought of the impending chaos of battle.

Feeling slightly repulsed at his own fear, his thoughts turned to his brother, Jutaar, at that moment leading a legion in Salphoria somewhere. As youngsters it had always been Jutaar that would be the first into any potentially dangerous situation, whether investigating caves in the mountains above Askh or sneaking into the private gardens of the neighbours to spy on the women-folk getting dressed. When faced with own his hesitance, Urikh reassured himself that it was natural for a sane and intelligent man to feel fear; and that his brother was too stupid to know when to be properly afraid.

Far from the steady glide Urikh had experienced on the previous days of the journey, the ship crashed through the water in a series of surges, hurled across the water with every draw of the sweeps, the whole vessel shuddering as the drumbeat boomed and two thousand and four hundred men threw their weight forward in unison. The alternating sensations of acceleration and slowing put Urikh in mind of a charging ailur, legs bunching and releasing, muscles tensing and relaxing.

He took a deep breath and turned his attention to the other ships, many so close to each other that their oars were almost touching. His apprehensions about fighting evaporated as he looked at the might of Askhor crowded around him. Urikh could appreciate the sense of power and achievement his father felt when he led a legion into battle; though he could not quite comprehend Ullsaard's apparent addiction to war that had driven him to personally lead the invasion of Salphoria.

This was what being a governor – being a Prince of the Blood – was meant to feel like.

The prince gloried in the spectacle of thousands of men, the effort and resource represented by this fleet and its crew, all bent to a common purpose: the execution of Urikh's will. To rule was not to sit on chests filled with askharins, or to have one's pick of any maiden for the royal bed. The reward for being in charge of the greatest empire ever created was not the politics and the negotiations – though Urikh enjoyed manipulating others. The simple exercise of power, the ability to enact one's plans and desires without hesitation, to command the loyalty and effort of countless servants, was the benefit of the Blood.

Urikh realised he was grinning, hand slapping the rail in time to the oar-drums. He glanced around the aft deck to see if anyone had noticed; standing next to the three men hauling on the tiller, Eroduus caught Urikh's gaze and smiled back with a wink.

"And those limp pricks back in Askh wonder why I bought a fleet," the captain called out. "There is not a race or blood duel at Maarmes that could match this, eh?"

Urikh laughed back, forgetting for a moment to appear stately and in control. He sneered at himself for the indiscretion and turned his back on Eroduus, his mood soured by the captain's intrusion.

Other than exchanging shouts with the crews of the closest ships, there was no way for the fleet captains to communicate with each other. Urikh could see nothing of the enemy ships from his vantage point, forced to listen for the sporadic shouts coming from the mastheads. He heard the cry of sails being sighted two miles downriver and waited impatiently for the number to be confirmed. The merchants who had been forced back by the pirates had claimed they were set upon by at least six vessels. Urikh hoped they were all in the water to be sunk; if he could deal with this situation with one act, it would be all the better.

"Four sail ahead!" came the next call.

That was good enough, to Urikh's mind. Even if the Mekhani were left with two ships, they were probably not going to threaten a well-crewed Askhan vessel. His only worry was that the pirates would realise their plight and flee too soon. Nightfall was no more than three hours away and darkness would allow the Mekhani to slip from the trap.

"Six sail ahead!"

Urikh smiled and rubbed his hands together. He felt the presence of Eroduus at his side and glanced at the captain.

"We have drawn them all out," said Urikh. "Now all you have to do is sink them."

"I think we can manage that, prince," replied Eroduus.

With the flagship leading the fleet like a mother swan followed by her cygnets, the twenty Askhan warships swept down the Greenwater. A mile ahead, the two galleys that had been despatched as bait were turning upriver, their spear throwers and catapults launching missiles at the low-beamed Mekhani ships trying to encircle them.

Though outnumbered, the Askhan vessels were handled better, oars moving with efficient strokes while the sweeps of the Mekhani ships had little coordination, some thrashing, others plunging deep into the water. Someone had shown the Mekhani how to build the ships, but not how to crew them. The desert tribesmen also had no war engines and were subjected to a hail of spears and boulders as they closed to board the Askhan ships. Fountains of water erupted around the closest pirate as boulders plunged into the river, while ropes were parted and the dirty white sail was torn by the flight of barbed-tipped bolts.

"Eight sail ahead!"

Both Urikh and Eroduus looked up at the masthead in surprise.

"Count them again!" roared the captain between cupped hands. Urikh directed an accusing glance at his admiral, who answered the glare with an innocent look of incomprehension.

"Sorry, captain!" came the next call. Eroduus shook his head in disappointed resignation. The eyes of both men widened at the next cry. "Nine sail!"

There was muttering through the crew and the legionnaires on deck; the news must have permeated down to the oar decks as a babble of voices drifted up from the open hatches.

"Stop their noise," Eroduus snapped at the officers standing below the aft deck rail. They headed into the mass of men, cursing and snarling.

"Your mastmen do know how to count, yes?" said Urikh.

The captain ignored the icy remark and strutted to the starboard side to bellow at the trireme surging through the water alongside. Listening to the short exchange, Urikh heard it confirmed that there were at least nine galleys ahead.

"Doesn't matter," said Eroduus on his return. "We still have more than a match for them."

As if given a cue by fate, another shrill cry sounded from the mast top.

"Three sail to aft!"

Sure-footed on the rolling ship, Eroduus reached the aft rail beside the tiller a few strides before Urikh. Nothing could be seen of the ships themselves, but three white patches against the forest canopy on the bank were sliding along the coast. They were headed for the merchant ships that were now nearly a mile behind.

"They must have been hidden in one of the side channels," said Urikh. He rounded on Eroduus. "Why were they not seen?"

The captain could only answer with a nonplussed shrug and a shake of the head. Eroduus stared back up-river, lips pursed tight, jaw clenched; he stood so still that he might have been mistaken for a carving set to look over the stern of the ship.

"What should we do?" said Urikh, keeping his voice calm, though inside he was seething with anger. Blame and punishment could be meted out later; his first concern was to deal with the rapidly-changed circumstance in which he found himself.

"That is your choice, prince," said Eroduus, suddenly springing into life again. "Three options. One: split the fleet. Two: turn back and save the traders, leaving the galleys ahead to fend for themselves. Three: keep on ahead and hope that the merchants can deal with three galleys on their own."

Urikh looked fore and aft repeatedly, trying to weigh up the best course of action. The purpose of the expedition had been to get the cargo to Cosuan. Losing two galleys with nearly a thousand legionnaires on board would not go down well with his father and would lose Urikh the respect he had tried to maintain with Harrakil.

Urikh looked along the deck and saw the First Captain glancing back at him from where he was stood next to the company of legionnaires left on board. It was obvious to the prince that Harrakil knew what was happening and the choice Urikh faced. The prince desperately wanted to ask Eroduus what he would do, but that would be a terrible abrogation of leadership from which Urikh might never recover.

The choice was Urikh's alone, and if he was to be king one day, it was the sort of choice he would have to be prepared to make.

"Destroying the pirates is why we came here," he told Eroduus. "Send the four smallest ships back to help the merchant fleet. That still gives us enough ships to send those bastards ahead to the bottom of the river."

"Right you are, prince," said Eroduus, giving the briefest nod of agreement.

Urikh studied the captain's face for any sign of disagreement, but saw nothing in the few moments before Eroduus spun away, bellowing orders. These in turn were shouted to the nearby ships and on to the others, passing to the rest of the fleet.

Turning his direction downstream, Urikh could clearly see the Mekhani war galleys. Even to the prince's untrained eye, they were poorly proportioned, front heavy vessels that ploughed through the water like an abada fording a stream. Two of the galleys were foundering already, one with a mast snapped, another with a gaping hole in the starboard bank of oars. This second vessel was listing badly, doubtlessly holed below the waterline. At this distance, Urikh could see nothing of the crew, but imagined with some satisfaction the desert-dwelling Mekhani trapped on board as their galley sunk.

From their positions and directions of travel, Urikh guessed the Mekhani vessels had emerged out of another side channel behind the bait ships, which were attempting to sail around the incoming flotilla by steering close to the dawnwards bank of the river. Having seen the full number of foes facing them, the two Askhan captains were sacrificing the accuracy of their war engines for speed, but the closest attackers were less than two hundred paces away; the main fleet still had half a mile to travel before their catapults would be in range.

"No need to look so worried, prince," said Eroduus, joining Urikh again. "There are nearly five hundred men from the Seventeenth on each of those galleys. Those boys are an Okhar legion; they have been fighting up and down this river for years."

Urikh resisted the urge to glance aft at the galleys turning back towards the trade fleet. There was nothing he could do to influence the outcome of that battle. He brought this line of thought up short, realising that there was little he could do to chart the course of the battle about to engulf him. He was in the hands of Eroduus and his captains. Such was the nature of leadership, he told himself; if done well, everybody else did the work.

It was a frustrating time waiting for the fleet to close with the enemy. He had not felt so tense since he had watched his father march away with his legions to take Askh from King Lutaar. Remembering the sense of impotence that had plagued him during the long days before hearing word of Ullsaard's victory darkened his mood even further.

While resigned to simply waiting, Urikh saw that the situation ahead was changing quickly. The Askhan galley furthest downstream had stopped in the water, hull leaning at a slight angle, grounded on a rock or shelf under the surface of the water. Two Mekhani ships were slowly and inexpertly closing in through the shallows, suffering the wrath of the beached vessel's catapult and spear throwers.

The other Askhan ship was almost clear of the Mekhani, sail taut with a following wind, oars crashing into the water with relentless rhythm.

With a slap of ropes and a crack that startled Urikh, the fore catapult of the flagship launched a rock. The prince watched the blurred arc of the rock, following its course until it hit the river with a tremendous eruption of water just in front of the closest Mekhani galley.

More boulders descended on the enemy from the rest of the fleet, pocking the surface of the river like children throwing pebbles into a stream. One shot hit the side of a galley near the stern, sending up a cloud of shattering planks and splintering oars. A short cascade of bodies flopped into the water from the ragged hole in the oar deck.

Two of the Mekhani ships started a slow turn downstream, giving up their pursuit of the closest Askhan vessel. Three others continued on their course, hoping to reach their prey before the reinforcements arrived. Beyond them, the other two galleys were drawing along the port side of the grounded Askhan ship. Distant shouts carried up the river, announcing the commencement of the boarding action.

Following the instructions passed by Eroduus earlier, the main fleet split into two lines. The ships closest to the duskwards bank steered towards the shore, seeking to close off the Mekhani's route back to the channel from which they had emerged. The rest of the ships, headed by Urikh's flagship, continued directly towards the scattering Mekhani flotilla.

Acrid smoke wafted along the ship from braziers lit next to the spear throwers. The war engine crews loaded bolts swaddled in oil-soaked cloth and stood ready with brands, their machines trained as far to forward as possible. Fire flickered on the decks of the other vessels and soon trails of smoke drifted behind each warship.

The fighting on the beached galley was in full ferocity, a swarm of red-skinned warriors battling against the legionnaires on board to gain a foothold. The purpose behind the higher fronts of the Mekhani ships became apparent as the savages leapt down from the bow of their vessels, into the heart of the defenders. More swung across from mast to mast, many to be cut down as they arrived by sailors waiting in the rigging of the beleaguered galley.

Eroduus gave the order for the spear throwers to shoot, the command repeated like an echo from one end of the ship to the other. Crewmen put their brands to the tips of the bolts while others made last-moment adjustments of aim and elevation. With the general order given, each team was free to shoot when they bore on their target. Timing their shots between the thrusts of the rowers, the two spear engines hurled their flaming ammunition at the closest Mekhani ship. One spear fell astern of the target, the other slammed into the planks beneath the aft-deck; the successful crew jeered the poor aim of their shipmates even as they were loading the next bolt and winding back the firing arm.

The blur of more boulders against the blue sky followed swiftly as the flames from the embedded bolt licked along the pirate vessel. Timbers exploded from two direct hits, planks rupturing with a storm of splinters. The yard arm of another ship snapped, dropping the tattered sail onto the red-skinned men below, the two parts of the heavy wooden beam smashing through the decking.

Urikh smiled at the destruction and felt relief that it was unlikely he would have to tangle with the Mekhani face-to-face. Askhan ingenuity was again triumphant over savagery.

"Brace for ram!" bellowed Eroduus.

"What?" Urikh turned on the captain, aghast at the announcement.

The prince realised he had been so intent on the target of the catapults and spear throwers, he had paid no heed to a Mekhani galley directly in front of the flagship. Debris hung over the stern of the enemy ship in a tangle of wood and rope, dragging through the river like an anchor. Powerless to stop the huge trireme bearing down upon them, the Mekhani crew were lining the side of the ship, stone-tipped spears and crude hide shields in hand.

They were so close now; Urikh could see the wild anger of the foe, their crimson faces contorted in screeches and howls, spears clattering against shields in defiance of the massive vessel looming over them. The drumming and pounding of the oars had quickened beneath Urikh's feet, the ship constantly a-shudder as it reached ramming speed. The sailors manning the fore catapult secured their engine against the imminent impact and scurried back along the length of the ship. From the mastheads, soldiers with bellows bows loosed bronze-tipped shafts into the massed Mekhani.

As the flagship continued on its course, oar blades a blur of wood and water, most of the savages quietened, backing away from the side of their ship. Quite a few jumped into the river rather than face the terrifying six-rammed monster bearing down on them, only to thrash wildly for a few moments before they disappeared beneath the water.

"Hold on to something," said Eroduus, snatching hold of a line running tautly from the masthead to the stern of the ship. Urikh wrapped an arm around the wood of the rail and braced himself as the Mekhani galley vanished beneath the foredeck.

With a deafening crash, the flagship smashed into the galley almost directly amidships. Pieces of broken wood and mangled bodies sprayed over the bow, the impact hurling Urikh against the rail, almost sending him over it. The fore of the flagship rode up over the galley, tipping the prince backwards, driving the Mekhani vessel downwards. The deck heaved violently underfoot, the mastheads swinging, a clatter of cracking oars joining the creak of straining timbers and panicked shouts of the Mekhani.

With a snapping of ropes and tearing of canvas, the Mekhani ship's mast sagged and broke as the vessel keeled over under the weight of the flagship. Air escaping from the galley's fractured hold burst through the river, the water bubbling and frothing as if boiled. The wails of wounded tribesmen were piercing, and Urikh could see dozens of Mekhani stumbling around the slanted deck of their ship, blinded by splinters, limbs sheared off, bodies punctured and pierced with wooden shards.

"Hold boarding!" Eroduus called out as Harrakil headed up the tilted deck towards the enemy vessel, his companies of legionnaires right behind him. "That bastard's going to sink any moment."

The First Captain accepted this judgement with a raised hand and a look of disappointment. Sailors gathered on the foredeck, pointing down at the ruined Mekhani ship, laughing at the predicament of the barbaric tribesmen. The red-skinned natives dashed to and fro as their vessel slipped further and further into the embrace of the river, the current tearing away planks, widening the gaping holes in the galley's structure. Some cowered by the stub of the mast, clasping each other in horror, screaming in terror at the water surging up between the deck planks; others sought the sanctuary of the listing foredeck, delaying the inevitable by clambering up to the highest remaining part of the galley. The marksmen in the flagship's mastheads made sport of the tribesmen, easily picking off the red-skinned warriors with their bellows-bows.

"It will be a long time before these bastards come back on the water," said Eroduus.

Urikh only half-heard the captain. He was still in a semi-trance, enraptured by the destruction wrought on the Mekhani galley. It had taken only moments, but the whole plateau was inscribed on the prince's memory in vivid detail.

He wandered across the aft deck as the flagship settled back into the water, spumes of water from the sinking galley spraying up over the ship's bow. Urikh lowered himself down to the main deck and advanced, pushing his way through the throng of sailors and legionnaires crowding towards the foredeck. His hands trembled as he grabbed the rope ladder to pull himself up to the bow. One hand on the rail to steady himself, he advanced cautiously to the prow and peered over to examine the wreckage of the enemy. All but the tip of the galley's fore-deck was beneath the water. Red-skinned bodies bobbed amid the tangle of shattered wood and split rope; a few of the Mekhani clung to the debris, kicking fitfully at the water to reach the shore.

Hands tightly gripping the rail, he leaned further, casting his gaze down at the six trunk-like rams jutting from the hull of the flagship. They were draped with ruin, mangled bodies crushed against the hull, the water foaming red from under the keel. The pounding of feet shook the ship as the oarsmen were ordered to reverse their stroke. Slowly, the flagship was backed away with long sweeps, leaving a trail of corpses and broken wood.

Urikh laughed. It was quiet, barely audible above the scrape of the oars and the sluice of water along the hull. The prince looked up to starboard and saw the rest of the fleet hounding the other Mekhani ships. Two were boarded, legionnaires advancing along their decks, cutting and hacking with ruthless determination. Another three were sinking, the current at the centre of the Greenwater pulling them apart, dragging a slick of blood and dead downstream.

Clenching his fists to hide the shaking of his hands, Urikh turned aft. He was met with a sea of faces, jubilant and expectant. *I'm supposed to say something,* Urikh thought. *A speech, to punctuate this moment of victory.* The prince was at a loss; what would his father say? Urikh had no idea. He looked at the companies of legionnaires, Harrakil at their front, and the gangs of sailors up in the rigging and standing on the rail to see their prince. Over the heads of the crowd, he could see Eroduus on the aft deck.

It had been brutally easy. For all their guile, the Mekhani had been outclassed from the moment they had attacked. Urikh wondered if all victory felt like this; to him it was a job done and nothing more. The expedition would be a success, but it was just a small step on a long road for Urikh. The men he looked at cared nothing for that. They wanted to be told how magnificent they had been; they wanted to be reassured that they were invincible; they wanted to hear how they would be rewarded for the triumph.

Urikh looked at them, their faces shining with sweat, and felt cold inside. The excitement of the battle was ebbing out of his body, leaving his stomach tied in knots, his throat tight, his mind numbed. He could think of nothing to say.

A small part of his brain prompted Urikh into action. He raised his arm into the air, fist clenched. A simple sign of approval. It was all the excuse the men needed. They answered his signal with a roar, the deck shaking as the sailors stamped their bare feet and the legionnaires hammered spear shafts of shields.

Urikh heard someone shout his name, and the call was taken up. He grinned, yet knowing inside that he had done nothing to earn such tribute. Hearing his name shouted from all around, Urikh headed aft, the crowd of his men parting in front of him, all the while their praise ringing in his ears.

A day ago he had been a troublesome governor, making people's lives miserable with his demands. Today, he was a hero. It did not make any difference that he had been near rigid with terror throughout the experience. This victory and his name would forever be entwined. There was no secret to being a ruler. No amount of money, influence and politics could replace the power of victory. Give the people an enemy to hate and then rid them of that enemy; that was all a ruler had to do.

One day, his father could be that enemy. The empire could be turned on him as they had been turned on Lutaar. All Urikh would have to do is point the finger; the weakness of everybody else would do the rest for him.

All too easy, he thought.

CARANTATHI
Late Winter, 211th year of Askh

I

There were voices coming from the fire pit. They were laughing, saying spiteful things. Aegenuis lifted his head from the table and stared at the flames with bleary eyes. He could not quite make out the words, but he felt their mockery. The only other sounds were the rain on the roof timbers and the crunch of the dogs gnawing at bones.

"Go away," the king muttered, pushing upright.

He grabbed the nearest jug and tipped it to his mouth. It was empty. Casting aside the ewer, he grabbed another, but there was only a dribble of ale in the bottom. Aegenuis let the beer drip onto his lips and then licked them, his tongue feeling thick and furry.

A sad-faced hound nuzzled his leg. Aegenuis reached down and tickled it behind the ear, scrunching long grey hair between his fingers.

"Just us, eh?" said the king. The dog stared back at him with thoughtless devotion and said nothing. "They deserve to die, all of them. Turn their backs on me, their king? They've made their choice. Ullsaard can fuck their grandmothers for all I care, and their grandfathers too, if that's what he wants."

Aegenuis surged to his feet and swiped his arm across the tabletop, sending plates and cups clattering to the floor. He took a step and stumbled, falling against a wooden carving of his father – one of many former kings whose likenesses lined the long hall.

"Sons of pig-fuckers! Accuse me of trying to grab their lands? My own son!" Aegenuis rounded on the dog, eyes narrowed. "What's that? Yes, I'll show them why I am their king. I'll have that bastard Ullsaard's head on a plate, and they can come grovelling back, begging me to help them. I'll wear that Askhan bitch-whoreson's balls around my neck and they'll come running."

Feet dragging through the rotting straw, Aegenuis lurched to his ceremonial seat at the head of the table. With a lunge, he flung himself into the furs, dangling one arm over the back. His head pounded.

Or perhaps it was thunder.

The king looked up as light spilled through the door at the far end of the hall. Four men entered, their hair and fur cloaks soaked through, leaving trails of drips on the dirt floor. Aegenuis squinted against the sudden light.

"It's morning?" he said.

"Yes, king," said the first man. Aegenuis did not recognise him. Looking at the others, he realised he did not know any of them.

"Who are you? Why do you come into my hall without permission?"

"We were knocking, king, but you gave us no answer," said the man. "My name is Furlthia. I am here to help you."

Aegenuis laughed.

"Perhaps the four of you are from the spirits, eh? Men of the crow and the tree and the wind? You'll be stopping Ullsaard's armies on your own, then?"

Furlthia looked at his companions and then back at the king.

"We should come back later, when you are sober," he said.

"No, no, stay," said Aegenuis. He heaved himself from his throne and waved them to the benches alongside the great table. "Be welcome in my hall. I've seen nobody but maids for many days. Do you want to be a chieftain, Furlthia? Is that it? It's not worth it. I'll make you one anyway, if you like. Why not? The Askhans can kill you as a chieftain just the same."

"I don't want to be a chieftain, my king," said Furlthia. While the other men sat down, he approached Aegenuis and laid a hand on his arm, guiding him back to his chair. "I don't want to be an Askhan, either. That's why we're here."

"The others all ran away, left me," said Aegenuis.

"They were idiots, king," said Furlthia. "You are right. The peoples must unite if they are to turn back Ullsaard and his legions."

"Can't be done," said the king. "Too late, even if it could. Half the tribes are dead, the rest are scattered."

"That is true," said Furlthia. He took two cups from the table and dipped them into a water butt set on the opposite side of the hall from the fire pit. He handed one to Aegenuis and drank from the other. "But Ullsaard cannot beat the winter. He has only reached as far as the Daruin Hills and the weather turns on him. He will stop where he is and tighten his grip on the lands he holds already."

"And we'll never take them back," said Aegenuis with a shake of the head. "Winter will be harsher on Salphors than Askhans. Our stores are gone; the tribes are foraging and hunting in the woods and hills. They will starve, and come the spring Ullsaard will sweep away those poor few that survive."

"This is pointless," snapped one of Furlthia's group, an aging man with soft features and hard eyes. "He's drunk, and worse, he's given up!"

"Never!" roared Aegenuis, pushing himself from his chair, hurling the cup of water to the ground. The king stopped, swayed for a moment and then broke into laughter as he collapsed back into the throne. "I'll just march off to see Ullsaard now. Maybe he'll stop if I ask him nicely."

"Maybe he'll stop if you give him a reason to," said Furlthia. He looked around the hall, seeing the mess on the floor, the dirt in the fire pit, the squalor. "Go to your chambers, king. Sleep and don't drink. We will see you tonight, and you will hear things that will make you a lot happier."

Aegenuis eyed the group dubiously and snorted.

"You? You miserable lot are going to give me something all the chieftains and all their armies can't?"

Furlthia nodded and waved for the group to leave. The king watched them file out of the door. The door closed, plunging the hall into the gloom of lamplight. Aegenuis looked around. He smelt the burning fat of the candles, the smoke of the fire, the shit of the dogs. He could smell himself as well, stinking of piss and vomit and grease and sweat. It was all a mess. Not just the hall, everything.

He recalled Furlthia's words, like a shadow in a fog. The man had seemed very sure of himself.

Throwing off his matted coat of furs, Aegenuis pushed himself to his feet and staggered over to the water barrel. He took a breath and plunged his head into the cold water. Rearing up with a gasp, droplets spraying from hair and beard, the king stepped back. Head clearing, he was intrigued by the visit.

Someone had mentioned sleep. Nodding to himself, Aegenuis headed for the doors, one hand on the table to keep himself upright. Yes, sleep seemed a good idea.

II

A hand gently caressed Aegenuis's cheek, rousing him from doze to full wakefulness. It was dark outside the narrow window of his bedchamber. His eyes moved to the woman cupping his face. It was Aleoin, one of his daughters. She sat on one side of the bed, dressed in a heavy woollen gown, a shawl around her shoulders. Aleoin had her mother's green eyes and her father's dark hair. She also had much of her father's broad build, and his flat nose, which was another factor on a considerable list of reasons why she had not yet found a husband. Her saving grace was her royal status, which ensured a line of desperate if not entirely desirable chieftains who wished to court her.

"Hello," said the king, sitting up. "Why are you here?"

"I heard you telling mother that you had to be woken at dusk," said Aleoin. "It seemed very important at the time."

"So why isn't she here to do the job?" the king asked. He pushed aside his blankets and swung his feet to the floor. The tiles were cold on his soles. Looking down at himself Aegenuis realised he was naked.

"I undressed you as well," said Aleoin. "The servants are too scared of you at the moment."

"Where's your mother?" Aegenuis found a washed shirt and trousers on a stool beside the bed.

"She doesn't want to see you."

"How so?"

"You don't remember?" asked Aleoin as she helped her father belt his shirt around his waist. "You beat her, two days ago. Broke her jaw."

"Oh." Aegenuis sat down on the bed to pull on his boots. "I was drunk. I'm sure there was a reason."

"You accused her of sleeping with another man, to give birth to a bastard like Medorian. You've been drunk for a long time. Half the people in Carantathi have left to follow the chieftains. Nobody calls you the king anymore."

Aegenuis detected more hurt in this remark than could be justified by what she was saying. He looked more closely at Aleoin and saw yellow bruising on her throat. There were scratches on her arms as well.

"What happened to you?" he demanded.

"Nothing important," said Aleoin, taking a step toward the door. Aegenuis grabbed her wrist and turned her back. He said nothing, but his intense stare repeated the question. "Last night, some men came for me on the way back from the market. They beat Cassuli and raped me. One of them said his seed would make a stronger king than any son of yours."

Aegenuis's first instinct was to demand to know who had done such a thing, but he stopped. What would be the point, he asked himself. By the sound of things, nobody in Carantathi, probably all of Salphoria, considered him king any more.

He corrected himself. The man who had come to him that morning, Furlthia; he had called Aegenuis 'king' and promised something that would stop Ullsaard and his Askhan dogs. Aegenuis could not remember exactly what had been said.

"I have to go to the long hall," he muttered. "Not sure why. Something about Ullsaard."

"You should eat first," said Aleoin.

"Later. You should find yourself a priestess of the dove; make sure you haven't been left with something by those bastards."

"I will, father." Aleoin looked uncomfortable. "It might not be Ullsaard that we have to worry about. If Medorian can get the chieftains to support him, he'll have you killed, maybe all of us."

"Medorian's a fool if he thinks he can get the chieftains on his side at the moment," said Aegenuis. He cast about the room for his cloak but could not see it. Opening the door, he turned back to Aleoin. "Never mind the Askhans; it's the chieftains that are the worst enemies of Salphoria."

Aegenuis left the house without looking for his wife or other daughters. Whatever he had done to them – and he could not remember any of it – his actions would take more than a swift apology to fix. He needed some air, now that his head was clearer than it had been for longer than he could recall.

Outside was cold. It was always chill in Carantathi, even at the height of summer. Perched atop a mount at the coldwards tip of the Ualnian Mountains, the Salphorian capital was constantly swept with wind and rain, the bare stone leeching away any warmth from the day while trapping the cold of night. There was cloud overhead, blotting out the stars and moons, draping the settlement with gloom.

Fires burned further down the hill and windows glowed with light, but there were dark patches where whole neighbourhoods had left with their ancestral leaders. There were even gaps in the areas where his own people, the Laeghoi, made their homes. Looking even further, the king could see warriors still patrolling the stone walls, passing through the glow of torches as they walked their rounds in small groups. At least someone still wanted to protect the city. The other houses arranged in a ring around the long hall stood empty. Looking down the spiralling street, no lights burned and no smoke drifted from chimney holes. Every other chieftain had left.

Looking across the street to the great hall right on the summit, Aegenuis could see that the doors were open and bright firelight flickered within. Shadows moved across the glow and he could hear loud chatter over the quietness of the rest of Carantathi. Curious, he hurried through the mud and up the wooden steps.

Within, the four men who had visited him earlier were sat at the table, eating and drinking. Platters of meat, loaves of bread and bowls of vegetables were laid out as if for a banquet. A few men and women were working at the fire pit, tending to half a roast pig and the great cauldron hanging over the flames.

Aegenuis recognised Furlthia, sitting to the right of the throne, where the king's heir would normally sit. All four of the men looked up as Aegenuis entered.

"So you think you can…" Aegenuis's rebuke died away as he saw the state of the hall. The dogs crunched fresh bones in the newly laid straw. The great chimney had been scrubbed; Aegenuis's embroidered banner had been strung between two poles behind the throne; the benches and table had been scoured clean and the gilded plates and cups gleamed in the light of a hundred fresh lamps.

The men stood together, the benches scraping across the floor. Furlthia raised his cup and the others followed.

"King Aegenuis!" Furlthia announced. "The blessings of the spirits upon this hall and its master."

Frowning with suspicion, Aegenuis stalked along the hall and sat in his throne, eyes never leaving Furlthia. The man passed a cup to the king with a short bow. Aegenuis sniffed the red liquid within, smelling rich fruit.

"Wine?" he said.

"Askhan wine, king," Furlthia replied with a sly smile. "From grapes that were grown in Ullsaard's own vineyards."

Aegenuis had to laugh. He took a mouthful of the wine and swilled it around his mouth before swallowing.

"It's good," said the king. "I must remember to congratulate that cat-fucker when he gets here."

"He won't get here," said one of the other men.

Aegenuis had not paid much attention to the man that morning. He was dressed in a hooded robe, much like the ones worn by some of the hermits that had dedicated their lives to the worship of one spirit or another. The cloth was a flawless black and hung from bony shoulders. The hood was drawn back, showing a face with high cheeks and a narrow nose; typically Askhan features.

The king balanced the cup on the arm of the throne, noticing as he did so that the grime had been cleaned from the deep grain of the wood and his lion's pelt cloak had also been freed from the muck and grime of drunken tumbles. He leaned towards his self-invited guests, hands in his lap.

"Tell me all your names," he said.

"I am Furlthia, as you know. The elderly man next to me is Serbicius, a chieftain from the Altes hills. My companion in the robe is Leraates; an Askhan, as you have guessed. The last of us is Kubridias, until recently of Magilnada."

This last name Aegenuis actually recognised, though he could not recall the man. He was one of the chieftains of the Free Country; or had been, until Ullsaard had started his invasion.

A serf appeared at Aegenuis's shoulder, a bowl of chicken stew in hand. With a glance at Furlthia, he set the meal down before Aegenuis, brought a platter of bread closer and quickly retreated to a place next to the fire pit.

"You run my hall better than me," said the king. "Think that you might run my lands better as well?"

"Not at all," said Leraates. "It is because we want you to stay king, and Ullsaard to leave your lands, that we are here."

"Go on," said Aegenuis, waving a spoon at the Askhan, mouth full of chicken.

"Ullsaard does not have total support within Greater Askhor. His attack on Salphoria is against the wishes of many. We would rather the agreement of King Lutaar was maintained."

"I'm not the one that broke the treaty," said Aegenuis, dunking a fistful of bread into his stew. "You can take that up with your oath-breaking king."

"We plan to do better than that," said Leraates. He pushed his plate to one side and leaned his elbows on the table. "When Ullsaard is defeated in Salphoria, we will restore the true line of the Blood to its proper place."

"You have Kalmud somewhere, do you? Or maybe Erlaan."

Leraates was taken aback.

"Don't mistake a drunkard for an idiot," growled Aegenuis. "And I'm not drunk at the moment. Carry on."

"It's simple," said Furlthia, raising a hand to hush Leraates reply. "Ullsaard's rule in the empire is new and weakly held. It is only fear of his legions that brings him anything like loyalty from his governors. Without the threat of the Askhan armies, he is nothing. Those inside Askhor want to see him fail as much as we do. If we can deal a blow to Ullsaard in our lands there are those who are backing him that'll withdraw their support."

"Sounds fine when you say it like that," said Aegenuis. "Simple enough, yes. All I have to do is defeat the most powerful army in the world, and this Askhan cat-buggerer will do the rest?"

Leraates took the insult without reply. Furlthia picked at the scraps on his plate as he continued.

"If you can retake Magilnada, the whole campaign fails."

Aegenuis laughed, spearing his knife into another piece of chicken. He plucked it from the blade with his teeth and chewed noisily.

"You might have noticed," the king sprayed gravy as he spoke, "that the whole Askhan army is between Carantathi and Magilnada. Oh, and I don't have an army. "

"You wouldn't have to lift a sword," said Serbicuis, talking excitedly over Furlthia. "Anglhan will turn on Ullsaard."

"Anglhan?" The king's voice dropped to a harsh whisper, the name forced through gritted teeth. "That oathless, traitorous, shit-eating, corpse-fucking smear of an arse stain! He steals a city from me and then promises to give it back?"

"By right of the treaty with King Lutaar, Magilnada was not your city," said Leraates.

"None of that matters," said Furlthia, cutting in before Aegenuis could react. "At the moment, like it or not, Anglhan is governor of Magilnada and the lands around the city. He's offering to return to the Free Country agreement that existed before Ullsaard moved in. Anglhan's a greedy bastard, don't forget, and I wouldn't trust him as far as I could spit, but if we can offer him something that makes it worth his while, it gives us all chance to get what we want."

The other men looked to Aegenuis for a reply. The Salphorian king said nothing, still fuming at the gall of Anglhan trying to trade off a stolen city. Aegenuis chewed laboriously as he considered his options. Part of him wanted to walk away without anything further said. Being king had brought him wealth and influence, but ruling over the Salphors was an uncertain privilege at the best of times. The most likely reward for turning back the Askhans, if it could actually be done, would be a knife in the back from Medorian or one of the chieftains looking to become king over a newly secured Salphoria.

"Perhaps Anglhan has the right idea," said the king. He held up his hand to silence Furlthia, who was leaning forward eagerly. "You misunderstand me. Perhaps I should treat with Ullsaard directly. It seems to me I'd be better off as a governor for Askhor than a defeated king."

"No, you cannot do that," said Kubridias.

"Why not?" said Aegenuis. "Seems to be that the future of an Askhan governor might not be so bad."

"Let me make myself clear," said Kubridias. "There are those of us that will not suffer Askhan rule by any means. We consider any man who works with the Askhans as a traitor to our people. You would not live long enough to make such a deal with Ullsaard, and if you did you would not enjoy the position for long."

Aegenuis's plate crashed across the table as the king rose to his feet, smashing dishes and cups.

"You come to my hall and threaten me?" roared Aegenuis. "You deal with that cock-hungry mongrel in Magilnada and call me a traitor? I'll cut your balls off for that!"

Kubridias stood as well, angrily wiping spatters of wine and gravy from his face. Serbicuis lunged across the wide table, snatching at the other chieftain's arm as he reached for his knife.

"Everybody sit down," said Leraates. His voice was like a blade on stone, cutting through the snarled insults and posturing of the men around him. Aegenuis looked incredulously at the Askhan, astounded by the man's affront; the others quietened immediately, cowed by his tone.

"Have I fallen so low that even here, in my own hall in Carantathi, an Askhan is telling me what to do?" Aegenuis said.

"Yes," replied Leraates. "Sit. Down."

The Salphorian king's eyes bulged with anger, but his stare was met with a look of such cold malice from the Askhan that his ire froze in his gut. In that moment, Aegenuis realised that he had misjudged the situation.

Furlthia was representing Anglhan, and both were mistaken in their view that they were in charge. As the other Salphors heeded the Askhan's command like hunting dogs called to heel, the king saw where the true power in this group was found. An Askhan did dare to give him orders in his own hall, and with good reason; in time these lands would belong to Askhor, one way or the other. Leraates was offering Aegenuis an alternative to direct rule by Ullsaard, though the deal had not yet been spoken.

Aegenuis knew who Leraates was, in type if not individually. His robes, his style, his wish to see the plans of Ullsaard dashed pointed to one conclusion: the Brotherhood. What little Aegenuis had heard of the strange Askhan sect had been unpleasant. He had not the slightest doubt that Leraates was here because he had a use for the Salphorian king. If Aegenuis proved unsuitable to that use, he might as well slit his own throat on the spot.

Hesitantly, Aegenuis lowered himself back onto his throne, his eyes never leaving Leraates.

"Thank you, king," said the Askhan. He studied Aegenuis for a moment. "Everything you are thinking is true, Aegenuis. Anglhan is not to be trusted, but that is not your concern. One step at a time, king. Let me make the situation clear for you. Ullsaard has overstretched his reach. He thought he could conquer Salphoria in a single season. At this moment he is making winter quarters hundreds of miles to dawnwards, tightening his grip on the lands he has held. Masons and engineers and labourers will come in the winter. They will build roads and towers, fortify towns and erect bridges over the rivers. By the first sun of spring, armies will be able to move from Magilnada to Daruin in thirty days rather than sixty. Grain carts and other supplies will be like the cord of a newborn babe, linking them to the life of Greater Askhor."

Throughout, Leraates spoke in a measured tone, his language the tongue of the dawnwards Salphorian peoples tinged by his Askhan accent. His eyes pinned Aegenuis to his throne, but his voice, his words, were intended for every man at the table.

"That cord must be severed if you wish to keep Ullsaard from being at your door within the year. You cannot do that from here. Your son tries to convince the chieftains to attack Ullsaard, but that attack will fail. Only Anglhan is in a position to hurt Ullsaard. He is a toad of a man, and your reputation will suffer dearly, but you must give Anglhan what he wants in return for his cooperation. Refuse and you will be dead before the year is out; either by the hand of Ullsaard or one of your own chieftains. That is a warning, not a threat."

Aegenuis cleared his throat and took a mouthful of water. There was no reason to believe that Leraates was lying about the situation. Whether Aegenuis held true to his word later, it was clear to the king that he had no choice for the time being. When the immediate danger was passed, he would find a way to bring Magilnada back into Salphorian hands and kill Anglhan. Until then, he would allow this Brother of Askh to weave his plots. Division in Askhor could never be a harm to Salphoria or Aegenuis.

"Very well," said the king, addressing his words to Furlthia. He made an educated guess at what the governor of Magilnada desired. "Tell Anglhan that he is to leave Greater Askhor and become ruler of the Free Country, with my support and the blessings of the spirits. Tell me, Furlthia, how does he intend to keep Magilnada safe from Ullsaard's vengeance? I hear the new Askhan king has a short temper, and two legions are not enough to hold Magilnada against the might of Askhor."

"He did not tell me, king, but I have no fear on that account," replied Furlthia. "Anglhan has a talent for self-preservation. He knows that Ullsaard will come at Magilnada with everything and will have some means to counter this. If he didn't, he wouldn't dare cede from the empire, not with a hundred thousand legionnaires within forty days' march of his city. No, believe me, Anglhan has something up his sleeve."

MAGILNADIA
Late Winter, 211th year of Askh

I

Moving up the wide stairs to the upper storey of the governor's house, Furlthia felt his skin crawl. Marble busts of Anglhan stood on pedestals flanking the stairwell, and as Furlthia turned onto the narrow landing, he saw a mural of his former master on the far wall. It depicted Anglhan standing at the gates of Magilnada, an Askhan army behind him. Anybody who had ever suffered dealings with the governor would see the lie for what it was; Anglhan had come to the city amongst an army of ragtag rebels and Hillmen, and not entered until several hours after the fighting had been concluded. He had not even raised a finger to stop the Askhans when Ullsaard had revealed his full intent and Askhan legionnaires had scoured the city of the last remaining Salphorian nobility and warrior-chieftains.

Coming to a set of double-doors, ornately carved with a view down upon the city from the great mountain on whose shoulder it was built, Furlthia took a breath. He fought down his irritation at being kept waiting for three days since making his presence in Magilnada known to Lenorin, the governor's chief aide. Eventually, a runner had come with a message demanding that Furlthia attended Anglhan at his home as soon as possible.

Furlthia knocked three times and waited, rehearsing what he would say to the governor. He wanted to deliver Aegenuis's agreement and then leave with as little fuss as possible. The more time Furlthia spent in Magilnada, the deeper his distaste for what Anglhan had done to the city.

"Come in!" came a strained call from within.

Furlthia opened the door and stepped inside. He halted with just one foot over the threshold on seeing what was within; the sight made him almost physically sick.

Anglhan bent over a large desk, kilt pulled up around his ever-growing waist, his voluminous body pinning a naked youth face down amongst the scrolls, wax tablets and official stamps of office. Sweat rolled from the governor's face in streams, his thinning hair plastered to his face as he thrust and grunted. Anglhan had the lad's face pressed against the wood with one hand; in the other he held a red candle held so that wax slowly dripped onto the youth's back.

Anglhan's face was a grimace of deviant pleasure, eyes wide, mouth snarling. Worst of all was the expression on the young man suffering such grotesque attention; Furlthia saw neither pleasure nor pain, just a bored look of indifference as Anglhan huffed and heaved his bulk against the youth.

"Spirits take my eyes," cursed Furlthia. He backed out and slammed the door closed. He had taken two steps towards the stairs when Lenorin reached the landing at a run. The chancellor stopped as he saw the expression on Furlthia's face.

"I'm sorry," said Lenorin with a knowing, weary look. "I meant to catch you before you came up here, but something distracted me."

"I should just stick a knife in the pig right now," said Furlthia, feeling his loathing for Anglhan reaching a new low.

"I would help, but for the bigger picture," said Lenorin, ushering Furlthia into a small study on the far side of the stairs.

One wall was covered with a canvas map of Magilnada, every building coloured to indicate the type of dwelling or business. Wooden shelves heaped with yellowing parchment scrolls lined the rest of the room, save for a small window through which the noon sun shone weakly. Pots of inks and brushes stood on a small stand beneath the window, a half-finished painting of a gate tower on an easel beside it.

"This is where you work?" asked Furlthia, allowing himself to be guided to a wooden stool by the flustered chancellor. Lenorin looked around as if seeing the chamber for the first time, but nodded.

"Yes, this is my office," he said. He closed his eyes for a moment, shaking his head slightly. "It serves me better than sharing a chamber with… that man. I'm within shouting distance when he needs me."

"Why do you even stay here?"

Lenorin smiled sadly and sat behind his small desk. He busied himself arranging wax tablets into a neat pile as he replied.

"It's the same as with him. Better the dark spirit that you know. Where I am, what I do, I can temper some of his worst excesses."

"You call what I just saw an excess?" said Furlthia. "No chieftain would behave like that to his men."

"That? That's small enough sacrifice to keep him content. A few serving boys now and then. I pay them off; send them out of the city if they want. There's a couple, like Amarin there, who don't seem to mind, so I make sure they're on hand when it looks like Anglhan is getting frustrated and frisky. Believe me, it's better that way. When he can't get his cock into some poor boy, he gets vindictive."

Lenorin cleared his throat, turned on his stool to put the tablets on a shelf behind him and directed his attention back to Furlthia.

"I'm worried," said the chancellor. "Ullsaard is coming back here soon from his winter camp. There's still snow in the air and he's getting ready for the next stage of the invasion. Anglhan has come up with reasons to keep his legions close to the city for the moment, but in his last letter, Ullsaard made it clear that he would be taking them duskwards on the next campaign. Without them, Anglhan has got no way to secure the border with Ersua."

"Like I told you when I arrived, Aegenuis is agreed to the plan. He's spent the winter regaining as much favour with his warlords as he can get. Kubridias and Serbicius have done as we wanted and pulled in every chief and warrior they can from their peoples. As soon as Anglhan makes his move, Aegenuis can persuade the rest of the chieftains to follow him again. Half the tribes have already agreed to send warriors against the legions to coldwards. Caught between the counter-attack and being cut off from Askhor, Ullsaard will have no choice but to fall back to a stronger position."

"And that's when Leraates does his thing, is it?" said Lenorin.

"I hope so," said Furlthia. "I can't figure that one out, not properly. I know Ullsaard disbanded the Brotherhood, but I don't see what Leraates and his allies have got against their new king that makes them so determined to topple him."

"Who cares? As long as Ullsaard's worried about his rule back in Askhor, he'll be too busy to be invading anywhere else. Knowing that the Free Country agreement with Askh is now worth less than dog shit, Aegenuis and his chieftains aren't going to let anyone just wander in and take over again."

There was a muffled ring of a bell from outside. Lenorin looked up sharply, looking like a guilty man.

"Anglhan's finished his rutting," said the chancellor. "You can see him now. Just tell him about the agreement with Aegenuis and get out; I'll deal with the details."

"Thank you," said Furlthia, standing up and offering his hand. Lenorin shook it limply. "Don't worry, friend. Once Ullsaard is seen to, that fat boy-fucker is next on our list."

"Hurry up, don't keep him waiting."

Furlthia headed straight for Anglhan's chambers and found the doors already open. Cautiously peering within, he found the governor sat on a low couch beneath the window, a plate of food propped up on his belly.

"Sorry about that," Anglhan said with a smile, waving for Furlthia to enter. "Lenorin was meant to tell me when you had arrived. Close the doors would you, wouldn't want any passing stranger to hear us."

Furlthia did he was asked and sat down on a padded seat indicated by Anglhan. The governor moved the plate to a side table and sat forward, hands on knees.

"So, my friend, what news?"

Trying to forget the image of Anglhan's ruddy, sweat-soaked face, Furlthia sat straight, arms folded tight across his chest. A draught from the window brought a waft of sickly-sweet perfume from Anglhan, but it failed to wholly mask the underlying smell of stale sweat and sex. Suppressing a wave of distaste, unclenching his fists, Furlthia looked Anglhan straight in the eye.

"The king says yes."

"Good, good," said Anglhan, chins and cheeks wobbling as he bobbed up and down enthusiastically. "That's just what I wanted to hear, my friend."

Furlthia squirmed at being called 'friend' by this loathsome pig of a man. He said nothing, fearing that if he were to open his mouth he might say something ill-advised.

"You don't look so happy," said Anglhan. "Don't worry, I've been thinking about this all winter and it's the best course of action for everybody.

"Everyone keeps telling me not to worry," said Furlthia. "I like to worry. Worrying has kept me alive."

"So keep worrying. I didn't mean anything by it. You spend your time worrying and I'll spend my time actually getting things done."

"I will," said Furlthia, standing up.

"Where are you going?" Furlthia couldn't tell if Anglhan's shocked expression was genuine or not. "You're not leaving yet, are you?"

"You've got Aegenuis's answer and I've got other people to see."

"But I need you to do a few things for me," said Anglhan.

"Get Lenorin to do them," Furlthia replied, taking a step towards the doors. "That's why you have him, governor."

"But I don't trust him like I trust you, Furlthia." Anglhan rose quickly and hurried over to his desk. "You know, this is a very delicate situation. I'm not totally sure where Lenorin's loyalties lie. But you and me, we have history together. We have a mutual interest."

Furlthia sighed and sat down again at Anglhan's insistence.

"What do you want?" he said, knowing that he was likely to regret asking.

"At some point, Ullsaard is going to come for me," said the governor, fishing though a stack of letters on his desk. Watching him, Furlthia had a momentary recollection of the youth who had been bent over the same desk less than half an hour earlier. He suppressed a shudder.

"Perhaps you want me to stand at the gates and welcome him in?" Furlthia said before he could stop himself.

Anglhan looked up sharply, but then grinned. He held up a folded piece of parchment, sealed with a blob of blue wax.

"Something like that, my friend. You know that as soon as I make my move, Ullsaard is going to fall on Magilnada like a cart-full of abada shit. This," he waved the letter, "is a better defence against that than all of the warriors in Salphoria."

Anglhan held the letter out to Furlthia, who folded his arms and refused to take it.

"What is it?" Furlthia demanded. "What are you offering him to stay his hand?"

"Better that nobody else knows, especially you," said Anglhan.

Furlthia looked at the letter. To his mind, it was a dagger aimed at Aegenuis's back; there was nothing else it could be. Furlthia had seen how Anglhan was a master at positioning himself between sides, just keeping to the edge of the abyss of everybody's disfavour whilst playing them against each other. The letter had to be an offer to Ullsaard that would give him some advantage over his Salphorian rival, back-tracking on Anglhan's commitment of support.

"I know what you're thinking," said the governor. "But you're wrong about me. Long before this letter reaches Ullsaard, I will be committed to the cause of Aegenuis and Salphoria. My legions are going to attack Askh's.

That's not something even I could wriggle out of, especially as Ullsaard has made it clear to me in the past that any hint of disloyalty will end with my death. In fact, I remember what he said very well: 'If you fuck around with me, I will come back and not only kill you, I'll burn this whole place to the ground.' Strong words, and we both know that Ullsaard does not make idle threats. This letter is the only thing that can stop that happening."

Furlthia shook his head.

"I'm not touching it," he said. "It's just a letter. Get someone else to take it to Ullsaard."

Anglhan crossed the room and laid a hand heavy with rings on the shoulder of his former first mate. Furlthia shrank away from the touch, causing Anglhan to sigh.

"I know that you do not approve of what I've done, my friend," said the governor. "I know I've got us both into some trouble, but have I ever done anything to wrong you personally? I've always looked after you, Furlthia, you know that. I need you to help me."

Earnestness was etched into Anglhan's face but Furlthia remained unconvinced.

"How can anybody trust you?" he said. "How can I trust you, when you won't tell me what you are up to? You are always looking to get ahead of everybody else, and I'll not have you do that at my expense."

"And I never would," said Anglhan, appearing aggrieved. "I know I play a dangerous game, but I always weigh up the risks before I do anything, and I always back a winner. There was an advantage in allying with Ullsaard, but it was only while something better came along."

Anglhan went back to the window seat and flopped down, dropping his letter on the side table. He linked his pudgy fingers together on his gut and looked at Furlthia for some time before speaking again.

"Have you ever considered what would have happened if Aroisius had been allowed to take Magilnada? Aroisius would be a thorn in the side of Aegenuis, and the matter of Magilnada would have divided the peoples just as much as this Askhan attack. He had no love of Salphoria and might have aided Ullsaard anyway. Chances are, the Askhans would have taken the city one way or the other and one of their own would be running it now. I am sympathetic to Aegenuis, and the only one that can help him now. Ullsaard will have to reply to what is in that letter, and you are the only man I trust to bring that answer to me unvarnished and untainted."

Listening to what Anglhan said Furlthia knew that it was true, as far as it went. He had no doubt the governor had much in mind that he was not saying, and had sidestepped the issue of what was in the letter. Every instinct in Furlthia told him to get up and walk out, but a nagging doubt remained. When all was done, someone would take that letter to Ullsaard and it would serve Furlthia's interests if it was he that delivered it. He could not bring himself to leave Anglhan alone, to plot and scheme without scrutiny, and Furlthia enjoyed a privileged position with the governor in comparison to Lenorin.

With a growl of irritation, Furlthia pushed himself up, strode across the room and snatched up the letter. He glared at Anglhan, who simply smiled.

"When do I deliver this?" said Furlthia.

"Ullsaard is coming here soon. You must wait until he returns to his main camp and is about to launch his next offensive. I don't know what his plan of attack is, but this letter will stop him in his tracks. He must receive it before he finds out what is happening back here."

"And what will be happening back here?"

"Just what you asked; my legions will seal the border to Greater Askhor and cut off Ullsaard's supplies. It's up to Aegenuis to make the most of that in whatever way he can."

Furlthia nodded his agreement and tucked the letter inside his shirt. Anglhan jabbed a finger at Furlthia.

"You must deliver that letter," said the governor. "If you don't, Ullsaard will destroy my legions, take Magilnada and sweep away any army Aegenuis can muster. Keep it safe."

II

Rain drummed on the stone courtyard outside the window, an elemental reflection of Allenya's mood. A small square of embroidery sat in her lap, not even half-finished, untouched for several hours. She watched the rain running down the long leaves of the bushes outside, each droplet a tear from the sky, shed for those she could not cry herself. She barely noticed the servant adding logs to the fire, only dimly aware of someone else in the room with her.

"Is there anything I can fetch you, mistress?"

Standing at the door Allenya saw Laasinia, her chief handmaiden, greying hair tied back tightly, dressed in a simple robe of dark wool. Allenya shook her head and turned her gaze back to the window.

"Perhaps some broth or a cup of honey tea?" Laasinia continued. "I would not forgive myself if you caught a chill, mistress."

"Nothing," said Allenya.

She heard Laasinia crossing the room and flinched as the maid laid a hand on her mistress's arm. Allenya pulled away.

"Forgive me, mistress, but you do not appear to be well," said Laasinia, crouching down in front of Allenya. "For many days you have been afflicted by this melancholy. I fear that with winter upon us, your mood will worsen."

"Can you fetch my husband and sons?" Allenya said quietly. "Will you do that for me?"

Laasinia said nothing, for there was nothing for her to say. Allenya looked at her servant and saw a face creased with concern, hands gently trembling. Suddenly noticing that the room was cold, Allenya gestured towards a shawl bundled carelessly on one of the other chairs.

"You are right, it would do no good to fall ill," Allenya said as Laasinia helped her pull the shawl over her shoulders. She grabbed the maidservant's hand in both of hers. "Do you have family, Laasinia?"

The handmaid was taken aback by the question and took a moment to answer.

"I have two daughters, mistress," she said. "They work in your kitchens."

"And their father?"

Laasinia glanced away for a heartbeat and could not look at Allenya when she answered.

"He was a sergeant in the legions. He died in Mekha, mistress."

"One of the Thirteenth?"

"No, mistress, he was in the Seventeenth."

Allenya patted the woman's hand.

"Though it is little comfort to the heart, your husband's death pension must make it easier to keep your daughters," she said. Laasinia twitched, jaw clenching. "Is that not the case?"

"My brother..." Laasinia stopped, gently pulled her hand away and stood. "I am sorry, mistress. It is not important. You have no need to bear my problems as well as your own."

"Talk to me, Laasinia," Allenya said suddenly. "Talk to me about the market, and your daughters, and your brother, and the city. Meliu shuts herself up with Noran all this time; Luia is in Okhar with Urikh. My other sons are not here. Ullsaard... I have nobody to talk to."

"Let me fetch you that tea, mistress, and we can talk as much as you like," said Laasinia.

The handmaiden left with a shallow nod and a weak smile. Allenya looked down at the embroidery. She had finished a blue sky and was working on the gold and greys of the palace atop the Royal Hill in Askh. With a sigh, she tossed the needlework aside onto the couch. Hugging a cushion, she curled up her legs and laid back, her gaze returning to the window.

Hearing a knock on the main door, she sat up, halting her slide into melancholic trance. She listened intently as the door was opened, but could not make out the voice of the visitor. Someone walked across the hall and a moment later one of the young serving boys appeared at the door of Allenya's sitting room.

"Governor Anglhan has arrived, mistress," the boy announced. "I have asked him to wait for you in the main chamber."

"Thank you," said Allenya, stirring herself from the couch.

She paced over to the polished bronze mirror beside the fireplace and checked her appearance. She adjusted a few of the ruby-headed pins keeping her hair in place, straightened her golden necklace and wiped away the dampness at the corner of her eyes. It had been some time since she had seen Anglhan; not since Ullsaard had last been in the city at the start of the summer. She wondered what had brought him here.

Attended by Laasinia, Allenya crossed the hall into the main function room. Anglhan stood admiring the fresco of a hunting scene along the wall and turned with a smile as Allenya entered. His hair and clothes had a fine mist of dampness from the rain and his face was flushed, the tip of his nose a vivid red.

"My queen," said Anglhan with an extravagant bow. Allenya laughed, surprising herself that she could.

"Governor," Allenya replied with equal formality. She darted a look at Laasinia. "I am sure our guest would like food and wine."

Laasinia departed with a silent bow, leaving Allenya alone with Anglhan. She waved him to a seat and took up station next to the fire, one arm resting on the mantel.

"Is this visit social or business?" she asked.

"A little of both," replied Anglhan, sinking down into the low couch with a grunt of effort. The chair creaked under his weight, which had continued to increase dramatically since she had last seen him. "First of all, I wished to check on the wellbeing of you and your family. Also, as I have heard nothing so I assume that Noran's condition remains unchanged?"

"What I know of my family, they are doing well," Allenya replied. "I am sure you hear more from Urikh, Ullsaard and Jutaar than I do."

"I doubt that," said Anglhan. "I am sure that you are far higher in their thoughts than I am, and certainly much deeper in their affections. I have come here to check that you have heard from Ullsaard; that he will be back in Magilnada in the next ten days."

"He sent a letter telling me as much, yes," said Allenya. "Do you have any better idea of when he is due to arrive?"

"The weather to duskwards remains changeable, but I have heard nothing of any serious storms or other conditions that might delay his return. I trust that you and

Meliu will be joining us when I welcome him back to Magilnada with proper ceremony?"

Allenya nodded. Laasinia came back at that moment, followed by two servants; one carried a tray with a pitcher of wine and crystal goblets, the other a platter of meats and cheese. These they laid on the table. Laasinia lingered for a moment, directing a look of inquiry at her mistress.

"You may leave us for the moment," said Allenya. "Please prepare a bath for me."

"I must confess to an ulterior motive to my visit, said Anglhan.

"If you confess it, it is no longer ulterior," replied Allenya. She walked around the table and sat at the other side. She poured wine for the both of them as Anglhan heaved himself out of the couch and sat opposite. "Forgive my pedantry. Carry on with your confession."

"One of my aides informed me yesterday that you have been making certain inquiries of the city merchants; inquiries that suggest to me that you are planning to leave Magilnada."

"Your assumption is correct. I will be returning to Askh in the spring."

"I see," said Anglhan. He frowned as he took a mouthful of wine. "I am disappointed to hear that. What of Meliu and Noran? Will they be travelling with you?"

"I do not think so. The surgeons do not think it wise to move Noran in his condition, and Meliu is bound to stay here with him. Why such concern for our whereabouts?"

"Let me be frank, Allenya. I see that being here is difficult for you, and perhaps Askh may offer greater comfort, familiarity and support. Forgive me if I speak out of place, but I do not think Ullsaard will be happy with your decision. I am sure he feels the distance between you already, and to return to Askh will only make him feel worse."

"You are right; it is presumptuous of you to say such things. If Ullsaard wishes to discuss the matter with me, he will do so."

"Forgive me again, but I do not think he will. We both know that he loves you deeply, and he would rather increase his own pain than impose more on you. He will agree to your departure because it is what you desire and will be all the more sorry for it."

"I do not see how that is any concern of yours."

"To be blunt, an unhappy Ullsaard makes my life more difficult. One of the benefits of the current situation is that his visits to Magilnada are tempered by your presence here. I am worried that his mood for this place will worsen if you are not here. He faces a challenging time; the Salphors will not give in easily. The king needs every support he can get, and no support is more important to him than yours. If you return to Askh, he will take it badly."

Allenya twirled her goblet and watched the wine swirling inside, red reflected against the gold. Ullsaard had shared concerns over Anglhan's ultimate motives before he had left, and warned Allenya not to trust him. She knew she could not take what he was saying at face value, though he made a good point.

"You are right, of course," she said. "It is important to Ullsaard that he knows he has people he can trust here. I will consider what you have said."

Anglhan stood and gave a shallow bow.

"We have entrusted our lives to your husband's endeavours. It is in both our interests to see that he succeeds. If there is anything I can do, any service or comfort I can provide to make your time in Magilnada an easier ordeal, just let me know. I am, of course, your servant as well as the king's."

Allenya nodded but did not stand up.

"I will see you again when Ullsaard returns," she said. "Thank you for visiting."

When the governor had left, Allenya finished her wine. She had never thought she would miss Luia, especially her venomous attitude to Ullsaard and her flagrant disrespect, but at that moment she wished dearly that her sister was around. She had a mind for the sorts of games Anglhan was playing, while Allenya did not. She would be much better at keeping an eye on the governor.

Sighing, Allenya left the table and headed towards the bath chambers. Luia was not here; she would have to do the best she could to look after Ullsaard's interests. If that meant staying in this dismal city, that would be the price.

FREE COUNTRY
Early Spring, 211th year of Askh

I

A pealing horn signalled the turning of Dawnwatch. Jutaar stayed in his bed, eyes closed, enjoying the privilege of his rank. It would be another hour before he had to get up, but nearly ten years in the legions meant that he could never get to sleep again after that wakening call. Sometimes he even still caught himself stirring at the change of Gravewatch, finding himself halfway out of bed before realising that it was no longer his duty.

Being First Captain was nothing like he had expected. He had been Third Captain for most of his life, a deputy leader to the bodyguard company of Governor Allon. He had been responsible for the kit and drill of one hundred-and-sixty men; the taskmaster that ordered the watch rotations; the oft-hidden force that ensured meals were on time, latrines were cleaned, foraging was undertaken, and patrols walked.

He had imagined that being First Captain was more of the same, in charge of companies rather than men, overseeing the human machine that was an Askhan legion. The reality had been far easier, yet somehow more disconcerting. He realised now that a First Captain only had work to do when things went wrong; while the Second and Third Captains were performing the duties, there was nothing for Jutaar's attention. He oversaw the punishments, signed the stores manifests, checked the paymaster's sums, but little else. He received his orders from his father, and his only job was to tell his subordinates to move the camp where it was needed. His legion, the First Magilnadan, had not yet been involved in a battle.

On this morning, he wondered at this inactivity. Both of the Magilnadan legions had been kept back in the Free Country. His father had explained that he wanted them fresh and ready if needed, but Jutaar was not convinced. He received news from the other legions and had heard that there had been setbacks. Some of the new legions, the ones raised earlier in the year by the nobles, had proven their inexperience, allowing themselves to be beaten by coalitions of Salphorian tribes. Surely, Jutaar reasoned to himself, an established commander like himself was better employed in the fighting, rather than overseeing a glorified garrison spread out over hundreds of miles of Free Country.

Jutaar knew that the supply route between Salphoria and Askhor was vital, but there was no threat to defend against. The Salphorian tribes of the Free Country lowlands had soon sworn allegiance to his father; any other attacks would have to come around or through the main Askhan advance.

As he did most mornings, Jutaar lay in his cot and wondered if today would be the day he received fresh orders; instructions to gather the legion together and march duskwards to join the proper campaign. It was a distant hope, but Jutaar knew that one day it would have to come true. As Ullsaard advanced, it was inevitable that the Magilnadans would have to move up into the space left behind to protect the rear. If Jutaar was lucky, there might even be a foolish Salphorian tribe or two to test his men against.

These thoughts, cogitations that occupied him every morning, were interrupted by the stamp of the sentries outside his pavilion. He jumped out of his cot and threw on a shirt. Belting his kilt around his waist, he strode into the main section of the tent just as the door flap was pulled back and a grubby-looking Salphor entered.

Jutaar knew Kubridias well, much to the First Captain's distaste. His bearskin furs stank and his poorly braided beard was always thick with dirt. The chieftain tucked his thumbs into his belt, his long and grubby fingernails fidgeting with the colourful wool weave of his trousers.

"I greeting you, First Captain," said Kubridias, in strained Askhan that made Jutaar want to wince. However, despite his efforts, the prince had failed to grasp all but the basics of Nerghian, the language of the lowland tribes.

Before Jutaar could reply, another man entered. He wore the red sash of a king's herald over his bronze breastplate. The First Captain's heart skipped a beat; the messenger's presence could only mean fresh orders.

Ignoring Kubridias, Jutaar took the letter offered by the bowing herald.

"Do you need to wait for a reply?" asked Jutaar as he pulled open the wax seal.

"No, prince," said the herald. "No reply is expected."

"Very well," said Jutaar, unfolding the parchment, eyes fixed on the revealed scrawl. "One of the sentries will guide you to the first company's mess."

"Thank you, prince," the messenger said with another bow.

Jutaar did not notice the man leave. He was intent on the letter he had brought. Reading slowly, he took in the usual platitudes and form that started all official orders.

Other officers would have skipped over them, but Jutaar read every name and phrase, committing them to memory, keen not to miss any important detail. Eventually he came to the meat of the orders.

He was, by order of the king the letter claimed, to move his headquarters fifty miles to duskwards, to a town called Arondunda. The name was familiar, but Jutaar could not place it until he caught the whiff of flatulence from Kubridias; Arondunda was the chieftain's capital.

He read on, and then re-read to ensure he had understood everything. The First Magilnadan and Second Magilnadan legions were to join forces at Arondunda. They were to prepare a march camp and stand ready to launch an offensive campaign. It was, according to the letter, likely to be a temporary posting lasting only a few days before further instructions would be sent.

This is it, Jutaar thought. This is when we get involved in the conquest. He smiled to himself and read the letter again.

"You come with me, eh?" Kubridias said with a grin, spoiling the moment. "You see how good my town be."

"You know about my orders?" replied Jutaar, eyeing the chieftain suspiciously. "How could you know?"

"I get letter from big man in Magilnada," said the chieftain. "He tell me come here. Show you way to Arondunda."

"Governor Anglhan sent you?"

"That the one." Kubridias looked perplexed, as if Jutaar has overlooked something obvious.

The First Captain looked the chieftain up and down, and wondered what to do with him. Jutaar knew exactly where Arondunda was, he had no need of this ignorant Salphorian to show him the way.

"Get someone to take you to Second Captain Allas. He will look after you."

"No, not look after me," said Kubridias, shaking his head, the beads in his beard cracking together and slapping against his chest. "Anglhan say I stay with you. You prince, yes? I look after you."

"I do not need you to look after me," snapped Jutaar. Kubridias's frown deepened. Jutaar held up a hand in apology. "I have a whole legion to look after me."

"Yes, big man say that," said Kubridias. "But not good here. Some tribes, not like you. I make them happy, yes? Got gold."

"You have gold?" said Jutaar, unsure where the conversation was heading. "Why do you have gold?"

"Pay chieftains, yes? Some chieftains not like me. They stupid. Chieftains not want gold from king, get spear in arse from you!"

Realisation slowly seeped into Jutaar's brain. It seemed a waste of money to bribe the Salphors when the legions could just as easily force them into line. Jutaar shrugged to himself; it was not his place to doubt his father's plans.

"Yes," Jutaar said with a sigh. "I will have a sharp spear ready, in case the other chieftains are not as smart as you."

II

The sun was still burning off the morning haze that surrounded the camp. It was a little past the third hour of Dawnwatch and the legionnaires had already dismantled a third of the camp in preparation for the day's march. According to the maps – and the unasked-for testimony of Kubridias – they would come to Arundonda late in the coming afternoon.

Most of the tents had been packed away already, the forges and kitchen fires quenched, the abadas harnessed to their carts and the kolubrid riders sent out on patrol. Everything was happening smoothly and quietly, a source of pride to the legion commander as he walked through the dwindling camp with his senior Second Captains; Luusin, Bariilin, Kasod and Daariun.

The four of them were tested officers, brought in by Jutaar's father from other legions to help him run the legion. To stiffen the resolve of the Magilnadans – a mixture of men descended from Salphors, Hillmen and Ersuans – the captains had brought their companies with them, forming a core of legionnaires that had fought across the empire and who Jutaar knew were loyal Askhans. Their presence served as an example to the other companies to live up to, and Jutaar, taking the advice of his father, had been forthright in his praise and reward of them in the hope that it would persuade the newer companies to come up to the level expected.

Legionnaires and Third Captains barely paid any heed to the officers in their midst as the captains made their way towards the main gate. Jutaar looked for anything out of place or badly done, and knew that his subordinates were doing the same. There was no cause for complaint; no poorly stacked supplies, no errant legionnaires slacking off, no discarded gear or slovenly behaviour.

"Have any of you seen… that filthy chieftain?" Jutaar asked his companions. He used the epithet rather than make a mangled attempt at pronouncing Kubridias's name, an issue that had caused the chieftain umbrage several times since coming to the camp.

"He left last night," said Kasod. "I think he's gone ahead to make sure there's a suitable welcome celebration for our arrival."

Jutaar grunted with displeasure.

"We are not here for feasting and drinking," said the First Captain. "There is no cause for celebrations yet.

When my father stands in the hall of Carantathi we can break out the wine."

"Of course, prince," said Kasod. Jutaar detected an unusual surliness to the Second Captain's tone.

"You have something to say about the situation, Kasod?"

"Just a little frustration, prince," the captain replied. He looked at the others before continuing. "I speak for us all when I say we wish we had something more to do. Ever since the legion was raised, these men have done nothing except march to Maasra and back, and guard a few roads. I would be happier once we've seen them in proper action."

"I understand," said Jutaar. He smiled at the group. "I will let you into a small secret. Although Anglhan has given gold to that bestial man to bribe the other chieftains, it is my intent that we do not spend it. I am not happy about paying off tribesmen with gold that could be spent paying legionnaires and building towns. My standing order to the legion is to attack any Salphorian settlement we come across. If they want to surrender, we will give them the chance, but nothing more."

"A good decision, prince," said Daariun. "If word gets around that the chieftains can earn themselves some coin by playing hard to get, it will only make matters worse. I'm surprised Anglhan would be so generous, he's not usually that free with his money."

The group had reached the gatehouse, which was being quickly dismantled as they passed out of the camp. Clouds filled the sky and Jutaar could barely see half a mile in the pre-dawn gloom; the fog around the base of the hill swathed everything in grey. Sounds of shouted orders, axes, hammers and the jangle of abada harnesses emanated from the camp behind.

Jutaar stretched to ease the ache in his shoulders. After the previous day's full march he had been a mess of sore feet and cramped muscles, unfit from the long days of in-activity. He had longed for a hot bath, but the lack of lava fuel made such a thing impractical on the move.

"I reckon it's going to be a fine day," said Jutaar. "Once this cloud has been burned away, it'll be good marching weather."

"Campaigning in the spring, you can't beat it," said Bariilin. "Warm days, cool nights, dry ground underfoot."

"It'll be nice to get an early test of the men," said Kasod. "Drill is all good, but it's only proper battle that sorts out the best."

Jutaar cast a glance at Kasod, wondering if the cap-tain's comment was somehow directed at him. Kasod was looking down the hillside, nonchalant with one hand on his sword hilt, the other on his hip. The prince said noth-ing, but knew that his ability to command was as untested as the fighting skills of the legion he led. He was under no delusion about his own talents; everything he knew about battle tactics he had learned from treatises or his father. He was also aware that he was not blessed with the active imagination and far-sighted vision of the truly great commanders.

Such deficiencies did not worry Jutaar too much; his father had assured him that winning a battle was more about doing things properly and efficiently than extrav-agant manoeuvres and wild plans. And, considering all things, Jutaar did not believe his father would put him in charge of the legion if the king did not think he was capable.

Knowing that he could lead an army on the field was one thing, showing it to his men was another. A victory, however gained, would be of benefit to everybody.

"Let us hope that some stupid warlord decides to make a stand," said the prince. "Nothing too dangerous; like a spar before a wrestling bout to get loosened up, work out the stiffness."

"There are half a dozen tribes within three days' march," said Luusin. "It would be easy enough to go and pick a fight with one of them."

"I would be all for it, captain, but those are not our orders," Jutaar replied with a sigh. "Not yet, at least. I hope that my father loosens the leash with new orders soon."

The group stood for a while in silence, each man enjoying the view and weighing the prospects of the future. A shout from a sentry patrolling outside the wall to their right broke the reverie. Looking to where the legionnaire was pointing through the thinning mist, Jutaar saw a lone outrider heading towards the camp at some speed, urging on his sluggish kolubrid.

In the clearing haze, the officers did not need the outrider to tell them what he had seen; a dark mass was coming into view across the crest of a ridge to hotwards, above the trail leading to Arondunda. Several thousand tribesmen were assembling on the hillside, no more than two miles away.

"It looks like our Salphorian allies have decided to join us," said Jutaar. He watched for a little longer. "Why are they stopping on the hill?"

"Why are they here at all?" said Kasod. "I don't think they are allies, prince."

Jutaar considered this. It seemed odd that the Salphors would attack now, when the legion had been camped only another day to dawnwards for the whole of the winter. On the other hand, there did seem to be quite a lot of them, several thousand at a rough guess; more than would be accounted for if Kubridias had brought just his own tribe.

"I'll have the men stand to arms," said Kasod, taking a step towards the gate.

"Yes, do that," said Jutaar, eyes on the expanding crowd of warriors extending along the ridge. "Surely they realise I am not going to simply march down there and let them attack? And I do not think they are foolish enough to come at us. What are they hoping to gain?"

The Second Captains offered no suggestions as horns sounded around the camp. The legionnaires dropped what they were doing – literally in the case of those men pulling down the walls – and gathered in ranks behind their company icons. The clatter of a breaking camp was replaced by the drum of sandaled feet, the clatter of spears and shields and a general murmur of confusion and suspicion. Bellows from the sergeants and Third Captains silenced the rowdier soldiers and harangued the slowest. Kasod prowled amongst the companies, sword in hand, shouting orders to the other Second Captains.

Watching the Salphors, Jutaar confirmed that they were massing on the hill but coming no closer.

"Do you think they are waiting for something?" he said.

"It looks like it, but waiting for what?" said Luusin.

Jutaar headed back into the camp, assessing the situation. Half of the wall had been brought down already. To stay within would be more of a hindrance than a help.

"I find the Salphors' timing remarkable," said Luusin, trailing behind the prince with the others. "It seems more than coincidence that they turn up right when we're in the middle of breaking camp."

Jutaar said nothing, but the thought put in his mind by Luusin did not sit comfortably. The timing was too neat, and contrary to what he had learned in general about the Salphors from the reports of the other legion commanders; their warriors took considerable time to prepare for battle and were rarely ready to fight before mid-morning. Thinking along this line in his own plodding way, Jutaar added in the fact that there was obviously more than one tribe gathering on the ridge. Only rarely had the Salphors been able to put aside their traditional differences even in the face of the Askhan advance.

Making pretence of looking over his army, the prince tried to put together the pieces he had at hand. It felt like one of those sums his tutors had tested him with as a child, but with some of the numbers missing; what he knew just did not add up to any plausible answer.

"Move the legion to a defensive position on the slope facing the enemy," he told his subordinates. "Leave three companies as rearguard in the camp."

The Second Captains thumped fists to their chests in salute and headed off to spread the word. Horns and drums signalled the orders to the army as Jutaar pondered the possible outcomes. He always found things worked out better if he had time to think them through in advance rather than make hasty decisions.

If the Salphors remained where they were, Jutaar decided he would force their bluff with an attack. If they moved away, he would order a pursuit; such aggressive behaviour could not be ignored. If they attacked, that would be the simplest solution of all; the army would hold the hillside and repel the tribesmen from the position of advantage.

Happy that he had all eventualities covered, Jutaar joined the front rank of the first company as they headed for the gate at the head of the march. They led the legion out of the camp and turned coldwards towards the enemy, taking up position on the far left of the line at a place a third of the way down the slope. More companies fell into position to their right, stretching around the hill for a quarter of a mile, each phalanx arranged ten wide and sixteen ranks deep, spears piercing the sky like a bronze-tipped thicket with large, round blue-and-black leaves.

Having been brought back from the picket by the clarions, the kolubrid company positioned themselves just behind the centre, ready to sweep around either flank as necessary. The thump of mallets on wooden pegs announced the war machine crews setting up the spear throwers and catapults a hundred paces behind the legionnaires, from where they would be able to fire over the phalanxes. Flames crackled and smoke climbed into the clouds as the rearguard set fire to the remaining camp defences. With this job attended to, the guard companies emerged alongside lines of abada wagons; they filed away slowly to hotwards, carrying essential supplies of food, ammunition, weapons and water, as well as the heavy bound chests holding the paymaster's coins. Everything else was left in the camp, to be taken by the flames or recovered after victory as fate decided.

The weather was warming quickly, as Jutaar had predicted. The clouds and mist that had obscured the approach of the Salphors were now all but gone, leaving the air chill but clear. The spring sun was not quite hot enough to make things comfortable, but the wind was light and there was no sign of worse weather on the horizon. If the Salphors wanted to wait out the patience of the Askhans, Jutaar was content to oblige them.

The morning dragged on laboriously, each hour of the passing watches called out by the timekeepers with their shuttered watch candle lanterns. Dawnwatch crept into Low Watch, when Jutaar issued the order for the army to take a water break. On the opposite side of the shallow valley, the Salphors seemed to be in no hurry to move either. Though it was hard to be sure, it looked to Jutaar as if many of them were sitting down, enjoying the sun and fresh air. It certainly was not the build up to a battle he expected.

It was impossible to keep the legionnaires at full focus for any length of time, and the Salphors were in plain view and thus unable to launch a sudden attack. As the second hour of Low Watch passed, Jutaar sent word to the Second Captains to stand down from battle formations. Staying in their companies, the legionnaires stacked their spears, piled their shields and gratefully took off their helmets. Conversation drifted along the hillside; Jutaar ignored the usual mix of boasts, complaints and tall stories as he left the First Company and walked the line, signalling for his council of Seconds to gather.

"Perhaps they are waiting for us to send an embassy," Jutaar suggested, as the five of them sat down on a clutch of rocks, water canteens in hand.

"If they wanted to talk, they would've sent someone to us," replied Daariun. "I think they are just fucking about with us. As soon as we make a move on them, they'll be off into the plains quicker than a run to the latrines after a night of bad beer."

"I just don't see what they think they can gain," said Luusin. "Do you think it's a feint? Maybe they've got a whole bunch more tribes hiding behind that ridge and they want to lure us into an attack before springing them on us."

"Maybe something is happening to duskwards, and this lot are just here to delay us," suggested Kasod. "Could be that Kubridias's neighbours have got bored of him playing whore and they've attacked his town."

"Which is it?" snapped Jutaar. "If it is a trap, we should not attack; if it is a diversion or delay, we should drive them off as soon as we can and head after Kubridias."

"You can rule out a trap by sending some scouts over that ridge," said Kasod.

Jutaar looked at the lay of the land. The ridgeline was bare of anything larger than bushes and rocks; any scouts would be easily spotted as they tried to cross it. The closest woods were at least four or five miles away to hotwards.

"That would take another hour, perhaps two to know for sure," said the prince. He turned to Luusin. "We may as well do something. Send half a dozen kolubrids through those woods down there. They should be able to see any army lying in wait once they get to the other side."

Luusin nodded and headed off towards the kolubrid company, waving to attract the attention of their captain. Soon the scouts were slithering away on their scaled mounts, heading down the blindside of the hill to avoid being seen by the Salphors. Luusin returned to the group.

"They'll burn lavaleaf torches if there are no enemy," the captain reported. "We should see the smoke from here if the wind doesn't get any stronger."

Jutaar nodded, pleased with his initiative. It felt good to be doing something, even if that something was only taking a better look at the situation. He wondered what his father would do. Probably attack first and worry about the consequences later, he decided. Jutaar did not like taking risks, and knew it would be better to wait than to commit to something foolish.

The third hour of Low Watch came and went without event. The small council broke apart, the captains walking amongst their companies and the other legionnaires, joking and passing the time as best they could. Jutaar stayed where he was, sitting and staring at the Salphorian army. He was forced to wonder if he was being tricked. If the Salphors had even more warriors, it made more sense that they would not have shown several thousand of their number on the hill; better to leave just a few hundred as more tempting bait. If that was the case, the Salphors were on the ridge for a purpose, and that could only be to protect something behind them.

"We are going to attack," Jutaar announced loudly, jumping to his feet. "Stand the legion to arms."

"Bored of waiting, prince?" Daariun called out from the third company.

"If the Salphors want to sit on that hill all day, we are going to make sure that they cannot," Jutaar replied. "Second Captains! To me for orders of battle."

When the company commanders had assembled, Jutaar outlined the plan of attack he had been devising throughout the whole morning. Like the commander that had thought of it, the plan was simple. The right wing of the legion would engage the Salphors directly and hopefully draw them down the ridge on to the centre. The left wing would extend past the Salphors' flank, gain the crest and attack the Salphorian rear from above.

"The enemy outnumber us," Jutaar warned. "The best way that this will work is for the centre and right to take up position at the base of the ridge. The war engines will move down onto level ground and attack the Salphors. They will have to either withdraw or come to meet us head on, straight onto our spear tips, which will suit us just fine. Either way, the left wing will move up the shallower slope and press their flank. If the Salphors move to head off this attack, the right wing will have to advance around the other side instead. Does everybody understand?"

There was agreement from all the captains and with no questions to be raised they headed back to their companies. Drums rolled to sound the advance as the legionnaires pushed themselves to their feet, took up spears and shields and fell into rank again. Advancing in formation, the First Magilnadan flowed down the slope towards the enemy as a solid line of bronze.

The legion had covered the first quarter-mile when Jutaar saw a ruddy smudge in the air, drifting up behind the Salphors. It was the smoke from the scouts, indicating that there were no enemy hiding behind the hill.

"I knew it was a ruse," Jutaar laughed to his icon bearer, Kaasin. "They would never catch me out with such a simple trick. We will see how clever they think they are."

Kaasin nodded and smiled but said nothing. Ahead, the Salphorian army was engulfed by a flurry of movement as the warriors gathered in their tribal bands, roused by the Askhan advance. Jutaar could hear crude hunting horns, but they were just blaring randomly, not the pre-arranged signals of the Askhan musicians. Watching the enemy movements carefully, Jutaar concluded that the Salphors were going to hold the ridgeline; they made no attempt to retreat but neither were they coming any closer.

The advance continued until the legion was a quarter of a mile from the enemy. Here, Jutaar called a halt while the war machines were erected again. All the while, the Salphors seemed content to allow him to organise his battle line and prepare his engines.

"Idiots," Jutaar said happily to the men around them. "They just wait there, like a rabbit in a snare not realising that the knife is coming down."

A tremor of words suddenly rippled through the army, seeming to originate from the far right flank.

"What is happening?" Jutaar called out to Kasod, who was in the company to his right.

The Second Captain shrugged and passed on the question to Daariun, but before anything was shouted back, Jutaar received his answer. Men from every company were turning around and pointing back up the hill. Jutaar craned his neck to look over the men behind and saw something in the air to hotwards; a slim arc of black smoke. It was the trail of a warning arrow, shot by a bellows bow in the rearguard.

The import of this quickly engulfed the legion; the baggage train was in trouble of some kind. Jutaar chided himself for advancing, leaving the supplies almost two miles behind. Had that been the Salphor ploy all along? He did not panic, even though around him the legionnaires were wildly and loudly speculating on the demise of their baggage.

"Restore order, captains!" Jutaar bellowed, stepping out of the first company to face the army. He waited for a moment while the chastised legionnaires fell silent. He pointed at Salphors in front of the army. "If we turn back, those crafty bastards are going to come down that hill after us. More than five hundred of your companions guard the baggage. We wait for the report from the rearguard. Until then, you will maintain ranks and be prepared to fight the enemy to our front. Company punishment for the next man to speak out of turn!"

There was no need to issue further orders; messengers on kolubrids were already guiding their scaled mounts up the hill to see what, if any, enemy was attacking the baggage and to intercept any rider or runner the rearguard were sending with news.

Jutaar attempted to affect the same air of nonchalance he had seem his father employ in such situations; though he was sure that in the case of Ullsaard his calm disregard was real and not feigned. Though he strove to appear unflustered by this development, Jutaar's stomach churned and his heart raced. It was not fear that caused this reaction, but excitement. Jutaar fought to concentrate, to remember the lessons he had been told and had read in the treatises of the old commanders. He kept telling himself that a rash reaction to events was the worst thing he could do. A real commander assessed the battlefield as it developed, based his decisions on what he knew for sure, and did not overreact.

The loss of the baggage would be an embarrassment more than a strategic disaster; every legionnaire was required to carry everything he needed for living and war-making. Each had food and fresh water for five days, and amongst the men of each company were more than enough whetstones, spare spear tips and knives, extra sandals and shield straps, and other such tools and supplies of maintenance needed to keep them in fighting shape. Whatever happened, Jutaar was determined that the legion would withdraw in good order, all the way back to Magilnada if needed.

There seemed to be some confusion amongst the scouts; some were turning back already while others were continuing on back up the hill towards the rearguard. Jutaar could plainly see the riders arguing with each other. It was ill-disciplined behaviour at the best of times and inexcusable during the current circumstance.

"Council captains, gather on me!" Jutaar called out. Bariilin, Luusin, Daariun and Kasod broke from their companies at a quick jog, quickly converging on their general. "Luusin, go and find out what that scouts think they are doing and report back immediately."

The Second Captain set off with a quick salute. Jutaar turned his attention back to the Salphors.

"It doesn't look like they're ready to come and play yet," said Kasod.

What he said was true. The Salphors stood at the top of the ridge, some of them laughing and pointing at their Askhan foes.

"If they think this is some kind of joke, they will learn that it is not," said Jutaar. "They are trying to goad us into an attack. We will remain here until the matter with the rearguard is settled."

There were nods of approval from Daariun and Bari-ilin, but Kasod looked unconvinced.

"You think we should attack?" Jutaar snapped at the Second Captain.

"I think we should do something, prince," replied Kasod. "If the baggage is being attacked, we look like a bunch of prize pricks waiting for the whores, standing here doing nothing."

"But what can we do?" said Jutaar, pacing in agitation, all thoughts of a calm presentation forgotten. "If the Salphors want us to pull back, we should attack. If they want us attack, we should pull back."

"Fuck the Salphors," said Kasod, grabbing Jutaar's arm to bring him to a halt. "What do *you* want to do, prince?"

"Yes, yes, you are right," said Jutaar, tugging free his arm. "We will continue the attack. The baggage guard will have to look after themselves."

"Are you sure, prince?" said Daariun. "We have unknown enemies behind us. If they come at us while we are engaged on the ridge, we'll be trapped."

Jutaar cleared his throat.

"All right," he said. "The most prudent stance will be to withdraw back to where we were and provide support for the rearguard. However, we will be prepared to turn if the Salphors come off the ridge."

A shout from a returning Luusin broke the deliberations. The Second Captain was approaching at a full run, helmet crest flapping madly. As he reached Jutaar, he flopped to one knee, fighting for breath.

"It's the Second," he managed between gasps. "Coming up from dawnwards."

"Well, that's all right," laughed Daariun. He nodded towards the Salphorian army. "That lot are fucked now. I bet they weren't expecting two legions."

"Nor should they be," said Jutaar. He pulled Luusin to his feet. "You are sure it is the Second Magilnadan? From Dawnwards?"

"Yes, prince," said Luusin. "Blue and black shields, with Anglhan's stupid silver bosses on them. Pretty much following in our footsteps."

"But they should already be at Arundonda, ahead of us," said Jutaar. He looked at his captains, bewildered by the news. "What are they doing here?"

"Delayed, maybe?" suggested Daariun.

"No, they were wintered more than fifty miles hotwards of where we were," said Kasod. "There's no reason they should be behind us, and certainly not with the orders they were given."

"They must have received new orders," said Jutaar. "But orders from whom?"

"Prince!" Luusin burst out having regained his breath, drowning out Kasod's reply. "They are marching on the rearguard. They're not just following us. They look like they're going to attack!"

"Well, that's clearly nonsense," said Daariun. "Why would they do that?"

"Anglhan," said Kasod. "Prince, where did our orders come from?"

"From the king," Jutaar replied, confused by the question. "Who else would have sent them?"

"From the king himself? Directly?"

"Well, no, not directly. They came in a letter, via royal courier." Jutaar swallowed hard, the implication of what he had just said sinking in. "You mean they were forged?"

"Yes," snapped Kasod. The Second Captain darted a look over his shoulder at the legion. In the absence of orders, they milled around, uncertain and restless. Several companies had broken up, some soldiers looking back towards the rearguard, others keeping an eye on the Salphors. "We have to get out of here. It isn't safe!"

The captains degenerated into a hushed, snarled argument. Jutaar was at a loss to say anything. He still found the situation highly unlikely. If Anglhan wanted Jutaar dead, there were other ways to achieve it. Even the pretence of having him slain by the Salphors was dubious, considering the cost and damage of setting two legions against each other. Jutaar could not figure out what was to be gained by pitching the two Magilnadan armies into battle with one another.

An answer trickled slowly into his mind, bringing with it a chill feeling in his gut. Jutaar stared at his army with suspicion. Some of the captains had left their companies and were gathered in their own group. They occasionally cast glances at their commander and his council.

"Captains, return to your companies," said Kasod, noticing the same. "Prince, we have to withdraw now."

"You are not in command," said Jutaar. "I am your general and prince."

"We don't have time for this," said Kasod. He turned on his fellow captains. "Anglhan has paid off the Magilnadans. Look at them! They're going to turn on us."

In fact, the Magilnadan officers were returning to their companies, calling them to order. Looking back to dawnwards Jutaar could see thicker smoke rising from where the rearguard had been; they had either destroyed the supplies or the other legion had reached the baggage train. On the ridge to the front, the Salphors had also seen this and obviously knew what it meant. Horns clamoured again and the tribal warriors stirred themselves, picking up shields and spears in readiness for battle.

"First through Fifth companies, assemble on your prince!" Kasod bellowed, running back to his men. The other Second Captains scattered, repeating the order, leaving Jutaar standing on his own in front of the army.

The prince hesitated, unsure what to do. He was wrenched from his indecision by the jangle of armour as the first company gathered around him. The legion was quickly splitting as both sides realised what was about to happen; the Magilnadans formed a tight line slightly further up the gentle slope while Kasod and the other loyal captains set their companies in a solid block around Jutaar.

The prince felt hopeless. This was only his first command and his legion was in revolt. His father had entrusted this army to him and he had failed miserably in his duties. Out-thought and outmanoeuvred, he had blundered into Anglhan's trap like a boar into a pit. The king had tried to warn him, but he had fallen victim to his own trusting stupidity.

Urikh had been right all along; he was a disappointment to his father. A mediocre son, a poor brother, a pathetic husband; that would be his appalling legacy. Worse than any of that, Jutaar knew he would be remembered as the commander of the First Magilnadan, a legion of traitors.

Jutaar's eyes stung as he held back hot tears. Through misted vision he could see the turncoat companies advancing in wide formation, spears lowered for the attack.

III

"Shield up, prince," muttered Kaasin next to Jutaar, lifting his shield in front of the prince, legion icon in the other hand. "No point going down easy."

The standard bearer's words cut through Jutaar's grief. That calm defiance rooted in the prince's spirit, reminding him that he was a prince of the Blood, but more than that, he was a legionnaire of Askhos. His father had told him with pride of how Cosuas had refused to surrender, preferring to die than witness defeat. Jutaar could remember listening to the old general's war stories, sitting on the veteran's lap as a child, his earliest memories filled with tales of blood and glory.

"Men of Greater Askhor," Jutaar bellowed, bringing up his shield. "Make your king proud!"

The prince watched the traitors advancing at an angle. There were four times as many of them as those loyal to Jutaar and their line extended far beyond the right of the prince's phalanxes.

"Watch the flank," warned Jutaar. "Fourth company, advance twenty paces. Second company, withdraw twenty paces."

The order was quickly passed through the companies. The loyalists adjusted accordingly, the echelon of phalanxes arranged to steer the renegades back towards their extended flank. Jutaar knew that it would make no difference in the result of the fight, but true to Karin's urging he would not allow himself to do anything less than the best he could.

The traitors accelerated to a steady run when they were fifty paces away.

"Receive the charge!" bellowed Jutaar, pulling free his sword. Despair had been swept away by anger; anger he had never felt before in his life. The affront of the traitors burned his pride; the insult to Jutaar and his family raged through his blood. "Let's make these cunts pay!"

With a roar from both sides, the legionnaires crashed together. Jutaar angled his shield to deflect a spear point away from the man to his left. The prince lunged forward, driving his sword into the narrow gap in the opposing line of shields. Shields rattled and spears clashed all around, accompanied by the shouts of loyalist and traitor.

Having weathered the brunt of the impact, the First Company pushed back under Jutaar's urging, stabbing with their spears. The prince hacked at the shield of the man in front, the repeated blows driving him backwards. A spear thrust over Jutaar's shoulder from the man behind, point ramming into his opponent's exposed shoulder. The prince swept his sword into the traitor's face as he fell back, the blade carving a deep wound across cheek and nose.

A shield rim smacked into Jutaar's hand, jarring his arm. Spitting with pain, the prince kept his numbed fingers tight in their grip and thrust his sword into the arm of another man. To the prince's right, Karin went down with a shout, the snapped haft of a spear jutting from his chest. Jutaar pounced sideways, warding away another attack with his shield as a legionnaire in the second rank stepped forward, dropping his spear to take up the golden icon of Askhos.

In the thick of the fighting, Jutaar had no idea what was happening to the other companies. It made no difference. Even if, by some twist of destiny, they were to prevail over the traitors, they would not survive against the Salphors and the other legion closing in. He chopped through the wrist of a hand holding a spear. With blood spraying, sweat dripping, everything in tumult around him, a strange thought occurred to Jutaar; he could not be taken prisoner.

It was his last duty not to be used as a hostage against his father. The situation made things very simple, and that was just how Jutaar liked things. All he had to do was fight until he was dead.

At that moment of realisation, pain lanced through his body as a spear clattered from the shield of the legionnaire next to him and punched into the right side of his ribs. He smashed the shaft apart as the enemy pulled out the spear, and turned his wrist to bring his blade crashing against the cheek guard of the traitor's helmet.

The edge of a shield caught Jutaar below the brow of his helm, stunning him. Blood trickled into his eyes as he stumbled back. Two legionnaires quickly stepped in front to protect their commander, shields and spears at the ready. Wiping blood from his eyes with the knuckle of his thumb, Jutaar pushed back to the front. His hand was sticky with gore and more blood seeped down his right leg, pooling into his boot. His breaths came as laboured gasps and he wondered if his lung had been punctured.

"Keep fighting," he growled to himself.

He parried a spear thrust aimed at his groin and stamped on the haft, wood exploding in a shower of splinters. Both sides had abandoned any attempt at co-ordinated action as the phalanxes shattered, the combat degenerating into clusters of men fighting each other.

Jutaar drove ahead, using his shield as a ram, knocking the man in front of him off his feet. Plunging into the gap, the prince sliced to the left and right, slashing at the traitors without any thought to where his blows landed.

Something pierced the back of his left thigh, bringing him down to one knee. Twisting to bring up his shield against this fresh attack, the prince left himself open to a spear from the right, which caught him in the right shoulder, bronze scraping against bone. Sword slipping from dead fingers, Jutaar roared in pain and surged to his feet. His shield caught a legionnaire beneath the chin, snapping his head back, bone cracking. Driving his knee into the man's groin, Jutaar tossed his shield at the next enemy to come at him. In the moment this bought him, the prince snatched up a fallen spear in his left hand and swung in a wide arc, the tip catching another foe in the eye.

He heard a snap of wood behind and dimly registered a spear point sliding into his lower back. A heartbeat later, pain seared down into Jutaar's legs and he collapsed, face hitting the ground. Sandaled feet trampled him, kicking the spear from his grasp. Agony burned through every part of his body as more spear tips sank through skin and muscle.

Coughing blood, feeling splinters of bone moving in his flesh, Jutaar rolled to his back. He could barely breathe and both his eyes were quickly swelling, his face a bruised mess. He was surrounded by a ring of shadows, silhouettes of crested helmets against the light blue sky. Jutaar fumbled for the knife at his belt but his fingers would not work. A foot pressed down on his chest, igniting a fire of pain in his heart and lungs. Through squinting eyes, the prince saw the glitter of sunlight on a bronze blade.

The last drops of Jutaar's life leaked from his wounds and he died, even as the sword sliced across his throat.

SALPHORIA
Summer, 211th year of Askh

I

Wood smoke drifted between the mud-stained tents and through the line of legionnaires waiting at their company kitchen. Gelthius queued beside his friends, bowl and spoon in hand. Though tradition entitled a man of his rank to cut the line ahead of the rank-and-file he was still uncertain about taking advantage of most of the privileges of being Third Captain, to the amusement of both legionnaires and fellow officers.

Not that such benefits would make any difference in the present situation, as he pointed out when Muuril reminded him that he did not have to wait in line with the rest of them.

"First in line for slop?" said Gelthius. "What's the point of that? Now, if the foragers had found a bit of meat or some nice vegetables or fruit, you can be sure I'd be up front quicker than a dog after a hare."

"This isn't right," said Loordin. "How long's it been now since the last wagons came in? Fifteen days?"

"More like twenty since we had a proper resupply," said Muuril.

They shuffled forward a few steps with the line. Up ahead, a legionnaire loudly voiced his discontent at the poor fare the legion had been enduring lately. There was nothing the men serving the plain boiled oats and heavy bread could do but shrug.

"It's not right," Loordin said again. "Within two days' march I reckon there's plenty of Salphorian food. What's the king wasting his time for?"

"How would I know?" said Gelthius.

"Thought you were best friends now, captain," Muuril said with a grin. "Special advisor, isn't it?"

Gelthius took this with a disconsolate shake of the head. His friends knew well enough that being a 'special advisor' was more of a chore than a blessing, but there were others in the company who genuinely believed Gelthius had some inside line to the workings of command; they would pester him for news that he did not have, or demand that he take up their complaints with the First Captain and King Ullsaard.

"Advancing without secured supplies is risky," said Muuril, answering Loordin's question as the line took a few more paces towards a bench sagging under three soot-stained pots of gruel. "Come on, you've been on enough campaigns to know that. Like when we was down in Mekha, we couldn't go nowhere less we had enough water. What if there's a caravan coming right now? They know where we're meant to be. If we head off from here, they might never find us."

"Yeah, but it's not right," said Loordin.

"Say that again and I'm going to batter you," said Muuril.

"Look, we're all hungry, right enough," said Gelthius, feeling that as Third Captain he had some responsibility to keep the men in the best spirits possible. "We can moan about it, or we can do our best to find some proper food next time we're on forage rotation. Other than that, you might as well work your jaw less and save yourself the energy."

Loordin looked for a moment like he was going to continue complaining, but contented himself with an annoyed huff. Gelthius knew Loordin was far from alone in his view. Walking the rounds of guard and hanging out with some of the captains from other companies, he felt the discontent. There was the griping that legionnaires were always prone to, and then there was genuine dissent.

Having had a hand in spreading a fair bit of unhappiness through the legions that had stood against Ullsaard's bid for the throne, and spent a dreadful winter with the Thirteenth when they had been beset by blizzards and plague, Gelthius knew how easy it was to tip the balance from discipline to desertion. Nobody had fled the legion yet, but with all of Salphoria to get lost in, it would only be a matter of time. It was only the presence of the king in the camp that was holding the legion together. As the Thirteenth, Ullsaard's chosen legion, the royal bodyguard, pride currently won over hunger, but there was a point at which pride would fail; when that happened, Gelthius was not sure which side he would be on.

II

The appearance of Maalus silenced the chattering in the king's pavilion. The gaggle of captains and commanders that made up Ullsaard's war council parted in front of the arrival, horror on the faces of a few, pity on the faces of others. The self-appointed general was supported between two Second Captains, thick bandages beneath his breastplate, his right leg ending in a bloodstained, swaddled stump just above the knee. The men carrying him were no better off, one with an arm in the sling, the other with a long cut across his cheek, his helmet scored by the same blow. Anasind was first to his feet, gesturing for the men to carry the commander to the vacated chair. Nobody said a word as Maalus hobbled across the stained rugs, wincing with every movement.

Since receiving news of Maalus's defeat, Ullsaard had expected the worst, but to see the man himself so badly injured brought home the disaster that had happened. The king poured wine for the nobleman and took it to him. Maalus took a grateful mouthful and sat back, waving away his orderlies. The two captains retreated to the door with bows and concerned looks.

"How many left?" said Ullsaard, getting to the point.

"Three hundred, maybe three-fifty," said Maalus. "I do not know how many escaped the rout, but I would not expect to see them again."

"The messenger said you were attacked by a tribal coalition," said Anasind. "What happened?"

Maalus took another drink.

"Lukha's dead, his legion destroyed as well," he told them. "Scouts reported a Salphorian army, maybe two thousand strong, twenty miles duskwards of where we were camped. I sent word to Lukha, and we combined our legions for the attack. It should have been easy. Such a small force of barbarians against two legions? Just the sort of fight you told us to pick. About six or seven thousand more Salphors had moved through the forests coldwards of Lukha's camp. They came in behind us the day before we were going to attack. Our only chance was to break through the small army and head duskwards into the wilds."

Maalus bowed his head and stared into his cup, lips tightly pursed. He did not look at any of the other men as he continued.

"Seems the scouts were wrong there, too. Not two thousand, but four thousand. They had dug ditches in the fields and fortified the farms. Lots of bows, thousands of them. Savage hound packs, chariots drawn by shaggy creatures I've never seen before. There was no way we could fight. Lukha and I agreed to split. He went to duskwards and hotwards, I went dawnwards. We thought that one of us might get away with our legion intact, maybe mount some kind of rearguard. I think the Nemurians decided to stay to make a fight of it. I hope they killed plenty of those Salphor boy-whores."

"But that didn't work," said Ullsaard, returning to his campaign throne. He snapped his fingers. "Two legions lost, just like that."

"Probably three," sighed Maalus. "The Fourteenth were on our coldwards flank, about another two days' march away. I sent Canaasin word of what we were planning to do, but there was no time to despatch a warning when it went wrong. I would not count the Fourteenth in any of your plans."

"Fuck!" Ullsaard's goblet flew across the pavilion, clanging into one of the carved poles holding up the roof. "Fuck and shit. The Salphors must have been mustering all spring to mount such an attack; and just now, when supplies are so low. It seems too convenient for this to be happenstance."

"You think that the Salphors have something to do with the supply caravans being waylaid?" said Aklaan, First Captain of the Third Legion. "We have the Magilnadan legions protecting the roads, how could that be possible?"

"It doesn't matter, not for the moment," said Ullsaard. "Whatever the reason, we can't carry on like this. The enemy have managed to gather their strength, to coldwards at least, but probably elsewhere. Too strong for the legions to take on individually. Something or someone is cutting off our supplies. If word gets out, and it will, those tribes behind us that we've got under control at the moment are going to start making trouble."

"So, what do we do?" asked Ullasand, another noble-turned-general who had joined the campaign only that spring. "I've emptied the family coffers to fund my legion. You can't call off the advance now, not with everything I've invested."

"Look at him!" snapped Ullsaard, pointing at Maalus. "He's lost a fucking leg, and you're worried about the return on your investment? If we press on now, the only coins you'll be counting are the ones your widow puts in your grave urn."

"I can't keep paying for my legion just to stand around with their thumbs up their arses," said Ullasand. "You promised us conquest; so far I've had eighty days of shuffling my legion around and making camps while roads and bridges get built."

"The empire wasn't built in a day," Anasind said quietly.

"We fortify," said Ullsaard. He looked hard at Ullasand. "The further we advance without sure supplies, the further we stick our necks out. I'll take the Thirteenth, Fifth and Twentieth back dawnwards to find out what's happening to the caravans. If it comes to it, I'll bloody escort the meat and grain through myself. Send word to the other legions to invest for an extended encampment, no legion more than ten miles from another. We'll have to give ground for the moment, but it's better that than lose everything."

"And then?" asked Maalus. "These bastards took my leg; please tell me I get to kill some of them."

"Once every legion is safely back to quarters, we'll have to assess their strengths, maybe combine a few of them. Then we organise into two forces. The first is heading directly for Carantathi. The sooner we have Aegenuis's head on a spear, the quicker the tribes will fall apart. The second will follow behind, mopping up any tribes that were missed by the first army."

"When?" said Ullasand. "It's almost new year already, half the summer wasted."

"It's sixty days to Magilnada and back," said Anasind. "Judging from earlier in the year that should still give us more than eighty days of good campaigning weather in these parts."

"We'll carry on into winter if we have to," said Ullsaard. "It'll be a bitch, but it'll be worse for the Salphors than us. Next time we won't give them the space to lick their wounds."

The talk carried on past Midwatch, into the early hours of the morning. Orders were drawn up for every remaining legion in Salphoria, logistics were arranged to pool the meagre resources, and the positions of the defensive line were agreed.

Ullsaard was exhausted by the time his head hit the pillow of his cot. Still dressed in his armour, he was instantly asleep.

III

The sand beneath Ullsaard's feet was the colour of rainbows, swirled into hypnotising curves by steady waves of golden water. Whichever way he looked, he gazed out across that auric sea, the spectrum of the beach stretching out endlessly on the periphery of sight. Ullsaard held up his hand. The air shimmered around his fingers like quicksilver. There was no breeze. Even looking directly up he saw nothing but sparkling tide.

"It's a fucking dream," he said. "Where are you?"

"Where I will always be, Ullsaard," Askhos replied behind him. "In your mind."

Ullsaard turned quickly. The dead king sat on a rock of black glass shaped like two cupped hands. He wore a plain white tunic and kilt of dark leather, sandals on his feet and a sash of red across his chest. Jewels glittered in Askhos's braided hair and beard. He seemed younger. The light of the golden sea reflected in dark eyes made them dance with life.

"I thought I was too far from the Crown," said Ullsaard. "I thought I was rid of you."

The apparition of Askhos shrugged.

"I do not know how this works anymore than you," said the empire founder. "We both march across uncharted lands. In your case, quite literally. It is disappointing that you have had to halt your advance."

"So you know what has been happening?"

"I only know what you know. I told you that last time. Oh, and thank you for sparing me the embarrassment of rutting with your wife."

Ullsaard leapt at the king and seized his throat in one hand, dragging him to his feet. Ullsaard was shocked that such a thing was possible. He had acted out of instinct, half-thinking that Askhos would be formless and his hand would go through him as if he were smoke.

"I am real, as much as any man's mind can be said to be," said Askhos, unperturbed by his predicament. "What do you hope to achieve?"

"Perhaps if I kill you here…" Ullsaard squeezed tighter, until his fingertips touched thumb, the king's neck impossibly constricted.

"Your mind is not made up of flesh and bone, is it? Throttle me for as long as you like. Neither of us has bones to break, or lungs to choke."

The former king illustrated his point by poking a finger in Ullsaard's eye. He felt nothing except a sense of pressure, much like when skin is prodded. Letting go, Ullsaard stepped back.

"Did I bring you here? Did you bring me here?" he asked.

Askhos directed a patronising look at his dream-companion and said nothing.

"You said your tomb was a real place," Ullsaard said, kicking the multicoloured sand with his bare foot. "Is this a real place somewhere as well?"

"What is your obsession with reality, Ullsaard? You say things are real, as if that has any proper meaning. Are thoughts real? Are dreams real? Is love real? You are a terribly narrow-minded man."

"Everything I know tells me that this place is impossible. It is just a dream. It is… unreal."

"Do not confuse reality with the physical. You might just as well ask why water is wet, or what air tastes like." Askhos waited, but received only an uncomprehending glare in reply. The former king sat himself down again and crossed his arms and legs. "Let us talk reality. Your army is stuck, you have no supplies, and your campaign will fail."

"It has stalled, but it has not failed," said Ullsaard. "I will put things right soon enough."

"For the moment, perhaps, but what about the next setback, and the next? Do you think I was able to create Greater Askhor by sheer force of will? Of course not. Empires need to be organised. Endeavours need to be coordinated. No single man can control something as vast as Greater Askhor. Even your governors struggle to maintain their provinces."

"So, we are back to this? You will tell me to restore the Brotherhood. I'm not an idiot. I see where this conversation goes."

"But you will not admit the truth that can be found at its destination. I was the greatest leader Askhor has ever seen. The loyalty amongst my subjects was absolute. I wielded powers you do not know exist, had allies you are not aware of, and even *I* needed the Brotherhood. They are the empire."

"Not any longer."

"You are all muscle, but you have no skeleton. The Brotherhood is the bones that keep everything else together. This little supply problem of yours? Expect it to get a lot worse. You have more enemies than you realise; the ones you know about and the ones you do not yet see. A thousand and one tiny cuts will destroy you. The Brotherhood is the salve for those little wounds."

"And your means to dispense with me completely and restore your immortal rule. You think I would sharpen the axe for my own execution and freely hand it over? No, I will never do that."

"Then you will die, and I with you, and the empire will fall. It is that simple."

"So be it."

IV

It took a further three days for Ullsaard to finalise his plans and despatch orders for the entrenchment of the Askhan position. When all was set in motion, the king lifted his camp and marched dawnwards with the Fifth, Thirteenth and Twentieth Legions. Along newly-laid roads, across bridges whose stones glistened with fresh whitewash, the eighteen thousand-strong army snaked back towards Magilnada.

On the nineteenth evening of the march, as the scouts returned bearing news of sites suitable for camp, one patrol brought back disturbing intelligence. Atop a hill a few miles from the road, the ruins of a legion camp had been seen. On hearing this, Ullsaard rode out on Blackfang, accompanied by Anasind and a bodyguard of five hundred legionnaires. Following the scouts, the detachment turned coldwards while the rest of the army continued on to set up camp.

"We should have made contact with the First Magilnadan by now," said Anasind, stepping easily alongside Blackfang's loping gait. "They were stationed to guard this stretch."

"Jutaar will have followed his orders," said Ullsaard. "He would have sent word if something was amiss."

As they continued, the blackened walls of the camp visible in the distance, the king doubted the truth of what he said. His second son was loyal and dogged, but Ullsaard was under no illusion regarding Jutaar's slowness of thought. It seemed incredible that some disaster might have befallen a whole legion without some news of it spreading, but the charred palisade on the hill ahead spoke a strong testimony; burning the camp was established practice when faced with an unexpected threat and something Jutaar would not have ordered without good reason.

Pressing on further than the scouts had investigated, the small column crested the hill. Ullsaard dismounted and walked amongst the ruin with his First Captain. The exact state of the camp at the time of its destruction told its own tale. Every legion broke camp in the same manner, and it was easy to decipher exactly when the site had been abandoned.

"This is a march camp," said Anasind. "The ditch is too shallow, the gatehouse not reinforced."

"No abada or wagons," said Ullsaard, pointing to the empty remains of the main corral. "They had time to send out the baggage train."

"Why were they here? They were meant to be thirty miles to dawnwards. What made them start out on a march?"

They wandered along rows of burnt canvas where piled tents had been set alight; between charred stacks of logs; past clouds of flies swarming over the latrines. The stench of smoke clung to everything, but Ullsaard was heartened that he did not smell rotting flesh. There was not a body to be found. It was further proof that the legion had torched their camp rather than been overrun.

"No way of telling how long ago this took place," said Ullsaard. "Perhaps the same thing that happened to Maalus happened here. They marched duskwards to confront a Salphorian army. They made camp after one day. In the morning they found the enemy stronger than they expected, abandoned the camp and retreated dawnwards with their baggage."

Anasind nodded, silent and not wholly convinced by this explanation. Through the ragged gaps in the wall, Ullsaard could see several miles further to coldwards. There was a smudge of forest in the distance. Seeing that green canopy reminded Ullsaard again of what had befallen Maalus and Lukha's legions. A quiver of nervousness over Jutaar's fate was becoming an insistent nagging in the king's gut.

A shout from past the collapsed remnants of the gate drew his attention. From the back of his kolubrid, a scout hailed Ullsaard and waved for him to approach. Sensing the soldier's agitation, Ullsaard strode quickly through the debris, booted feet kicking up ash. Anasind followed on his heel, his silence expressing concern more than any words could.

"What is it?" Ullsaard picked his way across the fallen timbers of the gateway.

"Bodies, king," replied the scout. He pointed down the hill to duskwards, one hand held to the brim of his bronze cap to shield his eyes, the leather of his light armour creaking as he twisted in his saddle. His mount's forked tongue flickered in and out, excitedly tasting the air, no doubt the reptile's hunger roused by the closeness of carrion. "Legionnaires. Just left in the open."

Ullsaard swallowed hard but did not ask whether Jutaar was amongst the dead.

"Show us," said Anasind.

He made to lay a reassuring hand on Ullsaard's arm but pulled it back at the last moment, remembering that he was the king. Ullsaard nodded dumbly and waved for the scout to set off. The First Captain and king followed a little way behind, and then came the bodyguard, marching mutely, their questions and gossip silenced by the stares of their officers and the mood of their commanders.

The flash of metal sparkled far off at the bottom of the hill. The long grass that covered the slope had been flattened by the tread of many feet. It was clear that most of the legion had left the camp by this route, marching down the hill. They followed the trail for some time, until Ullsaard noticed a change. The trampling of the grass spread out. He called the scout to a halt for a moment and pointed out his discovery to Anasind.

"They formed line," said the First Captain. He paced away to the left, measuring each stride. At a hundred paces he turned and called back. "Looks like they were in formation, drawn up for battle."

"But no fighting here," Ullsaard muttered. There was some litter still around; mouldy apple cores, a few bits of bone, broken sandal buckles. All of the things that would have been left behind after a break in a march. But there was no blood, no bodies.

"Over here!"

Ullsaard turned at Anasind's shout. The First Captain was further down the slope. He held up what looked like a stout stave banded with bronze. It took a moment for Ullsaard to register what it was: the broken shaft of a legion icon.

Knowing that Jutaar would give his life rather than let the legion icon be taken, Ullsaard broke into a run, almost tripping over as he sprinted down to the level plain where Anasind stood.

The corpses were easy to see now. Clouds of flies hovered over them, their black bodies crawling across red cloth and bronze armour. The bodies were piled together, marked by wounds and the attention of scavengers. Ullsaard ran past them, paying no heed to the story they could tell. Scavenging birds hopped lazily away, gorged by the feast, their featherless faces slick with blood.

In his wake, the other legionnaires broke ranks, walking amongst the dead in amazement. Some – the most experienced – wasted little time on wonder and grief; they began to pull belts free, hooked off sandals and searched pouches for food. Ignoring the cloying clouds of insects, with knife tips they loosened spearheads from broken shafts and cut armour straps to free breastplates. Soon, the whole bodyguard were committed to the grim task; the officers organised their men into parties to pile shields and spears, collect water canteens and begin the gruesome job of bringing the bodies to one place so that they could be properly cremated.

Oblivious to the looting behind him, Ullsaard slowed to a stop beside Anasind.

"Where is he?" the king demanded. "Have you found him?"

"Over there." Anasind jerked his head to the left, eyes downcast, unable to meet Ullsaard's gaze.

The king took a few steps, scouring the haphazard corpses for Jutaar. He stopped in stunned recognition as his gaze fell upon his son's mutilated remains. Had it not been for the First Captain's insignia on the battered helm he might have missed him altogether. Ullsaard knelt down, pulling the helmet free, part of him still believing that the man wearing it was not his son.

The dried blood was almost black and maggots crawled in the many wounds inflicted upon Jutaar. His eyes were missing – probably taken by birds – and his skin writhed with larvae and beetles. Ullsaard could not bring himself to touch this disgusting thing, his hand held just above Jutaar's chest.

Shadow enveloped him as Anasind came up from behind.

"He died fighting," said the First Captain.

For a moment Ullsaard felt a burning rage. The mangled remains of his son were a horror he had hoped never to see. He was about to turn his anger on Anasind when the words sunk home. Those three words were a tribute; perhaps the finest any legionnaire could make of another man.

He died fighting.

"His sword has gone," the king mumbled.

With a ring of bronze, Anasind drew his weapon. He stepped past Ullsaard and crouched to place the hilt in Jutaar's dead grip.

"Now he has one again," said the First Captain.

Ullsaard slumped back, arms limp by his sides. It did not matter what had happened. Answers would come later. For the moment, all that filled Ullsaard was the certain knowledge that his son was dead. Anger melted into the bloodstained grass and was replaced by tears. Head bowed, the king sobbed, while Anasind stood beside him, watching over father and son.

V

Furlthia wanted to turn around the cart and head back into the wilds. Never before had he felt so scared. Even when he had been caught up in the madness with the rebels, and watched the fires spreading across Magilnada, he had felt safer than now.

The Askhan army stretched across the hills for half a mile to either side of the road; right flank anchored against the river, left flank secured by the still smoking ruins of a Salphorian settlement. Perhaps it was Furlthia's knowledge of why they were here that gave the blocks of legionnaires a vengeful air. The thousands of Salphors driven back to Magilnada were a sure sign that King Ullsaard was very unhappy with the current course of events. Tales of the Askhans' brutality had been brought along by the lines of ragged women and children, spread by the warnings of terrified old men, carried from the fighting like the refugees' packs and handcarts.

He was well aware of the strange sight he must present, emerging from the line of Magilnadan legionnaires and Salphorian tribesmen on his small, lupus-drawn wagon like a peddler who had lost his way. The lupus itself, a larger black-furred cousin to the wolves of the Altes Hills, was unknown in Greater Askhor; a gift from Aegenuis.

A mile separated the two armies, a short enough distance in itself, but the journey from one side to the other seemed to take forever and Furlthia's skin crawled with nervousness the whole way.

Ahead, Askhan companies drilled and shifted, as adjustments were made to the line. Squadrons of soldiers on kolubrids passed back and forth in front of the phalanxes, the shimmering bodies of the serpentine creatures catching the morning sun. At the heart of the Askhan line Furlthia thought he could see a small group of officers gathered beneath a shining icon, one of them mounted on an ailur. His gut clenched and his sphincter tightened at the thought of approaching the Askhan king. He patted the letter inside his jerkin and whispered an entreaty to the spirits that Anglhan knew what he was doing.

221

When he was halfway across, Furlthia noticed several of the skirmishers redirecting their steeds in his direction. They closed in fast, ten of them, hefting heavy bellows bows to their shoulders, bronze arrowheads pointed at his wagon.

He pulled back on the harness and called the panting lupus to a halt. The beast settled to its haunches, a growl in its throat as it watched the circling kolubrids with slitted eyes, its ears folded back. The kolubrids hissed and swayed their heads, their riders hauling tight on their reins to keep their distance a few dozen paces away.

"Are you lost?" one of the riders called out.

"I bear a message for King Ullsaard." Furlthia's declaration was greeted with harsh laughter. He held up a hand to shade his eyes against the glare of the sun reflecting back from the speaker's helm. The man's face was heavily tanned, creased with age, his eyes alive with amusement.

"I don't think the king is welcoming visitors just at this moment," the man said, affecting a cultured accent. "Perhaps if you made an appointment you would have more luck."

"The message is from Governor Anglhan."

The humour fell away like a dropped stone, replaced with such an air of hostility that Furlthia's stomach turned another somersault.

"Nobody cares what that treacherous cunt has to say. Best turn around now, you dog-fucker, before we send you back to your master with a bit more bronze to decorate your guts."

Furlthia dearly wanted to comply, but he knew that he had to deliver the letter. He tried a different approach.

"Anglhan isn't my master. I think he's just as much a cock-loving traitor as you do. I'm just doing a job. Please, the king has to read this letter."

The scout's sergeant urged his mount closer and leant forward, eyes burrowing into Furlthia. The kolubrid and lupus eyed each other with similarly deadly intent.

"What's the message? We'll pass it on."

"Doesn't work like that. I have to deliver it myself, and get the reply. Please, it is very important. Thousands of lives depend upon this letter being delivered; maybe even yours."

The sergeant sat back. With a barest flick of the head, he sent one of his men heading back towards the Askhan line, a sinuous trail of flattened grass left in the kolubrid's wake.

Furlthia wanted to break the uneasy silence as they waited, but all small talk fled his mind. He watched the scout racing up the road, following his progress all the way to the king. It was impossible to see any reaction from this distance, but it was only a matter of moments before the rider had turned around his mount and was heading back. Furlthia did not know whether such a brief exchange meant good news or bad.

As the scout approach, Furlthia's bladder added to his discomfort. He could not let go of the lupus's reins, fearing what the creature might do if he let it out of control for a moment, and so had to sit on the board, squirming with the growing urge to relieve himself.

The scout and sergeant had a brief conversation, their eyes turned on Furlthia. The sergeant nodded and reined his kolubrid away.

"Follow us," he snapped back over his shoulder.

Furlthia gratefully flicked the reins and the lupus strained into its harness, black furred shoulders bunching as it pulled against the wagon's weight. The cart rocked from side to side along the rough road while the kolubrids slithered through the grass to either side, the scouts' bows still trained on Furlthia.

When they were some fifty paces from the king, the scouts formed a ring around the wagon again and motioned for Furlthia to dismount. He did so, moving forward to hobble the lupus. A group of orderlies approached from the throng of Askhan officers. Two of them stood either side of the cart, two more gesturing for Furlthia to accompany them.

Taking one reluctant step after another, Furlthia walked towards Ullsaard, trying to gauge the king's next action. The ruler of Askhor appeared impassive, but Furlthia knew not to be fooled by looks alone; he had seen before the instinctive way Ullsaard had despatched those that displeased him, having shown not the slightest sign of murderous intent in the preceding moments. He comforted himself with the thought that had the king wanted Furlthia dead, Ullsaard could just as easily ordered his scouts to shoot him where he had been.

"So, here's Anglhan's little whelp come to beg terms," said Ullsaard. "Does he take me for an idiot? Perhaps you are going to lie to me? Tell me that I have come to the wrong conclusion about what's happened? You are wasting your breath."

"I will not lie to you, king," said Furlthia. "I am only a reluctant associate of Anglhan. What you believe to have happened is true. Your former governor has betrayed you. He has brokered a deal with King Aegenuis, and between them they have agreed to return Magilnada and these lands to the status of Free Country."

"You know that his actions have killed my son?" Ullsaard growled.

A quiver of panic shot through Furlthia.

"I did not know, king. I am sorry to hear that. I can't begin to think what that must be like, I have no children myself, but I wouldn't wish that on any father. But there are a lot more sons and brothers going to be killed unless you choose to accept Anglhan's new position."

"Accept his new position?" Ullsaard's voice dropped to a hissed whisper that sent another shudder of dread down Furlthia's spine. The king's brow was knitted in a deep scowl, his teeth clenched, as he continued. "I gave him that city. I made that ungrateful whore-bastard governor. I'd sooner let my whole legion take turns fucking my wives than agree terms with that snivelling little bitch-cunt."

The king swung off his ailur and tossed the reins to one of his officers. He stalked towards Furlthia, shoulders hunched, hands clenched in massive fists. It looked likely that the king would beat him to death and spare himself the effort of unsheathing his sword. Faced with a beast of a man bearing down on him, Furlthia could hold his bladder no more. A trickle of warmth soaked his groin and seeped down the left leg of his trousers.

He snatched the letter from inside his jerkin and thrust it towards Ullsaard, holding out the folded parchment as if it were a ward against all the evils in the world.

"You have to read this!" Furlthia's voice was almost a squeal. The letter flapped in his trembling hands as he fought to control himself. He took a deep breath and spoke again with a little more dignity. "Please read the message."

Ullsaard stopped, barely two paces away, fully a head taller than Furlthia. The Salphor looked up into the king's face and considered dropping to his knees. He's going to kill me, thought Furlthia, over and over, the words bouncing around inside his head.

Plucking the letter from Furlthia's grasp, the king cocked his head to one side.

"This will fix everything, will it?"

Furlthia shrugged helplessly. He sincerely hoped it would, but he had no idea what was contained in the letter. His breath came in short gasps as Ullsaard inspected the seal and then broke it with his thumb. The king held the letter in one hand and rubbed his chin with the other. Furlthia followed every movement, watching Ullsaard's eyes flicking left and right as he read. The king's scowl deepened and his jaw worked as he ground his teeth. The veins in Ullsaard's thick neck stood out like cords and his eyes moved to Furlthia, windows into pure fury. For a moment, Furlthia believed he saw tiny flickers of flame in the king's murderous gaze.

He stepped back out of instinct, but not quick enough. Ullsaard's fist caught him square in the chest, smashing him to his backside, all the wind driven out of his body. Coughing, he struggled to get up and was met by a booted foot in the ribs.

"You delivered this? To me?" Ullsaard's accusation was a deafening roar, punctuated by another kick.

Furlthia curled up, arms across his head, knees to his chest.

"I don't know what it says!" he wailed. "I don't know what it says! I'm a messenger, you can't hurt me. I'm protected!"

Ullsaard's next kick caught Furlthia in the kidneys, sending a spasm of pain up his back.

"Please, king, please! I'm just delivering the letter. It's from Anglhan, not me!"

Ullsaard grabbed a handful of Furlthia's hair and dragged him up to his knees. With his other hand, the king thrust the letter into Furlthia's face.

"Can you read, you little shit?"

"Yes, king, yes."

"Then read it! Look what message Anglhan has sent me."

Through tears, Furlthia tried to make sense of the scrawled marks. It was written in Askhan, and used some words that he did not understand. Forcing the fear from his mind, he concentrated, trying to understand what had provoked such a reaction.

The start of the letter laid out what Furlthia had already explained: Anglhan's secession from Greater Askhor. It went into some detail on this, which Furlthia skipped over on the second reading. The letter went on to make various demands for the withdrawal of the Askhan legions across the border into Ersua, and insisted that Ullsaard agree to take no military action or other reprimand against the city of Magilnada or its territory.

It was not until the end that Furlthia realised what Anglhan had done. The letter ended pleasantly enough, assuring Ullsaard that as a free city Magilnada would uphold its previous trade agreements with Askh. The last line was the guarantee that made Anglhan so confident. On the face of it, the words were innocuous enough. Furlthia read them several times, realising how much weight could be put into a single sentence, and why Ullsaard was so enraged.

The parting comment simply read: *Also rest assured that I will continue to protect your family and friends for the remainder of their stay in my city.*

Furlthia turned wide, disbelieving eyes to the king. Ullsaard let go of Furlthia's hair, stepped back, took the letter from his weak fingers and folded it crisply before tucking the parchment into his belt.

"I had no idea…" said Furlthia.

"That just makes you an idiot, not an accomplice," replied the king.

Ullsaard turned away and Furlthia let out an explosive breath of relief. He looked up at the cloudless sky and let his hands drop to the dirt, feeling it between his fingers, the grass rubbing against his palms.

Almost quicker than Furlthia could follow, Ullsaard span back, sword sliding from sheath. In one motion, the king struck, plunging the tip of the blade into the flesh between neck and shoulder, driving it down into Furlthia's chest.

Furlthia felt only a moment of pain before he died; his last vision was of the Askhan king's hate-filled eyes boring into him, blood spattered across his bearded, weathered face.

VI

The wreckage of clay pots, plates, tables and chairs littered the pavilion. Ullsaard's campaign throne lay upended against a roof pole. The ornately carved and painted panels were stained with splashes of wine, running down the vistas of Askhor like blood.

The king lay in a stupor, surrounded by crushed goblets and shattered jugs, his shirt wet with sweat and wine. His breastplate lay where it had been flung, his helmet at the other end of the room. Ullsaard murmured in his sleep, grunting and growling; his gnarled hands clenched and unclenched in torment, as the king was gripped by wine-fuelled nightmares.

Askhos walked out of the flames that engulfed Ullsaard's dreams, clad in the finest robes of state. A red cloak trailed behind him, edged with white fur. Upon his breastplate snarled the etched face of an ailur and his hair hung in oiled curls about his shoulders.

Naked and shivering, Ullsaard looked up from a bed of hot ash.

"Not now," he snarled.

"Neither of us seems to have a choice," replied the dead king. "I would rather leave you to your unpleasant fantasies."

Ullsaard rolled away, eyes screwed shut.

"I do not think it works like that," said Askhos.

With a deep-throated growl, Ullsaard sat up, bringing his knees to his chest, arms clasped around his legs. Smoke from the all-encompassing fire swirled into a column and formed a stool for Askhos to sit.

"How do you do that?" asked Ullsaard.

"Practice," said Askhos. "I have a lot of time on my hands at the moment. It gives me plenty of opportunity to explore every dark corner of your mind. I would have thought you had more control over it, but apparently not."

The fires burned white as a wave of irritation swept through Ullsaard. He flinched at their sudden ferocity. As the king's mood settled, the flames quietened.

"So, what are you going to tell me now" he asked, resting his chin on his knees.

"I think you already know."

"I am not going to attack Magilnada."

"It seems my purpose has become that of bearer of bad news, Ullsaard." Askhos ran the fingers of one hand through his beard, tugging at the tight loops of hair. "Maybe that is why we keep getting brought together."

"You're my conscience?"

"The opposite. I have been cast in the role of the truth-teller. You cannot let Anglhan hold hostages against you. It is a never-ending negotiation from which you cannot escape. Call his bluff. Attack the city."

"And he will kill Allenya, and Noran, and Meliu. Anglhan is sly, but he never lets go an advantage without a fight. I can't do it."

"You think Allenya is special? She is not. How many wives have I had over two hundred years? Save for the first, my darling Ausieta, I have chosen none of them. And I have outlived them all. It is a sad thing to lose one you love, but you must be stronger than that."

"Jutaar is dead. Allenya probably doesn't even know yet. This isn't her fault. I can't have her death on my hands as well."

"Fault? What has fault go to do with anything? Was it that messenger's fault that he happened to carry Anglhan's letter?"

"I acted in anger. I'll not repeat the mistake with my wife's life."

"And so we come back to where all of these conversations seem to end. You did so much to take my Crown, but now that you have it you have become weak. Perhaps we are seeing the lie of your ambition. You did not kill Lutaar because the empire was growing soft. You stole the Crown for yourself. The first small hurdle, the first obstacle Anglhan throws in your path, and you cringe from what you have to do."

"I will find another way," said Ullsaard. He stood up and faced Askhos, fists balled at his sides. "Anglhan will pay for what he has done."

"Words, words, words! Do what you have to do, Ullsaard. Destroy Magilnada; kill this traitor that makes a mockery of you. I felt the shame you felt, when you had to order your army to stand down. It sickened me more than you can imagine. I heard those Salphor bastards laughing, heard the discontent amongst our men. And you explain nothing to them. You cannot. You know they will tell you the same thing I am telling you know. Destroy Anglhan. Pay the price you have to pay."

"I will not!"

"And you will fail. Piece by piece, Greater Askhor will crumble without strength, without the respect for the Blood that held it together. The governors will see your weakness and they will take your power. They will fight like dogs over the scraps of the empire's carcass. If you are lucky, you will not live long enough to see it."

"And you? When I die, what happens to the almighty, immortal Askhos? Perhaps it is that fear that drives you? When I am gone, will you be gone as well?"

Askhos sagged, the point of his gaze moving into the flames.

"I do not know. Perhaps the end of Ullsaard will be the end of Askhos." He turned his attention back to the king. "It will certainly be the end of Greater Askhor."

"Then we both have good reason to keep me alive," Ullsaard said. He smiled grimly and folded his arms across his scarred chest. He wondered briefly why his dream-body was still marred by the marks of his worldly injuries while Askhos seemed untouched. The thought fluttered away as it soon as it appeared. "Maybe now you realise you should be doing everything you can to help me, rather than arguing against every course I choose?"

Askhos laughed and shrugged.

"Maybe I will have to accept that. It is such a shame that you did not kill Kalmud and Ersuan as well as Aalun. With my mind and your body, I could have done great things."

"There's no reason we can't do great things as we are."

The dead king studied Ullsaard shrewdly for some time. He gave a slight nod and smiled.

"No reason at all."

TEMPLE

I

The words meant nothing, yet the incessant chants reverberating from the stone echoed within Erlaan's bones and skittered along his nerves. He lost himself in the monotony. There were no days and no nights, no mealtimes and no need to sleep. Time did not pass, yet his heart beat, his lungs filled and emptied, the invocation changed in pitch and tempo. This place was timeless, yet it was eternal.

He watched over his father, from a stool set beside Kalmud's bed. Like all else, Erlaan's father did not move, his condition neither worsening nor improving. In the Temple, he felt closer to his father than ever before, an almost physical link between them. When he laid his hand upon Kalmud's chest or brow, Erlaan's flesh tingled at the touch. He felt the flickers of fevered dreams that raged in his father's mind.

"It is the power of the Blood."

Erlaan looked to the doorway and saw the withered high priest Lakhyri, standing motionless in the square arch as if he were a statue that had always been there. When he spoke, only his lips moved, the barest twitch of muscle beneath the taut skin of his face, every other part of him frozen.

"The same energy that fuels the Blood is the source of the Temple's power," Lakhyri continued. "That is why you feel its presence, why you feel that you belong in this place."

"The chanting, it draws in the energy of the world," Erlaan said. "I sense the ebb and flow of its tides. I feel something else, though, a tugging at my spirit, like a hole that opens up beneath us."

"The power of the Temple is weakening," Lakhyri said with a single, slow nod. "It took much of the remaining energy to bring you and your father to this place."

"Why did you? Why are we so important that you would do that?"

"You are the true heirs to the Blood. It is imperative that you survive. The Blood must rule the empire. You will be restored to your rightful place and the course of the empire shall be corrected, returning to the path that has been laid down."

"What of Ullsaard? He is king now. Why is he so wrong for Askhor?"

The tiniest flicker of agitation passed across Lakhyri's face, so fleeting that Erlaan wondered if he had imagined it.

"He is a usurper," said the high priest. "He does not belong. He is not part of the plan. Your father is the true heir to the empire, and you after him."

"That's why you're keeping him alive?"

Lakhyri's lips twisted fractionally at the corners, distorting the runes carved into his cheeks. Erlaan realised it was a smile, more grotesque and frightening than anything he had seen. What could amuse such a creature?

"It is not I who sustains your father, nor the powers of the Temple. It is from you that he draws sustenance. You give over to him your own life. Every moment that you feed him with your spirit is a moment taken from your mortal span."

Erlaan instinctively drew back his hand from Kalmud's chest, and felt a sudden pang of guilt that his natural reaction was so selfish. Even so, he did not put back his hand.

"Why did you not tell me sooner?" the prince asked.

"So that you would know what it feels like to make such a decision."

"Decision? What decision?"

"Whether your father lives or dies."

As horrifying as the idea was, Erlaan felt no shock at the thought of his father's life being in his hands. This was a place that teetered on the line between life and death, existence and oblivion. The idea of responsibility, of becoming king, had terrified Erlaan, but in the Temple there was nothing that felt more natural.

"The choice you face is harsher than you think," said Lakhyri, breaking Erlaan's train of thought.

"Harsher? What could be harsher than life or death?"

"A quick or slow death. I see from your eyes that you already are considering whether it is worth the expenditure of your life to perpetuate this half-existence of your father. There is another option. That flutter of life that still beats in your father's breast, it is weak, but it exists. It is in your power to take it for yourself."

"Steal his life force?" It was a genuine inquiry, not an admonishment. Erlaan wondered why the suggestion did not fill him with disgust. Why did he spend even a moment contemplating such a thing?

"Your father's opportunity has passed, Erlaan." It was the first time Lakhyri had addressed him by name. The high priest stepped into the room. His words were delivered in the same flat manner as before, without pity or distaste, but his eyes betrayed just a shred of lingering humanity as he continued. "Your chance is now. To let your father dwindle away would be doubly disrespectful.

End his suffering now, and use the last of his strength for yourself, to reclaim that which belongs to you."

Erlaan said nothing, but his mind was awhirl with the implications. His father's life hung by a narrow thread, all that remained between Erlaan and becoming the heir to Askhos. Was it selfishness to cut that thread, or was it a mercy? He turned back to Kalmud and placed the tips of his fingers on his cold brow.

"The empire has already taken his life," said Erlaan. "It would be a waste to let what remains slip away without purpose. What do I do?"

"You already know."

Taking a breath, Erlaan stared at his stricken father. He could feel the tremor of a pulse, not in his fingers, but somewhere deeper, in his veins. It took no effort, Blood calling to Blood, drawing to its own. Erlaan felt the slightest shift within, a momentary change of current between him and Kalmud.

His father's heart stopped and a last breath whispered from Kalmud's lips.

"I have little to offer," said Erlaan, closing his father's eyes before turning to Lakhyri.

"What are you willing to give?" said the priest.

"I have no experience as a leader of men, and I am no great warrior. I would not call myself brave by any measure."

"These things I can give you, if you are willing. It will not be easy, and it will not be pleasant. What will you do to reign as king?"

Erlaan looked at his father and thought of his dead grandfather and uncle. He was the last of the Blood, save for the bastard who now wore the Crown. It was Erlaan's birthright to rule, and he recalled Ullsaard's words to him, an assertion the general had made to assuage the prince's doubts, which Erlaan had etched into his memory during the long days and nights he had spent in Askh, fearfully waiting by his father's side. 'You are what you are, and it is in you to embrace that destiny. You owe it not only to yourself, but to the people you will rule and your forefathers.'

The prince met the implacable glare of Lakhyri.

"My family have given their lives for the Crown. I would offer nothing less. My body and my spirit, if needed."

Lakhyri accepted this declaration with a slow blink.

"Your life will not be necessary. Your spirit, your body... that is a different matter."

GERIA
Summer, 211th year of Askh

The herald waited with his helmet under one arm, eyes roving around the great hall of the palace looking at the murals on the walls and ceiling, examining the delicate tiles of the mosaic underfoot; his eyes looked everywhere except at Urikh.

The prince carefully read the missive from Harrakil, deciphering the First Captain's infantile strokes. When he was finished he leaned across from his chair and handed the letter to his mother, sat on his right.

"You know the contents of this?" Urikh asked the herald.

"Yes, prince. Captain Harrakil said I was to add anything else you might ask."

"These Mekhani attacks, how frequent are they?"

"Before I left, there had been seven in thirty days, prince. All along the border. Raids, mostly."

"Raids? Three towns have been destroyed!"

"Yes, prince. No survivors. We don't know how big the Mekhani forces were. There have to be several armies, to attack so many places so quickly. Leviira and Hanalun had garrisons of three hundred men each, prince. Wiped out to the man."

"Captain Harrakil tells me that captives were taken."

"Yes, prince. Slaves, most likely."

Luia stirred, folding her hands in her lap, the letter in her grasp.

"The Mekhani do not take slaves," she said. "Not before now."

"That's right, queen. We don't know why they've started."

"What else don't you know?" asked Urikh, keeping his tone mild.

"I don't understand, prince."

"Who is leading these Mekhani attacks? What is Harrakil going to do about them? What extra forces does he need?"

"He was waiting on your orders, prince, which I'm supposed to return with. There's no way of telling where the next attack will come, or when. The border's more than five hundred miles, from the Greenwater to the mountains. The captain's worry is that if we split up, we'll be picked off like the garrisons."

"Three quarters of the legion is already in the area," said Luia. "Are nearly five thousand troops not enough for Harrakil?"

"Though he would never say it himself, queen, I think the captain would need at least twice that number to patrol the border. More, if you want him to head into Near-Mekha and chase down the bastards."

"Three legions?" Urikh laughed. "Where does he think I can get another ten thousand men?"

"Perhaps you could send word to the king?" suggested the herald, eyes fixed firmly on a detail of the mosaic.

"Thank you, we will send for you," Luia said before Urikh could reply. The governor glanced at his mother, annoyed, but recognised the intent look on her face.

"Yes, refresh yourself and return this evening," said the prince. "I will have a message for you to take back to captain Harrakil."

The herald bowed and departed, his hard-soled kohbrid boots clicking on the tiled floor. When the tall double doors of the hall closed behind the messenger, Urikh turned to Luia.

"Do you really think it is a good idea to request legions from Ullsaard at the moment? He is probably a thousand miles into Salphoria by now, and no doubt having immense fun."

"He will thank you little for allowing Okhar to be overrun by Mekhani savages while he is away conquering new lands," Luia replied. She smoothed her long dress, hands running over the dark blue Maasrian silk. "There could be another way to get the soldiers you need."

"No, not the other governors," Urikh replied with a shake of the head. "You know they would insist on payment, over the odds. The cost would be extortionate. Trade is barely half what it was two years ago and there are some parts of Okhar that have not paid their taxes since I took power. There is simply not enough money in the city vaults and I am not going to the moneylenders."

"Sometimes you will have to delve deeper than the official coffers, Urikh."

"Family money?" Urikh almost choked on the suggestion.

"Nobles have been raising new legions all over the empire to join my husband on his jaunt," said Luia. "Thanks to Nemtun's exploits trying to stop your father, Okhar is woefully under strength. The Greenwater is vital, the border with Mekha volatile, and to duskwards you have the hill tribes on the Salphorian border; and to deal with all of that you have barely a single legion. Maasra, peaceful Maasra with her Nemurian neighbours, boasts three legions. Enair has four. The situation is unsustainable."

"I will write to Ullsaard," said Urikh, deciding that any solution that did not involve spending his own money was preferable.

"It could be the end of the summer before we receive his reply." Luia stood up, adjusted the slender silver chain that served as her belt, straightened her necklace and fixed her son with a hard stare. "You best hope that your father is in a generous mood, and that nothing drastic happens to hotwards. Make no mistake, if Ullsaard thinks you are not up to the task of being governor, he will replace you, son or not."

"You would never let him do that."

Only Luia's look offered argument to Urikh's assumption. She turned away, saying nothing, and left the hall by a side door. The patter of bare feet announced the arrival of several servants, buckets of water and brushes in hand. As they set to work scrubbing the floor tiles, Urikh sat deep in thought, composing the letter he would have to send his father. If he could find some way to make it look like he was taking assertive action and needed the soldiers for expansion, not defence, his message was more likely to be welcomed.

With the proper phrasings coming to mind, Urikh strode from the great hall with determined steps, heading for his study.

FREE COUNTRY
Midsummer, 211th year of Askh

I

More than a dozen heralds crowded into the king's pavilion. Ullsaard's scribe, Lasok, sat behind a small field table with a pile of scrolls, handing one out to each messenger in turn before crossing off a corresponding entry on a wax tablet. Ullsaard sat on his campaign chair watching the proceedings with a dour expression, chin cupped in his hand, elbow on the arm of the throne.

Anasind pushed his way through the throng and bowed quickly. He glanced over his shoulder at the heralds.

"Fresh orders?" he asked. "Will we be moving out soon?"

"No," Ullsaard said with a slow shake of the head. "The legions are staying exactly where they are."

"I understand that you do not have to tell me what's going on, but if I can help?"

Ullsaard beckoned the First Captain closer and waved to one of the stools arranged around the throne. Anasind swept his cloak out of the way and sat down, leaning close to hear the king's soft words.

"Our woes are not restricted to Salphoria," Ullsaard said with a heavy sigh. "I received word last night from Urikh.

Those Mekhani we left behind are stirring up trouble on the hotwards border."

"Surely Urikh can cope with a few troublesome savages," said Anasind. "It doesn't say much for his suitability as a governor, if you forgive me saying."

"I would think the same, but from what Urikh has reported, these are not your normal summer raiders. Someone has been bringing the Mekhani together, organising them. Most of the legions are with us, trapped this side of Magilnada. I can't abandon the campaign wholesale to sort out the Mekhani without giving the Salphors an opportunity to take back everything we've conquered already."

"I see that. I still don't get what all the messengers are for."

"I'm assembling the council of governors in Askh. Urikh can't ask them to pass on their legions to him, so I'm going to have to."

"You're going to Askh?" The First Captain's brow furrowed. "Who's going to be in charge here?"

"I was going to speak to you later about that," said the king. "Since you're here now... I'm going to name you my general. You'll be in command."

Anasind rocked back, making no attempt to hide his happiness.

"I'll be general? Thank you, king!"

"Don't thank me yet," Ullsaard replied with a sour look. "It's not going to be easy for you. The situation here is fragile, and I don't know what Aegenuis or Anglhan are going to do next. You can expect the Salphors to make something of the situation. You're also going to have your hands full with these amateurs, the merchants and nobles, trying to get their own way and tell you what to do."

Ullsaard levered himself out of his throne and stepped forward to lay a hand on Anasind's shoulder.

"I trust you with this. You need to keep the army as intact as possible. Supplies will be low, and you need to keep a lid on desertions. Some might be up for a fight, wanting to advance again. You can't let that happen. If the army starts to break apart, the Salphors will pick off the legions on their own. I don't expect them to launch a major counter-attack this season, because they've had plenty of time to do so while we were readying our defences. That said, I'm sure they'll try to bait some of our commanders out of the line. Sit tight. It could be for the whole winter, I don't know yet. Keep everyone safe and ready for me."

Anasind stood and rapped his fist against his chestplate, eyes gleaming with pride.

"You can rely on me, king."

"I know," Ullsaard replied with a smirk. "I wouldn't have picked you, otherwise."

"No, I suppose you wouldn't."

"You also need to keep my departure secret. The less people that know I've left Salphoria, the better. Let's say I'm going on a tour of inspection around the other legions. That should explain my absence for plenty of time."

"When are you leaving?"

"Tomorrow," said Ullsaard, returning to his throne.

Anasind looked worried, realising how soon he would be left in command.

"You'll be taking the first company as bodyguard, I assume."

Ullsaard shook his head.

"No, I want to leave them with you. They'll help keep the legion in order. I'll be taking a few dozen men from across the other companies. Lasok already has a list of names. I want them assembled and ready to go by the second hour of Dawnwatch."

"And how do you think you'll get back to Askh without being noticed?"

Ullsaard patted the arm of the throne.

"I'll be leaving this behind, for a start."

II

The glow of campfires could be seen to hotwards, a smudge of red in the night amongst the shadows of the foothills overlooking the road between Magilnada and Ersua. Anglhan's legion stationed to guard that road were making no secret of their location, and from what other travellers had said, Gelthius knew that the other legion was keeping an eye on the other road running to dawnwards, forty miles to coldwards of where he walked along the base of a low hill.

The early evening air was warm and sweat beaded Gelthius's brow as he pulled a handcart over the humps and dips of the plains, the solid wooden wheels occasionally catching on a rock or thick tussock of grass. A few paces ahead, a handful of other legionnaires waded through the thigh-high grass, their uniforms hidden under long shirts, mud-stained robes and ragged cloaks; their weapons and armour were in the handcart, buried beneath a pile of pans, canvas and other gear.

Twenty of the king's bodyguard had forged ahead several miles, looking for a likely campsite. Fifteen more followed behind, broken into small groups to avoid attracting too much attention. King Ullsaard travelled in Gelthius's band, and had been relying on the Salphor's knowledge of the terrain to pick the best route back to Ersua, balancing speed of travel against the need to avoid settlements and the likely outlying garrisons of the Magilnadan legions.

The king fell in beside Gelthius, moving up quickly from behind with long strides. He grabbed one of the shafts of the handcart.

"Let me pull that for a while, take a rest," said Ullsaard.

"It's all right, king, I can manage," replied Gelthius, horrified by the thought that Ullsaard would drag around the legionnaires' gear.

"I insist," Ullsaard said with a smile, gently shoving Gelthius out of the way and taking up position between the two handles. He ducked his head under the yoke-strap and easily lifted the cart. "I have to keep in shape, you know."

"We'll be making camp soon, I suppose," said Gelthius, feeling put out by the king's interference.

It was hard for the Salphor to reconcile the different sides of Ullsaard he had seen. His first encounter with the king had ended with the massacre of thousands of Salphors and hillmen that had refused to join his legion. As a man of the Thirteenth, Gelthius had learned more about Ullsaard's history; how he had started out as a simple legionnaire and worked his way to the position of general. Gelthius could not help but respect that achievement. Fighting for the king had felt like a privilege despite the manner he had been pressed into Askhan service.

And then had come the death of Furlthia. Anglhan's ex-mate had been a good man, as far as Gelthius knew. Furlthia had always treated him and the other debtors with respect if not actual kindness, and he was loyal to his fellow Salphors. To see the king cut him down out of hand, to see a man Gelthius had once considered a friend murdered in cold blood, had dented the pride he had felt to be one of Ullsaard's chosen legion.

Ullsaard was unpredictable, and that made Gelthius uneasy. How could he ever feel truly safe around the king, knowing that the wrong words or a mistake might see him butchered the same way as Furlthia? It was too easy to forget the man's bloodthirsty nature, seeing him hitching up the straps of the handcart, marching through the dirt and filth with his men. Gelthius knew he would never be truly at ease around his new king, but it would not be a good idea to show it.

"A few more miles, I reckon," Ullsaard said, pulling forward with powerful strides. "Three more days to Magilnada, you reckon?"

"Right enough, king. The road loops coldwards a ways ahead. We can cut across and ford the Lasghin, or follow it around and use the bridge at Furath. Takes about the same time, either way."

"The bridge'll be busier, eh?"

"Most likely, king. But there's been rain up in the mountains the last few days, can't say for certain the ford'll be crossable yet. Might be quite a few folk waiting for the river to quieten down."

"Less chance of Anglhan's soldiers keeping watch at the ford. We'll keep heading that way."

Gelthius plodded through the grass on tired legs. They had left camp thirty two days ago, and for the most point had avoided the newly laid roads, crossing the rugged countryside instead. Having spent most of the summer in camp, the exertion had taken its toll on the aging legionnaire, and though he would never admit it, he was grateful that the king had relinquished him of the hand cart's burden for a while.

"When we're near the border, we can wear our armour, not carry it," said Ullsaard, as if reading Gelthius's thoughts. Glancing across at the king, Gelthius saw that Ullsaard was almost talking to himself, eyes fixed ahead, thinking aloud. "I'll requisition the first abada we come across, too. That'll make things easier."

"Still a tidy walk to Askh, king." Gelthius didn't know

if he had been heard at all. Ullsaard continued with his monologue, the words coming in time with his strides.

"We'll turn coldwards and take ship in Ersua, head down to the Greenwater and get off at Narun. That'll take fifteen days at the most. We'll be in the capital well before the rains start, gives us at least thirty days to sail down to Okhar and sort out Urikh. Might even get a legion or two to Near-Mekha before things get worse to coldwards."

"We're going to Mekha?" Gelthius couldn't hide his surprise.

Ullsaard glanced across at the legionnaire, almost as startled by the interruption.

"Of course, you've never been, have you? You weren't with us the last time the Thirteenth was there."

"Is it true that there's these giant lizards the size of a house, and the Mekhani have skin as red as an apple?" Gelthius had always doubted some of the stories his fellow legionnaires had told him about the desert lands, and he figured the king would tell the truth. "Do the women really have three tits?"

Ullsaard laughed and almost tripped. He paused for a moment, regaining his balance before striding on.

"No, they've got two tits like other women. The lizards though, that's true. We call them behemodons. Killed one myself, I suppose you heard."

"I did, right enough," said Gelthius with a chuckle. "Some of the lads admitted they thought you was a goner that time, when that big old thing tried to bite your head off."

The king turned his head and winked.

"I'll let you into a secret. I didn't fancy my chances much, either."

Ullsaard fell quiet, perhaps remembering the occasion, a wistful expression on his face. In the moonlight, he seemed older, the lines in his face, the sunken sockets of his eyes, the creases in his brow deeper than normal.

Not wanting to disturb his king's thoughts, though filled with questions about Mekha, Gelthius walked alongside the cart in silence. Up ahead, the scouting party had stopped beneath a stand of scattered trees, the light of the stars and moon shining from waxy-leaved branches. The first glimmers of a fire flickered in the shadows.

"Looks like we're making camp here," said Ullsaard. He coughed and spat. "We need to be off before dawn. We're close to Magilnada now, better to move under cover of night when we can."

"They can't patrol the whole border, king, not with just two legions."

"Anglhan raised a third legion," Ullsaard replied with a soft growl. "Fat bastard's got more money than I have. We'll have to watch our step all the way to Ersua."

"Right enough, king. I'll head out tomorrow and have a word with some of the locals, see if they know where this new legion's kicking about."

Ullsaard stopped and straightened suddenly, his height almost toppling the baggage out of the handcart's open back. The king turned a penetrating gaze on Gelthius, who took a couple of steps back, scared by the scrutinising glare.

"You've had plenty of chances to slip away between camp and here," said the king. "Why haven't you? You're a Salphor."

"Not rightly sure, king," Gelthius replied with a relieved shrug. "My family's still in the followers' camp with the Thirteenth. No point going anywhere without them. I don't think deserting ever occurred to me, king. Just loyal, I guess."

Considering this, the king started walking again, the cart wheels rattling as the ground became rockier underfoot.

"No other reasons?" Ullsaard asked as the turned up the slope towards the copse where the fire was now burning brightly.

"I suppose I like to be on the winning side, king. Who doesn't?"

"You know the current situation, don't you? Most of my legions are trapped in Salphoria, between Anglhan's and Aegenuis's armies. The Mekhani are on the brink of all-out invasion of Okhar. The empire's straining to the limits just to keep trade moving and supplies flowing. And you think you're going to be on the winning side?"

"Well, yeah." The question seemed pointless to Gelthius. "You wouldn't be here if you weren't going to win, would you? I mean, nobody thought you could become king, did they, but you did. I don't reckon this is half as hard as that, is it?"

Ullsaard did not reply straight away. With a grunt of effort, he dragged the hand cart the last few paces to the trees. He gently lifted the yoke over his head and lowered the handles into the grass. The king grinned at Gelthius, eyes flashing in the moonlight, his whole demeanour wolfish, feral. He cracked his knuckles and rolled his shoulders.

"When you put it like that, I can't lose."

TEMPLE

I

Circle after circle stood around the Last Corpse; men, women and children, staring vacantly ahead, flesh pallid. Atop the slab of black stone and bone, Erlaan lay staring at the ceiling, ignoring the silent, unmoving people around him. Beneath him, the Last Corpse was almost freezing to the touch, gradually leeching his energy from him, absorbing the life force he had taken from his father.

He was not sure what was going to happen next, but was certain that he would not regret it. Lakhyri would not explain the details of the changes that would be wrought on Erlaan, or the method by which they would be made, but the high priest had been adamant that it was the only way to reclaim the empire.

Erlaan could not hear the captives breathing, but he could feel their presence, their life in this dead place. Each of the two hundred and thirteen was like a candlelight in darkness, burning with vitality. Ten times that number had been taken, but they had been judge unworthy and sent to the deepest bowels of the Temple. Erlaan did not know what would happen to those that had been rejected, and did not dare to guess. He focussed on what was important: himself.

He had a feeling now for how the Temple worked, had experienced the transfer of energy between himself and his father. It was another sense, like touch or taste, somewhere inside him, its secret held within his Blood. Lakhyri skirted on the edge of existence, barely present, and even the youngest acolytes were dull embers compared to the prisoners that had been taken by the Mekhani.

"We will begin," announced Lakhyri, entering from one of the many dark corridors that led away from the main chamber. Behind the high priest came Asirkhyr and Eriekh bearing the tools of their craft; slabs of grey metal trays upon which glittered blades and hooks, styluses and ingots of silver and gold.

The two hierophants stood to either side of Erlaan while Lakhyri took his place at the prince's head. Erlaan shuddered as chill, dry fingers settled lightly on his brow, their touch as light as the scuttle of an insect on his flesh.

A distant chant echoed into the chamber, funnelled down into the hall through the maze of stone passageways. There was a different timbre to the invocation, a greater sense of urgency.

"Will this make me immortal, like you?" Erlaan asked.

"Better," replied Lakhyri. "You will think with the speed of lightning. The words that spill from your lips will be taken as truth by all that hear them. Every command you utter will be obeyed without question. You will run as swift as the wind. Your skin shall be as iron. Your lungs will be as the bellows of the forge. You shall be as strong as the behemodon. Your eyes will be as sharp as the hunting bird. All these gifts, our masters shall give to you. Speak no more."

The chanting washed through the chamber, bouncing from the walls, overlapping, growing in power, ripples of sound that disturbed the air like a wind on the water of a lake. Around and through Erlaan the chanting moved, rebounding from the circles of people around him to create eddies and currents that drew swirling lines of life from their bodies.

Erlaan could feel the energy, spiralling faster and faster, whirling towards the Last Corpse. Its touch was warm on his skin, seeping through his flesh and into his bones. This is not so bad, he thought.

Eriekh and Asirkhyr set to work. With slender knives, they gently flayed the skin from the soles of Erlaan's feet, peeling them as assuredly as a fruit. Around the toes, over the ankles and on to the shins they moved. Erlaan barely felt the bite of their blades as his skin sloughed sway in translucent sheets, unfolding from exposed fat and muscle like petals. Lakhyri worked on his head, moving with even greater speed and deftness, slicing away scalp and face.

So skilled were the priests that Erlaan's skin was left hanging over the Last Corpse like a diaphanous sheet. His limbs unmoving, as stiff as wood, Erlaan was rolled to one side and the next as they continued their bloody cutting on his thighs and back, his neck and buttocks, until not one part of his skin remained attached.

He could not blink, nor swallow, nor move his tongue or wiggle a finger or toe. Bereft of skin, his body felt exposed, every slightest breeze touched on raw nerve, but the sensation was not unpleasant.

With Erlaan's skin removed, the priests swapped their blades for shorter, thinner knives. Erlaan felt the first pierce of blade into muscle at the base of his skull. That was not so pleasant. With the same precise care, the priests separated tendon and muscle, fat and artery, nerve and vein. Erlaan was feeling some pain now. It was everywhere, an irritation, an itch that could not be scratched, a pain of the mind as much the body.

Piece by piece, they disassembled him, revealing bone and organ. As with the skin, Erlaan's flesh was kept intact, separated into a few bloody ropes of sinew and muscle. He did not wonder that he still lived; the energy of the Temple, and the life of the captives, formed a shell around him, tingeing the air with a glitter on the edge of vision, replacing flesh and blood with pure power.

Lakhyri brought forth a burned crucible, in which was held a pool of bubbling gold. Erlaan was confused for a moment, until Asirkhyr and Eriekh produced a needle-fine blade and a nib-like tool.

If the pain from having his flesh cut away was an irritation, the touch of pin and molten gold was an agony, a conflagration lit within his mind. The power of the Temple flowed into every stroke of blade and stylus, first crawling into his heart, every golden rune searing into the organ, a wisp of smoke quickly vanishing in the wake of every pen stroke.

Erlaan wanted to shriek as the priests moved on to his lungs. He knew that he was not breathing, not in any sense that he understood, and yet when the first runes were etched into his lungs every breath he was not taking was like breathing in the vapours of a lava-thrower. The pain was almost overwhelming, choking and internal, impossible to escape.

The torment became a never-ending coruscation of agony as brands were brought forth and sigils burnt into liver and stomach. Drills and awls buried themselves into his bone, through to the marrow, scoring an interconnected web of lines and symbols, each turn and piercing a white-hot needle of pain in his spirit.

He wanted to black out, to blot away every sensation

by the time they had progressed up every vertebra and started work on his skull. Lakhyri prised open his jaw and used a tong to pull out his tongue. Sigil-headed pins were pressed into his gums and the roof of his mouth, and lines of silver sliced and melted into his tongue and lips. A shower of gold enveloped all that he could see as they laboured on his eyes, pricking and cutting, delicate strokes that were each an eternal torture he had to endure.

He thought that his torment would be ending soon as they re-clothed him with his flesh, but the cessation of pain was all too brief. They branded and carved, stitched him back together with hair-thin wires upon which gleamed even tinier runes. Nails and rivets, their tips similarly etched, heads moulded in impossibly fine zodiacal emblems, reattached muscle to bone, tendon to joint. Every finger and toe, strung back together like the parts of a puppet.

They wrapped his skin across him, covering the grotesque beauty of their handiwork, using molten wax and stitches of hair to reattach his outer shell. Still they were not done. Upon his newly reapplied skin, they cut yet more symbols and patterns, down to every fingertip. They slid his fingernails and toenails back into place, now carved with swirling devices. With knife and needle, they scarred and tattooed, covering every part of Erlaan, each prick feeling like a sword thrust through him.

And then they stopped.

The agony became pain, became an ache, and then subsided.

Lakhyri held him down with his bony fingertips on his brow again. Erlaan still could not move, not the least twitching of an eyelid or the wiggling of a toe.

"It is not yet over," whispered the High Brother. "All we have done is to make you ready to receive the gifts of the eulanui. Now comes the hardest part."

Terror filled Erlaan. Tears welled in his scarred eyes at the thought that all he had endured had not been the worst.

The pain came again, forced into Erlaan through Lakhyri's fingertips, as if they delved into his brain. He felt the sheen of energy pouring over him, channelling down the lines and sigils like rivulets of water down a mountainside. Where they passed, the streams of energy left agony in their wake. They soaked through skin, drawn down into muscle by the devices wrought upon them; and through muscle into organ and bone.

Flesh bubbled, contorted, expanded. Bones lengthened and strengthened, pushing his flesh apart from the inside. Erlaan felt as if he were being ripped apart from within, unable to contain his elongating skeleton.

And then organs and flesh writhed with their own power, adding to a pain that was already too much to bear. His heart hammered, beating like a clap of thunder. He drew in a breath, a gale forced into his expanding lungs. Muscle bulged, testing the sutures in his skin, before it too was forced to change by the power of the Temple, cracking and hardening, like the crust on a lava flow, splintering and reforming constantly as Erlaan's muscles continued their distorted growth.

Life, true life, returned with a last implosion of power and pain.

Erlaan hurled himself from the slab of the Last Corpse, howling and shrieking, the last adjustments of his body settling into place. He roared, baring teeth like an ailur's. He opened eyes that were slit-pupiled and golden, and saw a world of startling colour and texture. He un-clenched his fists, uncoiling fingers with extra knuckles, each digit tipped with sharpened bronze.

Panting, knotted chest heaving with effort, Erlaan pushed himself to his feet, his skin rustling like dead leaves. Around him, the desiccated corpses of the sacrifices were crumbling into whirls of dust, each a tiny storm of particles, until they too were gone, every last part of their energy flowing into the reformed beast that had been Erlaan.

"We are done."

Lakhyri's voice, once so heartless, so monotonous, was a harmony of notes, more touching than any music Erlaan had heard. The Temple blazed with rainbows of light, dancing from every surface like a sheen on oil. Erlaan moved his hand, feeling the touch of the air on every fibre of his fingers, the tiniest breeze as obvious as a fold in cloth.

Erlaan laughed to see and hear and feel the world as it really was.

ERSUAN BORDER
Midsummer, 211th year of Askh

I

Streamers of cloud clung to the Altes Hills, lit by the warm glow of the rising sun. The mountains reared just over the horizon, bright to dawnwards, shrouded in shadow to duskwards. As Ullsaard's small troop broke camp, the king looked coldwards, knowing Magilnada lay nestled at the foot of those peaks, though he could not see the city.

The thought of it made him fume. He had expected Anglhan to skim off a few taxes, perhaps aggrandise himself a little; this betrayal went far beyond anything Ullsaard could tolerate. The king's feelings went beyond resentment at the man's ingratitude, into a deep well of anger fuelled by personal loathing. Anglhan's alliance with Aegenuis was almost understandable; Ullsaard was well aware that he had turned on the previous king. That was, he had painfully learnt, the simple facts of power and politics. But to hold Ullsaard's family hostage, to threaten the lives of his wives, made the matter personal.

He wondered if Allenya was aware of the danger she was in. Was she being held prisoner, or was she blissfully going about her normal life, ignorant of the knife that Anglhan held to her throat? Ullsaard was thankful for one small mercy; his mother, Pretaa, had left Magilnada to return to her home in Enair. At least she was beyond Anglhan's reach.

And there was the matter of Noran. Ullsaard felt enough guilt on behalf of his friend without any need for further burden.

"Are you ready, king?"

Ullsaard turned his attention to the legionnaires around him, their tents packed away, the fire smothered. He realised he had been staring coldwards for quite some time.

"We'll get the bastards, won't we?" asked one of the soldiers.

Ullsaard looked coldwards again, picturing the walled city sitting at the base of the cliff. In his mind's eyes he saw the Hill of Chieftains and the governor's palace; Anglhan within, pleased with himself for his manoeuvring, doubtlessly plotting his betrayal of Aegenuis.

The former governor had every right to be smug. Anglhan held the one thing that could keep Ullsaard in check, dragging tight like the reins of an ailur. Ullsaard had not the first idea how he was going to change the balance of power. Anglhan had seen how easy the city had fallen to infiltration before and would have agents scouring every visitor for signs of subterfuge. A full-scale attack was out of the question. The merest hint of a legion approaching the city would spell death for Allenya and the others.

For the moment, Ullsaard was powerless, but he knew that there was no such thing as a sure guarantee. The situation would change, and when it did Ullsaard would find a way to even the score.

"Yes," said the king. "We'll be getting the bastards."

II

The hotwards reaches of the Magilnadan Gap were dominated by heavily wooded hills, heaping upon each other until they became the shoulders and ridges of the Lidean Mountains. The dawnwards extent of the forests marked the edge of the Free Country, running along the Saol River. Ullsaard had no idea how closely Anglhan and his allies were watching the roads and rivers into Ersua, but had to assume the worst.

A long detour into the mountains would add at least twenty days to the journey, so at some point the king and his bodyguard would have to dare a crossing. The easiest way would be to find some boats or a ship rather than rely on one of the bridges. In this circumstance, the careful cartography of the Askhans would prove its worth. From studying the map he had brought with him, the king knew he was three days from the Soal, and if they cut straight to dawnwards through the forests, his group would avoid any settlement larger than a logging cabin or hunting lodge.

In double file, the legionnaires wound between the trees, heading towards the glimmer of the rising sun that could be glimpsed through breaks in the leaves above. The soldiers were armed and armoured, having abandoned the handcarts when they entered the forest. It was better that they were prepared for confrontation, in Ullsaard's opinion; so many men would arouse suspicion in these parts regardless of how they were dressed.

A summer shower had swept down from the mountains just before dawn and the trees were alive with the patter of water falling from the canopy. The ground was wet enough to leave tracks, but there was little Ullsaard could do about that; there was only so much secrecy available to a body of fifty men. Confident that the Magilnadans and

Salphors were unaware of his presence, Ullsaard felt that it would only be blind chance for a hunting party or patrol to come across them now.

The going was not easy, as Sergeant Daesio led the way, pushing through brush and bush. The trees here were old and moss-covered; their huge roots a tangle waiting to trip the unwary. A thick layer of mulch clung to the king's boots as he followed the men in front, while rotted branches, hidden rocks and uneven ground threatened his footing every few steps. The chorus of birds that had welcomed sunrise had died down, but still the arboreal gloom echoed with shrieks and chirrups from all around.

They pressed on without stop until the sun was directly overhead, at which time Ullsaard called a brief stop. Sitting on a rock slick with lichen, the king pulled out the map stowed in the top of his pack and unfolded the stained parchment. As best as he could reckon it, they had covered fifteen or sixteen miles; slow going for a normal march but a good distance considering the terrain. Calculating this position on the map, Ullsaard figured they needed to turn more to coldwards in order to avoid a Salphorian village about twenty miles further dawnwards. He fixed his mind on the direction they would have to travel and put away the map, pulling out an apple in its stead.

Even as he took the first bite, the sound of a hissed warning cut the quiet, coming from the sentries off to the king's right. Ullsaard dropped the apple and pulled out his sword, rising to his feet. Others were standing and he whispered a command for them to stay low, the order passing quietly from man to man. Treading softly through the undergrowth, Ullsaard made his way to the three men that had issued the warning.

They were crouched behind the aging remnants of a fallen tree, looking to hotwards. Ullsaard came up to them in a stoop, eyes scanning the trees for a sign of what they had seen. He stopped beside the rotting trunk and lowered himself to one knee, leaning across the flaking wood of the dead tree.

"There," said one of the legionnaires.

Ullsaard's gaze followed the soldier's pointing finger and he immediately saw the glimmer of bronze through the trees, in a clearing about two hundred paces away. The midday sun was glinting from spear points but Ullsaard could see nothing more through the undergrowth and long grass.

"How many?" he asked.

The legionnaire answered with a shrug and a shake of the head.

Thinking that he had glimpsed the crest of a legionnaire for a moment, Ullsaard considered his options. Further investigation risked discovery. An attack would be foolish without knowing how many foes they faced. Either choice would likely lead to confrontation, and although the king was sure his men would overpower whoever was out there, they would probably be missed sooner rather than later.

He tapped the shoulders of the men with him and with a flick of the head sent them back to others. He remained at the fallen tree for a while longer, trying to catch another glimpse of the men ahead, but saw nothing more revealing than a few obscured figures moving back and forth.

Turning around, he saw that all eyes were on him; most of the legionnaires had gathered together a few dozen paces back and crouched with their shields and spears at the ready. Ullsaard sheathed his sword and raised a finger to his lips, before jabbing a finger to coldwards.

The sergeants quickly divided the group into parties of five, and each of these slipped away into the woods at short intervals. Ullsaard stayed until the last group was ready to head off. He noticed that Gelthius was amongst them, a strange smile on his face.

"What's so funny?" the king asked, hunkering down next to the captain.

Gelthius looked as if he was not going to answer for a moment, but then did so, his eyes innocently looking up at the trees, not meeting Ullsaard's annoyed gaze.

"Was just thinking that you can't have had this in mind when you wanted to be king," Gelthius said with a chuckle. "Sneaking through woods with wet boots and all."

Ullsaard glanced over his shoulder, back towards the strangers, now out of sight. He gave Gelthius's shoulder a comradely squeeze.

"No, it wasn't high on my list of ambitions."

He waved the group of men away and lingered as they stalked off into the trees. Gelthius was right. He hated having to skulk around like a thief. Part of him wanted to call back the legionnaires, march into the clearing and confront whoever was out there. He was king of the most powerful empire in the world, and it stuck in his throat to be so meek. He closed his eyes and pictured Allenya's face, calming himself.

"Patience," he muttered with gritted teeth. "One thing at a time."

Pride tempered with this thought, he turned and slinked away into the woods.

DEEP MEKHA
Midsummer, 211th year of Askh

I

The waters of the great lake were covered with petals and leaves, a multicoloured carpet of offerings that undulated with the swell of the wind. Two-thirds of the lake's edge was filled with pitched tents amongst the lush greenery; domed structures of dark behemodon hide painted with blue and yellow designs, held up with reed poles that swayed in the wind. At the centre of each group of tents had been placed totems and fetish staves with bones and feathers and skulls hanging from them, identifying the shaman-chieftains who were present.

Some way back from the water's edge, where the short trees gradually gave way to bushes and grass, thousand of Mekhani tribesmen and women had made their camps, sleeping in rough bivouacs around their fires. Behemodons ambled at the edges of the camps, hobbled by thick ropes passed through rings in their noses to shackles on their forelegs, their dung heaps attracting thick swarms of flies. Smaller lacertils and xenosauri sunned themselves in their corrals, tongues flicking, their dappled bodies crusted with sand and dirt.

The Mekhani mingled freely, rivalries both ancient and

recent temporarily set aside by the neutrality of the Calling. Some entrepreneurs took the opportunity to trade their wares, free from the threat of banditry by other tribes. In the spirit of harmony, elders discussed territorial boundaries and water rights. Dressed in their finest head feathers, tasselled arm and leg bands rustling, their red bodies painted with black and blue swathes, unmarried braves strutted from camp to camp attracting the attention of potential wives; such displays usually met with derisive hoots and whistles from wrinkled-faced matriarchs watching over their daughters and granddaughters.

Sitting cross-legged beneath his totem, Nemasolai gazed out over the great lake, lost in thought. Another Mekhani looking at the craggy, vacant-faced shaman-chief of the Allako tribe might have thought he pondered the ancient secrets of the waters, or perhaps contemplated the riddles of life, or even communed with the souls of his ancestors to divine his as-yet unknown successor.

In truth, his thoughts were prosaic. His latest mistress had left him before the journey to the Calling and the sun had risen more than thirty times since he had last been with a woman. As a holy man, he was forbidden from taking a wife, so his manly needs were met by the unmarried women of the tribe. He reviewed the potential candidates in a mixture of cataloguing and lewd daydream, trying to figure out which of the twenty-two available women best blended the virtues of beauty, athleticism, creativity, naiveté and experience he desired. He was engaged in mentally sodomising Olloroa, daughter of Mainamoa, unconsciously rubbing himself through his sarong, when a shadow fell across him.

Nemasolai opened one eye and squinted at the silhouetted figure standing over him. He recognised Manamosalai, the shaman of the Kallalo. The young chieftain held his ceremonial stave over his right shoulder, his other hand with thumb hooked into his belt of woven beads.

"Piss off," said Nemasolai, trying to retain the image of Olloroa bent willingly before him. "Can't you see I'm busy?"

In reply, Manamosalai stretched out his arm, pointing his stave towards the setting sun. Nemasolai saw that the red disc was almost touching the horizon. The pale crescent of the moon was visible in the clear sky.

"Shit," Nemasolai said, scrambling to his feet, all erotic thoughts dispelled.

"The others are gathering," said Manamosalai. "I have a boat waiting."

"Thank you." Nemasolai slapped a hand to his companion's arm. "Wouldn't want to miss this, would we?"

The shaman's gaze moved past Manamosalai, out across the lake to the far shore on the edge of visibility. That side of the great lake was bare of trees and tents; not even grass pushed through the arid earth. A single structure stood a short way back from the shore; an arch of white stone five times the height of Nemasolai, yet no wider than his outstretched arms. In the dying light of dusk, the desert beyond could be seen through the arch, yet distorted as if by a heat haze, despite the cool air around the lake.

"You're very lucky, you know," Nemasolai told his fellow shaman as they walked quickly down to the shoreline. "To be brought to a Calling happens less than once in a lifetime. To witness one at such a young age is very fortunate. I have lost count of my years, and this is my first."

"I have spoken with many of the other chieftains, and none is old enough to remember the last Calling," said Manamosalai. "We are privileged."

Nemasolai was not so sure of that. The previous incumbent of his position, Katokalai, claimed to have been to a

Calling but refused to speak of what had happened, always turning away with a shudder whenever the young shaman-to-be had questioned him on it.

Holding the bow of a shallow reed canoe, Manamosalai gestured for his older companion to get into the boat first. When both of them were sat inside, they took up the rough paddles and headed out across the lake, parting the layer of devotional flora behind them.

Neither of them spoke. Not one shaman at the Calling could guess why they had been brought together, and idle speculation was not encouraged in Mekhani culture. Each wise man had received the dream of the lake and the arch thirty-five days ago, and knew instinctively what it meant. All hostilities between the tribes had been called to a halt and the shamans and their tribes' favoured families had packed up camp and moved here, marching across the hot desert without question.

The tales of the tribes described that forbidding arch as a gateway, though to what place was much in debate. Through discussions with the leaders of other tribes, Nemasolai had learnt that some shamanic tradition believed the arch led to Oogaro, the world-oasis that had spawned the Mekhani. To others, including Nemasolai, it led directly to Samonao, the everlasting fire beneath the desert that stole the water and burned the souls of the Mekhani when they were dead. A few shamans even believed that a man who passed through the arch would find himself on the moon or the sun, but they were generally ridiculed if they openly offered this view.

Glancing over his shoulder, Nemasolai saw that they still had time to cross the lake before the sun would be extinguished by the waters of Oogaro. When that happened, when the light of the new moon alone touched the arch, the shaman knew something would take place. What that something might be, he had not the faintest idea.

They drew up their boat amongst several dozen others. Clambering to the sand, Nemasolai joined the other shamans hanging around the arch. Some he knew, some he knew of, but most were completely unknown to him.

Nobody seemed sure what was meant to happen next. The casual conversation died away as the last glow of the sun disappeared. All eyes turned towards the archway. The white stone glittered, far too bright for the little moonlight reflecting from the lake.

"Where are the stars?"

Nemasolai did not know who asked the question, but immediately everybody's gaze was directed upwards. Utter blackness stretched across the sky. The air was still. The sound of the distant camps had been silenced. Not even the lapping of the water disturbed the strange night. Glancing at the lake, Nemasolai saw that everything was still, the ripples in the water unmoving. His skin prickled with cold and his breath frosted in the air.

The shamans exchanged dread-filled glances, but none spoke, frightened of breaking the frozen tableau.

"Kneel."

Two figures stood in front of the arch and had spoken in unison. Unthinkingly, Nemasolai obeyed the command; he fell to the sand and prostrated himself along with the others. He dared not look up, filled with terror by the men he had glimpsed; their rune-carved bodies unsettling, their gold-flecked eyes seared into his mind. He shivered, head pressed into the cold ground, fingers clawing into the sand.

"Long you have suffered." The voice was like the scuttling of a scorpion over a dune. "The desert sands swallowed your cities. The hot winds scoured your history from time. None of you remember that age of glory. We do."

"You were once the chosen people, and you have been chosen again." The second voice reminded Nemasolai of wind sighing across the desert, the quiet whisper of shifting grains. "A thousand years before the Askhan upstarts took your lands, you ruled over more than dust and sand. The greatest city of the world was not Askh, which even today is but a shadow of the glories found in Akkamaro. Behold, your city lives again!"

Hesitantly, Nemasolai raised his eyes from the ground. He saw first the archway, still glimmering in false moonlight. Now the arch was part of a building, an opening into the bottom tier of a mighty ziggurat that stretched into the dark sky on five levels. Flanking the arch were two sets of steps, leading up to the highest point of the building, where something bright could be seen. Looking closer, Nemasolai saw that it was an immense throne from which a man could look out over the city. Glancing to his left and right, the shaman found himself in a massive plaza, the sand beneath him now just a thin layer scattered across thousands of flagstones. Columned buildings appeared around the square out of the gloom, with high-peaked roofs of black slate and red tiles. Frescoes were painted on the white walls, showing long caravans trekking between bountiful oases and mighty armies in red cloth purging savages from verdant forests.

The gasps of the others proved to Nemasolai that this was no mirage; or if it was, one that was shared equally with his fellow shamans.

Movement and sound returned. Stars twinkled against the black velvet of the night sky. The wind keened from the buildings. Light glowed from windows, glossily lacquered shutters thrown back to reveal intricate, multi-coloured panes of glass that cast rainbows dappling on the ivory-coloured stones of the square. Lanterns hung from the broad eaves, glimmering.

And there was the sound of water; not the sluggish lapping of the great lake, but the tinkle of fountains. Sitting up to his haunches, Nemasolai looked over his shoulder at where the great lake had been. It had become a vast cistern lined with blue and white tiles, artificial islands of red wood tethered upon its surface. Water flowed down channels from this immense well, disappearing down wide streets that led into other parts of the sprawling city that now surrounded them.

Tears welled up in Nemasolai's eyes. He was filled with an overwhelming sense of fulfilment and accomplishment. More than that, he felt as one might after coming upon a familiar sight after many years of starved wandering. Every fibre of his being told him that he was home.

Nemasolai heard distant shouts of surprise and fear; the tribespeople could see the city too.

"Akkamaro, your capital, birthright of the Mekhani."

At the sound of the first voice speaking again, Nemasolai directed his attention back to the archway. The two figures had not moved, but in the warm glow of the city they appeared less dreadful. The runes upon their flesh still disturbed Nemasolai's thoughts, but their demeanour was as stern fathers not sinister oppressors.

Some of the shamans were getting to their feet, gazing in wonder at their new surrounds. A few laughed childishly, pointing without comment at one feature or another.

"The revelation is not yet done," said the second man. All eyes turned on him. "We have brought back Akkamaro for you, but a capital needs its ruler. There are none among you worthy of forging a new future for the Mekhani, so we bring to you another gift. Look upon him and weep for your enemies, shed tears of joy for your future generations. You shall have a Great King again, as you did in the forgotten past."

A shape moved in the darkness of the archway.

"Kneel down and give praise to Orlassai, undying monarch, Great King of the Mekhani!"

The man that eased his way through the arch was barely a man at all. He stood almost twice the height of the two sigil-etched priests, with shoulders so broad he had to twist slightly to fit between the stones of the gateway. His eyes gleamed gold in the lantern light and his fingernails glittered as bronze. Like the other two, his skin was heavily marked with spiralling lines and convoluted runes; where they were wizened and frail, Orlassai was bulky and strong. Bloated muscles contorted beneath the Great King's skin as he moved towards the kneeling shamans. Veins like rope corded his flesh. His skin had the rough texture of tanned leather. Teeth like diamonds shone as he grinned at his new subjects.

Their new master had a boyish face, though much warped with prominent brows and hard-edged cheekbones. His head was bald, his scarred flesh bulging with bony nodules like a bag of pebbles.

The newcomer was clad in a high-collared robe of deep yellow, bright against his tanned skin. A belt of black bound the robe around his thick waist, its ends hanging with jewel-bound tassels. Gold and gems were hung on his wrists and ankles, and a chain of rubies and sapphires set into red gold adorned his bulging neck.

"I am Orlassai, reborn again in new flesh," the Great King declared. His words, the sound of his voice, were like a flow of honey, mellifluous and beautiful. Nemasolai heard the love of his mother, the pride of his father in those tones and he wept again, filled with memory.

"Who here would swear allegiance to me?" Orlassai continued.

Nemasolai shouted out that he would, eager to make himself heard above the clamour of affirmation and praises offered by the other shamans. Orlassai stooped to one knee and extended his hand to one of the shamans abasing himself. Nemasolai felt a pang of jealousy that he had not been chosen for such attention as the Great King gestured for the shaman to stand with a five-knuckled finger. Nemasolai did not recognise the other man, who shuddered under Orlassai's golden gaze.

"What is your name?" asked the Great King.

"Akannasai, your greatness," said the shaman, almost falling to his knees again, kept from doing so only by the intervention of the Great King, who placed a finger under Akannasai's chin and lifted his head.

"Will you obey me, Akannasai?"

"I will worship you as Great King, mightiest of lords," gushed Akannasai. "Your every word shall be the command that rings in my ears."

"That is good," said Orlassai. Nemasolai felt a thrill of pleasure at this simple praise, sharing Akannasai's dedication. "My first order as your king is this: go to your people and bring them here to Akkamaro."

Nemasolai was filled with an urgency to comply. He shouted more words of praise as he stood up, bowing his head over and over, backing away from the Great King without averting his gaze from the stunning apparition that had been brought before him. He heard the rapid pattering of feet around him and saw that some of the others had broken into a run, eager to bring the news of the reborn ruler to their tribes. With a last adoring, lingering look at Orlassai, Nemasolai also turned away and urged his aging frame into an awkward lope.

II

As the shamans disappeared into the night, Erlaan breathed a sigh of relief. The sense of adulation, the roar of so many hearts, the stink of their sweat had been almost overwhelming. Even now he could hear the slap of sandaled feet and the shamans' gushing whispers to each other.

Eriekh signalled for him to follow and mounted the steps up the face of the ziggurat, Asirkhyr just behind. Erlaan followed slowly, his long stride taking the time-worn steps four at a time. He marvelled at his improved body, enjoying the grace and power with which it moved; so different from the gangly pubescent form he had left behind. He remembered admiring the athleticism of men like Ullsaard and chuckled to himself. It would be others that longed to have what he now possessed.

"Everything Lakhyri promised was true," said Erlaan. "They were hanging on my every word, not a question of doubt in their eyes."

"We have made you Orlassai reborn," said Eriekh.

"Who was he? Was that true, what you said about an ancient Mekhani civilisation that was greater than Askhor?"

"It is true, Great King," said Asirkhyr. The use of that title sent an almost sexual thrill through Erlaan. "Many times have we raised up the savage tribes of men to be the masters of the world."

"And what happened to the Mekhani? Why have I never heard of this?"

"They failed," Eriekh replied. Both of the old priests were panting hard from their exertions, their haggard breaths like the rasp of saws in Erlaan's ears. "The history of them all – Askhan, Mekhani, Erdutian, Connamite and many others – is kept in the Archive of Ages at the Grand Precincts."

"I would have learnt all of this when I became king of Askh?"

The two men exchanged a glance with a meaning Erlaan could not read.

"The king of Askh is privy to all of these secrets," said Eriekh.

"You said that they had failed," Erlaan continued. "Failed at what? Is that why you've done this, because Askhor has failed as well?"

Again there was that knowing exchange of looks, mixed with a hint of impatience at Erlaan's questions. Eriekh gave Asirkhyr a subtle nod of approval.

"Our masters, the eulanui, once ruled this world," said Asirkhyr, his breathing so laboured now that Erlaan thought the hierophant might collapse. "They... lost their grip on this realm. Since that time, many thousands of years ago, we have endeavoured to bring about their return. When we are successful, it is better that there is an empire ready for the masters to rule, for should they need to create one for themselves, it would not go well for our kind."

"Our kind? The eulanui's sect?"

"Mankind," Asirkhyr said quietly.

"And before you ask about it, let me tell you of the city," Eriekh said with a wheezing sigh. "We have not created it from thin air. It has always been here, since it was first built. When the Mekhani's enemies ravaged their empire and the grasslands had become desert, Lakhyri chose to save the city rather than see it swallowed by the sands or razed by barbarians. We moved it to a safer place."

"A place that is here, but cannot be visited by normal men," said Erlaan.

Eriekh glanced back, pleasantly surprised.

"Yes, something like that."

"And the Temple…" Erlaan thought aloud. "That is here as well, and in the Grand Precincts, and I suppose many other places that are one step aside from the world I knew."

Eriekh actually smiled at this.

"Your understanding is correct, Great King," said the priest.

"I do not understand much," confessed Erlaan. "But these eyes you have given me, they let me see things… differently. There are spaces within spaces, coiled up tight within the grains of sand, like a whole city hidden in the crack of a brick. The world normal men see is a vast empty space to the eulanui, and it is in these vast gaps that they dwell."

They had reached the summit of the ziggurat. Eriekh waved a hand towards the golden throne, whose back was shaped like a great bird of prey with wings spread wide. Erlaan ran his hand over the smooth red cushion of the seat, feeling every tiny fibre on his fingertips. He turned and sat down to gaze across the vast city in the desert. It was larger than Askh, radiating out to duskwards in a semi-circle of boulevards. He could see splashes of green where parks broke the procession of white domes and coloured roof tiles.

"And I am to found a new empire from here?" he asked. "I am to wage war against the city of my birth?"

"You are to wage war against Ullsaard, who has stolen from you that which you were born to possess," said Asirkhyr. "You will take back what is yours, Great King, mighty Orlassai."

Erlaan gripped the arms of the throne with his strange hands and turned his gaze to coldwards, picturing the mountains of Askhor and the city of his birth. He had wondered so many times if he had been fit to rule; wept into his pillow at the fear of his weakness. The Blood had proved its strength, with the aid of Lakhyri.

He smiled. He was ready to take his rightful place.

ASKH
Late Summer, 212th year of Askh

I

The blare of a hundred trumpets split the air from the walls of Askh, heralding the return of the king. Leading a bodyguard of five hundred legionnaires picked up from the governor of Ersua, Ullsaard marched back to his capital; the fifty men that had accompanied him through Salphoria had been given ten days' leave in Askh as reward for their service.

Even before he had reached the massive gatehouse Ullsaard could hear the sounds of the crowd waiting within the city. Drums pounded and music skirled against a backdrop of voices echoing from the tall buildings. He could barely hear the tramp of the legionnaires twenty paces behind him.

Plunging into the darkness of the gate, the king was surrounded by the sound, ringing from the arched tunnel. Thirty paces ahead the light of the sun made a bright arch in the gloom, through which Ullsaard could already see coloured banners waving and lines of soldiers keeping the Royal Way clear.

Emerging into the sunlight, the roar that greeted him was deafening. Dancing girls, naked save for a few wisps of silk, twirled across the cobbles in front of him, scattering petals in his path. Thousand were shouting his name, calling for his attention, clamouring with each other for a glance or a wave, while legionnaires with linked arms strained to hold back the mass of people. Children threw handfuls of salt and grain at his feet from baskets wreathed in ivy leaves. The street was packed, a path less than ten strides across open before him. People had clambered onto every roof and garret, hung from every window and shouted down at their ruler from dangerously full balconies.

Ullsaard stopped in his tracks, dazed by the sound and spectacle.

He looked at the sea of excited faces, seeing women with tears rolling down their cheeks and men pumping their fists in the air, chanting madly. Poles carrying effigies of Salphors danced above the crowd, the stuffed figures upon them jerking on the end of nooses tied from thorny vines.

Amongst the throng, Ullsaard spied a familiar face a short way off to his left, hanging back on the near side of the legionnaires' cordon.

"Leerunin!" the king called out.

The man smiled briefly but without conviction, obviously distressed by the attention. Ullsaard's former treasurer, appointed court chamberlain by the king before he had departed, wiped a cloth over his balding scalp and scuttled forward at Ullsaard's beckoning finger.

"What the fuck is this?" the king asked out of the corner of his mouth, still grinning at the jubilant crowds.

"It is a celebration of your victories in Salphoria, king," said Leerunin. He bobbed apologetically. "Is it not to your liking?"

"How much is it costing me?"

"Not a tin, I assure you," said the chamberlain. "The city merchants and the nobles have offered this parade as a gift in recognition of your accomplishments."

Ullsaard started walking, Leerunin hovering at his shoulder like an obedient hound.

"So you haven't passed on the contents of my last letter to them?" said the king.

"I deemed it unwise to apprise the council of the severity of the current setbacks of the situation with regard to the continuing heroic campaign in Salphoria and the problems arising in Okhar," said Leerunin, once again amazing Ullsaard with his ability to spin out the simplest of answers into the longest of sentences.

"Why would it be unwise?"

"The imperial economy had been soundly boosted by your exploits to duskwards and many contracts and transactions have been sealed on the understanding of the accruement of wealth from future conquests and discoveries."

"I see," said Ullsaard, though he didn't but was sure a better explanation could wait. "Let me make sure I have this right. None of the nobles or powerful merchant houses know that the Salphorian campaign has stalled and the Mekhani are giving us grief?"

Leerunin hesitated for a moment, struggling with the concept of giving a simple answer before sighing heavily.

"That is correct, king," he said.

"And they have spent a lot of money – money they don't actually have yet – throwing me a welcome back gala?"

Again Leerunin squirmed.

"That is also correct, king."

Ullsaard said nothing more, allowing the chamberlain to silently writhe in a misery of his own making, until they reached the bottom of the Royal Hill, where the broad road split around the mound.

"I am going to take the long route, through Maarmes, while you are going to head straight up the mount and assemble as many of the nobles and merchants as you can find in the next hour. Bring them to the Hall of Askhos so that I might address them."

"Yes, king, I shall do as you say forthwith and wi–"

"Now," Ullsaard growled. Leerunin set off at a brisk jog, breaking away from the route of the parade.

Ullsaard had faced down many foes in his time, and had gladly marched to battle against each and every one of them. The thought of disgruntled merchants and out-of-pocket nobles filled him with a deeper agitation than any confrontation he had yet encountered. His grip on the Crown was loose at best, and it had been the promise of Salphoria that had secured the backing of the most powerful families in the empire. Now he would be forced to explain his failure, yet at the same time not reveal the true secret of what held his wrath at bay; the nobles would care not one jot for Ullsaard's family and would be likely to take the matter out of his hands if they knew the truth. Add to that the risk of Mekhani attack in Okhar – from tribes he should have subjugated when instead Ullsaard had been warring against his own king – and the situation looked even worse.

Despite the triumphant shouts, the placards with their mottos of victory, the swirling streamers, the laughing children, Ullsaard did not feel much like celebrating.

II

The chipping of the mason's chisel rang coldly from the marble walls and floor. Ullsaard sat alone at the end of the Hall of Askhos, lounging in a large, plain chair of black wood. Around him had been carved the names of the fallen, those who had given their lives for the glory of

Askhor since the founding of the First Legion. Line after line of tiny script named more than two hundred thousand casualties of Askhor's wars. There were so many that the walls were nearly half-filled.

Ullsaard had only come here once before, during his investiture as a general of the empire. He had read some of the names, wondered about the men they represented. Several thousand were simply listed as 'Legionnaire of the Empire'; these came in blocks signifying the few defeats sufficiently disastrous that the dead could not be distinguished from the deserter.

Had they been brave or cowards? Had they died on the field, from their injuries, or swiftly despatched by their companions to ease their suffering? The weight of so many dead was a terrible burden, and the knowledge that the names being constantly added were now Ullsaard's responsibility was heavy on his shoulders. As a commander, he had led men to their deaths for the ambitions of others. As king, it was his ambition that waged bloody war.

That was the point, Askhos told him. Since returning to the capital, and closer proximity to the Crown, the dead king had been a constant presence in Ullsaard's thoughts. *A leader of men must ask others to sacrifice their lives for his cause, but he should never treat their deaths cheaply nor allow their deeds to go unrecorded.*

Ullsaard said nothing. He was tired. He had slept little, fearful of Askhos's influence, retiring to his bed only when he was so exhausted he fell into dreamless sleep. He was fatigued from a day of dealing with dignitaries and petitioners; of having to tell the great and the good of Askh that the war in Salphoria was not progressing well and that the expenses they had incurred would not be recouped for a considerable time. He had chosen this place for his audiences to remind the nobles and the merchants, the bankers and the fleet captains, of the price others were paying for the campaign. Some had been moved by the sombre memorial; many had been so self-absorbed they had barely considered their surroundings as they whined about the money they were losing.

Ullsaard's thoughts turned to the Crown. It was locked in the palace vaults along with the dwindling treasures of the king. He did not know whether it was the presence of Askhos or his own fear that prevented him from wearing it, but its absence from his brow had been remarked upon more than once since he had returned.

"Leave me," Ullsaard called out to the mason. The wiry man nodded, packed his chisel and padded mallet into his belt and clambered down the scaffold on which he had been sitting. When he was gone, Ullsaard addressed Askhos.

"I can't deal with the situation in Magilnada and the Mekhani at the same time. The treasury is almost empty, and the nobles will not be putting up any more money for the campaign any time soon. Tax revenues are low, and slow to come in. I'm paying legions in Salphoria to stand idle. Anglhan is strangling trade through the Magilnada gap. I had hoped to hire some Nemurians to bolster the armies, but there is not the money for more than a handful. I thought the resources of the empire were inexhaustible. It seems I was woefully wrong."

Are you asking for my advice, or simply complaining?

Ullsaard hesitated, kneading his knotted brow with his fingers.

"I need your help," he admitted. He sighed heavily. "There are so many decisions to make. Everyone has plenty of advice, but every piece comes with another demand for action, another choice to make."

You thought being king would be a mere matter of leading the armies to victory and everything else would fall into place?

Ullsaard grunted and slumped to one side, elbow on the arm of the chair.

"Maybe. I have a chancellor, governors, paymasters, engineers all filling my head with information, expecting me to make sense of it all."

You know the advice I would give.

"The Brotherhood." Ullsaard shook his head. "How can I trust them?"

You misjudge them, and their loyalty. The Brotherhood is dedicated to the success of the empire and not one man. Only one, the High Brother, knows the truth of my existence. With the line broken, you are the rightful king. The Brotherhood will ease away the many pains of rule, allowing you to concentrate on the matters that are truly important. I could not have founded the empire without them. Like you, I have no mind for figures and commerce, though I have picked up much strategy over the years. Do not carry burdens others are willing to bear for you.

Ullsaard sorrowfully shook his head and scratched at his chin.

"It's too late," he said. "I do not know how to start the rebuilding of the Brotherhood. Most of the Brothers fled, some are under house arrest, and I have several thousand of them under guard in a camp at Parmia. I don't know what to do with them, or how to start things moving again."

You are the king. There is still one right you have yet to exercise. Go the Grand Precincts and demand entry, as is your sole privilege.

"The Grand Precincts are as deserted as any of the others. My men had no response from within. The High Brother has fled, no doubt, with the rest of his cronies. No food or other supplies have passed into the building for more than a year; there's nobody in there."

The Grand Precinct is never deserted, Ullsaard. Have you gone yourself to the great door and demanded entry?

"No, why would I? The knock of one man is the same as any other."

You are not any other man, you are the king! You accept your responsibilities with furrowed brow and sagging shoulders, but make no use of the rights that you possess. Go to the Grand Precincts. I will guide you.

The king considered this. There was no assurance that Askhos could be trusted; in fact, every reason to believe the opposite. Similarly, the Brotherhood was Askhos' tool, and had used every means they had to thwart Ullsaard's claim to the Crown. It was likely they would continue to resist his rule.

Your are wrong, Askhos interrupted his thoughts. *The Brotherhood opposed you because you were a usurper and, as Lutaar, I instructed them to. You still act like a usurper, not a rightful king. Re-establish the Brotherhood and command them as I did. Show the Brotherhood that you do not fear them, that you have every right to wear the Crown as any man that came before you. You think that the Brotherhood is inactive, simply because they do not carry out your bidding? Better to bring them back into the light of your gaze than leave them to foster their own plans in the shadows.*

This last comment struck a chord with Ullsaard. In Askhira, with the burning of Ullsaard's fleet, the Brotherhood had demonstrated their power to work unseen. Even now they could be manipulating the people of the empire. Somewhere, Erlaan and Kalmud were still alive, and no doubt there were those amongst the Brotherhood who would see the previous line restored. Askhos was right. If Ullsaard was to be treated as a king, he had to act like one.

A bell chimed the second hour of Duskwatch. The thought of going to the Grand Precincts as darkness fell unsettled Ullsaard.

"I will sleep on the decision," he said, though the laughter of Askhos in Ullsaard's mind revealed that the dead king knew his true reasons for delaying until the light of morning.

III

Only the drip of the water clock disturbed the silence within the mausoleum-like bowels of the Grand Precincts. Consisting of two bowls set one above the other, the clock sat on the table in the chamber of the High Brother.

Lakhyri stared at the drops of water as they fell, his golden eyes following each from the top bowl to the second. It intrigued and irked him in equal measure, this passing of time, the slow wearing of mortality and entropy. In the Temple he was immortal; here in the world every passing drip was a passing moment of his life. It did not wear on him heavily, but was a slow erosion of his existence like the wind wearing down a mountaintop. The runes carved into his flesh itched, leeching life-giving power from the thousands of small creatures and insects that infested the deserted Grand Precincts, sustaining him with their tiny contributions of force.

He dismissed thoughts of time and turned his mind to more pressing matters. Erlaan was installed as the new figurehead of the Mekhani. He was under instruction to begin a more concerted campaign against Okhar before the end of the year. The situation in Salphoria was confusing to the high priest. He could fathom no reason why Ullsaard had stalled his advance so swiftly. By Lakhyri's calculation, the king should have been smashing down the gates of Carantathi by the end of the summer.

Lakhyri wondered if he had moved too soon. Had encouraging the Mekhani distracted Ullsaard from his campaign? It seemed unlikely. The raids had been carefully planned to add impetus to the king's war, not delay it. Ullsaard was meant to crush Salphoria swiftly so that he could return to deal with the Mekhani attacks. Instead, he had called a halt to his conquest and returned to Askh.

Like many things of late, it perturbed Lakhyri that matters were progressing in ways he had not foreseen. Ullsaard was so unpredictable. Other men, even his brother Askhos, had been simple to manipulate; acting and reacting in ways that had been laid out in Lakhyri's mind like a map. This new king, he caused problems. He was an anomaly. He should never have been born. From that moment, things had started to go awry, even if the full extent of his deviation from the great plan of Lakhyri was not yet fully known.

The high priest reined back his thoughts from such amorphous speculation. He had to focus. The dripping of the water clock rang loudly in his ears, reminding him that the eulanui were losing patience. He could not allow himself to be distracted by the longer consequences of what had gone wrong. The empire had to be complete. Ullsaard needed to conquer Salphoria. At the moment of Ullsaard's triumph, Erlaan would sweep hotwards with his Mekhani horde and take over Greater Askhor, thus uniting the new empire of Askh with the ancient realm of Mekha. As foretold, a single king would rule all of the lands between the seas.

And when that happened…

A gong echoed along the corridors. For a moment, Lakhyri thought that he was back in the Temple, hearing the call to prayer. The moment passed and as the gong sounded twice and thrice, he realised what was happening. The lingering presence of Udaan stirred in a corner of the body Lakhyri had stolen from the High Brother and the meaning of the three gong notes became clear.

The new king was paying a visit.

He picked up the silver mask lying next to the water clock and pulled its straps over his head. Lifting up the hood of his robe, Lakhyri stood, mind abuzz with concerns at this development.

With long strides, he navigated his way along the corridors and halls until he came to the large double doors of the Grand Precinct's main portal. Pulling a rope, he activated a series of counterweights. The doors ground inwards, sweeping two arcs through the dust that had settled on the stone floor.

Morning light streamed inside, silhouetting a large man stood with legs braced apart, arms folded across a muscled chest. He was dressed in a simple tunic and kilt. Lakhyri noted with interest that he did not wear the Crown, and there was no sword at his waist.

So this was Ullsaard, who had stolen the Crown of the Blood. Lakhyri measured up the man in an instant. Physically powerful, self-confident, ingrained with the assumption of command. Prideful. He had come here unarmed, which showed that he was either arrogant or naive. Lakhyri detected the singular presence of the Blood, lingering beneath the surface of the man.

Remembering that he currently played the part of the High Brother, Lakhyri dropped to one knee, eyes locked on the newcomer.

"Welcome, King Ullsaard, to the Grand Precincts of the Brotherhood."

IV

Lakhyri ushered the king into the reception hall, noting the man's roving eyes and tenseness in his body that conflicted with his affected air of confidence.

"You're not Udaan," said Ullsaard. "Even without the eyes, I can tell you're someone else by the way you hold yourself."

The high priest did not waste his precious time with denial.

"My name is Lakhyri. I am the custodian of the Brotherhood's secrets. If I can be of any service, please inform me."

Ullsaard paused for a moment, the slightest of frowns creasing his brow, as if he was listening to someone whispering in his ear. He gave a slight, involuntary shake of the head.

"Show me everything," said the king. "The Archive of Ages, the lava tanks, the ailur pits."

"There is little to see, my king. There are no Brothers here except for me."

"And we both know that you are not really a Brother," said Ullsaard, a lopsided smile briefly twisting his lips. "You are something far more important, aren't you? And you can dispense with calling me 'king'; I know that you have no loyalty to me."

Lakhyri stifled a hissing intake of breath. He scoured the king's face, searching for clues as to his intent. The high priest detected amusement, curiosity. And something else, something Lakhyri could not place, momentary distractions of attention.

"You are well-informed," said Lakhyri. A glimmer of an answer was born in the depths of the priest's mind, but it was indistinct, as yet nascent. "Unnaturally so."

"King Lutaar was very helpful before I slit his throat," said Ullsaard.

The implied threat was immature, an unnecessary reversion to basic animal instinct. Lakhyri smiled thinly behind his mask, certain that the usurper was far less sure of himself than he was pretending.

"It is not a tour of the Grand Precincts that brought you here," said Lakhyri. He waved for Ullsaard to follow and turned towards the corridor that led to his adopted chamber. "If you would come with me, we can discuss these matters in more... comfort."

Ullsaard stepped forward quickly; catching up with Lakhyri in four strides, anxious not to be trailing behind the man he considered his inferior. Again, the king's eyes were taking in every detail; the stonework, the dust on the tiled floor, the faded murals all were subjected to his active gaze.

"The Grand Precincts are older than Askh, right?" said Ullsaard.

Lakhyri glanced to his left to see the king trailing his fingertips along the wall, perhaps trying to get a sense of the place by touch when eyes and ears had failed. Lakhyri considered something else. Ullsaard clearly had the Blood, and as one of the Temple's interfaces in this world, the Grand Precincts resonated with the king on a level he probably did not understand.

"Many thousands of years older," said Lakhyri.

He sensed that Ullsaard already knew this. He was probing, questioning Lakhyri in a manner more subtle than his questions suggested, trying to get a measure of the priest, judging his honesty. Lakhyri was happy to be open for the moment. The more Ullsaard understood about what he faced, the better the chance that he would accede to Lakhyri's demands when they were made. Already the high priest was reconsidering his schemes, intrigued by the possibility that Ullsaard might be prepared to take up where Askhos-as-Lutaar had failed, without the need for too much subterfuge.

They reached a junction in the passageway and Lakhyri noticed that Ullsaard was turning to the right, towards the chamber, before the priest had indicated the path they needed to follow. It was a small thing, but it raised fresh suspicions in Lakhyri's mind; Ullsaard already knew this place. It was impossible. No mortal save for the members of the Brotherhood had stepped foot inside this building, and even the most gruesome torture would not make them reveal their secrets. For all that, Ullsaard's existence had meant to be impossible, yet here he was, literally as large as life, towering over the wizened priest as they reached the study chamber.

Lakhyri held aside the curtain of beads across the door, dipping his head to indicate to Ullsaard that he should enter. As the king passed, the priest's golden eyes bore into Ullsaard, looking past the flesh and bones, trying to see the web of energy within. The Blood glittered in Lakhyri's altered vision, and there was an odd haze about the king's head that he had not seen before. It was another clue, but the meaning and importance Lakhyri could not yet divine.

Ullsaard sat on a stool beside the table with the water clock, smiling at something unknown to Lakhyri. The priest sat on the other side and laid his palms on the worn wooden table, achieving a moment of stillness that calmed his racing thoughts.

"This place, the Brotherhood that inherited it from its founders, is dedicated to a single purpose," said Ullsaard. His eyes were fixed on Lakhyri, never once straying to look at the bound scrolls on the shelves around the walls, nor the cracked mosaic underfoot. "You desire an empire; one that covers all of the lands from dawn to dusk, cold to hot, sea to sea. Our goals are in accord, and there is no reason for us to be enemies."

Lakhyri thought about this, sitting absolutely still, allowing his mind to swiftly process this new information and gauge a response. On the face of things, Ullsaard spoke the truth. He had not once claimed personal ambition for taking the Crown, but pretended that he had done so for the benefit of Greater Askhor. The priest detected no deception in the king, but self-deception was always a possibility. For the moment, Ullsaard believed the truth of what he said.

"They are, and there is not," said Lakhyri. "Yet you made an enemy of the Brotherhood. You chose to set yourself against the king that they supported."

"A king that you supported also," said Ullsaard. "Perhaps I wish to make peace with my enemy. I am king now. Support me."

The king's tone hovered between request and demand. Never one to take such things at face value, Lakhyri took stock of his options, appraising Ullsaard's intent and sincerity. Taking all the factors into account, the king's offer was an unexpected boon. He was clearly feeling the pressure of two costly and potentially disastrous wars. For a brief moment, Lakhyri was conflicted. If he refused his support, his plan with Erlaan and the Mekhani might bear fruition even sooner than he had calculated. On the negative side, such a victory would still leave the necessary conquest of Salphoria unresolved. The best outcome would be to help Ullsaard defeat the Salphorians whilst leaving him open to being toppled shortly after. Lakhyri had two plans in motion and it was in his best interest to keep them both moving forwards. He made his decision.

"If you wish to rebuild the Brotherhood, I will assist you in whatever way I can," said the high priest. "Under my guidance and your leadership, the empire will prevail over its current problems. I would see you conquer all of the lands between the seas, as Askhos decreed."

Again Ullsaard hesitated before speaking, distracted for a moment, a smirk playing across his lips for a moment.

"Then it is agreed," said the king. "I shall remove the injunction against the Brotherhood, release those under arrest and restore the power of the precincts. You will use the means you have to inform the Brothers that their oaths of allegiance to the empire apply equally to me as they did my predecessor."

Ullsaard stood and held out his hand. Lakhyri looked at it for a moment, confused, before he remembered that it was a gesture of trust. By accepting it, he would be symbolically sealing the nature of their agreement. His spindly, rune-etched fingers closed around the rough hand of the king and they shook on the deal.

"The agreement is reached," said Lakhyri, glad that his mask concealed his satisfied smile.

He moved to withdraw his hand from Ullsaard's grip, but the king's fingers remained tight for a little longer. He pulled Lakhyri slightly closer, the high priest unable to resist the much stronger man.

"If I have the slightest suspicion, just the smallest whiff of betrayal, yours will be the first head to be separated from its neck," Ullsaard said with a pleasant smile that was not matched by the murderous glint in his eyes.

Released, Lakhyri took a step back, his smile gone. Such juvenile threats were usually pointless, but there was something about the king's manner that unsettled Lakhyri. He definitely knew more than he had said, and Lakhyri realised the threat had not been idle nor should it be lightly dismissed. There was something oddly familiar about the way Ullsaard acted, the way he carried himself and the things he said, but the high priest could not yet identify exactly what it was. He would have to watch the situation – and this new king – very closely.

GERIA
Autumn, 212th year of Askh

I

The docks were thick with ships and boats, the cranes swinging above, loading and unloading the last surge of trade before winter. A grey sky thick with dark clouds hung over Geria, bloated with a coming storm. One wharf was conspicuously empty, and it was to this that the captain of Ullsaard's ship directed the tillermen.

The king prowled the foredeck and scanned the dockside for any sign of ceremony or other nonsense. He had been clear in his letter to Urikh that his arrival was to be conducted with the minimum of fuss. Ullsaard saw a few companies of legionnaires arranged along the open area beyond the quays; his son's ceremonial guard. Other than this obligatory gesture, it seemed as if the docks were operating as normal, much to Ullsaard's relief.

As the boat swung towards the quay, Ullsaard watched the labourers going about their work. He saw the distinctive black robes of the Brotherhood amongst the half-naked men. Askhos had told him that Lakhyri's response would be swift, but the king had still been surprised by the speed with which the Brotherhood had resurfaced. Within a few days, long before Ullsaard's letters to the governors had arrived, the Grand Precincts in Askh had been bustling again. For most, Ullsaard's change of policy had been a relief, and he had been inundated with visits and messages of approval from across Askh as the news had spread.

In part, it was to escape the confines of the palaces that Ullsaard had come to Okhar. He had reason enough to be here; the Mekhani attacks had subsided but had not stopped and it was the king's opinion that they were gathering their strength for some greater move. Urikh had assured him by herald that the extra three legions brought in from other provinces at the king's command were sufficient to contain any threat, but Ullsaard had little faith in his son's military acumen.

With a grind of wood on wood, the ship slid along the wharf, shaking beneath Ullsaard's feet. As ropes were tossed to the waiting men ashore, Ullsaard headed down to the main deck, impatient to be on dry land again. The deck thudded with feet as his accompanying guard of a hundred legionnaires from the First assembled behind him. As soon as the gangway had been lowered, the king strode from the ship, his bodyguard's captain calling out a hasty order for the soldiers to fall in behind their king.

Turning along the wharf, Ullsaard saw Urikh stepping out from his own guard. The king could see Luia standing a little behind her son. She seemed to be in conversation with one of the company captains. Judging by the officer's nervousness, the topic was not to his liking with Ullsaard bearing down upon them with a body of armed men. Ullsaard wondered for a moment if Luia was offering some new proposal, or simply making conversation with a current partner. The king dismissed the thoughts; he had more important things on his mind.

Urikh waited for his father where the quay met the dockside. He looked relaxed and his skin was tanned from the Okhar summer. Forgetting for a moment that he was a king meeting one of his governors, Ullsaard smiled with pride. In his official white robes, the green-and-gold sash of Okhar across his chest, Urikh seemed to have matured by ten years. Gone was the scheming boy who used to trick his brothers into taking the blame for his misadventures; gone was the gambling teen who used to fleece his friends with his wrestling wagers and loaded set of bones; gone was the speculating trader who would risk a fortune on a rumour of a bad harvest or the loss of a cargo ship.

A sudden thought struck Ullsaard and he stopped in mid-stride. He did not just look at his son as a respected governor of the empire; he looked at the future king.

Gathering his wits, Ullsaard continued and reached the end of the wharf. Urikh welcomed his king with a short bow. He looked as if he was about to say something, but the words were caught in his throat. Ullsaard was similarly tongue-tied, unsure whether to be formal or not. The two of them suffered an awkward silence before Urikh finally resolved whatever dilemma had plagued him.

"Geria and all of Okhar greet you," he said. "You have made good time from Askh. May I present my guard of honour?"

Ullsaard nodded and Urikh turned and gestured to his senior captain. At a shout from their commander, the legionnaires raised their spears with a cry of "Askhor! Ullsaard!" and returned to attention.

Luia drifted over, her carefully tailored red dress clinging to her shapely body, slits in the woollen gown showing her arms and thighs. She drew up a white shawl from her shoulders as scattered drops of rain began to fall onto the stone of quayside.

"Greetings, husband," she said with a nod of the head. She directed a look at Ullsaard, which the king found difficult to read for a moment. At first he thought it was anger, but realised it was a look filled with desire, an almost predatory hunger. He found it quite disconcerting coming from a woman who had regularly pronounced her hatred of him and scorned him so vigorously in the past.

"Greetings, wife," he managed to reply, confused by the unexpected desire her glance had roused in him. "You are well?"

Unbidden, she turned next to Ullsaard and linked her arm in his. They strolled towards the riverside warehouses as Urikh dismissed his guard with an irritated order and followed behind.

"I find Geria to be most satisfying," said Luia. "The weather is more favourable than Askh, and the governor's palace, though austere from the outside, has all of the comforts a woman could desire."

"All of the comforts a *queen* could desire?" Ullsaard asked with a lopsided smile. Her grip on his arm tightened for a moment and the feel of it sent an unusual thrill through the king.

"Perhaps all a queen desires is her king," said Luia. There it was again, that look of animal need.

Ullsaard knew that she was trying to manipulate him. He could not remonstrate with her, not in such public view. And there was part of him that enjoyed it. Always she had craved a powerful, important man, and yet sought her physical pleasures from elsewhere. Perhaps on becoming king, Ullsaard had finally managed to make himself a man worthy of Luia. They had copulated before – Urikh was testament to that – but never before had Ullsaard sensed such desire in her. It had been more than half a year since he had last lain with a woman, and Luia's attentions were reminding him of that fact.

"I know that you do not wish there to be any fuss, but I have organised a formal reception for you tonight," Luia told him. "You presence here would be more widely remarked upon if you were not to have some kind of banquet."

"You're right," said Ullsaard. "Tongues will wag, whatever I do, so best not give them more than necessary to wag about. The usual merchants, nobles and dignitaries?"

"Yes, and a few Second Captains from the palace guards. Oh, and Lerissa will be there too." This news brought an instinctive tension to Ullsaard. Luia laughed at his involuntary reaction. "I always thought there was something between the two of you."

"I've never laid a finger on her," said Ullsaard, pulling his arm free from Luia's.

"Touchy subject," she said. "You have certainly laid eyes on her, haven't you? There is no shame in it."

"I love Allenya," said Ullsaard, as if that was all the explanation that was needed.

"And yet you have slept with me and Meliu," answered Luia. "You have a strange sense of loyalty, Ullsaard. You treat a simple physical act as if it was something to be treasured."

"It is important to me."

They reached the plaza beneath the concourse leading up to the palaces. Turning up the roadway, Ullsaard again took Luia's arm in his, feeling oddly guilty about his outburst. He remembered that Luia knew nothing of her sisters' predicament in Magilnada. It was time that she did.

"Have you had any letters recently from Allenya or Meliu?"

"Just the other day, from Meliu" replied Luia. "They seemed to think you were still in Salphoria. She complained about the lack of news coming to them regarding your war. She said that Anglhan had visited several times, but had not offered any answers to their inquiries. Allenya is in a melancholy state, she informed me. She had been keen to return to Askh, but Anglhan convinced her to remain. Why have you not written to Allenya to tell them that they can leave that wretched city?"

The thought of his wife's sadness brought an ache to Ullsaard's chest. The moment was lightened only a little by the knowledge that his family did not yet know that they were being held hostage. He stopped and turned Luia to face him, gesturing for Urikh to step forward to join them. He gripped each of them by an arm.

"You must not let anyone else know what I am about to tell you," he said. They nodded and he continued. "Anglhan wishes to remove Magilnada from the empire. He uses Allenya, Meliu and Noran as bargaining chips for that freedom."

Luia moved to break his grasp, but Ullsaard held firm, fingers dimpling the soft flesh of her arm.

"Tell no one!" he snarled.

"What are you doing about it?" demanded Urikh. "Is this why the news of the campaign is so dubious?"

Ullsaard ignored the question for the moment, concentrating on Luia. Anger flashed in her eyes and she bared her teeth. The king swayed back, expecting her to strike him, but she simply quivered in his grip, her whole body shaking with rage. This mood lasted for a few moments before her fury gave way to despair. She sagged against Ullsaard, her tears flowing fast, soaking into the weave of his tunic, her fingers clawing at its hem. Taken aback, he let go of her arm and placed it around her shoulders, kissing her on the top of her head.

"I'll not let anything happen to them, I promise," he

said. Stroking Luia's hair, the king turned his attention to Urikh, who had taken a step back, arms folded tightly across his chest, eyes narrowed. "We are at an impasse for the while. Anglhan controls my supplies and my family, so I cannot move against him. His hostages are only of value if alive, so they are safe enough if I do nothing to move against Magilnada."

"But that is an intolerable situation!" All of Ullsaard's earlier pride was swept away as Urikh seemed to revert twenty years, back to when he used to have tantrums as a child when denied.

"Act like a man!" the king snapped. "The world does not simply exist the way we want it to; we have to make it that way."

Luia had calmed herself and parted from Ullsaard, her cheeks and eyes red. She sniffed loudly, wiped her face with the cuff of her dress and tidied her hair.

"How are you going to make them safe?" she asked.

"I don't know," Ullsaard confessed. "I just don't know yet, but I will think of something. I'll find a way, even if it means giving up Salphoria."

Luia nodded, sniffed again, and stroked a hand along his arm.

"I know you will, husband." She glanced up at the palace and then at her son. "Not a word, we are agreed. We have a royal feast to attend. There have been supply problems in Salphoria, but now that the Brotherhood has been restored, that will not last. Other than that, there is nothing to concern anyone with regard to Salphoria."

"As you say, mother," said Urikh, his whole demeanour sullen.

The three of them continued up the road, Ullsaard's hand clasped with Luia's, his son at his shoulder. Though he hated himself for thinking it, the king could not help but wonder what he might have done if it had been Luia in Magilnada rather than Allenya? He cursed himself for entertaining such a notion, knowing that no good could come of it.

II

Ullsaard prodded an Okharan spiced fish head around his plate with a spoon, not feeling the slightest touch of hunger. Rain pattered at the window shutters and the occasional distant growl of thunder announced the coming storm. The reception room was abuzz with conversation amongst the two dozen or so special guests who had been chosen to take part in this post-feast discussion. Two First Captains were present – Harrakil of the Seventeenth and Meesiu of the Sixth – along with several fleet owners, a handful of warehouse landlords, three local noble family heads, the chairmen of the city's two rival merchant boards and Thasalin.

This last cut a strange figure amongst the gaudy refinery of the others. Dressed in his severe black robe, the head of Okhar's Brotherhood precinct meticulously selected an apple from a bowl on one of the low tables, turning each fruit over in his hand, inspecting it precisely before replacing it. Having made his decision, the chosen apple was carefully pared away with a small knife, each sliver deposited neatly between the Brother's fleshy lips and chewed dispassionately.

Ullsaard hated the man; not just because he was a Brother. The qualities that made him such an admirable civil servant were vices in good company. He was fastidious to the point of pedantry; he had the habit of repeating any question asked of him, rephrased with subtle changes of nuance; his watery blue eyes regarded everything with suspicion and every person with mild disdain.

He was just the sort of man that Ullsaard had long despised for their miserly allocations of funds and grain, their undisguised contempt for men that shed blood for a living, and their self-important inflexions and sneering comments that the king had never understood. For all that – because of that – Thasalin was also just the sort of man Ullsaard needed to run the empire on his behalf.

Sensing their liege's sour mood, the guests invited into this inner circle had not approached Ullsaard, though clearly nearly all were anxious to do so. Ullsaard was content to let them wait. He remembered when he was last in this room, exchanging barbs with Nemtun, terrifying Noran. He looked at the fish head and smiled at the memory of Nemtun's indignation and the pleasure of causing it.

"If I may have a word, king?"

Ullsaard looked up and saw Thasalin, who had evidently taken Ullsaard's brief display of humour as an indication that the king was now amenable to interruption.

"Have several," Ullsaard sighed, depositing his plate on the side table next to the couch. He slouched back, rested his hands on his belly and crossed his ankles. "Have as many as you want."

Thasalin turned slightly and gestured to Harrakil and Meesiu. The two captains approached, helmets under their arms.

"I wish to clarify a few points, king," said Thasalin. That was another thing that annoyed Ullsaard. Thasalin always wanted to 'clarify'; never 'sort out', 'check' or 'confirm'. "It is with regard to the provisioning of the legions you are despatching to the Mekhani border."

"What of it?" said Ullsaard, not bothering to conceal a yawn. His sleep had not improved much, even though he was now several hundred miles from the Crown.

"I can understand the need to provide full camp supplies for the Seventeenth and Eleventh, as they are stationed upon the border itself. The Third and Sixth are to make camp in far more fertile areas. They will be able to forage without concern, yet you have ordered that they be provided with enough provisions for a sixty-day campaign. This seems to be a waste of much-needed grain, meat and other comestibles."

"Food," said Ullsaard. "We like to call it food. The Eleventh and Seventeenth are our front line against the Mekhani, but they are more of a garrison force. The Third and Sixth are a mobile reserve. They may be in fertile lands now, but I want them to be ready on any given day to march out and take the fight to the Mekhani. That could mean many days of hard march with no forage time, and might even take them into Mekha."

"I see," said Thasalin. His expression conveyed his understanding of the policy, if not his approval.

Ullsaard looked up at the First Captains, standing just a little behind the Brother.

"You have concerns you wish to raise?" asked the king.

"Are we to be quartered in Okhar for the whole winter?" asked Meesiu. "The Third have marched directly from Ersua and we have not yet received cold weather kit."

"Okhar is not as cold as Ersua," replied Ullsaard. He waved a hand at Thasalin. "That said, I'm sure the Brother here can make the necessary arrangements to provide extra blankets, storm sheets and all of the other stuff you might need."

"There is something else, king," said Harrakil when it was clear that Meesiu was not going to say anything further. "My orders are to patrol the border in force, keeping my legion together. It seems counter-productive to do so, when we could cover more ground if I split the Seventeenth into patrol marches. Say, two companies in each?"

"No," said Ullsaard with a shake of the head. He sat up and fixed the First Captain with his stare. "The Mekhani could pick off any number of those marches at will if they choose; they'll think twice about attacking a full legion."

"The savages are crossing the Nakuus at will, king," said Thasalin. "They burn farms and towns, and have waylaid caravans on the roads and ships on the river. It is more efficient to garrison the crossing points and the settlements than send two whole legions marching back and forth for no purpose."

"No purpose?" Ullsaard forced himself to remain calm. "Was I just speaking Salphorian or something? The Mekhani want to divide us and we must not allow that to happen."

"With respect, king, the Mekhani are a bunch of half-brained barbarians," said Meesiu. "You attribute them with a greater sense of strategy than they possess. They are raiding in force, yes, but nothing a strong garrison could not repel."

"And I made the same mistake in Salphoria," Ullsaard growled. "They're just a bunch of idiots, right? No strategy, no tactics, right? Wrong! I lost whole legions because I underestimated what a rabble can do if they get together."

"The Mekhani do not have a single leader," protested Thasalin. "We know that they attack each other as much as they attack us. This is not a concerted effort, it is simply opportunism. They have doubtless heard in some way that we are heavily committed in Salphoria and they have scuttled out of their holes like mice when the cat is busy chasing rats. I think you grant them too much credit, king."

"I'd rather give them unearned credit than see a Mekhani army marching on Geria," said Ullsaard. "Besides, what makes you think I'm happy about sitting around and waiting for them to attack?"

"You aim to launch a campaign in Mekha come the spring?" Thasalin could not hide his incredulity. "You wage war on two fronts?"

"Something like that," grunted Ullsaard. He stood up, forcing the men back a few steps. "My strategy is my own, but my commands have been clear enough. Is there any reason why you cannot carry out your orders?"

The three exchanged glances. No objection was forthcoming.

"Good," said Ullsaard. "Now I will attend to some of my other guests."

With that, the king headed towards the beaded curtain over the door. Pushing through, he came to the main feasting hall. The event was more boisterous here, the wine from Urikh's cellars flowing freely, the naked dancing boys and girls giving great entertainment. Here were the lesser entities of Geria, including the sons, wives and daughters of some of the men within the other chamber.

Ullsaard looked across the crowd of people gathered in groups, circulating slowly and lounging on divans and couches. Men with flushed faces, women with pale make-up, serving staff with dark red tunics and dresses weaving through the mass.

Beside one of the open doors, the darkening evening sky behind her, stood a beautifully proportioned woman with flowing locks of auburn hair, her slender body barely concealed by a few veil-like wraiths of silk, a rainbow-coloured shawl about her shoulders. She regarded the handful of fawning men around her with blatant disinterest, her eyes frequently straying to the other guests. Her gaze met Ullsaard's and stopped roaming, a coy smile turning the corner of the woman's mouth.

"Lerissa." Ullsaard barely breathed the name to himself. When last he had seen her, briefly glimpsed across a banquet, he had been a general summoned by her husband, the governor. Now he was king.

He pushed through the cluster of people that had gathered around the king at his appearance, paying them no heed. At his approach, Lerissa's clamouring consorts scattered like rabbits before a fox, and those folk trailing hopefully behind Ullsaard broke off their following and turned away with disappointed grunts and sighs.

Alone with Lerissa, Ullsaard took her hand and lightly kissed her palm in greeting. She bowed her head in return.

"It is an honour to meet our king," said Lerissa. "I hope that this latest visit to our city is fruitful."

"It has had its ups and downs," said Ullsaard. He winked. "Currently, things are up."

Lerissa smiled again, indulging the bad joke, her eyes roving up and down the king for a few heartbeats before settling again on his face.

"You have the whole of the empire at your disposal, but if there is anything I can do to make your stay here more pleasant, I am happy to oblige," she said.

"Oblige?" Ullsaard almost choked on the word. He looked away for a moment, and his eyes met those of Luia, who was stood at the beaded doorway, one arm on the frame, the other on her hip. She gave him the subtlest of nods, smiled and turned back into the other room. Ullsaard returned his attention to the red-headed woman before him, standing so close he could smell the perfume upon her skin.

"I have a few matters I wish to discuss with you," she said, raising her voice slightly. Ullsaard was confused by this change until she continued. "They are of a private nature, perhaps you would walk with me a while in the gardens."

"I would be happy to," Ullsaard replied, a little stiffly, catching on to her intent. "I could spare a short while to listen to any petition."

Lerissa waved for Ullsaard to proceed out of the door. The rain was falling hard but a black-lacquered roofed path crossed the lawns, lit every twenty paces by blue-glassed lanterns. Ullsaard said nothing at first and instead listened to the pattering of the rain on the wood above his head. Thunder rumbled and lightning flashed in the distance, silhouetting the trees and hedges that bounded the dawnwards extent of the gardens.

"I love Allenya," he said, and instantly wondered why.

"I'm sure if I was to know her, I would love her also," replied Lerissa. She caught Ullsaard's intrigued glance. "As a sister."

Ullsaard nodded and chuckled.

"Why would you speak to me of love?" Lerissa asked.

"Because I want to fuck you," said Ullsaard. Lerissa stopped and turned to him, and the king cursed his lack of subtlety and scant knowledge concerning the finer phrases of seduction.

"A soldier's proposal," laughed Lerissa.

"I'm sorry," said Ullsaard. "You are right, I speak with a soldier's tongue, and very clumsy it is."

"Do not apologise," said Lerissa. "Your honesty is as alluring as your body. Not the sweetest-tongued man in Geria has the courage to speak his intents so plainly to me, though their desires are every bit as obvious."

"Still, it was blunt, and I should not have said it."

Lerissa hooked her arm in Ullsaard's and led him along the path again, taking a fork towards a covered bench set within a tall hedge.

"I think I should very much like to fuck you as well," she said. "It has been a long time since I have had the benefit of a soldier's directness. All of these preening suitors have multiplied since you killed my husband, and there's not a man amongst them."

"I am sorry if my act has deprived you," said Ullsaard.

"Killing Nemtun? Think nothing of it. He was an odious toad, and I have fine apartments and many luxurious clothes and glittering jewels to keep me company now."

"It must have been a hardship, sleeping with such a man."

Lerissa laughed, and the sound was not pleasant.

"If you mean having sex with him, do not worry on my account. Nemtun had only half a cock to his name, and so I was never forced to endure his sweaty attentions."

"Half a cock?"

"An Anrairian warlord caught him through the kilt with the edge of his sword, almost severing the poor member. He had barely enough to piss out of, and nothing to put inside a woman. I feel a little sorry for him in that regard, for his inability to take me as a man doubtless added to his misery and frustration and fuelled his eating and jealousy."

"And yet he was content to share you with other men?"

They had reached the bench and sat beside each other. Lightning and thunder was growing in strength and the rain was hammering at the peaked tiled roof protecting them. Rivulets of water were flowing down the path and between their feet. Their shelter was incomplete and gusts of wind brought the rain onto them, dampening their clothes.

"And that was part of his sickness of mind," said Lerissa. "I was a trophy, and so he gloried in other men being able to sample the delights of my company without ever being allowed to possess me as he did. For my part, I was happy to indulge his perverse needs."

"Why?"

Lerissa ran a hand into Ullsaard's tunic, stroking the muscles of his chest.

"Because I am a woman who has needs like any other."

The wind was blowing stronger, opening the front of Lerissa's flimsy dress, exposing the cleavage of her pert breasts. Ullsaard reached out and mirrored her, placing his hand inside her gown. Rain was coming under the roof steadily, soaking into their hair and clothes, and Ullsaard was fascinated watching the droplets running in trickles down Lerissa's tanned skin.

"Yes, if you would like to fuck me now, that would be good," Lerissa said with a chuckle, lifting back the leather of Ullsaard's kilt to expose his erection.

She turned and slid sideways, straddling him on the bench. He raised his hips, eager to be inside her, pulling aside the last scrap of cloth concealing her chest so that he could engulf a breast in his mouth. She lowered a fraction, giggling as the tip of his member touched her, before she rose up again, teasing.

Ullsaard growled in annoyance and grabbed Lerissa's hips, pulling her down onto him. There was a moment of resistance and then he pushed up, this time growling with delight at the sensation of penetrating her. She rocked back and forth, head swaying from side to side, her wet hair like lashes across his face and chest. Hands clamped to Lerissa's buttocks, Ullsaard lifted her and then pulled her down, timing the movement with thrusts of his hips.

"I've never fucked a king before," Lerissa said with a laugh. She gently dragged her fingernails through his beard. "It's much better than a governor with no cock!"

Ullsaard barely heard her. He grunted and thrust, mind only occupied by the feeling of being inside her, the pressure mounting in his body for release after so much time.

With a snarl, he stood up and swung around, pinning Lerissa to the back of the bench, his hips moving faster and faster. Her hands clawed at his hair and her teeth sank into the exposed muscle of his shoulder, almost drawing blood. The pain added to the pleasure and Ullsaard's loins exploded with his climax, a drawn out, stuttering exclamation torn from him.

"Allenya!" he snarled.

Lerissa slapped him across the face, spitting curses. Ullsaard ignored her, thrusting several more times to expel the last of his seed into her.

"You fuck-happy piece of shit!" Lerissa hissed in his ear, struggling to free herself from his tight grip.

With a final shudder, he pushed into her once more. Legs buckling from his release, Ullsaard flopped to the bench, a broad grin on his face. Another slap brought him to his senses.

"What the fuck are you doing?" he demanded, batting away her next blow with his arm. "Stop that or I'll hurt you."

"You called me Allenya, you pig-son-of-a-whore!" Lerissa shrieked, jumping to her feet and pointing accusingly at the king. "You were thinking of her while you fucked me!"

Recollection of his outburst returned to Ullsaard. He shrugged, unable to deny the image that had been in his head while he had been inside Lerissa.

"I told you that I love my wife," he said in explanation.

"Then go fuck your wife, and every other slut in Askhor, you bastard. I hope your cock shrivels off." Lerissa stormed away, cutting across the grass, the rain quickly soaking her.

Ullsaard watched Lerissa disappear into the blue-tinged gloom, the post-climactic glow assuaging any guilt at what he had done. He thought of Askhos, lurking in the recesses of his mind somewhere.

"I hope you enjoyed that as much as I did, you dead cunt," he whispered.

As he sat there, the rain soaking his skin and clothes, Ullsaard thought numbly about doing one thing and thinking another. An idea struggled to the surface amidst his post-coital fugue. Rubbing the rain into his face to clear his senses, the king stood and looked up into the sky. The idea formed more fully and he smiled.

For too long he had been reacting to events. It was time to take the initiative.

III

It was with some satisfaction that Urikh stood on the balcony of a waterfront house and looked over the activity of the docks. The Brotherhood could take some credit, but not much; many of the duties they had reclaimed had been fulfilled perfectly well by the governor's own measures in the Brotherhood's absence. It was with some reluctance that he pulled his eyes away from the scene and turned to Thasalin, standing to his right.

"You see how the king's ship has been given priority?" said Urikh, pointing to his father's trireme. A flotilla of boats crowded around the vessel, attended to by the floating crane-barge Urikh had commissioned. "With five more of those loading ships, we could double the dock's capacity by freeing up wharf space for smaller vessels."

"To what purpose?" said Thasalin. "The majority of trade ships of that size continue upriver to Narun."

"And that is my purpose," replied Urikh. "Your order spurned the needs of the large merchantmen for decades, forcing them to load and unload at Narun. Now they can do so here with equal ease."

"To what advantage? The traffic on the river will not increase, and so your facility will simply diminish the trade passing through Narun."

Urikh looked askance at the Brother, vexed by his attitude.

"What advantage? We take five per cent of value of all goods unloaded in tax." Urikh shook his head, surprised that he had to explain himself to Thasalin. "More goods equal more tax revenues."

"Taxes taken in Geria or Narun both go into the imperial coffers," said Thasalin, frowning at Urikh's reasoning. "It is more efficient that we build individual centres of excellence for specific tasks. Considerable resources have been invested in Narun; an expense that you have needlessly duplicated here. Over the sum, the empire's wealth has been diminished not enhanced by your actions."

"My father thinks otherwise," said Urikh. "He is keen to foster a spirit of competitiveness, of rivalry, between the provinces. He believes that it breeds better discipline and more productive policies. In allowing the private raising of legions once more, he has sent a signal that men of wealth and influence should take a wider role in the machine of the empire. It encourages the nobles and governors to each take greater responsibility for the development of the provinces."

"While a laudable policy in a marketplace, it is one that is not suitable for the management of the empire," Thasalin said huffily, crossing his arms. "As several would-be legion commanders have discovered in Salphoria, taking risky ventures upon oneself has its dangers. Are you suggesting that we should allow the economy of a province to fail, simply because it lacks the inherent resources? That may be a fine idea for you, as governor of Okhar. What of Anrair and Enair? Do you think your father's homeland should struggle to build roads and raise cities because the wealth of the empire is concentrated in Nalanor, Maasra and Okhar? Askhos founded the empire on the principle that the burden is shared by all and the profits earned by all."

"A noble cause, if ever there was one, concocted in a time of scarcity and famine," Urikh replied with a lofty wave of the hand. "I mean, I would not have any man starve while his neighbour has bread; no more than would I see a man who tills his field tirelessly give half of his money to the lazy man in the next farm who allows his crop to go to ruin."

A twitch of a smile marred Thasalin's severe look, and for a moment Urikh thought he had been caught in some trap of logic by the Brother.

"It matters not," said Thasalin. "As governor you are only the nominal raiser and distributor of monies. The administration of such matters will be applied by the Brotherhood in the manner and form laid down at the founding of the empire."

"No they won't," said Urikh, eliciting a look of surprise from Thasalin that gave the governor a thrill of pleasure. "I have spoken to the king on this matter, and the powers of administering and spending taxation will be retained by the governors, though the application of the governor's policies will be enacted by your sect."

Thasalin was at a genuine loss for words, his mouth opening and closing several times before he finally managed to collect his thoughts enough for an indignant outburst.

"But this is a terrible decision! Your father will set province against province, like wrestlers in the arena. If Enairians were forced to pay a proportionate amount to what they receive from the imperial treasury, they would have to suffer taxes of fifty per cent or more. The province will be dead within three generations as the wealthiest leave to take their business and homes to other provinces!"

The Brother paced back and forth along the balcony, remarkably agitated, giving voice to his concerns in a near-continuous stream of snarled words.

"The governors have no principles. They will waste money on aggrandising and enriching their own positions. What if they start raising more legions in competition with each other? Who would protect the people against the vested interest of their rulers? No, no, this will not be tolerated! Such powers lead only to corruption. Look at Salphoria, or study the history of the tribes before the enlightened wisdom of Askhos. Men are selfish and they are greedy. The Brotherhood exists to temper the worst excesses of that base nature. Give a man free access to the imperial purse and he will invest in those things that further his own ends and profits, and disregard those that are of no interest or use to him."

"I think you are too late to raise your disagreements," said Urikh, pointing down to the docks.

Preceded by his guard, Ullsaard was disembarking from one of the troop boats onto his trireme. A blue flag with the golden face of Askhos fluttered free from the masthead as he stepped aboard.

Urikh glanced across at Thasalin, who gripped the balcony rail with white fingers, his face a mask of trembling anger. The two of them watched as the trireme weighed anchor and slipped out of the docks into the main current, swinging majestically downstream. In silence, the governor and Brother kept the ship in view until it disappeared around a bend in the river.

Urikh knew that he had exaggerated his father's position; the governor was loathe to relinquish more powers to the Brotherhood than were necessary and was adamant that it would be he that controlled the provincial coffers. He expected resistance, from Thasalin and his Brethren, but he was prepared to fight them if needed.

His father had made a mistake bringing them back, at least as far as Urikh's plans were concerned. The power he held as governor, the wealth of Okhar, would be needed when he made his own bid for the Crown.

"It was my belief that the king was returning to Askh," Thasalin said quietly.

"Yes, he told me that he has further discussions to have with the head of your order," said Urikh. He looked at the Brother, whose anger had been replaced with an expression of suspicion. "What of it?"

"Why has his ship just set sail to Hotwards?"

NEAR-MEKHA
Winter, 212th year of Askh

I

It was a sight almost as glorious as an Askhan army. On a litter carried by ten men, Erlaan-Orlassai surveyed his Mekhani warriors; fifty thousand near enough, arrayed in the best war gear their tribes could provide. Under the reign of their new king, the people of Mekha had responded swiftly, gathering what resources they could. With bronze taken from Askhan settlements, forged by armourers and smiths held as slaves from the same raids, the Mekhani made spear and arrow tips that could pierce the armour of a legionnaire. Under the guidance of the great Orlassai and his two strange companions, the Mekhani had learnt afresh how to best cure the hides of the behemodons, fashioning shields and armour almost as strong as metal.

Gone were the stone axes and howling mobs, the infighting and wildness. In quiet warbands led by their shaman-chiefs, the Mekhani horde waited on the dunes for their lord and commander. Behemodons stood sullenly at their chains, their backs heavy with howdahs, catapults and enormous spear-throwing bows constructed under the direction of their returned masters.

Around totem-standards bedecked with bones and feathers, the groups of warriors knelt in the sand, hands raised to their brows as their king approached from dawnwards, the sun at his back.

At Erlaan-Orlassai's command, the bier-bearers stopped and lowered him to the ground. Wood creaked under his massive tread as he rose from his throne and strode down onto the sands of his adopted kingdom. Armoured he was, a few scant patches of rune-etched flesh visible between hard leather plates and rings of bronze and iron. His bizarre, boyish face regarded the army from beneath a helm crested with a dozen long feathers of red and blue and black.

The king grinned his approval, revealing teeth like ailur fangs.

"See the glory of Mekha restored!" Erlaan-Orlassai shouted, raising his arms into the air, the runes upon his tongue twisting his words into the guttural language of the desert people. "Feel now the strength that lies within these lands; a strength long-forgotten but now recalled."

Erlaan-Orlassai drew a curved sword almost as long as a man is tall and held it up, its gilded blade gleaming in the rising sun. Fifty thousand spears were raised in return.

"Who shall rule again?" bellowed the Mekhani king.

"Orlassai!" came the reply, the sands shifting at the thunderous noise.

"Which land shall rule again?" The king's sword swept in an arc, encompassing the surrounding deserts.

"Mekha!"

The blade stopped, pointing to coldwards; neither at the dunes, nor the scrub, nor even at the river that glittered at the edge of the horizon, but at the lands beyond, and a city encircled by mountains.

"Who shall fall to us?" Erlaan roared.

The answering cry was even louder than the others, fuelled by generations of scorn and hatred, powered by fifty thousand grievances and two hundred years of subjugation.

"Askh!"

II

Tossing the gnawed remnants of a bone into the fire, Eriekh reached for another haunch of goat from the table. He sank his teeth into the roasted meat, savouring the taste and the juices running down his chin. He chewed ferociously, enjoying the grinding of flesh between his teeth. Swallowing, he took up a small clay cup half-filled with immon, a Mekhani spirit made from the bark and leaves of various oasis bushes and flavoured with spices. He swilled the liquor around his teeth and gums with eyes closed, delighting in the burning sensation on his tongue and in his throat.

"That is not wise," said Asirkhyr.

Eriekh opened his eyes to see the other hierophant standing at the door of their high-sided tent. Asirkhyr wore only a loincloth, the tattoos on his flesh were barely visible against his sunburnt skin, but the scars stood out in stark relief. In contrast, Eriekh was clad in a skirt of woven grass fibres, a poncho of the same around his shoulders, his head enclosed within a hat of goat hide and feathers.

"What is not wise?" asked Eriekh before taking another bite of goat meat.

"Indulging in the physical pleasures of this world," said Asirkhyr, waving a hand towards his companion's clothes and the meal upon the table.

"We must eat here if we are to live," Eriekh replied, pieces of meat tumbling from his mouth. "What is unwise about enjoying this necessary bodily function?"

"It will be hard to forget when we return to the Temple,"

argued Asirkhyr as he sat on a stool beside the small fire. The hierophant looked up into the clear skies. The air was chill, but he looked to suffer no discomfort. "There is life in this world to sustain us, but you choose to partake of this crude biological process."

"Lakhyri gave us strict instructions not to drain our new allies," said Eriekh, eyes narrowing with suspicion. "It would be unwise of you to forget that."

"I have not leeched a single drop of their essence." Asirkhyr reached a hand out to the low flames burning in the small circle of stones in front of the tent. Runes glowed on his fingertips and the fire flickered for a moment, the flames bending towards his outstretched hand. "Simple combustion; a wasteful method for transmission of energy. And that food you eat? It is inefficient. For us, there are better ways to exist."

"More efficient, yes, but better?" Eriekh smiled and licked a dribble of fat from his fingers. "So you soak the life from a few plants here and there, and maybe the odd reptile or goat? I would say it is a waste of the tongue and belly with which you were born."

"Such pleasures of the flesh are not our concern," snapped Asirkhyr. "Next you will be singing and dancing, and fornicating with the females. It is not our purpose here."

"You think that our great leader does not indulge the needs of his fleshly carcass when he is in this world? How do you think he controls them so well, these bags of instinct and desire? By sharing that world and understanding the failings of it! Do not be concerned for me; I am still focussed on our task."

"And the imbibing of alcohol helps does it?" Asirkhyr looked meaningfully at the earthenware jug next to Eriekh's plate. "Almost a third of that ewer's contents have been consumed. You are drunk."

"Not at all," said Eriekh. "Though I have consumed enough to intoxicate a normal man, I have left only enough alcohol in my system to attain a mood of relaxation and a small increase in confidence, no more."

"We do not have the luxury of these fanciful distractions." Asirkhyr turned his gaze to the sea of campfires surrounding them, his eyes ending upon the huge black pavilion a short distance away, inhabited by Erlaan. "Lakhyri's last communication urged us to action. He has succeeded in persuading the usurper to reinstate the Brotherhood."

"I know this as well as you, as you are aware," said Eriekh. "I do not need reminding of the plan."

"And so why is it that you sit here gorging like an animal instead of discussing the strategy of the upcoming campaign with our new underling?"

Eriekh belched and pushed back his plate.

"The essence of life may sustain us, but it does not wholly sate our natural hunger or thirst. I find that they are more distracting here than in the Temple. Having assuaged these discomfiting sensations I am now able to think more clearly. You should try it; perhaps it would alleviate some of your tetchiness."

"Tetchiness?" Asirkhyr sneered at his companion. "Do not confuse a rightful sense of urgency with short patience."

"And do not confuse my attitude with complacency or indolence!" Eriekh turned on his stool to face the other hierophant directly. "The king of the Mekhani is addressing his shamans. When he is finished, he will attend to us here, as I have instructed him. All things considered, I believe this plan to be more satisfactory than Lakhyri's last attempt. The immortalisation of Askhos was an unnecessary complication. This new approach will reap quicker results."

"I know that you held little regard for our leader's brother, but he achieved a great deal for our cause." Asirkhyr matched the other priest's stare. "When Erlaan is dead, we shall need to find another to replace him. The line of the Blood did away with such considerations."

"Erlaan can produce a successor if needed," said Eriekh. "He is the continuation of the Blood."

"Not while the usurper still lives. When Ullsaard is dead, the full inheritance of the Blood will become Erlaan's."

"You think that Askhos still lingers on in the Crown? No, he is gone, lost to the voids of nothingness. He has paid the price for wanting a worldly life, but in his loss there is opportunity for us."

"We do not know for sure whether Askhos survives or not. It is not without cause to believe his essence may yet exist in this realm."

"It is impossible to say." Eriekh stood and went to the tent, emerging a few moments later with a blanket around his shoulders to ward away the growing cold of the night; an action that earned himself another scornful look from Asirkhyr. "That Ullsaard is himself is certain. On that basis, it is hopeful speculation and nothing more that Askhos remains with us. He may yet be tied to the Crown, but it is not Lakhyri's intent to retrieve him. He has served his purpose, but time grows short for our masters and we need a more aggressive policy."

"You think that a youth can succeed where Askhos failed?"

"No," said Eriekh. "But he is merely a tool, a figure-head. For too long Askhos was allowed to do things his way. With the return of Orlassai we can operate in the open. This will be the final attempt, and it will succeed. The need for secrecy is no more."

"You are correct, this is the final attempt. It is a gamble that Lakhyri takes with all of our futures. Should it fail,

319

there will not be time to engineer another opportunity; the eulanui will return and take what is theirs, and we know the consequences of such a catastrophe. Only by strenuous efforts have we held them at bay for so long. I feel their patience with Lakhyri wears thin indeed. Not for much longer will they believe it is best to wait for the world to be offered as a gift."

Eriekh saw a large figure approaching through the gloom.

"No more of these matters, Erlaan approaches," he warned.

The warped king of the Mekhani strode into the dim light of the hierophant's fire. There was an earnest expression on his twisted face.

"You have received fresh news from Askh?" he asked, sitting on the ground beside the table, his head still level with the priests' such was his size. "The tribes are entranced by my speeches and the shamans are ready; I fear such enthusiasm will wane if that energy is not shortly unleashed."

"We leave tomorrow," said Asirkhyr. "All is in place. We have received confirmation from the Brotherhood that Ullsaard has positioned his legions and they await an attack on Okhar."

"We even know the towns they garrison and the roads they march along," said Eriekh, smiling at the thought of the usurper bringing about his own downfall by the reinstatement of the Brotherhood.

"How?" Erlaan's question caught Eriekh by surprise.

"How do we know these things?" said the hierophant. He glanced at Asirkhyr, who nodded in agreement. "Every Brotherhood precinct contains the Chamber of Words. In that chamber are a number of wax slates inscribed with runes taught to us by the eulanui. When one Brother makes a mark upon those slates, they appear on corresponding tablets at the Grand Precinct."

"They are the same slate in different places? Like the city you hid away in and the Temple?"

Eriekh was again pleased with Erlaan's grasp of the multi-layered nature of reality unveiled by the works of the eulanui.

"That is correct, and thus communication is instantaneous," said the priest. "Your grandfather's killer has laid out his battle plans and the Brotherhood move to enact them. Without even knowing of our existence, they pass on this information. Every shipment of grain, every sandal and nail that goes to the legions is remarked upon by a Brother somewhere, and so we have a clear picture of Ullsaard's movements and plans."

"And where is the man himself?" Erlaan's question was innocently asked, but it caused the priests a moment of consternation.

"He left Geria some time ago, but has not been seen since," admitted Asirkhyr. "Most likely his absence is explained by a return to Salphoria, where as yet there are no Brothers. Believing his hotwards border to be secured, he doubtless has returned to his army to resolve the cause of his delay in his campaign against the Salphors."

"So we still do not yet know what has halted his advance?" Again the question was asked with no guile, but Erlaan was proving to be shrewd in strategic matters.

"The war is beholden to the whim of the usurper," said Eriekh. "To attempt to divine the mind of such a capricious man would be difficult. For all we know, he was struck by a period of nostalgia and simply wished to return to Askh, but not trusting his subordinates in his absence ordered them to pause in their attacks."

"Or perhaps he simply found the climate not to his liking," Asirkhyr added scornfully. "Who can read the motives of such an ill-disciplined and selfish person?"

Runes curved upon Erlaan's brow as he frowned. He shifted his bulk and looked earnestly at the two others. He grinned in lopsided fashion, exposing pointed teeth.

"I have known Ullsaard since I was a child, and marched to war alongside him," Erlaan told them. "Do not underestimate him. That a man of such ill temper and poor education is now ruler of Greater Askhor is evidence of his abilities and his ambition. Some of that we might attribute to the power of the Blood, but at least an equal proportion must be given as credit to the man. He was always competent, more than competent. He can be exceptional, and in overthrowing my grandfather he displayed a grasp of politics equal to his mastery of warfare."

The king-messiah paused and looked at the small fire, his face growing serious.

"He outmanoeuvred Lutaar and all of the governors, dissolved the Brotherhood and took the Crown. If I were you I would look to make an ally of him and not keep him as your enemy."

Eriekh resisted the urge to glance at his fellow priest. Both knew that Lakhyri was doing just such a thing; supporting both Ullsaard and Erlaan, the high priest knew that whichever triumphed would mean victory also for the disciples of the eulanui. If Ullsaard proved himself the more capable ruler and defeated Erlaan, nothing was lost. For all of the effort that had been directed at the Mekhani resurgence, that support could be withdrawn quickly and the threat from hotwards allowed to wither and die if it served the order's interests better to do so.

"You are the rightful heir," said Asirkhyr, filling the silence left by Eriekh. "It is you who has the right to fulfil Askhos's legacy and no other."

Taking this assurance with a slight nod, Erlaan stood, stretching up to his full height.

"We set out for Okhar tomorrow to bring about that day," said the Great King.

"Not so," said Asirkhyr. He continued as Erlaan's monstrous frown returned. "We will cross the Nakuus into Okhar, as agreed, but then turn duskwards into Ersua. Ullsaard has Okhar well guarded and expects any attack to head for the Greenwater and Geria. We shall not oblige him."

Erlaan laughed and punched one hand into the other.

"From Ersua we can strike at Nalanor, Okhar or Anrair. Ullsaard will have to pull back his legions from Salphoria and even then he will be stretched thin protecting every approach to the Askhan Gap. He will have to either pull his forces back to the Wall to guard Askh, giving us free reign over the rest of the empire, or his legions will be spread out and easily overcome. I assume that with your information from the Brotherhood you have a route through Okhar that will keep our intent secret for as long as possible?"

"We do," said Eriekh. "Any small measure of resistance the Askhans can muster will be swept away by your army. Ullsaard forgets that the weather is much kinder in these parts and does not expect any attack until spring. By the start of summer, the empire will be yours again, and with the combined might of Mekha and Askhor, Salphoria will fall by next winter."

"I wish I could see Ullsaard's face when he realises he's lost the empire even more quickly than he won it." Erlaan's cracked lips curved in a bestial grin. "His reign will be so brief, it will make the rule of a Salphorian king look like an ageless dynasty!"

OKHAR

Late Winter, 212th year of Askh

I

Seeing his army marching across several rough wooden bridges thrown across the Nakuus, Erlaan wondered if Askhos had enjoyed the same feeling of power when he had loosed the First Legion against the tribes of Askhor. This was the start of something new, a fresh force of nature arising to claim the world.

The king-messiah strode at the head of the Mekhani host, tens of thousands of warriors following him onto Askhan-claimed soil. Behemodons waded effortlessly through the sluggish river, urged on by the goads of their mahouts. The wood of the bridges shook with the tramp of so many feet.

The last time he had passed this way, Erlaan had been wrapped up in concerns for his father and himself. Though he had come of age, he realised now that he had still been a boy in mind. When Ullsaard had defeated Cosuas's army and Lakhyri – masquerading as high brother – had ushered Erlaan and his father to safety, he had been afraid and uncertain. He had doubted whether he would ever see Askh again.

Certainly he had not foreseen the manner of his return at that bleak time. Now the fear and doubts were gone.

He had lain to rest the worries of his father and taken up the mantle of a true king. As his body had been strengthened, so had his ambition and resolve. He could scarcely believe that he had once thought himself unfit to become a ruler. Perhaps that was the price of a position inherited, not earned. Not so on this day. It was not by right of the Blood or accident of birth that he would become lord of the world, but by his own hand and his own will.

His thoughts strayed from Askh to Ullsaard. He admitted that he was thankful to the usurper; for his strong words, his guidance and for forcing Erlaan to fight for what he believed to be his. The priests thought Ullsaard was blunt, if not outright stupid, but Erlaan was going to assume nothing. After so much effort to take it, the Askhan king would not relinquish his grip on the Crown without a hard fight.

The horde of Mekhani warriors were chivvied into a more organised column of march as they struck out into Okhar, heading almost directly coldwards in accordance with Eriekh's information. Midday had passed and the army was still divided by the Nakuus when Erlaan's rune-gifted sight spotted his scouts returning from dawnwards. Skittering through the grass on the backs of their lacertils, the outriders were returning with speed and purpose.

The only reason for such haste would be a sighting of Askhan forces. It was inevitable that an army of the size Erlaan commanded could not progress unseen, but it was a blow that their first encounter with the enemy was so soon. As the lizard-riders approached, Erlaan passed the word for the army to halt and wait for those on the other side of the river to catch up.

"If we are discovered, we cannot allow the Askhans to escape to take word to their king," Erlaan told the cabal of the oldest shamans that served as his general staff. "We must obliterate them entirely."

"As you say, mighty Orlassai," one of them replied, Erlaan could not remember his name; the shamans all appeared as shrivelled, near-dead husks to the king-messiah's eyes, their font of life energy almost spent. "We shall slay them all."

Several of the shamans left to help with the mustering of the army from the march, leaving Erlaan with two hunched, aging companions. He ignored them, wondering where Eriekh and Asirkhyr would be found. They were probably still with the rear of the column, ensuring that there was no dawdling.

Riding up to their ruler, the handful of scouts leapt from the backs of their lizard mounts and prostrated themselves in the patchy grass. Their obeisance gave the king-messiah mixed thoughts; such unthinking dedication was gratifying, but having been raised in the court of Askh where there was little formality Erlaan could not help but feel a small amount of embarrassment at their abasement. He signalled for them to rise.

"You have sighted Askhans?" said the king.

"Yes, divine Orlassai," said the chief of the scouts, a haggard-faced elder called Inomasai. He turned and pointed back to where he had come from. "Soldiers riding on giant snakes, in the hills towards the dawn."

Erlaan said nothing about the vagueness of this report, consoling himself that when the new empire was established the Mekhani would learn of such things as hours and miles. He looked to where the scout pointed and saw that the ground rose up to a steep, scrub-filled slope about four miles away. If the scouts were there, the Askhan force for which they were the eyes would be another five to ten miles behind.

"Did they see you?" he demanded.

Inomasai shrugged and looked at his underlings, who cautiously shook their heads.

"They gave no cry of warning, so it is not likely, mighty Orlassai," said Inomasai. "I stayed for a while hidden in the grass and they did not change direction."

"And which direction was that?"

The scout hesitated before replying. The Mekhani used landmarks and well-known trails to describe places in the desert; without such references, Inomasai was finding it difficult to explain what he had seen.

"They move along the hills, from the cold to the hot," said the chief of scouts, waving his hand in the direction of the scouts travel. "They head towards the river."

Absorbing this information without comment, Erlaan turned his gaze back to the Nakuus, several miles behind. At a rough guess, there were still more than a tenth of his army to cross the river. He had to make a decision.

"Send word to the rear to cross as soon as possible," he told the remaining shamans. "The rest of the army will march to dawnwards. If the enemy scouts spot us they must not be allowed to give the Askhans too much warning. We will fall upon them like a scouring wind and sweep onto whatever force it is they protect."

"As you command, mighty Orlassai," the shamans said in unison, bowing low before scampering away.

While the orders rippled through the army, Erlaan loosened his sword in its sheath. The thought of battle excited him. This magnificent body he had been given by the sect of the Temple had not been truly tested yet. He wanted to know just what sort of ruin he was capable of unleashing.

It took a while for the Mekhani to settle on their new course, and there were a few disagreements as shaman-chiefs argued over who took which position in the line.

While he waited, Erlaan sent Inomasai to round up the scouts and press into the hills ahead of the main attack. From all around, the lizard riders converged, more than four thousand of them advancing as a screen.

Eventually the desert-dwellers arranged themselves on the new line of advance and with a signal from Erlaan the army set out at a fast pace towards the hills. Erlaan loped to the front with long strides, golden eyes scanning the hillsides for signs of the Askhans. The lacertil riders had reached the bottom of the slopes when the king-messiah spotted the first kolubrids.

Even from this distance, Erlaan could see the exchange of arrows and slingshots as the two skirmishing screens clashed. Far from sweeping away all before them, the Mekhani advanced faltered quickly, losing dozens to the volleys of the Askhans' bellows bows. This was the first thing to give Erlaan pause; the number of kolubrid scouts present indicated a larger force than he had anticipated, perhaps even a full legion. It made little difference, he decided. Even a full legion numbered no more than five or six thousand legionnaires; little match for the tens of thousands at Erlaan's command.

Despite their best efforts, the lacertils were driven back down the slopes, and then further onto the grassland, harassed by the bellows bows of their foes. Erlaan reckoned his main army was a mile away, no more. Even if the Askhan force had already received warning, they would have no more than a six or seven mile head start over the king-messiah. Certainly that did not give them enough time to prepare a march camp or other defensive position, and though a smaller, nimbler force, the armoured legionnaires would not move as swiftly over the rough ground as Erlaan's warriors. It would only be a matter of time before they were caught.

When the king-messiah was half a mile from the foot of the closest hill, he saw the sun glinting on spear points and shields ahead. It seemed that the enemy commander had come to the same conclusion as Erlaan and had decided to fight instead of flee. Phalanx after phalanx of legionnaires appeared at the crest of the hills, their standards flapping.

The soldiers were as easy to see to Erlaan's eyes as if they were no more than an arm's reach away. He recognised the standard and colours of the Seventeenth. Things may have changed since he had left the empire, but when last Erlaan had been in Askh, the Seventeenth had been commanded by Harrakil. Dredging through his memories, Erlaan recalled that he was a good commander – bad commanders did not become First Captains – but not of remarkable talent or great achievement. He had spent most of Ullsaard's war for the Crown guarding Governor Adral of Nalanor.

Raising his hand, Erlaan called for the army to halt and spread out for attack. As the order rippled through the tribes, the Mekhani moved into position, placing behemodons between their warbands, while the crews in the howdahs readied their war machines.

While this continued, the Askhans were also preparing. Erlaan could see kolubrid riders hurrying back and forth between the First Captain and the company commanders, carrying the details of the battle plan. Positioned at the top of the steepest slopes, the legion had the advantage of ground; the kolubrids were trying to push back Erlaan's skirmishers and gain the flanks, but so far were being held between the two armies.

"Let us see how you fare against a commander who knows how you fight," Erlaan growled.

He had spent much of the winter preparing the

shaman-chiefs for such an encounter, impressing upon them the need to avoid challenging the Askhan spear blocks head-on. It had taken some considerable time, but the king-messiah had hammered home the importance of tactics and manoeuvre over individual bravery and strength. The Mekhani could not hope to defeat a phalanx one-to-one, on attack or defence; with his subordinates, Erlaan had drilled his troops to feint against the front of the enemy before using their speed to get between the Askhan formations to attack from the side and rear.

Erlaan flexed his fingers in anticipation and was about to draw his sword to signal the attack when a doubt stole into his thoughts. Seeing through the cloud of pleasure that had filled his mind at the prospect of battle, he paused for a moment to think about the situation.

"Why does he fight?" the king-messiah asked himself. "What can he hope to gain?"

One possibility was that Harrakil had despatched part of his force to take warning to Ullsaard while his legion acted as rearguard. That seemed a reasonable explanation. There was another, and it unsettled Erlaan. What if, against all expectation, the Askhan force was stronger than one legion? The kolubrids had fought so hard to keep the heights, it was not beyond the realm of possibility that more legionnaires lay in wait beyond the hills.

Growling in irritation, Erlaan weighed up the possibilities. The show of defiance could be an elaborate bluff by Harrakil, conceived to fool Erlaan into thinking the Askhans were stronger than they were; an act of desperation on being confronted by such an overwhelming force. Yet, if it was not a bluff...

Erlaan wished he had someone with which to discuss his thoughts, but his priestly companions were nowhere to be seen, and the shamans were incapable of providing any useful insight with such a conversation. The decision remained Erlaan's alone, without advice or encouragement.

His instinct was to attack and have the matter settled, but he knew that good commanders did not act on instinct alone. Harrakil thought that he faced the Mekhani of the past; barbaric and impetuous. His plan would be based upon that assumption. Thinking further along this line, tugging at his thoughts like a stray thread, Erlaan considered the consequences of what might happen. The Askhans knew the Mekhani would attack, and that was what they wanted to happen, for whatever reason. It followed, Erlaan concluded, that if he was simply to withdraw, Harrakil would be left with the difficult choice of coming down onto the grasslands, revealing his true strength in the process, or simply letting the Mekhani move away to wreak whatever havoc they intended.

"We will withdraw!" Erlaan announced.

This proclamation was greeted with some consternation by his subordinates. The nearby shamans muttered briefly to each other until one was nominated as spokesman. He knelt before Erlaan, eyes fixed on the ground.

"Forgive us for doubting your wisdom, which is brought to you upon the winds from the sky, mighty Orlassai," the shaman began. "We seek only to understand your impeccable will. The enemy are few and we are many, and you alone could destroy these fools. Why do we not attack? Is it now your intent that they escape, to take word to their king of the great and terrible foe that they face?"

As he considered his next words, Erlaan looked at the Askhan legion intently, unsure whether he was making an error. It had been Asirkhyr's intent to keep their presence as secret as long as possible. Such a factor seemed less important now when judged against the losses that a battle would inflict, before the campaign proper had begun. A few days mattered little measured over a season of war.

"They are beneath us," declared Erlaan. "When we wet our spears, it will be with the blood of men, not dogs. If they are truly worthy of facing me, they will come after us, and we shall oblige them with the deaths they desire."

This seemed to satisfy the shamans, who nodded and smiled in reply.

"Pass on my will to my brave warriors," Erlaan told them with a wave of his hand. "The towns and people of Ersua should not be made to wait too long for our cruel attention."

As soon as the shamans had departed, they were gone from Erlaan's mind. He drew his sword and pointed it towards the icon of Askhos as the centre of the Seventeenth's line. Drawing in a deep breath, he roared his next words, the runes on his tongue and lips sending them clear and loud up to the legionnaires on the hill.

"Know that I am Orlassai, the reborn king of Mekha! Run like dogs to your cowardly master. Tell your king that his time is short. I desire his Crown and I shall take it. If he kneels before me and presents the Crown to me I shall be merciful and spare his people!"

While the Mekhani turned away and headed coldwards, there was movement in the Askhan ranks. Two companies parted and a figure rode forward on the back of an ailur. Even with his enhanced eyes, Erlaan could not make out the noble's features, but the glint of gold when the man raised his spear was an unmistakeable declaration. A shout carried on the wind, picked up only by the king-messiah's ears; words that amused and concerned Erlaan in equal measure, for the man who uttered them could not have known that they would be heard.

"You want my Crown? Come and take it, you goat-fucker!"

As the cry drifted away on the wind, the hills were alive with movement. More golden icons appeared, and the flapping standards of many companies. Rank after rank of spearmen marched up the crests of the hills, until the Askhan line was nearly a mile wide.

Four whole legions stared down at the departing Mekhani army.

Pleased that he had not fallen into the trap, Erlaan smiled. The priests had been wrong about Ullsaard. He was here, and he had a force almost the equal of Erlaan's. Almost equal, but not quite. In the past, four legions would be a match for fifty thousand Mekhani, but not now. With the advantage of the hills, he was safe, but on the level ground of Okhar the advantage was with the numbers. If the Askhan king wanted to come down and start a fight, Erlaan was happy to let him.

But he knew it would not be that simple. Ullsaard had already caught up a step, even if he could not yet match Erlaan. Given the chance, he would strike when the right opportunity presented itself; but that was not now.

"We will finish this another time!" Erlaan cried out.

With that, he sheathed his sword, turned his back on the Askhans and walked away.

II

The departing Mekhani army was soon obscured by the cloud of dust left in its wake. Ullsaard watched them for some time, ignoring the presence of Harrakil to his right. Finally the First Captain broke the silence.

"Are we going to let them get away?" Harrakil asked, his tone conveying his disapproval of this course of action.

Ullsaard turned slowly in the saddle and fixed the legion commander with his stare.

"Do you want to fight them?" said the king. "You can count as well as I can."

"Had we struck earlier, while they were still crossing the Nakuus, their advantage of numbers would have been less. Fifty thousand Mekhani are no match for four legions."

"You saw how organised they were," said Ullsaard. "These are not the Mekhani we have fought in the past. That creature, the one that called itself Orlassai, has changed the way they fight. They had war machines and armour. When I was last here, every legionnaire was worth five Mekhani. That isn't true with this lot. Why risk a battle when we can let them do as much harm to themselves?"

"I don't follow your meaning," said Harrakil.

Before Ullsaard could answer, several officers arrived to request orders from their commander, including messengers from the other First Captains. The king told them to wait and continued to voice his theory to Harrakil.

"This reborn king, whatever or whoever he is, knows how to forge an army, but he is ignorant in strategy. It's clear he intends to march on Ersua, which is a mistake."

"How so?" said Harrakil, concerned at the prospect. "From Ersua, they can attack at the heart of the empire."

"Possibly, but our opponent's thinking has been clouded by his time in the desert," replied Ullsaard. "Though the sun shines here and the weather is not so foul, remember that it is still winter. Once the Mekhani reach the Ersuan Hills, they'll find the climate not so much to their liking. The winter stores of the towns will be at their lowest. I'd like to see how he plans to feed an army of that size in the late snows."

"You would just let them run loose over Ersua?"

Ullsaard shrugged.

"Better one province is ravaged than we lose the whole empire," said the king. "We're still unprepared for a straight battle. There are half a dozen ways for them to head coldwards, so even if we could force march ahead of them, where would we set our next line of defence? We're no more secure trying to protect Ersua than Okhar. Give them time to lose a few thousand warriors to winter supply and then we'll see what sort of shape they're in for a fight."

"So what are we going to do now?" Ullsaard did not like Harrakil's accusatory tone, but chose to overlook it for the moment. Clearly the First Captain was disappointed at marching several hundred miles only to see his enemy allowed to walk away.

"We came here to kill some Mekhani, so that's what we're going to do," the king explained patiently. He signalled for the heralds to attend him. "Send word to the governors. They are to mobilise what legions they have to guard their borders with Ersua. We'll let the Mekhani have free rein for the moment, but I want the passes and crossings into Okhar, Nalanor and Anrair guarded. Also, I will have orders to convey to the army camp in Salphoria. I want a couple of legions to move closer to Ersua, just in case the Mekhani want to make trouble to dawnwards."

"And our orders, king?" asked one of the captains.

"Two thousand men from the Third will follow the enemy, with five hundred kolubrids. They are to harass them as much as possible and cause whatever trouble they can. Pick a captain that is good on his initiative, willing to be a bit daring; but warn him not to get drawn into a pitched battle. He is to raid and annoy, nothing more. He should create the impression that he has a larger force.

I want the Mekhani to think that all four legions are following."

Ullsaard smiled at the officers waiting on his next words.

"The rest of us?" said the king. He pointed hotwards, towards the Mekha desert. "We'll be teaching these goat fondlers not to leave their homes unprotected. I want every Mekhani town, village and tent within a hundred miles of the border razed to the ground. We'll show these bastards what it means to start a war with Askh. Prepare the army for night march; I want to be across the Nakuus by dawn without the enemy seeing us."

Their orders given, the crowd of officers dispersed back to their legions, leaving only Harrakil and his few staff captains. The commander of the Seventeenth looked perturbed by Ullsaard's chosen course.

"Thirty days," the king assured the First Captain. "Thirty days of fun while the weather improves to coldwards, then we'll come back and give this goat-fucker a battle he'll not forget."

When Harrakil and the others were gone, Ullsaard remained where he was, watching the dwindling bank of dust on the horizon. For all his outward confidence, the appearance of the Mekhani, and the monstrous creature that led them, concerned the king greatly. The timing of this attack was too neat; the Mekhani had to know their foes were heavily committed in Salphoria. Though he would never tell his subordinates as such, Ullsaard had another reason for staying hotwards of the empire. There was no Brotherhood here.

Whether directly involved or not, the king did not trust Lakhyri for a moment, despite the words of reconciliation he had offered. It was clear that the Brotherhood still had an agenda of their own. Kalmud and Erlaan were still unaccounted for, ready to be offered up to reclaim the throne for the heirs of Lutaar. Ullsaard was sure that Lakhyri knew where they were.

More than that, there was something about the High Brother that disconcerted Ullsaard, and it was not just those disturbing gold eyes behind the silver mask. There was a stench, a presence about Lakhyri, which Ullsaard could not put his finger on but unsettled him nonetheless. He had the same feeling about this Orlassai fiend. Something in the king's Blood was put on edge by both of them, and he was always ready to trust his instincts in such matters.

There was more than just Ullsaard's future as king at stake. He could not begin to understand fully the unnatural benefits and risks associated with the Blood coursing through his veins. He did not know the extent of Askhos's influence, or the implications of the First King's continued survival. The new Mekhani leader had called himself the 'reborn king' and that had struck a chord in Ullsaard's thoughts. He would have to tread carefully; not just militarily and politically, but personally as well. A wrong move could allow Askhos to gain more control, perhaps permanently, condemning Ullsaard to a future as a tiny fragment of spirit imprisoned within the immortal king.

He shuddered at the thought and turned his ailur back towards his army. The giant cat was a young creature called Storm, bought in Geria. She had a more placid temperament than Blackfang, but the king missed his faithful mount and for a moment wondered how she fared in the camp in Salphoria. Such thoughts led Ullsaard to his family unknowingly held hostage in Magilnada. His fingers tightened on the reins and Storm snarled in annoyance at the sudden tug at her mask.

One thing at a time, Ullsaard cautioned himself. First, the Mekhani. When that's settled, the reckoning with Anglhan would be had. As Ullsaard rode down the slope after his departing legions, he entertained himself picturing the many punishments he would inflict upon the treacherous Salphor; an exercise that lasted for several hours.

ERSUA
Early Spring, 212th year of Askh

I

Bedraggled and sullen, the winding column of Mekhani warriors laboured on through the unending rain, the narrow track they were following a slippery river of mud that made every step treacherous. Standing at the crest of the pass, looking back over his foundering army, Erlaan contented himself with the thought that another two days' of hard march would bring them to the fertile plains of Nalanor. His tired and hungry followers would find plenty to forage and dry beds when they fell upon the unsuspecting town of Aarisk at the coldwards end of the pass.

It had been hard going, but driven on by the speeches of their king the Mekhani had suffered the depredations of the march without undue complaint. The barns and farms of Ersua had provided little enough spoils, barely enough to keep the army going as it pressed coldwards, and the last of the looted supplies had been spent three days ago. Some hard rations remained, and three behemodons had been slaughtered for food; there was nothing for them to carry and their deaths were more useful than their continued lives. The promise of food and shelter, and the guiding words of their ruler, kept the Mekhani advance moving, when many had been keen to return to their homes.

Further down the defile, several thousand more Mekhani tribespeople followed the army. In groups they had fled coldwards, as families and tribes, driven out of the desert by Askhan attacks. They had brought with them terrifying stories of Ullsaard's assault; of women and children butchered and whole towns burnt to the ground; oases despoiled and the valuable groves along the wadis razed. As dozens of refugees had become hundreds and later thousands, Erlaan had been forced to make more speeches, turning the plight of the men's families into another wrong done to them that must be repaid by the Askhans.

It seemed to Erlaan a deliberate policy of Ullsaard to drive from dawnwards to duskwards, herding the fearful Mekhani over the Nakuus and after their army. More mouths to feed and woes from home increased the burden on the Mekhani king, but Ullsaard had not reckoned for Erlaan's rune-powered gift of speech, or his personal determination to reclaim the Crown of the Blood. Where a lesser man would be tempted to turn back and prevent the burning of other villages and the slaughter of more families, Erlaan felt no such compunction. He took it as good news that Ullsaard was fearful of confronting the Mekhani army in open battle.

The news from the fleeing tribes also confirmed the king-messiah's suspicions that the Askhan force that had been shadowing and raiding his army for the last twenty-six days was but a small force, also intended to slow the Mekhani advance and delay their attack into the heart of the empire. This too would fail. Annoying as the loss of foraging parties were, as irksome as the flurries of night-time ambushes on the camps, the threat from the Askhans was easy to dismiss.

Once they were over the mountains, circumventing the Askhan forces no doubt gathering at the coldwards border with Anrair, the Mekhani would have the riches of Nalanor to pillage at will. Even in his most pessimistic predictions, Ullsaard would not have considered the Mekhani crossing the mountains where the peaks were highest. In this respect he had not accounted for the Behemodons. Thought sluggish in the cool weather, the massive beasts could carry far more than a whole caravan of abadas, and such was the skill of their riders the treacherous paths and trails of the pass were no obstacle.

Erlaan turned to Asirkhyr and Eriekh, who had not left the king's side since his decision to decline battle after crossing the Nakuus. They had been soft in their admonition for the choice Erlaan had made, and were evidently becoming more aware of their precarious position, cut off from their fellow priests of the Temple and the network of the Brotherhood. Not that this stopped them from reminding Erlaan on occasion that he derived his power from their sorceries.

"The weather will improve once we cross the shoulder," he told the two priests. "The descent will be much swifter. We should be able to attack Aarisk in three days at the most, probably two."

"There is a Brotherhood precinct in that town," said Asirkhyr. "They will send word to the Brotherhood of our attack. It would be better if our passing across the mountains would go unnoticed."

Erlaan shrugged sending a stream of water cascading from his armour.

"There is nothing our foes can do to stop us," said Erlaan. "It would take twenty days for a legion to march around the mountains, thirty if Ullsaard wants to come up from Mekha, by which time we will be hundreds of miles away. I think it might be a wise course to spread the word of our arrival. We can save time and bloodshed if the towns in our path are given the chance to surrender."

"And who would you send on such a delegation?" said Eriekh. "The Mekhani cannot negotiate and you cannot leave the army."

"You will go," said Erlaan, pointing at Eriekh. "You will be my herald, with a bodyguard of, say, a thousand warriors."

"Your herald?" Indignation wrinkled the aged priest's face. "I am a hierophant of the eulanui, not your messenger boy."

"And you will be returning to Mekha," Erlaan told Asirkhyr, ignoring the other's protest. "This is, after all, just the vanguard of my army. At least another fifty thousand warriors will have gathered at Akkamaro. You will lead them against Ullsaard's forces, if they remain in Mekha. If not, a second attack towards Geria will meet little resistance. It would be foolish to think that a single army will win us Askh. I will subjugate Nalanor and Anrair, while you will secure Okhar and Maasra. Ullsaard knew what he was doing, isolating Askhor from the other provinces."

"I do not think he will repeat the mistakes of Lutaar and Nemtun and concede such territories without battle," said Asirkhyr. "I am no military commander, and we cannot trust the shamans to fare any better against the legions. You would throw away thousands of warriors for little gain."

"I do not need you to win battles, simply to fight them," said Erlaan. "Ullsaard cannot fight both us and the Salphors at the same time. If he withdraws his troops from Salphoria, his enemies there will sweep to the border and retake Magilnada, and I cannot see how the usurper will allow that to happen. His entire goal has been the conquest of Salphoria, and his arrogance is such that he will believe he can defeat me whilst maintaining his strength to duskward. He will bring together what legions he can to defeat me, leaving the hotwards and dawnwards provinces ripe for the picking. It is my intent to give him no opportunity but to surrender."

"You think that is likely?" said Eriekh. "He will not relinquish the Crown while he lives, that is the extent of his stubbornness."

"And should he refuse, he will make an enemy of the governors," Erlaan said with a toothy grin. "With certain assurances to their continued power, they will be happy to endorse me as the rightful heir of the Crown and withdraw their support from Ullsaard. He forgets how easy it was for him to turn the provinces against Lutaar, and I shall use the same weapon."

The two said nothing, searching for further arguments but finding none. Eriekh sneered as he spoke.

"Do not fall victim to overconfidence," said the priest. "It is one thing for the governors to accept a renegade like Ullsaard; it is another for them to bow to the rule of the Mekhani."

"That is why I will offer to send the Mekhani back to the desert if the governors recognise my claim," replied Erlaan. "I am monstrous and unnatural, and it will be hard for them to accept me, but I will offer no alternative. As my followers they will see the empire expanded with Mekha, and against such strength Salphoria cannot hold. As Ullsaard did, I will show them that the protection of the king is worthless. If they refuse, I will destroy them, one by one."

Obviously still rankled by his appointment to herald, Eriekh stalked away, sour-faced and grumbling to himself.

Asirkhyr remained, distaste at Erlaan's edicts written in his glare.

"What of the Brotherhood?" said the priest. "You cannot reveal to them the secrets you have learned, and they cannot be cowed by your threats."

"Lakhyri controls the Brotherhood, as he has always done. They are the least of our problems."

Erlaan was tired of the priest's protests and turned his back on Asirkhyr. The king called for his council to attend him and as the shamans gathered, he watched Asirkhyr hurrying off to catch up with Eriekh. The king-messiah was sure the priests thought he overstepped his mark with his plans and commands, but he did not care. Their schemes were convoluted and time-consuming. If Erlaan had learnt anything from his grandfather's faltering and Ullsaard's usurpation, it was that direct action brought the swiftest and surest results.

The army marched on up the pass, the rain unrelenting. Erlaan moved through the column, offering words of counsel and encouragement. Wherever the king-messiah passed, the hearts of the Mekhani were lifted, his presence enough to bolster their resolve.

A windy and wet night followed, during which Erlaan's followers found what shelter they could at the height of the pass. Though food was low, the meltwater and rain provided plenty to drink, and grumbling stomachs were easier to ignore with thoughts of Aarisk's large grain stores and fertile pastures just two days away.

Dawn brought some relief as the mountain storm dropped in severity, reducing to a constant drizzle. As the morning light spread up the pass, Erlaan could feel the hopes of the army rising as well. The path down was steep but widened quickly and the sun continued to strengthen, occasionally breaking through the clouds. By noon, the head of the column had reached the floor of the valley, and word came back that foraging parties had some success, killing deer, goats and birds by the score. They had also found two swift rivers, alive with fish, and with nets and ropes, more was added to the stockpile of food. It would be far from a feast, but little fare was better than none at all.

Erlaan renewed his promises of what was to come, and described the riches that awaited the Mekhani once Askh was theirs, though he knew that they would share little of such plunder. He felt no guilt at using them in this way. The red-skinned tribesmen were still lesser people. Despite everything, Erlaan considered himself still an Askhan; purebred of Askh and the legitimate heir to the Crown of the Blood no less.

As he walked along the files of warriors wending their way down the pass, he conceded that the Mekhani were not as savage as he had once thought, and the knowledge that they were but the remnants of an advanced civilisation gave him some pause for thought. For all that, an upbringing built upon prejudice and disdain could not be easily overcome and Erlaan considered his new allies clever animals at best. Their superstitions alone were reason enough to dismiss them as anything more than useful minions. Come the war with Salphoria, Erlaan would put his trust in good, honest Askhan legionnaires. If the Mekhani proved capable he would consider admitting them to the legions in due course.

With such thoughts occupying him, Erlaan passed the long day of marching. He felt not the slightest fatigue from his walking, his body sustained by the same aura of energy that the denizens of the Temple existed upon. Part of him hoped the people of Aarisk would put up a fight; he had already felt the small thrill of feeding upon his near-dead father and the thought of drawing on the essence of several thousand deaths filled him with excitement.

The day and night passed without incident; apparently Ullsaard's shadowing force had thought better of coming into the mountains after the Mekhani. They were most likely dashing back to hotwards to inform their master of Erlaan's cunning change of route. Though he tried hard not to listen to the false praise of the shamans and his warriors, Erlaan realised that he was truly marked out as special. Each day, testing himself against Ullsaard and the elements, Erlaan felt stronger and wiser. There was not a challenge he could not overcome.

Early in the following day's march the rain came again, hard and steady. At first the Mekhani had delighted in the water that fell from the sky, so rare in their lands. Now they endured the wet and cold in silent misery, quietly pining for their sun-drenched homes and the cool evenings of the desert. Erlaan barely felt the pattering on his thick skin, though the rattle of rain on his armour became a thunderous din if he concentrated on it.

Mile after mile the army trudged, down towards the plains of Nalanor. Though he had hoped to come upon Aarisk that day, the constant rain made even the surest path a quagmire to wade along, and the king-messiah was forced to call a halt at dusk; the terrain was too treacherous to press on through the night.

"The town will wait for us," he assured his followers with a smile. "Before the sun sets again, you shall see for yourselves our next prize."

Erlaan no longer had the need to sleep, though sometimes he would lie down and close his eyes, picturing the palace of Askh or the fields of Nalanor. There were coughs and sneezes from across the camp, each sounding near at hand to Erlaan's supernatural hearing. The thought of disease reared in his mind; something he had not previously considered. The chill and the damp might prove more of an enemy than he had thought. He would do well to head dawnwards from the mountains, towards the border of the Greenwater between Nalanor and Maasra, where the climate was hotter. He considered towns along the route that would make suitable stopping points and drew up a mental map to follow. When he had marched with Ullsaard, he had not paid a second thought to the problems of feeding and equipping an army; all of that had been carried out by lesser officers. The Mekhani had no such appreciation of logistics and so he would have to do his best in absence of quartermasters and caravans.

As dawn broke on the next day, the day when the Mekhani would fall upon Aarisk like a red storm, the scouts were sent out and the rest of the army prepared to break their makeshift camp. Erlaan was eager to get moving and chivvied the shaman-chiefs into action, impressing upon them the closeness of their goal. Aarisk was built upon the shoulder of a mountain at the far end of the pass, perhaps no more than four hours away. The Mekhani had already passed several huts and lodges and farms – abandoned for the moment – which had caused considerable interest and excitement in the desert warriors. They seemed as enthusiastic for the coming attack as their king.

Tasking the shamans to hurry up, Erlaan headed after the front of the column, wanting to be the first to lay eyes on the Nalanorian town that would become his base for attacks into the rest of the empire.

Midmorning, Erlaan guessed it to be around the second or third hour of low watch, a party of scouts returned. They were agitated as they reported their findings to the shaman council. Erlaan intervened to find out what was wrong.

"The town, it is broken," one of the scouts was saying.

"Broken?" said Erlaan, wondering if he had misheard. "What do you mean?"

"It is broken, great Orlassai, ruler of the skies," the scout said again, struggling for the right words. "It is empty. The walls, they are broken. The fields, they are no more. There is nothing but the dust and the smoke."

"Smoke? Dust? Make sense!" snapped Erlaan.

"Come with us, great Orlassai, and we shall show you." The scout pointed to a ridge that curved coldwards, cutting across the arc of the valley floor. "This way is quickest."

On foot, the scouts led their king up the slope and, picking their way carefully between the rocks and scrubs, they ventured out onto the narrow ridge. The wind was strong, but Erlaan was grateful that the rain was little more than occasional showers.

Following a well-worn goat track, the party made their way along the ridgeline, at times meandering around great cracks in the rocks, sometimes scrambling across fissures and over patches of loose scree. In places the slope dropped down sheer. Though he was certain his toughened skin and flesh could withstand sword and spear, the king-messiah eyed these cliff faces uneasily, not certain if even he could survive such a drop. The Mekhani were labouring by the time they reached the height of the ridge, though Erlaan's heart barely beat any faster and his breath came easily.

He pulled himself up the last stretch of an escarpment after the others. From here he could see down the length of the pass, and into the hills and plains beyond.

Aarisk sat on the shoulder of the pass entrance as it had always done but it was… broken. The scout had been right. The buildings were half-ruined and burnt, and there were gaping holes in the curtain wall. The streets and houses were blackened with soot, and the gateway was unbarred by gates. Towers had been toppled on to the road that wound up the hillside, and a pall of smoke hung over the mouth of the pass. Through the haze, everything was dark. The hillside pastures were dead. The woods further up the mountains were a swathe of stumps and still-smouldering fires.

Everything had been destroyed.

Erlaan growled and clenched his fists. This was Ullsaard's doing. The people of Aarisk had razed their town rather than let it fall into the hands of the Mekhani. The Askhan king was willing not just to sacrifice Ersua, but to employ a scorched earth policy wherever the Mekhani might advance.

"What has happened, mighty Orlassai?" asked one of the Mekhani. "What shall we do now?"

Erlaan looked down at the man's red face, eyes wide with doubt and pleading. It sickened the king-messiah. Every decision was his to make. Every detail, every smallest inconvenience, was his to resolve alone. The Mekhani were pathetic. They were like children, looking to him to solve every problem.

With a surge of anger, fuelled by Ullsaard's ruthless approach and the naive bleating of the scout, Erlaan grabbed the man by the throat. His fingers snapped his neck without effort, blood surging through the king-messiah's grip and splashing to the rocky ground. With a snarl, he hurled the corpse away, tossing it easily from the ridge.

The other scouts cowered back, both afraid and adoring, torn between their love and fear of their strange ruler. For a moment, Erlaan held his anger in check. What good would it do to lash out at these poor creatures? It was not their fault that the runes of the Temple made them slaves to the Orlassai's every whim; it was not their fault they were robbed of reason in the presence of their king-messiah.

The moment passed and loathing returned. What good would their deaths serve? They would sate the king's bloodthirst, which denied by Ullsaard's tricks now raged in his veins; that was cause enough.

Erlaan drew his huge sword and stepped towards the scouts, ignoring the shrieks of the terrified men.

CAVRINA,
NALANOR/OKHAR BORDER
Spring, 212th year of Askh

I

"You have to admire their persistence," said Naadlin. The First Captain of the Second shielded his eyes against the morning sun and smiled. "But I much prefer their stupidity."

"Don't praise stupidity too much," replied Ullsaard, walking up from behind the cluster of legion commanders. "Stupid men don't know when they're beaten and fight on regardless. If this amateur had any idea about strategy, he would have scuttled back to Mekha ten days ago when we nearly had him at Lastuun."

Harrakil looked unconvinced.

"There are still more than forty thousand of them left," he said. He looked at his king. "How far away did you say the Seventh and Twenty-First are?"

"Twenty miles, no more," said Ullsaard. "I sent the messengers back telling their commanders not to dawdle. They'll be here mid-Noonwatch at the latest."

"The Mekhani will get wind of it," said Aklaan, the commander of the Third. "They'll attack."

"Good," said Ullsaard. He turned and gestured to a nearby orderly to fetch his ailur. "If they commit, they won't be able to get away again. I want a fight, but that bastard over there is either too canny to fall for my lures, or too stupid to recognise a seemingly obvious opportunity for victory. I guess we'll find out in the next hour or two."

The Mekhani camp was a sprawling affair, disorganised and poorly defended in comparison to the march forts of the Askhans. For all that, the earth walls and ditches surrounding the disorganised spread of multicoloured tents were enough to give the king second thoughts about attacking. He counted fourteen behemodons at the centre of the camp, and rough revetments housed more than a dozen war engines of crude but lethal design. An assault would be costly, and if Ullsaard could tempt or taunt his foes out from under them, it would be for the better.

His officers' insults aside, the enemy commander had chosen to make his stand in a good spot. The plains stretched for several miles in every direction; the only two rises in sight being the hill on which the Mekhani had made camp and the shallower mound from which the king surveyed his enemy a few miles away. A river, though not wide, curved around the duskward side of the enemy-held hill and cut between the two encampments, and the slopes to coldwards, facing the Askhan army, were strewn with rocks and steep faces. The best approach would be to circle around to duskwards and attack from the other side, and wisely the Mekhani had sited their catapults and huge bows facing duskwards and hotwards to counter such a move.

"Should we send a parley, just in case they want to surrender?" suggested Naadlin.

"Not a fucking chance," said Ullsaard, his finger rubbing at the scar on his lip from his last attempt to speak terms with the red-skinned tribesmen.

"We could send out the kolubrids, launch some fire arrows into those tents. That'll stir them up." Aklaan seemed excited by his proposal. "Let a few of the bastards burn."

Ullsaard considered the idea.

"Not yet," he replied. He glanced up at the sky, trying to work out the time. The sun was hidden behind a swathe of low cloud. "I reckon the reinforcements won't be here for another four hours. We'll make our move in two."

The orderly arrived with Storm in tow. The ailur flicked her head, tugging at the reins in the captain's hand. She was feisty, but Ullsaard had not yet decided if that was a good or bad trait. He had known when he bought her from a nobleman in Geria that she was untested in battle; a symbol of prestige that had never hunted or fought but the only ailur in the city.

With a nod of thanks, he took the reins and swung up into the saddle. Storm took his weight with a swish of her tail, but no further protest. Ullsaard turned her along the slope towards the camp of the Third but stopped and glanced back over his shoulder.

"Best have the companies turned out anyway," he told his staff. "If the Mekhani decide to start things early, I don't want to be rushing about. Everybody has their orders?"

A series of affirmatives came in reply and the king nodded his appreciation and rode on, confident that the First Captains would follow their orders to the letter. A track wound down the hotwards slope of the hill just before the wall of the Third's encampment. Ullsaard turned down this path and continued down to the bottom of the slope. He stopped for a while, surveying the ground from this level, assuring himself that the gently undulating grasslands would be the perfect field for the phalanxes to move across. It was a pity that only the slender river provided any barrier with which to anchor a flank, but it would have to do.

He pictured the coming battle as he hoped it would unfold, running through the positioning and movement of his line and the kolubrid squadrons in response to the possible Mekhani actions. So engrossed was he in this, that he almost did not hear a warning signal being sounded from the camps above.

Looking back up the hill, he saw that the four legions of his army were almost assembled, rank after rank of bronze spears and polished shields. There was a calm effortlessness to the blocks of soldiers arranging themselves, like the intricate interweaving of graceful court dancers. There was certainly nothing of concern that he could see, and he turned his attention back to the Mekhani, expecting to see them mobilising from their camp.

There was movement, but not on the scale he would expect to precede an attack. The enemy encampment was situated around an abandoned farm and a paved road switched back and forth down the near slope before turning duskwards towards Cavrina, a town fourteen miles away. Something appeared at the gate leading to the road, large enough that Ullsaard could see it, and at first he thought it was one of the Mekhani's reptilian beasts, though smaller than a behemodon.

As it approached down the road, Ullsaard recognised what he saw: the huge man who called himself Orlassai. The enemy commander walked down the road with easy strides. There was no sign of a bodyguard. Eyes narrowed, Ullsaard watched the giant's progress.

He turned at the sound of footfalls on the trail behind him, to see Harrakil hurrying down at the head of a company of legionnaires.

"You're more of a fussing hen than Cosuas was," Ullsaard told the First Captain as the self-appointed bodyguard formed up around their king.

"I do not like the look of this," Harrakil replied with embarrassment. "This creature is unnatural."

"He is big, I'll give him that," said Ullsaard, returning his gaze to the Mekhani king, who had reached the plain and was now striding confidently across the grasslands directly towards the legion camps. "And his balls are just as huge, by the looks of it."

The other commander stopped about a mile away. Ullsaard heard his name called out. He glanced at Harrakil, who shook his head. Ignoring him, Ullsaard urged Storm into a trot.

"Wait there!" the king snapped as the bodyguard broke into a run to keep up. "It looks like we might parley after all. Let's not do anything stupid."

"Besides," he added under his breath, "I'm not sure you'll be any help against that bastard of a brute."

The Askhan king crossed the divide quickly and reined Storm to a walk a quarter of a mile away, holding up his empty sword hand in a gesture of peace. As he rode closer and closer, Ullsaard realised just how large the other man was. Distance had masked his true size the previous times the king had seen his foe. The Mekhani was more than twice as tall as Ullsaard, and past the ornate helm and armour the king saw that his skin was of normal colour. Whoever he was, he wasn't born to a Mekhani mother.

Ullsaard's nerve held out long enough for him to get within a spear's cast of his opponent, and then he pulled Storm to a halt. With such long legs, the Mekhani commander would be able to cross the distance in a matter of heartbeats.

"Bow down before Orlassai, the reborn king, rightful ruler of the world!"

The voice was a roar that rang Ullsaard's ears. Storm cringed at the noise, snarling a mixture of defiance and fear. The king knew how she felt. For a moment he was overawed by this apparition of a man and he felt his fingers twitch at the reins and his legs tense, his body moving to comply with the order even as Ullsaard's brain rejected it. Amidst the confusion, Ullsaard thought he recognised the voice, but could not place from where or whom.

"Go fuck whatever twisted bitch spawned you!" Ullsaard called back in return, his voice sounding thin and weak in comparison to the bellow of the other. "I'm the king of Askh, and I bow to no man. Or whatever you are."

Orlassai laughed, a much more human sound, and it triggered a half-formed memory in Ullsaard; he had heard that laugh before, somewhat youthful, in the palaces of Askh. He dismissed the idea. He would have noticed such a monster wandering the halls and corridors.

"What do you want?" he shouted.

"I want the Crown," Orlassai replied, his tone less menacing than before. "It belongs to me. You took it from me."

"You're wrong," said Ullsaard. "I prised it from the dead fingers of Lutaar himself. I'm sure you aren't him. That makes it mine now."

Again there was that familiar laugh and Orlassai came forward, long strides covering the ground quickly. Ullsaard didn't know whether to stay or run. Not since the behemodon had he faced such opposition, and on that occasion shock had spurred him to action. Seeing the gigantic warrior bearing down upon him filled Ullsaard with a fear he had not known before, as if dread itself washed over him from Orlassai's presence.

At his approach, he felt something else, and the fear subsided. The Blood fizzed in his body, strengthening his resolve, filling his muscles with power. More than that, it reacted to something else. It reminded him of the odd feeling he had from Lakhyri. He had no name for such a thing, but his ancestors might have called it sorcery.

With a start, Ullsaard saw the golden eyes in the shadow of the feather-plumed helm of his foe. It was too much, and immediately the king knew that Lakhyri was somehow involved. Had he been setting up Ullsaard simply for this moment? Was this beast of a man sent to kill him?

Storm went down to her belly, ears flat, hissing and spitting. She tensed and Ullsaard flung himself from the saddle a moment before she bolted. Landing awkwardly, the king glanced back to see the ailur racing off with his spear and shield still hanging from her saddle.

"Shit." There seemed little else he could do except face down the Mekhani king.

"I will kill you, Ullsaard." The Askhan king watched in fascinated horror the twisting sigil-carved lips of Orlassai as he spoke, and felt a tremor of uncertainty as rows of fangs were revealed. It was as if an ailur was speaking to him. With another part of his brain, Ullsaard recognised the impeccable Askhan accent of his foe; better than his own. "That much is certain. It would be a shame to waste the strength of your legions. I will need them to finish your conquest of Salphoria."

Like the laugh, the voice resonated with some part of Ullsaard's memory, but the bass rumbling obscured any recollection. Orlassai smiled, and it was a gruesome sight.

"Still you do not recognise me?" Orlassai reached up a hand with too many knuckles and pulled his helm from his head.

Ullsaard gasped, disgusted by the writhing, leathery flesh revealed. His shock increased as he looked more closely, seeing someone he knew amidst the etched runes and golden eyes. The face was boyish, handsome even.

He remembered the expression of triumph, on the face of a youth at the Maarmes circuit.

"That isn't right," Ullsaard said, even though he knew it was. Finally he had found out what had happened to Lutaar's heir. "Erlaan?"

The giant nodded and extended an arm, muscles moving like stones in a sack beneath his skin. The sun shone dully from metallic fingernails.

"It is impressive, is it not?"

"It's hideous. What happened to you?"

"I became worthy of the Crown, Ullsaard. Give it back to me and I will make your death quick."

Ullsaard took a few steps back and drew his sword.

"You don't expect me to die without fighting, do you?"

"You are a good warrior, Ullsaard, but you are not invincible." Orlassai-Erlaan drew his own weapon, its wickedly serrated blade catching the light. "Do you think you can stop me?"

Ullsaard swallowed hard and his mouth was dry. One stroke of that sword would cleave him in half. It was at that moment he remembered telling Erlaan that a warrior fought with his mind as much as his sword. He desperately wracked his brains for an idea.

"Have you become as savage as the army you lead?" said the Askhan king, sheathing his sword. "What would your father think of this behaviour?"

"I am no savage," Orlassai-Erlaan replied. "What do you mean?"

"Would you break the truce of parley? Do you remember what happened to the last man that crossed me in such a way?"

The monstrous king hesitated and he looked more youthful than ever in his uncertainty. With a coy smile, he lowered his blade.

"Forgive my manners, I have picked up some bad habits from my minions," said Orlassai-Erlaan. "My father is dead, Ullsaard. He thinks nothing of me now, but I would honour his memory. You wish to talk terms of your surrender."

Ullsaard forced a laugh.

"Not of *my* surrender, no," he said. "You might be able to kill me, but your army will be destroyed."

The other man did not share Ullsaard's humour. His frown was frightening to behold and for a moment Ullsaard thought he would be struck down regardless of his opponent's claim to civility.

"Little has changed from our last encounter, Ullsaard," Orlassai-Erlaan said. "I have a few thousand less men, but four legions are still not enough to match us. This is no barbaric horde you face, it is a trained army."

"Depends what you consider training to be," said Ullsaard. "I'm happy to put your tactics to the test if you are. I reckon the odds are pretty even. Let's see which of us is the better commander, eh?"

Again Orlassai-Erlaan paused, a flicker of nervousness crossing his face. Ullsaard felt a little glow of hope growing within and pushed home his point.

"You know how good I am, but how good are you, Erlaan? You've seen one battle, and a straightforward one at that. I don't doubt that sword of yours could match a hundred men of mine, but a commander wins battles with his plans, not his blade."

"This is a trick," said the other king, shaking his head. "You are scared and seek to outwit me."

"Or I have outwitted you already and I'm just pretending to be scared."

Orlassai-Erlaan's lips rippled with a snarl.

"Words, Ullsaard. You used to fight your battles with armies, now you use words."

"I'm told I have to be more of a politician if I am to be a good king," Ullsaard replied. "Come on, what's your answer. Kill me and be cut down by my avenging army, or are we going to do this properly?"

"I will rip you to pieces!" Orlassai-Erlaan's bellow almost felled Ullsaard with its ferocity. "I will destroy your army and all of the empire will know me to be the true king. They will beg me to take up the Crown and lead them."

"Fair enough," Ullsaard said with a shrug. He looked up at the sky. "Shall we start things in an hour? I wouldn't want to rush you."

"Your insolence earns you a slower death, Ullsaard. I will feed your balls to you and strangle you with your gizzards. When you are screaming for me to release you from your agony, remember your flippant remarks."

"I'll try to," said Ullsaard, tapping himself on the side of the head to indicate he was committing the words to memory. "When your army is shattered and you stand alone against ten thousand spears, *you* should remember that I offered you the chance to avoid it."

Ullsaard turned away and started back towards his army. He heard the Mekhani king's growl and tensed, expecting a blow to land upon him. He would not give Erlaan the satisfaction of seeing him look back. Heart hammering, Ullsaard fought the urge to run and kept his pace slow and steady.

He made it all the way back to his pavilion, shooing away his officers as they crowded around him, before his legs gave way. Unseen, he staggered into his bed space and flopped down onto the bedding, shaking uncontrollably. He wanted to throw up, and was glad that his body had not betrayed him earlier, because it had been an effort of will to stop his bowels from emptying themselves.

Taking deep breaths to calm down, he closed his eyes and rolled to his back.

"I better win," he muttered.

II

Orlassai-Erlaan stormed back into the camp, bellowing for the army to assemble. While the warriors gathered in their tribal groups, the war engines were lifted from their positions and the behemodons roused. Eriekh emerged from somewhere, dodging between the assembling fighter bands.

"We attack?" said the priest. "Your conversation with the usurper went so well?"

"Not well at all," Orlassai-Erlaan growled. "He has something planned, wanted us to fight in an hour's time. I suspect he has reinforcements arriving. We must crush his army before they arrive."

"Why leave the defences of the camp?"

"You call these defences?" Orlassai-Erlaan snarled, waving a hand at the ditches and earth ramparts. "They will not protect us. We are losing, Eriekh. Unless you have received some word from Asirkhyr that he has brought my second army from the desert, we do not have the luxury of waiting."

"We have yet to fight a battle, and you concede defeat?"

"Ullsaard has trapped us here, leaving a trail of unburnt fields and intact towns like a line of seed to capture a bird." The king-messiah smashed a fist into the side of his helm in self-remonstration. "And I walked blindly into his snare! While we remain here, more legions will descend upon us. We must break through Ullsaard's army and into Okhar, and send word to Asirkhyr to bring fresh troops to us."

"What is your plan, mighty Orlassai?" a voice asked from behind. He turned to see the group of shamans, eyes averted from him.

"All-out attack," replied the king. "Extend the army past the right flank of the Askhans and envelop them. Use the behemodons to engage their left flank and stop them reinforcing. When we have encircled the end of their line, redirect the beasts against the centre and scatter all opposition."

"As you command, lord of the skies, watchful guardian of the deserts," said the shaman, bowing low and backing away. The group held a brief conference and then hurried off in different directions, calling out for others.

"And where will you fight?" asked Eriekh. "What if they withdraw to their camps?"

"I am going to kill Ullsaard," said Orlassai-Erlaan. "His death will not win the battle, but it will certainly shorten the war. He has brought us here for a reason; he cannot simply let us walk away this time. He needs to win this battle as much as we do."

The first tribes were already pouring from the camp, spreading out along the road towards the Askhan army. The ground trembled as behemodons lumbered forward between the clusters of warriors, the crews in the howdahs shouting and laughing down at those forced to walk.

"And have you anything to add to our strength?" the king demanded of Eriekh.

"I am not a master of the sword," the priest replied. "Our powers are subtle, and I possess no particular skill for battle. Remember the other gifts we have bestowed upon you, not just that fine body. Lead your army, let them hear your voice, let them see the slaughter you wreak. I shall do my part to aid you, do not fear for that."

"I heard rumour that when Ullsaard sought the Crown, Lakhyri visited upon him nightmares, and inflicted pestilence, snow and grief upon his legions," said the Mekhani king. "Can you not use such sorcery now?"

"Such things take time to prepare and to work their way into the hearts and bodies of men," said Eriekh. "You think that if we could conjure up storms in an instant, raze the ground in fire with a word, we would have kept ourselves secret for these thousands of years? These things, the eulanui could do, but we are only their servants. Be thankful for the powers you have already been given."

Orlassai-Erlaan grunted his disappointment and turned away. He joined the flood of warriors pouring out onto the grassland, taking up his position at the front and centre of the army. Harsh horns blared and the Mekhani shouted boasts and threats as their numbers swelled.

The king-messiah studied the Askhan formations. They did not move in response to the assembling Mekhani horde. Two legions formed the centre, arranged narrow and deep, the long spears of the phalanxes like a forest. On their left, the spear blocks were dispersed and Orlassai-Erlaan's keen eyes spied lava throwers between the legionnaires; to any other they would have been hidden from view. On the Askhans' right, the phalanxes fell back in echelon, each a few paces further back so that the line appeared to curve away from their foes.

From this, the king tried to discern Ullsaard's plan and work out if his own would succeed. On the face of it, the Askhan deployment favoured Orlassai-Erlaan's approach. The right would commit to attack, allowing the Mekhani numbers to spill out further and surround the phalanx. The left looked set to defend with the lava throwers, while the centre was poised to respond to either direction.

Checking his own troops, the king saw that they were almost ready. He glanced at the sun, judging the time to be close to noon. The king-messiah was confident his scouts would have spied any reinforcements within ten miles. That gave him at least two hours grace, probably more. Ullsaard had thought himself clever to set the timetable, but Orlassai-Erlaan was wise to his tricks now. He would decide when they would fight.

He waved to the chieftains of the lacertils and the lizard-riders set out, fanning across the grass in front of the Mekhani. As expected, the Askhan kolubrids issued forth from between the phalanxes to combat the approaching skirmishers. The lacertils closed fast, braving the clouds of bellows-arrows to bring their slings into range. With little room to withdraw and keep their distance, the kolubrid riders suffered in the exchange; their bellows bows hit hard but could not match the weight of missiles unleashed by the slings of the Mekhani cavalry.

Another lesson learned from the first encounter.

As the kolubrids fell back, the lacertils did not follow directly, but moved sideways, trying to force the Askhans back towards their own centre where they would impede any advance from the phalanx.

Orlassai-Erlaan drew his sword and raised it above his head.

"Attack now, my brave followers!" he roared. "End now the days of deprivation that have been heaped upon us. Take back your pride with your spears. Let your weapons feast on the enemy as we will gorge on their food and women!"

The king looked on proudly as the army advanced. No mad dash, no hoarse shrieking; just a steady push with shields held to the front and spears shouldered. It was not quite the in-step march of a legion, but it was better than what Erlaan-Orlassai had seen of the Mekhani the first time he had encountered them.

The ground was soft underfoot, still sodden from the spring rains. The Mekhani left a swathe of flattened grass nearly a mile wide in their wake, great holes left in the mud by the tread of the behemodons. Ahead, the Askhan legions shifted. Trumpets blasted and drums beat the orders as companies split along the left of their line, moving out to match the overlapping ranks of the Mekhani. In response, the legion next to them widened its lines, bringing forward the rear ranks of the phalanxes to fill the gap.

Urged on by their drivers, the behemodons moved ahead of the infantry, stomping across the soft turf, studded armour plates slapping at their flanks. They dragged sleds behind them laden with more ammunition, young warriors clinging on as they bumped over the uneven ground. Erlaan-Orlassai could see the brightly feathered headbands of the shaman-chiefs waving in the wind as the tribal leaders called to each other from their howdahs, their ceremonial staffs waving and pointing to keep a safe distance between the monstrous war beasts.

Startled birds launched from their hidden nests in front of the advancing wave of warriors, squawking and flapping madly. Gusts across the plain fluttered the feathers upon the army's totem standards and sent chains of bones rattling. The steady trample of thousands of sandalled feet set the ground to shaking, and as the Mekhani came within half a mile of the Askhan line sonorous chants lifted into the air; each tribe giving voice to its traditional war songs, rising in volume in competition with each other.

In the narrowing gap between the two armies, the kolubrid squadrons made a break towards the behemodons, enduring a hail of sling bullets for a while until their faster mounts took them clear of the lacertil-riding warriors of Mekha. Their bronze arrows flew up towards the giant warbeasts, joined by bolts hurled from the Askhan spear throwers on the hill nearly half a mile ahead. The advantage of height was with the enemy and the behemodon mahouts pressed their mounts on into the flurry of missiles to close the range. From the howdahs, the nobles of the tribes hurled spears at the harrying kolubrids while the lacertils closed in behind to drive away the enemy.

Two spears caught the foremost behemodon simultaneously, one lancing through its neck, another smashing into the woven cane howdah. Even as the beast slumped forwards, the structure fell apart, spilling red-skinned warriors into the grass. Several did not rise, but the rest recovered quickly and dashed away, bellows arrows chasing them from the kolubrids.

The beasts with catapults upon their backs halted first, five in all, Mekhani scrambling down ropes to secure the chains hooked into the skin of their beasts so that they could not move too much. The arms of the catapults were pulled back and piles of fist-sized rocks loaded into the cups. At the cries of their chieftains, the war machines were loosed, the catapult arms snapping forward under the power of twisted rope to hurl their projectiles far up the hill, dark blurs falling upon the raised shields of the legionnaires.

Onwards pressed the Mekhani, their chanting growing ever louder and faster, the shouted warnings of their leaders reminding them not to charge too soon. The hill occupied by the Askhans seemed to get steeper the closer the army approached. From here the Askhans looked like a wall of bronze and Erlaan-Orlassai realised that the front ranks were kneeling, so that the back ranks could angle their spears down the slope.

The king-messiah looked for gaps in the line as the ground sloped upwards. He searched also for Ullsaard, but could see no sign of the Askhan king. Instead he made directly for the icon of the legion in front, knowing that it was borne by the first company, the best fighters.

He would destroy the veterans and sow fear into the hearts of the others with the ease of their destruction.

To his left, the behemodons carrying spear throwers had also come into range. A fierce artillery battle had broken out, rocks and bolts raining down from the hillside and soaring up into the ranks of the spear companies.

A new wave of kolubrids emerged from behind the Askhan line, held in reserve by their commanders. The snake-like mounts swiftly circled around the end of the enemy line and joined with the others to drive back the lacertils. Into the space created, half a dozen spear companies advanced, guarding the lava throwers. The men manning the Mekhani war engines saw the threat and directed their weapons against this advance. Two black-red blossoms of fire erupted amongst the Askhan ranks as the machines found their marks on the fuel barrels of the volatile weapons. The engineless behemodons lumbered into the legionnaires, their crews jabbing down with long spears, the beasts crushing men with their bulk and snapping off limbs with fang-filled mouths.

Five of the lava engines had been dragged into range and gouts of flame spat out towards the enemy, engulfing three of the behemodons. The howdahs ignited swiftly, sending charred corpses tumbling, sticky fire clinging to the hide and armour of the monstrous lizards. Panicked, the creatures ran amok, smashing into the Askhans and lunging at each other in their madness.

Erlaan-Orlassai was no more than two hundred paces from the waiting Askhans and could spare no thought for the battle to his left. He looked in the other direction and saw that the left flank of the Askhan line was pulling back from the overlapping hook of the Mekhani right, anchoring their flank against the walls of their camp. More figures appeared at the rampart and arrows rained down on the desert warriors from above. The king-messiah heard the furious shouts of the shaman-chiefs and the Mekhani surged up the hill, straight at the retreating phalanx.

Erlaan-Orlassai fixed his gaze on the First Captain standing beside the legion icon ahead. There was nothing more the reborn king could do for the moment, save fight himself. Ullsaard had done well to defend against the advantages of the Mekhani, but his army was still outnumbered by at least ten thousand warriors, probably more. Erlaan-Orlassai would break the shield wall himself and the advantage of numbers would do the rest.

He broke into a run at a hundred paces, arms pumping, massive shield on the left, his sword gripped tightly in his right hand. His strides took him quickly clear of the sprinting Mekhani and a thicket of spears seemed to converge on him. He trusted to the gifts of the eulanui and charged straight in, head bowed, sword lifted for the attack.

Wood splintered as Erlaan-Orlassai crashed into the first company. Bronze spearheads bit at his flesh, pricking his thick skin like thorns of a bush would scratch a lesser man. The impact of his arrival hurled two legionnaires backwards with buckled shields and snapped spears. Sweeping down his sword, he carved through three more and plunged into the heart of their formation.

Metal screeched on metal as bronze spear tips met bronze armour. The king-messiah used his shield as a weapon, smashing aside the enemy, crushing their fallen bodies beneath his booted his feet; his sword severed heads and limbs with every wide swing, slicing through shield, armour and flesh without hindrance.

He howled his excitement, the deafening noise terrifying the legionnaires around him. Most of them broke and ran, overwhelmed by the nightmare warrior that confronted them, their bravery washed away by the ensorcelled cry that rang in their ears. A brave few mastered their terror to thrust their spears toward his face, but such was his height, it was easy to sway aside. Erlaan-Orlassai's sword descended in a flash, carving apart a legionnaire from head to waist. With a snarl, the king-messiah wrenched the blade free and swung backhanded, the edge of his sword chopping through a shield and decapitating another legionnaire.

Around and about their godlike king, the Mekhani poured through the breach in the line. The spear companies hurriedly adjusted their facing, turning their spears to confront the red-skinned savages wailing and shrieking in their midst. Some were successful, greeting the charging warriors with a wall of spears; others were caught in mid-manoeuvre by the lightly armoured warriors leaping between their ranks.

With his foes dead or fleeing, Erlaan-Orlassai paused for a moment to take stock. He caught a glint of gold out of the corner of his eye and turned. Kicking aside the corpse of a second captain, he found the fallen icon of the legion, the numerals of the Seventeenth etched into a plaque beneath the disc of Askhos's face. For a moment, he considered mangling the standard, crumpling it beyond recognition with his bare hands. He stopped, remembering that he fought to become king of the empire. He was not some Mekhani savage; he was the future commander of the legions.

He sheathed his sword and stooped to pick up the icon. The stylised bearded face of Askhos was half-covered in blood and spattered with mud. With barely any effort, Erlaan-Orlassai drove the haft of the standard through the body of the dead captain and into the ground beneath. He tore the officer's cloak from his back and used it to wipe away the filth from the face of his ancestor before casting aside the ragged scrap.

Shouts and the ring of weapons sounded out from the left and right, mixed with the cries of the wounded and the screams of the dying. Towering above the normal men around him, Erlaan-Orlassai could see some considerable distance along the line. From one end to the other, the Mekhani and Askhans were locked together. Several more companies advanced from a position in reserve to plug the hole opened by the king-messiah. Erlaan-Orlassai drew his sword and headed straight for them.

He met the nearest reserve company a few dozen paces from the mass of fighting. Perhaps having seen the destruction he had inflicted on their first company, the legionnaires did not wait for his attack but pressed forwards, both sides charging at each other.

Blood flowed from biting wounds as spear points found Erlaan-Orlassai's face and exposed flesh between the plates of his armour. He ignored the stinging pain and slashed left and right, hewing down the legionnaires with no finesse. He laughed at himself, thinking about the careful guards and postures he had learnt for use on the bloodfields. His raw strength was now such that brute power served him better than any amount of guile or skill.

It was like being swarmed by wasps. The legionnaires converged on him from all directions, jabbing and slashing with their spears, setting his armour ringing, grazing his leathery skin, probing for eyes and joints. He swatted away a handful of foes with a swipe from his shield, bones splintering through flesh from the blow. A spear drove up between the plates protecting his lower back, digging the length of its point into his flesh.

He whirled around, the movement ripping the weapon from the legionnaire's grip and sending him to his back.

Erlaan-Orlassai drove his sword point through the man's helm, slicing off the top of his head. Shields battered at his legs and more spears rattled and scratched as the legionnaires closed in again from every direction. Though he felt little pain, Erlaan-Orlassai could feel the trickles of blood flowing from under his armour, staining his hands and pooling in his boots. He swung his sword in a wide arc from right to left, not looking, the serrated blade savaging four men in a sweep of gore.

"Where is Ullsaard?" the king-messiah bellowed. A spear snapped, leaving its head in the side of his throat. With a growl, Erlaan-Orlassai kicked out, his foot crushing the chest of the legionnaire who had struck him. Hands grasped at his left arm, trying to drag down his shield, and he fought back, lifting two men from their feet, tossing them into their fellows with a casual flick of his shield. "I'll kill you all if I have to!"

Another spear point took the king-messiah in the back of his right knee, forcing him down for a moment. Before he could right himself, his ears picked up another sound amongst the cacophony of melee: a deep-throated growl.

He half-turned, just in time to see the ailur leaping for his shoulder, claws bared, mouth wide. Her weight slammed into him, pushing him to one knee whilst her claws left gouges across the bronze of his armour. Her masked face snarled and hissed a hand's breadth from his face, hot breath on his skin. With a snarl, he flung out an arm, smashing fist and sword hilt into the giant cat's chest, hurling her backwards. She twisted and landed and sprang again, claws raking a furrow across the king-messiah's cheek. He kicked her away again and raised his sword to cleave her in half.

He stopped mid-stroke, hearing the steady tread of booted feet to one side. He caught a whiff of a familiar smell. It was Ullsaard. Almost absent-mindedly, Erlaan-Orlassai caught the leaping ailur on the flat of his shield. He pushed against the momentum of her attack and drove downwards, crushing her against the ground at his feet with the rim of his shield. She scrabbled for a moment in the last throes of life, blood leaking into the mud, mewls escaping her red-flecked muzzle.

The king-messiah of the Mekhani rose up and turned to face the king of Greater Askhor. Erlaan-Orlassai's sword was smeared with blood, as was his shield and armour. A hundred dents and scratches marred the bronze of his war gear. He felt nothing of the dozens of small wounds leaking blood along the swirls of runes etched into his skin.

"You'll pay for that," said Ullsaard, hefting his golden-headed spear. "You killed my cat, you cock-eating son of a snake's cunt!"

III

It was hard to make any sense out of the confusion. Nemasolai sat upon the back of his xenosaurus, a blanket for a saddle, looking left and right across the groups of warriors fighting under the shadow of the Askhan camp. He tried to direct the attacks of his tribe with shouts augmented by gestures from his wand – a crooked branch from an irsakki tree tipped with the skull of a sand weasel. He could not tell if his orders were unclear, unheard, or simply being ignored.

From the parapet above, Askhan youths pelted the Mekhani warriors with stones. The slingers did their best to reply, but the protection offered by the wooden wall proved impossible to overcome. Nemasolai had sent fifty of his warriors around the camp to attack from the other side, but there was no sign of them and he guessed that they had been slain. Ahead, the melee surged back and forth, companies of Askhans giving ground and advancing with the tide of battle as the tribal warriors attacked and regrouped.

Dozens of dead and wounded from both sides littered the trampled grass and mud. Broken spears and discarded shields added to the debris of war. A few dozen paces to Nemasolai's left, the two sides parted for a moment and the shaman saw an Askhan crawling through the gore, dragging himself over the fallen with blood flowing from the stump of his right leg. A Mekhani warrior, himself bleeding from spear cuts across his arms and chest, heaved himself out of the murk and smashed his shield into the back of the wounded legionnaire's head. A spear thrust from freshly advancing Askhans finished him off in turn.

Nemasolai heard a shout to his right and turned to see Manamosalai waving frantically with his stave. Nemasolai grabbed the rope rein hooked into the fronds behind the xenosaurus's head and tugged in the direction of his fellow shaman, urging the beast into a waddling trot.

"What is it?" he called out as he approached.

"Are we winning?" Manamosalai asked. "I cannot see what is happening."

Glancing over his shoulder, Nemasolai could see nothing beyond the mobs of warriors around him; the lay of the hill obscured everything beyond a few dozen paces to his left, though the sound of fighting seemed to come from everywhere.

"I do not think we are losing," he told his companion with a shrug. "I saw Orlassai striking down the Askhan dogs without pause."

The clear notes of Askhan horns rang out over the din of battle, signalling some change or manoeuvre. Nemasolai had no idea what they meant, but as far as he could see, nothing changed. Shouting warnings, a cluster of red-skinned fighters fell back from a charging Askhan phalanx, some of them tumbling as they retreated down the slope. Manamosalai bellowed at his own warriors to press forward into the flank of the advancing spearmen, urging them on with shakes of his feather-hung staff.

"I think we have killed as many as we have lost," Manamosalai said, returning his attention to Nemasolai, his words almost lost in the whooping war cries of his followers as they leapt to the attack. "That must be a good thing."

"Watch out!" bellowed Nemasolai as he saw figures appearing at the camp wall not far from where he was. Manamosalai guided his reptilian mount away from the wall as a new hail of stones rained down on the Mekhani. The two of them rode a little bit further down the slope, out of range and were joined by a third chieftain, Annomasai.

"We have some of the bastards pinned up against the wall," the new arrival declared with a grin. "Push your warriors forward and we shall finish them off!"

"Which way?" asked Nemasolai, craning his neck to see what was happening. Annomasai pointed up and to the right, but nothing particular could be seen past the throng of bodies.

Manamosalai kicked his xenosaurus into motion and called out the names of the senior warriors under his command. He waved them in the direction Annomasai had indicated and several dozen Mekhani peeled to the right and headed back towards the camp, shields raised against the shower of missiles that greeted them. Nemasolai looked to see if any of his men were able to help, but they were all fighting hard, trying to encircle two Askhan companies, jabbing with their spears and hollering.

Nemasolai wiped the sweat from his face with the cloth of his poncho. It was hot work, even for warriors raised in the desert. The wind had died to nothing and the air was heavy with a gathering spring storm. As he turned his mount towards Annomasai, he happened to glance back to coldwards. He caught sight of metal and with a sensation that felt like a kick in the gut, he saw a column of Askhan soldiers curving around the hill on which the Mekhani had made their camp.

"Look! Look!" he shrieked, stabbing his wand at the enemy reinforcements. The other shamans gave startled shouts as they saw what Nemasolai had seen.

"What do we do?" said Manamosalai. "Do we press the attack? Do we turn?"

Annomasai seemed frozen in place, staring in horror as company after company of Askhans marched into view.

"I shall seek the wisdom of Orlassai," said Nemasolai. "Keep fighting! Break the Askhans!"

With that he wrenched on the rein of his mount and kicked his heels into its flank, forcing it into an ungainly run. Steering to the left, Nemasolai saw that others had witnessed the arrival of the fresh legion. Some were calling to their warriors to pull back; others were doing the same as he, running and riding in the direction of their king.

IV

With a casual thrust, Erlaan-Orlassai finished off Storm, driving the point of his blade into her throat. He stepped over her corpse and faced Ullsaard.

"Are you ready to fight this time?" asked the Mekhani king. "No parley? No clever words?"

Ullsaard answered with his spear, tossing it overhand at his opponent's throat. Erlaan-Orlassai brought up his shield, catching the spear with the edge, causing it to bounce harmlessly from the side of his helm. The twisted beast of a man laughed.

"You will have to do better than that? Look at what I have done to your legionnaires. Think you can fare better alone?"

Ullsaard pulled free his sword and broke into a run. He dodged to his right as Erlaan-Orlassai swung his sword, blocking the blow with his shield, rolling with the force of the impact. The Askhan king's momentum carried him back to his feet and he skidded in the mud, chopping his blade towards the exposed knee of his foe. Bronze bit dully at bizarre flesh, leaving the faintest of marks.

Erlaan-Orlassai kicked out, forcing Ullsaard back.

"You might need a sharper sword," said the king-messiah, grinning widely. He lunged, driving his blade at Ullsaard's chest, the blow ringing against the king's hastily raised shield, knocking him back two steps.

"You might need more friends," said Ullsaard, nodding to Harrakil who stood behind the monstrous warrior with several dozen legionnaires. The First Captain gave a shout and led the charge as Ullsaard ducked beneath another swipe of Erlaan-Orlassai's sword and brought his open weapon up and under the giant's wrist, the blade slashing through the bindings of a huge vambrace.

"Coward!" roared Erlaan-Orlassai as a handful of legionnaires barrelled into him, throwing themselves at the back of his legs. He staggered but did not fall, slashing behind with his sword to open the face of one of the men tackling him.

"Idiot!" Ullsaard snarled in reply. "I warned you never to accept a fair fight. Too late to learn now!"

With a grunt of effort, the king of Greater Askhor hammered the edge of his shield into his foe's right knee but still Erlaan-Orlassai did not buckle. The Mekhani's leader chopped down with his blade, moving with incredible speed for his size, the point missing Ullsaard's throat by less than the width of a finger. Startled, Ullsaard leapt back, shield raised against a return blow that smashed him from his feet. His breath exploded from his chest as he crashed onto the body of a dead legionnaire.

Erlaan-Orlassai turned sharply, driving his shield into the face of Harrakil, buckling the First Captain's helmet and shattering bone. Harrakil flopped to the ground, knocked out. His men swarmed around Erlaan-Orlassai, raking and stabbing with their spears. With another swipe of his blade, the enemy general cut through spear hafts and arms, sending both flying through the air in a shower of blood. Erlaan-Orlassai turned his back on the shrieking legionnaires and stepped toward Ullsaard, face twisted in a hateful snarl.

"Fight me like a man!" the warped warrior demanded, gesturing with his shield for Ullsaard to stand. "Let us see who is better now!"

Ignoring a sharp pain at the base of his spine, Ullsaard pushed to his feet. Sweat dripped from his beard and soaked the bindings on his wrists and hands. He relaxed his grip on his sword and took a breath, narrowed eyes never leaving the monstrous thing that confronted him. A few legionnaires made another attempt to fell the warrior, using their spear butts as clubs, breaking them over Erlaan-Orlassai's back and legs to little effect.

"You're an abomination," said Ullsaard, sword circling slowly in his hand. "Look at yourself. You're no prince of the Blood; you're an animal that talks."

Incensed, Erlaan-Orlassai closed quickly, drawing his sword back for a backhanded slash. Ullsaard met the charge head-on, driving the point of his blade at the warrior's armoured thigh. Metal screeched across metal but the armour held as Ullsaard dashed past, Erlaan-Orlassai's blow cutting air just behind him. The two spun to face each other, swords springing out on instinct, meeting between them. Ullsaard's arm went numb as the force of the blow reverberated through him from hand to shoulder.

Feet moving quickly through the mud, he side-stepped, flexing his fingers on the grip of his sword to restore some feeling. The Askhan king was having serious doubts about his course of action. His foe wore armour heavier than any normal man could bear and his flesh, covered with unnatural carvings, was like toughened leather. Still, Erlaan-Orlassai was bleeding from many cuts, and even if it took another hundred such blows, Ullsaard was determined to finish him.

If he had the chance…

The Mekhani warlord attacked with a combination of quick strokes, sword flashing, parried away by Ullsaard's shield and blade at each attempt. Erlaan-Orlassai towered over him, swathing the king in shadow. Without thinking, Ullsaard dropped his shield and grabbed his sword in both hands, swinging up into the beast's groin with all of his strength. Blade bit into flesh between thigh armour and loin guard, slicing deep.

Ullsaard had no time to dodge the downswinging sword of his foe – as he had known would happen – and did his best to twist away, the edge of his opponent's blade carving a slice from his shoulder. The king could not stop the shout the sudden pain wrenched from him, but Erlaan-Orlassai was badly wounded too, staggering back as blood streamed from the cut in his groin.

Snarling and cursing, his left arm useless, Ullsaard dropped to one knee, panting. Around him the battle still raged; neither side paused to witness the spectacle of their duelling generals. Ullsaard paid no heed to the ongoing fight, knowing that he had won the battle if he could bring down Erlaan-Orlassai.

The other man limped closer, leaving a trail of thick blood across the muddy ground. A charging legionnaire was caught in the chest by the Mekhani general's shield, ribs crushed, organs burst by the strike. Ullsaard roused himself, forcing himself into a run. He dived under his opponent's sword as it descended towards him, angling the point of his blade towards Erlaan-Orlassai's foot. Bronze pierced the leather bindings around his foe's ankle and he felt metal scraping on bone. The twisted warrior roared in pain, drawing his foot back as Ullsaard scrambled to his feet, the king expecting a crashing blow against head or body at any moment.

Ullsaard saw someone stirring just behind Erlaan Orlassai. Harrakil sat up groggily, sword still in hand. The Askhan king shouted wordlessly to attract his foe's attention, fearing for the First Captain. He need not have worried; Harrakil looked up from a mask of blood and slashed his sword at the back of Erlaan-Orlassai's knee. Wounded in thigh, knee and ankle, the beast's leg finally gave wave and the Mekhani general toppled to one side with a howl.

"Pin him!" bellowed Ullsaard, sheathing his sword to pluck the spear from the hand of a dead Mekhani. He drove its point into Erlaan-Orlassai's exposed ankle, heaving with all of his weight so that the spear buried deep into the mud.

Yet the warped prince was not yet done. From his back, he swung sword and shield, slashing off legs and snapping bone. Dozens of legionnaires pounced, dropping their shields to plunge their spears two-handed into their disabled enemy. The crack of splintering bronze and the wet splash of blood sounded loud in Ullsaard's ears.

"His throat!" he heard a legionnaire call out. "Cut his throat!"

That's the idea, thought the king, pulling free his sword again. He watched Erlaan-Orlassai thrashing desperately at more than a dozen spears piercing his arms and legs, as the legionnaire's cut through armour straps and used their spears to lever off plates of bronze; they gasped in amazement at the realisation that some of the armour was riveted directly into the monstrous king's flesh.

A surge of achievement rushed through Ullsaard as he pushed through the crowd, sword at the ready. The last of Lutaar's spawn was about to die, leaving no one to challenge him for the Crown. He stepped up onto Erlaan-Orlassai's chest, his mangled left arm hanging at his side, sword raised. Erlaan-Orlassai glared venomously at Ullsaard from under the rim of his helm, his golden eyes filled with hate.

"Time to join your grandfather," spat Ullsaard, bringing his sword down.

He checked the blow at the last moment, turning the blade aside so that it rang harmlessly from the fallen king's helmet, slicing off part of the feathered crest.

"Kill him, king!" shouted Harrakil, still on the ground. "Finish it!"

Ullsaard could not strike that fatal blow.

It was not mercy that stayed his hand, but self-preservation. In that moment as he swung his sword, he had realised what he was about to do: slay the heir to the Crown of the Blood. Aalun was dead, savaged by his own Ailur; Lutaar and Nemtun had both been slain by Ullsaard's hand; Kalmud had died according to the testimony of his son. The only two surviving descendants of Askhos were Ullsaard and Erlaan.

If Erlaan died, that made Ullsaard the true heir.

He stepped back, wondering what this would mean. Could he risk becoming the true heir now? What if Erlaan's death somehow completed the ritual that Askhos had devised, allowing the dead king to take full control of Ullsaard? So much was uncertain, it was not a chance the Askhan king was prepared to take.

"Bind him with chains," Ullsaard snapped at his men, fearful they would slay Erlaan-Orlassai themselves. "He gets to live for now."

"You are doubly a coward!" snarled the fallen warrior. "I do not want your mercy, usurper!"

Ullsaard ignored him, and the complaints of his men, who muttered their desire to avenge the many that had fallen to Erlaan-Orlassai's blade. The king stepped down from the giant's chest and walked over to Harrakil, extending a hand to help him up. The First Captain said nothing as Ullsaard pulled him to his feet.

"You have my orders, captain," said the king. "See that they are carried out."

Harrakil nodded groggily and joined his men as Ullsaard surveyed the progress of the battle. It was far from won yet, but victory was certain. The Mekhani had broken the line in many places and there were thousands of dead on both sides but on the plain below, he saw the two reinforcing legions no more than a mile away. Without their general and with a fresh enemy at their rear, the Mekhani were breaking away in increasing numbers, streaming to dawnwards in scattered groups.

Ullsaard found a rock to sit on. He glanced at his shoulder, wincing as he saw the extent of the wound. There were orders to issue, a pursuit to organise; he decided he could let it wait. He glanced over his shoulder to where

381

Erlaan-Orlassai's raving was growing weaker. Victory today was not the end of the king's problems, but it heralded the opportunity to sort out some more.

First on the list was the treacherous High Brother. Ullsaard had living proof of Lakhyri's involvement in the Mekhani attacks, though he was not sure what exactly it was that the High Brother had done.

With a sigh, the king stood up and called for his heralds to attend him. There was no point thinking about battles yet to be fought when he still had one to finish.

V

Back in his pavilion, Ullsaard sat on a stool while the surgeon, Luaarit, swabbed the wound on his shoulder. Harrakil and Meesiu, the First Captain of the Sixth, were in attendance; the other legion commanders were leading the pursuit of the broken Mekhani army.

"You were lucky," said Luaarit. "The blow just missed the bone. You could have lost your arm. As it is, you'll never have full movement again, there's too much damage to the muscle."

Ullsaard grunted in reply, gritting his teeth as he lifted his arms at the surgeon's gesture, allowing him to wind a long bandage across the king's chest and shoulder.

"Do we head hotwards again?" asked Meesiu. "We took Mekhani prisoners and they hint that another army is being raised in the desert. There's a lot of nonsense too, about this reborn king of theirs and a great city."

"Their new king lies in chains," said Ullsaard, wincing as Luaarit pulled the bandage tight. He considered the situation for a moment. "Without that twisted monstrosity, I don't think this other army will be as much of a threat. Five legions should be enough to keep them at bay. I'll make Harrakil general."

"And you, king?" said Harrakil, surprised. The commander's head was swathed in padding and bandages, one side of his face discoloured by a vicious bruise. "Do you not wish to oversee the campaign?"

Ullsaard shook his head. Luaarit finished his ministrations and stood back with a satisfied expression.

"You'll have to get those dressings changed every two days," said the surgeon. "Do you wish me to accompany you, or will a couple of my orderlies suffice?"

"You tell me," replied the king. "Are your orderlies up to tending to their king?"

Luaarit smiled, wiping his bloody hands on his apron.

"They can change bandages and apply unguents well enough," he said. "Should you get a fever, I would advise you find a more qualified physician though. The wound looks clean enough but there is always the possibility of mortification."

"I've had worse and survived," said Ullsaard, though that was an exaggeration. He didn't want to think about the consequences of blood poisoning; by the regulations of the legions, such ailments were cured with a blade across the throat and Ullsaard did not know if the same rules applied to kings. "You can go."

Luaarit nodded, gathered up his things and departed quietly while Ullsaard turned his attention back to the First Captains.

"I've been too long away from Salphoria," he said. "For all we know, Aegenuis has stormed the camps and destroyed my army."

"Is that likely?" asked Meesiu, horrified at the proposition.

"No," said Ullsaard, "but that does not make it impossible. I'm sure Anasind is doing a fine job of keeping those Salphor dogs at bay, but the longer the legions are stuck there, the more the war will swing against them. I've no idea what the supply problems are like, for a start."

"Is there any reason why the caravans from Magilnada would not be getting through?" asked Harrakil. Ullsaard cursed himself for his loose tongue.

"The Salphors are not easy subjects," he said hurriedly. "You think they've bowed down and accepted their fate one day, only to find them raiding your columns the next. While Aegenuis and Carantathi are free, the Salphors will keep fighting."

"Which legions will you be taking with you?" asked Harrakil. He had a wax slate in hand and was making notations. "The Seventh? Twenty-First? Both?"

Ullsaard shook his head and grimaced.

"Send them up to Anrair to wait for me," he said. "I can't go directly to Salphoria. I'll need a fast column, say five companies."

"I am sorry, king, I am confused," said Harrakil. "You are not heading to Salphoria?"

"No," replied Ullsaard with a heavy sigh. "First I have someone to deal with in Askh."

ASKHOS
Late Spring, 212th year of Askh

I

The shuffling of feet along corridors, the quiet breaths sighing from the stone of the Grand Precincts reminded Lakhyri of the Temple. If one looked at things in a certain way, it *was* the Temple, of course, but the high priest did not allow himself to be drawn into such metaphysical contemplation, as tempting as it was. As he sat in his sparse chamber, fingers steepled on the table, he felt calm. After years of his brother's timidity-disguised-as-consolidation and the setbacks of Ullsaard's coup, Lakhyri finally believed that the situation was again developing as he wished.

The best result of his plans would be the rise of Erlaan to take the Crown, the combined forces of Mekha and Askh extinguishing all resistance in Salphoria to bring about the time of the eulanui. At worst, the Brotherhood had been re-established and Ullsaard's dependence upon it would grow stronger and proper leverage could be applied.

All things considered, Lakhyri was pleased with the turn of events.

A fierce knocking at the main doors echoed down the passageways, disturbing the high priest from his thoughts.

He straightened and stood as feet pattered past the archway towards the front hall. With measured paces, he left his chamber and passed silently along the corridors as the pounding at the door continued.

"What shall we do?" asked a Brother as Lakhyri entered the vestibule. "Who could it be?"

By the urgency of the knocking, Lakhyri guessed that it was a messenger bearing important news; he smiled thinly at the idea that perhaps such news was the death of Ullsaard.

"Open the door," he declared.

The Brothers worked the mechanism and the two doors noiselessly swung in, bathing the hall with moonlight. Lakhyri had not realised it was night; it was so easy to lose track of time.

The opening doors revealed ten legionnaires, one of them a second captain who still had the pommel of his sword raised to beat upon the wood. He sheathed the weapon and stepped inside.

"Where is the High Brother?" the officer demanded, glowering at the closest priest.

"I am here," said Lakhyri, taking three steps towards the man. "What brings you here to disturb our work?"

"I have a message to deliver to you," said the captain, waving to his men. A wagon was pulled into view, the back covered by a thick awning.

"A message from whom?" said Lakhyri as two of the legionnaires unfastened the ties of the awning and pulled down a hinged tailgate. "What is this?"

Something large was pushed out onto the flags in front of the doorway. It took a moment for Lakhyri to realise what it was: the huge form of Erlaan-Orlassai bound in chains and manacles. The runes carved into his skin were obscured with scabs and dried blood and he writhed weakly against his bounds. It was then Lakhyri noticed his protégé's lips had been sewn up with wire.

"Recognise this?"

Lakhyri's eyes snapped up to the back of the wagon, where King Ullsaard stood in the shadow, arms folded across his chest.

"Close the doors!" snapped Lakhyri, but the legionnaires acted first, grabbing the nearby Brothers and throwing them to the ground.

Ullsaard jumped down from the wagon and approached, directing a kick at the helpless Erlaan-Orlassai as he passed. Behind him, more legionnaires mounted the steps up to the Grand Precincts.

Lakhyri said nothing, noticing the sword at Ullsaard's hip. The king stopped a pace away from him, his face an expressionless mask.

"Do you recognise this creature?" the king said quietly.

Lakhyri quickly considered his options. Denial was impossible; it was clear Ullsaard already suspected Lakhyri's involvement with the resurgence of Mekhani, or at least with the transformation of Erlaan-Orlassai. The question was, just how much did the king really know?

"That is Erlaan, former prince of the Blood," the high priest said calmly. "Why have you brought him here?"

"These... changes, are you responsible?" the king continued in the same measured tone.

"You have proof that I am involved with this?" Lakhyri said.

Like a striking serpent, Ullsaard grabbed the front of Lakhyri's silver mask and wrenched it from his head, throwing back the high priest's hood as he did so. Lakhyri sneered as his sigil-carved features were revealed; the snarl turned to a choked cry as Ullsaard grabbed him by the throat.

"There is my proof, traitor!" said the king. "Your eyes betray you, Lakhyri, as do the strange marks upon both of your bodies."

"Traitor?" gasped Lakhyri, weakly pulling at Ullsaard's tight grip. "What treachery?"

"You are behind the Mekhani attacks," said the king. "You raised up Erlaan to be their leader in an attempt to overthrow me. Do not waste your last breaths denying it!"

The high priest gave up his forlorn struggles and fell limp in Ullsaard's grasp. Though he feigned defeat, his mind was whirling, seeking a means to exonerate himself, to deny the accusation; to save his life. He could think of nothing, and chose defiance instead.

"What if I did?" he croaked. "Perhaps you are jealous of our young prince? Should I have offered my gifts to you instead?"

Lakhyri felt the fingers around his throat relax a fraction.

"Turn me into a monster?" said Ullsaard, seemingly amused by the thought. "I am scarred and ugly enough already."

Lakhyri met the king's hard stare with golden eyes and smiled.

"What I did with Erlaan was necessary, but extreme," said the high priest. "You are of much stronger basic stock. There are lesser gifts that I could give you."

The grip tightened again, sending pain through Lakhyri's jaw and back, the sudden pressure dizzying him for a moment.

"I do not desire your gifts, you cur," said Ullsaard. He stalked forwards, pushing Lakhyri ahead of him, the priest back-stepping quickly so as not to fall. "You would promise me anything to save your life."

They stopped when Lakhyri was backed up against the hewn stone of the archway leading into the depths of the building. His bony fingers scrabbled at the rough surface, seeking purchase as Ullsaard lifted the high priest to his toes.

"Yes, I would!" he managed to say between gritted teeth. "Name your price!"

The king was taken aback, dropping Lakhyri down though not releasing his hold. Ullsaard's brow furrowed in thought, eyes never leaving the high priest's. As Lakhyri had noticed in his last encounter with the king, Ullsaard paused for a moment, distracted.

"There are many things that I might do for you, Ullsaard," Lakhyri said, in the most soothing tone he could manage. "Strange and many are my powers, as you have seen."

"Leave us!" growled the king, still not turning his eyes away. The legionnaires and Brothers looked at each other before retreating through the main doors. Those Brothers that had been skulking at the other door to watch the scene disappeared back down the corridor.

Ullsaard pulled back his hand and Lakhyri flopped back against the wall, rubbing his throat. The king paced back and forth for a few steps, his lips moving as if in whispered conversation. As before, Lakhyri detected a strange double-presence around the king. With the threat of immediate violence withdrawn, the high priest's mind worked more smoothly. He wondered why Erlaan still lived; his corpse would be as much proof as his living body. Lakhyri wracked his mind for an answer but Ullsaard spoke before he came to any conclusions.

"There may be something you can do for me if I let you live," said the king, his voice quiet. "A problem I have that you might be able to deal with."

Lakhyri suppressed a smile of satisfaction.

"I shall serve in any way I can," he said, with a bow of the head.

"Stop that!" snapped Ullsaard, hand moving to the hilt of his sword. "No mock servitude, no false praise. Last time we spoke, you said that there was no reason our goals could not be joined. You lied to me then. Tell me now, truthfully, if you could ever accept me as king."

"I seek for the empire to cover all of the lands between the seas, and nothing else," said Lakhyri. "I only used Erlaan against you because I thought you were too weak. I was wrong. It matters not who wears the Crown."

Ullsaard flinched, as if in pain. He grinned at Lakhyri when the moment had passed.

"I am told that your words are worth less than abada shit," said the king.

"Told by whom?" said Lakhyri. "Who dares say such things?"

Resting one hand to the wall, Ullsaard loomed over Lakhyri, eyes wide, tiny reflections of the high priest's shocked face in his pupils. He tapped the side of his head with his other hand.

"Your brother," whispered the king. He nodded to himself. "I know everything about you, Lakhyri. Everything!"

The high priest looked at Ullsaard with narrowed eyes, searching for a hint of deception. What he said could only mean one thing.

"Askhos." Lakhyri barely breathed the word. "He lives."

"He continues," said Ullsaard, straightening. "That is the closest he'll get to living again if there's anything I can do about it."

Instinctively, Lakhyri's eyes drifted over Ullsaard's shoulder at the mound of humanity still lying sprawled beyond the open doors. The king noticed his gaze and grabbed his chin, forcing Lakhyri to look at him.

"I considered it," said Ullsaard. "Neither I, nor Askhos, nor you really know what will happen if Erlaan dies now.

390

Perhaps it is too late for your brother. Perhaps he is trapped between me and the Crown forever. All you need to know is that should Erlaan die, however it happens, and I remain myself, I will kill you. It is not only my future and your brother's that would hang on such a decision, it is also your own. Your grand plans for empire, you can forget all of them if anything bad happens to our young prince."

"What would you have me do?" Lakhyri asked, conceding defeat for the time being. "Protect Erlaan?"

Ullsaard nodded and laid a thick arm across the high priest's shoulders, dragging him away from the wall.

"And there is still the promise you made me; to help me with my problem."

"The campaign in Salphoria?" guessed the high priest, rewarded by the look of surprise from the king. "Come now, it is clear that something occurs to dawnwards that has held you in check. If I can remove any obstacle for you, I shall do so."

And so came the story from the king, of Anglhan's treachery and the hostages the governor held. The tale was told with a mixture of anger, regret and embarrassment, and when he was done, Ullsaard was trembling with the indignity of it.

"You see my dilemma?" finished the king. "I cannot prosecute the war while that venomous serpent lies coiled behind me."

"And you value your family too highly to risk any overt attack," added Lakhyri. His next words were directed at the spirit he now knew lurked inside Ullsaard. "Perhaps a weakness, but one I might once have shared. We sometimes make concessions for family that more ruthless men would discard."

"When I fought against Lutaar, or Askhos, or whoever, you visited woes upon my army to thin our numbers and sap our morale," said Ullsaard, ignoring the high priest's last comment. "From afar, could you strike down Anglhan?"

"The fact that you still live proves that it is not possible," said Lakhyri with a solemn shake of the head. "Do you think that if I could end a life in such a way, you would have lived past the moment I learned of your plans to become king? No, my powers cannot be so specifically directed, not against the living."

Ullsaard slumped, shoulders sagging.

"There is nothing you can do to aid me?"

Lakhyri examined his options. Perhaps it was time to do more than appear as Ullsaard's ally. If Askhos dwelt within him, he knew the secrets of the Brotherhood, perhaps of the Temple and the eulanui. Such knowledge had not weakened his desire for conquest.

"Your friend, the one that fell protecting you against my puppets, he still lives?" asked the high priest.

"Noran? Yes, last I heard he still lives. But he cannot help me; he is in a sleep that will never end."

"That is perfect," said Lakhyri, clasping his hands together at his chest. "That will be all I need."

"Really?" The hope on Ullsaard's face was almost pitiful. Not half an hour since coming here to slay Lakhyri, now he was desperate for his aid.

"There are some preparations we will both need to undertake," said Lakhyri. "Ready your men for an assault on Magilnada. Not too obvious, but be ready to act swiftly. We too must go to the Free Country."

"And what then?" said Ullsaard. "What will you do and how is Noran involved?"

"That is best demonstrated than explained," said Lakhyri. He hesitated before asking a question. "Do you trust me, Ullsaard?"

"No."

"You will have to learn, because if I do what you wish, you will have to place your life, your whole existence, into my hands."

"And why would you not simply extinguish it when you have the chance?" asked the king.

Lakhyri took a deep breath and smiled.

"The empire of Greater Askhor has taken longer than you can imagine to create, far beyond the two hundred years of its written history. For the first time, it is on the brink of succeeding in uniting the whole land under one banner. You are the man that can achieve that, Ullsaard. Erlaan has proven too weak and inexperienced. Askhos let himself get killed. If I kill you, Ullsaard, I will have to start again as your death would herald the fracturing of the empire. It has barely stood the strain of your usurpation, it cannot take any more. In short, you are my best chance to achieve my goals. Believe that and trust me, or do not, and slay me now."

The king drew his sword, but Lakhyri masked his shock as the point swung towards his chest. He faced down Ullsaard, meeting his gaze, unflinching.

"Only I can help return your family to you," said the high priest.

The sword tip lowered and Ullsaard stepped back.

"Magilnada, then," said the king. "We leave at dawn."

FREE COUNTRY
Early Summer, 212th year of Askh

I

The mountain wind flapped at the tent walls and howled over the rocks. Braziers lit the inside of the pavilion with a ruddy glow, the white fabric dancing with shadows as Lakhyri and Ullsaard entered. Outside, two companies of legionnaires stood guard watching the pass that led down towards Magilnada. They huddled around their fires, quietly wondering what their king and the High Brother were doing, yet reluctant to speculate too much.

Rugs had been spread over the ground, and a plain chair stood in the centre of the pavilion. Ullsaard sat himself at Lakhyri's invitation, dread and excitement warring within him. The high priest had explained nothing of the ritual he was about to undertake despite the king's persistent questioning. Even now, Ullsaard was not sure of Lakhyri, yet for the many days it had taken to travel from Askh the king had not come upon another means to secure his family's release.

It was this more than his life that occupied Ullsaard's thoughts; not that he was willing to die just yet. The helplessness that ever hovered on the edge of his mind returned as he settled back into the chair, and as before his anger at the situation swept away the doubts.

Lakhyri stood before him, a small canvas bag over his shoulder. His spindly fingers delved into the sack and pulled forth a handful of dried leaves.

"So that you understand the bargain we will make, I must tell you that what I offer is a chance, not a guarantee," said the high priest.

"I understand," Ullsaard replied with a nod. "That doesn't mean I won't kill you if you fail."

"If I fail, you will be in no position to kill anybody," Lakhyri said, his expression solemn. "Even if I succeed, there will be a price to pay, a physical toll upon your life. Do you agree to consent knowing this?"

"What sort of toll?"

"It varies," Lakhyri replied with a sight shrug. "A few years from your life at best; crippling at worst."

"How can I make such a decision? Both the terms of success and the price to be paid are uncertain. Only a fool would agree to such a thing."

Lakhyri shoved the leaves back into his bag and stepped away.

"I cannot offer you any better assurance," he said. "Yet it is not the final decision. First I will show you what is possible. It is then that you must decide if you wish to proceed further. You will have one chance to change your mind, but before that you must still place your life in my hands."

"In the spirit of honesty, I should tell you that the second captain of my guards has orders to slay you if I should die." The king smiled at Lakhyri's reaction. "Perhaps that is the extra incentive you need. Whether he will actually do it or not, I cannot offer you any better assurance."

Ullsaard gestured towards the priest's bag.

"What's with the leaves? Is there going to be much chanting and such?"

Lakhyri brought forth the bunched leaves again and placed them in Ullsaard's hands.

"This is not some primitive ceremony of superstition, Ullsaard," said the priest, showing repulsion at the thought. "This is a precise ritual, honed over a hundred lifetimes of mortal men. There will be no chanting or dancing or other nonsense. The leaves are a drug to ease you into a deep sleep. When you are there, I will join you in your dreams."

Ullsaard was becoming less keen on the plan the more he heard of it. It was no wonder Lakhyri had not offered any earlier explanation.

"So it'll be like when Askhos invades my dreams?"

"He does?" The priest could not hide his astonishment. Ullsaard had been aware of Lakhyri's casual yet constant inquiries regarding the exact nature of Askhos's state for the whole journey; inquiries that Ullsaard had met with the same silence with which Lakhyri had answered the king's questions.

"Sometimes," Ullsaard said, wishing he had said nothing. "If I'm going to do this, we might as well get started. How long will this drug take to work?"

He stuffed the leaves into his cheek and almost retched at the bitter taste.

"Do not chew," warned Lakhyri. "Let the juices mix with your spit, absorb it through your gums and mouth. It will not take long at all."

Within a few heartbeats Ullsaard was already feeling numb in the face. His pulse and breathing slowed as Lakhyri took the king's hands in his, for a moment looking like a parent standing over a child. The edges of the king's vision darkened, the red of the braziers deepening, the gold of Lakhyri's eyes growing brighter and brighter.

His whole body was limp and the world had disappeared to a tiny patch filled with the priest's rune-etched face. He could not feel Lakhyri's grasp, or the rug beneath his feet, or the chair he sat on. Ullsaard wanted to say something, give voice to the fear that he was dying, poisoned. Yet the dread was as dull as every other sense. He could not even hear his heart and the wind was a distant memory.

Greyness covered everything, a mist inside and outside of him, neither warm nor cool, until even that slipped away.

II

Ullsaard awoke in the pavilion, alone.

"Is that it?" he asked. His voice echoed oddly from the tent walls. He tried to stand but was paralysed. Panic swelled up. "Lakhyri? What have you done to me?"

There was no reply, save for his owns words ringing oddly around.

"Guards!"

Again there was no response. He was utterly alone. Paying more attention, Ullsaard saw that the flames in the braziers did not move, frozen in mid-flicker. There was no sound of the wind, no tramp of patrolling legionnaires, no strum of rope or slap of canvas. All was still, and he wondered if he had called out at all or if the sound had been only inside his head.

"How remarkable." He recognised Askhos's voice immediately. The tent flap pulled back and the dead king strode in; for the moment the door was open Ullsaard thought he glimpsed a backdrop of stars as he had seen from Askhos's tomb. The First King was dressed as if for a full ceremonial audience in an embroidered gown, gold necklaces and bracelets hanging heavily, beard and hair curled and oiled.

Ullsaard felt a light touch upon his right shoulder and found he could move. He looked up and saw Lakhyri standing behind the chair. The priest glanced at him only for a moment before staring at his brother. Ullsaard looked between the two and found little resemblance; perhaps the line of the jaw and nose but nothing else. Where the king was broad, fulsome and well fed, Lakhyri was a shrivelled husk, at least a head shorter.

"So it is true," said the priest, coming around the chair to examine Askhos more closely. "What a vain man you can be, brother, clinging onto this vision of your best days."

"While your desiccation is no less a badge of honour?" replied the dead king. "You wear your withered flesh no less proudly than I wear this appearance. Both are who we are."

"You faltered," said Lakhyri with an accusing glare. "You lost sight of what we set out to achieve and dallied in your duty."

"The problem of an immortal existence, one where I get to live again and again properly, not like the half-life you eke out, is that it becomes harder and harder to bring about its end."

"Our masters would gr–"

"We're not here for a fucking family gathering!" rasped Ullsaard. "Keep your bickering for another time. Get on with it, Lakhyri. What happens next?"

"I must leave you for a moment," said the priest. "I shall return."

With that said, Lakhyri faded away. Ullsaard glowered at Askhos.

"Your childhood must have been very fucked up," said Ullsaard.

A low reclining seat appeared and Askhos lowered himself into it, one arm behind his head.

"You cannot comprehend the lives we used to lead, Ullsaard," said the First King. "Yet it was not so different in some ways. We had a loving mother and a proud father, and a sister, though she drowned in a river when we were barely old enough to know her."

"And you decided one day that you didn't like the idea of dying and so you started to inhabit the bodies of your children while Lakhyri... well, does whatever it is he does to keep alive."

"We found something that opened our eyes to a wider world," said Askhos. "The Temple, ageless and ancient even when we came upon it. What happened next is not important. It sustained us and those who joined with us. I was once as Lakhyri is; perhaps a little less scrawny."

"I cannot pretend to understand how any of this is possible."

"How could you? It is as far from your experience as the life of a man is for an insect. At its heart it is a very simple thing. The physical world, the one you see and hear and touch and breathe and fornicate in, is but one part of a much larger world. There are gaps between everything, where the essence of life exists, where dreams are made. Its power is limited only by the span of the universe itself. We all live here too, but only from what we learned in the Temple were Lakhyri and I able to see it, to consciously explore it."

"And what is your brother up to now? Has he gone exploring?"

"I believe he has," said Askhos, shifting his weight and bringing his hands to his lap. "From what he said earlier, I think he has gone to look for Noran."

"Noran is here?" Ullsaard sat up and looked around, and felt foolish for doing so. He slouched back with embarrassment. "Here, in your world between worlds."

"His essence, his mind, his life, whatever you wish to call it, is separate from his physical state. He is not dead, and so that force that is Noran must still be here."

"It sounds like a big place," said Ullsaard. "It could take some time to find him."

"It is massive and yet tiny, that is one of its charms," Askhos said with a wistful smile. "The whole of everything within a grain of sand; yet also in every grain of sand and speck of dust and pore upon your skin. Everywhere is everywhere if you know how to walk properly."

Saying nothing, Ullsaard crossed his arms and legs and waited. He knew he was not an educated man, but he had never lacked for cleverness. He had learned quickly his lessons, though they were of a practical rather than philosophical nature. For all that, the things Lakhyri and Askhos told him were very confusing; he suspected he would never get any better explanation from either of them. There was one question that nagged at him as he sat tapping a finger against his arm, trying to be patient.

"The Blood," he said, startling Askhos who had closed his eyes. "I understand it is your link from generation to generation, through the Crown somehow. But what is so special about it? A man's seed carries him into his sons and daughters, not his blood."

Askhos smiled at the question and sat up, suddenly animated.

"Our bodies are but one thing given different forms," said the dead king. "Blood, seed, muscle, bone, all of it springing from the same place. We call it the Blood, but it is in everything that makes us, from the hair on our heads to the nails on our toes. The Blood we share is not the blood of normal men; not wholly the blood of men at all."

"You'll be spewing Salphorian myths about spirits coming down and fucking women in their sleep," laughed Ullsaard. "*Your* Brotherhood dispelled all of that myth. Talk sense."

"Myth is not the same as fact, Ullsaard," said Askhos. "The Brotherhood seeks to expunge superstition, legend, because it is a fabrication. Yet they are perhaps stories based upon truth, on tales first told by our most distant ancestors. They are corruptions of the truth, but they lead to questions that men should not ask. Our Blood comes not from men, but from something else."

Ullsaard was about to challenge this when he saw something out of the corner of his eye. Turning his head, he saw Noran lying on the rugs beside the chair, eyes closed, hands folded neatly to his chest. He appeared fresh-skinned and healthy, with none of the deathly pallor Ullsaard had seen when he had last visited his friend.

Seeming to step from the shadows cast by a brazier, Lakhyri reappeared, stooping down to lay his fingertips upon Noran's brow.

"Join us," the priest whispered.

Noran awoke with a gasp and looked around with frantic eyes for a moment before springing to his feet. His words were incoherent as he staggered a few paces, eyes roving until they fell upon the king.

"Ullsaard!" Noran seemed startled by the sound of his own voice, which was as mellow and enunciated as it had been before his injuries. "Ullsaard?"

The king jumped up and embraced his friend with a laugh. Noran lifted up his hands and examined them, wiggling his fingers with a smirk. The smile faded and he pulled from Ullsaard's arms.

"This does not feel right," said Noran. He looked around the pavilion room, eyes fearful. They stopped when they fell upon Lakhyri. "What are you?"

"Questions can wait," said the high priest. "Time is now being counted, Ullsaard. I have recovered your friend's essence from the pit into which it had fallen, but to do so

I draw on the strength of your body. Every beat of Noran's heart steals one from you."

"What does he mean?" said Noran. As he turned back to the king, he spied Askhos on the couch and gave a delirious giggle. "Do you know who you look like?"

"It doesn't sound like we have much time for explanations," said Ullsaard, grabbing his friend by the shoulders to gain his attention. "Think of this as a dream. That is King Askhos, and this is Lakhyri, the founder of the Brotherhood. You have been brought here to help me."

"How?" asked Noran. Ullsaard looked to Lakhyri for the answer.

"Outside of your dream, your body is in an unwaking sleep," said the priest. "You are in Magilnada with two of Ullsaard's wives and are being held hostage."

"Hostage?"

"Concentrate, Noran, please," said Ullsaard. "Listen to Lakhyri but save your questions."

The high priest waited for a moment, until Noran nodded that he was ready to continue.

"Anglhan had turned against your king, and to stop Ullsaard from taking back the city he threatens your life and that of Allenya and Meliu." Ullsaard frowned and raised a finger to silence Noran as he looked to speak again. Lakhyri carried on in a patient tone. "I will allow Ullsaard to give up some of his life to restore yours. Do not ask how; know only that it can be done. Through me, his energy will pass from his body into this dream and from this dream into your body, restoring some of your strength. You will revive and when you do so, you must escape the city with your queens."

Noran nodded uncertainly.

"I don't know if you are free to move around, if you're imprisoned, in Anglhan's palace or anything else," said

Ullsaard. "Nobody expects you to recover, and you must use that surprise to free Allenya if you can. I have troops outside the city, in disguise near the city gate, who will escort you here once you are out of Magilnada."

"Right," said Noran. "Lots of questions, no time. I understand, I think. So, what happens now?"

III

A bird was chirping merrily to itself nearby. Noran felt a soft mattress beneath him, a pillow under his head, sheets tight across him. Probably not a cell, he thought. He opened one eye and in dim, pre-dusk light he saw a ceiling painted with a mural of a boar hunt. He turned his head to look around. Even this slight movement sent a wave of nausea through him, causing him to lurch to one side, vomiting a small stream of liquid onto the carpeted floor.

Wiping his hand over his mouth, Noran noticed a yellow hue to his skin. He opened his other eye carefully, expecting more sickness but none came. His fingernails were brittle, cracked, the flesh wasted away to reveal bulging knuckles.

Noran raised his fingertips to his face, felt hollow, fleshless cheeks and a sheen of sweat. His body trembled from weakness and he lay still for a moment, his breath shallow, heart beating perilously weak. Hunger gnawed at him, every bone ached and his eyes burned even in the gloom, the calls of the bird shrill in his ears.

"Cannot stay here," he said, his voice a wheeze that shocked him. He took a ragged breath and sat up quickly, preparing himself for the wave of dizziness that struck. Glancing down, he saw that he was naked. Checking the room slowly he saw no wardrobe or chest that might contain clothes. "Not the first time I have had to run naked from a house," he reminded himself with a chuckle.

He gingerly swung his legs free and pushed himself to the edge of the bed. One hand on the wooden frame, he hauled himself up, steadier than he had expected. Movement seemed to help, quickening his pulse, strengthening fibres and sinews not used for a long while.

Noran slid his foot through the pile of the carpet in a faltering step, half-twisted to maintain his balance with the help of the bedstead. Like a child, he reluctantly released his hold and tottered forward a few paces, a smile on his face.

"Congratulations," he told himself. "Next you can teach yourself how to piss standing up. Come on, this is no time to be cautious."

His confidence fuelling his steps, he walked to the window and pushed back one of the shutters. Daybreak was not far off, the glow to dawnwards visible above the houses on the opposite side of the street. As yet the city was not awake. He dredged his memories for everything he knew of Magilnada from the time he had spent here before Ullsaard's pretend liberation. Noran had walked every street and alley and square over those long days of misery. The recollection brought a stab of pain as he remembered his depression, caused by the death of his wife and unborn son.

Holding himself up on the sill of the window, Noran bowed his head for a moment, the emotional agony of the memory greater than any soreness in his atrophied body. He fought back tears, fingers gripping the sill tightly, picturing the lovely Neerita. Looking back into the street, he realised Ullsaard's family were still in the house they had shared with Noran and his other wife, Anriit. He wondered if Neerita's older sister still lived here, and whether he would bother taking her from the city.

The creak of a foot on a floorboard outside the door caused Noran to spin. The handle turned and he staggered across the chamber as the door opened. A middle-aged woman in the garb of servant stepped inside, eyes widening in surprise and Noran lunged, grabbing her arm in one hand, clamping his other over her mouth as he dragged her inside.

She struggled and his weak body failed him, losing his grip on both her arm and face as he tumbled to the carpet.

"Master Noran!" the woman yelped, crouching beside him.

"Hush woman! Do not speak, but listen!"

With the maid's help, Noran regained his feet and leaned against the wall, signalling for the servant to close the door. When she had done so, he pulled her towards the bed and they both sat down.

"What is your name?" he asked.

"Laasinia," the woman replied, eyes averted from the noble's nakedness. "I am Queen Allenya's senior handmaiden."

"Yes, Laasinia, I am remembering now," said Noran. He took her hand in his, squeezing it in what he hoped was a comforting fashion. "Look at me, Laasinia."

She turned her head, eyes betraying her confusion.

"It is important that you listen to exactly what I say, and not to waste time with asking why," he told her. She nodded. "First of all, do not tell anyone of my recovery yet."

"But Queen Meliu…"

Noran hushed her with a wave of his hand.

"Not yet," he said. "I need you to get me clothes, first."

"A chest of your robes and shirts is in another room," said Laasinia, standing up. Noran pulled her back and she tried to step away.

"No, not my own clothes," he said, thinking as quickly as he could. "Is there a servant of right height and build?

Laasinia looked him up and down and nodded again.

"Saamiaris is about your size," she said. "He is a cook. He has already left for the market; I can get clothes from his room."

"Good," said Noran, standing up. "When you have done that you must find other clothes, for your mistresses."

Again Laasinia opened her mouth to speak and Noran raised a finger to silence her.

"Do not ask me how I know, but there has been threat made against Ullsaard's family," he explained, the words coming quickly. "They are in danger, right now. The longer we stay here, the more dangerous it will be. I have to get them out of the city, and servants' clothes will make a good disguise. Do you understand?"

"Not everything," Laasinia admitted, "but I will do as you say. Shall I wake my mistresses?"

"When I am more respectable, I shall attend to that," said Noran. "Tell me, does my wife, Anriit, still live here?"

"She left," Laasinia said, embarrassed. "She has returned to Askh to seek the annulment of your marriage."

"One less thing to worry about," muttered Noran. He focussed on Laasinia. "Try not to let on to the other servants what you are doing. The house may be watched, and I do not know if the man who wishes harm to your mistresses has his own people in the household."

Even as he spoke the words, Noran wondered if he could trust the woman. She had served Ullsaard's family back in Askh, he remembered, but it was possible that Anglhan might have turned her loyalties. It was too late now, he realised.

"Can you do these things?" he asked.

"I will," said Laasinia. "The kitchen staff have taken the cart to the market, but I shall send a boy for another to take you to the gates."

"Good thinking," Noran said, patting her on the arm. "Do not say what is for."

"Of course not," she said, offended by the suggestion. "If the matter is as serious as you say, I will see my mistresses safely away from the city, do not doubt that."

Noran leaned forward and kissed Laasinia on the forehead, startling her.

"You are a gem, Laasinia," he said. "I am sure Allenya and Meliu will be very grateful."

"Let us hurry," said the maidservant, stepping briskly away. "It is market day and the streets will be busy by mid-Dawnwatch. Better that we are on our way before then."

Noran nodded and watched her as she opened the door and slipped outside, closing it quietly behind her. It opened again a moment later, causing Noran to jump. He relaxed as he saw Laarisia's face peer around the frame.

"You look like you need food, master," she said. "I'll bring something with the clothes."

Before Noran could thank her, she was gone again, her footsteps fading on the landing beyond the door. He paced back and forth at the foot of the bed as he waited, trying to come up with a list of things he would need. A weapon of some sort would be good. He wandered back to the window, scrutinising the street for any sign of somebody watching the house. It was impossible to say; dozens of windows on the houses along the street could see the main gate to the courtyard. He consoled himself with the thought that at least they were not locked up in some dungeon somewhere. Compared to that, smuggling themselves out of the city would be easy.

He turned quickly as the door opened again. Laasinia entered with a bundle of clothes in her arms, some bread and fruit perched atop the pile. She laid these on the bed with a nod to the nobleman and left again without a word. Though now ravenous, Noran took a cautious bite of an apple. It tasted sweet as juice ran down his throat and he fought the urge to finish off in a few bites, wary of taxing his shrunken gut. He had heard tales of the ailments that had befallen legionnaires over-indulging after long campaigns on march rations. He dragged on a heavy woollen kilt, apple held between his teeth, and tied the roped fastenings, marvelling at how skinny he was. The fit was adequate; for a cook, Saamirias did not sample much of his labours it seemed.

Finishing off the apple, Noran tossed the core onto a side table and ripped a hunk of bread from the loaf. He stuffed this in his mouth and chewed laboriously as he pulled the shirt over his head. The coarse fabric itched at his skin, nothing like the fine clothes he had been used to. Resisting the urge to scratch everywhere, he pulled on the sandals, a little too big for his feet, and tied the thongs as tightly as he could. There was a heavy, sleeveless jacket too, and he dragged this on to complete the outfit. Taking another apple and the loaf, he padded across the room and opened the door a fraction.

He could hear the sounds of servants elsewhere in the house, but the landing was empty. Knowing that Allenya would be the calmer of the two queens, he tiptoed out and to the left, heading for her bedchamber, keeping to the wall. He stopped at the second door and paused as he heard footfalls on the stair behind. Coiling to pounce if need be, he waited with breath held, letting it out in a rush as Laasinia stepped onto the landing. She saw him and nodded, lifting up a sack in her hand.

Taking the bag, Noran quietly opened the door to Allenya's room. Any feelings of intrusion were washed away by Noran's urgency; both from fear of discovery and ignorance of how long he would be able to continue walking and talking.

Ullsaard's wife was sprawled on the bed, covers in disarray, one arm flung out, her face hidden behind a mass of dark curls on the pillow. Noran could not stop himself admiring the graceful curve of her exposed thigh. He quickly dismissed the distraction; having sex with one of the queens had been a mistake, lusting after this one would be suicide.

"Allenya," he whispered, crouching down in front of her. "Allenya, wake up."

She stirred, rolling to her back, eyes flickering open. There was a moment of vagueness before she sat bolt upright to stare at Noran.

"Yes, I'm back," he said, knowing exactly what thoughts were going through Allenya's mind. "There is no time to explain, and I do not know if I understand it myself."

"What are you doing in my room?" Allenya said, pulling a blanket over her body.

"Anglhan has betrayed Ullsaard." Noran spoke quickly but quietly, trying to keep calm. "He is keeping you in the city as protection against Ullsaard's retaliation."

Allenya ran her fingers through her hair, raking it back from her face, her expression half-asleep.

"What was that about Anglhan?" she said. She looked more closely at the man in her bedchamber. "And why are you dressed so badly?"

Noran stood and emptied the clothes from the sack onto the bed.

"You do not realise it, but Anglhan is using you as hostages against your husband," Noran said, stepping to the door. "We have to leave here as soon as we can, and get out of the city. Please, get dressed in these clothes and then get Meliu to do the same. Your maid is organising a means by which we can get out of here unseen."

"Wait." Allenya's call stopped Noran as he was about to leave. He turned back, one foot on the landing. "Anglhan has been very hospitable to us. Are you sure?"

"Ullsaard himself told me so," said Noran.

He saw the look of confusion that would herald more questions and decided to avoid them, moving onto the landing to close the door behind him. Laasinia was still waiting close by.

"Any luck with a wagon?" the noble asked.

"I've sent a lad to fetch one," she said. "He'll bring it up to the gate. How will you get on it without being seen?"

Noran thought about this for a while, hearing the sounds of Allenya moving around through the door.

"We will not try to hide," he said. "Find something that would look normal to load and move, a piece of furniture or something. We will just carry it out and climb on board with it."

"Why would two maids be moving furniture?" asked Laasinia.

"Think of something else, then," snapped Noran. The surge of strength that had propelled him so far was leeching away, leaving his limbs trembling and his head aching. "Use your head, woman."

Laasinia bobbed demurely and disappeared down the stairs. Noran leaned back against the wall, his hunger returning, his muscles twitching with the effort. On the floor below, a small bell tinkled to signal the start of Dawnwatch. More distant bells and calls could be heard from across the waking city. Noran fretted, gnawing at an overly long nail, fearing that they were taking too much time. Anglhan was no fool. He had chosen not to jail his hostages, probably for fear of provoking attention, but he would have the movements of Allenya and Meliu watched closely so that they could be prevented from leaving the city, even if innocent and ignorant of their predicament. The more people on the streets, the harder it would be to avoid attention.

Noran was chewing down a third nail by the time Allenya's door opened. She walked out garbed in the clothes of a maid, her face showing her full displeasure.

"I demand a proper explanation Noran," she said.

"Please, Allenya, keep your voice down," Noran replied. "It is very complicated. All you have to know is that Anglhan does not want you to leave Magilnada; he has made threats against you to Ullsaard. Your husband is less than a day from the city. I am going to take you to him."

"Ullsaard is near?" the prospect brightened Allenya's mood substantially and her further questions went unasked. "Really?"

"Yes, really," said Noran, trying not to sigh in frustration. "Please, take the other clothes, get Meliu dressed and we will leave the house. Make sure she causes no fuss."

"Wait here," said Allenya, heading to the other end of the landing. "You cannot be seen."

Noran bit back a retort about stating the obvious. He could hear Laarisia's voice from the bottom of the stairs, but could not make out everything that was said; something about the mistresses desiring not to be disturbed this morning until Low Watch. A wonderful woman, Noran thought, entirely deserving of some extra Askharins for her loyalty.

He lowered to the floor to sit with his back against the wall, resting his head in his hands in an effort the ease the throbbing at his temples. There was soreness in his chest and he lifted up his shirt and saw a jagged scar. No wonder every breath hurt.

"Shit," he muttered. He could barely remember anything of how he had been wounded. He recalled some soldiers trying to kill Ullsaard in camp and shouting a warning. The rest was all blurred.

A door banged open and he looked up to see Meliu dashing along the landing. He pushed himself to his feet and was almost toppled again as Meliu threw her arms around him with a gasp, the two of them saved from a tumble only by the wall.

"Oh, Noran!" Meliu gushed, kissing his cheek and neck ferociously.

"Hello," he said weakly, pushing her away.

Her brows furrowed, cheeks reddened and lips pouted. Recognising the signs of an impending outburst, Noran did the only thing he could think of to quieten her; her grabbed the back of her head and pulled her into a long kiss.

"Save that for later," said Allenya, hurrying to the top of the stairs.

Meliu pulled back with another shuddering breath, eyes moist.

"Allenya tells me we are in trouble and you have come back to rescue us!" she said. "You are so brave!"

Noran darted a look at Allenya, who shrugged in confession.

"Come on," said Noran, grabbing Meliu's hand. She squeezed it tight, painfully so in Noran's weak condition.

The nobleman led them down the stairs and found Laasinia sitting with some needlework on a chair in the hall below. She put the sewing to one side as they arrived.

"I have sent the other servants to clean the main feast room," she said, ushering Allenya towards the foyer. She looked at Noran. "Can you drive the wagon, or should I fetch one of the men?"

"I will do my best," said Noran, though he knew he was an inexpert teamster. "Rather that than risking the confidence of anyone else."

They hurried out into the courtyard, the flags still damp from overnight rain. Noran let go of Meliu to move ahead and open one of the gates. On the road outside a single abada stood patiently before its wagon, chewing on its leather bit, horn rope in the hand of a boy no more than ten years old.

"Take these," said Laasinia, ducking into a small storage shed at one side of the yard. She emerged with woven baskets. "Put them on the wagon and climb in."

"Try to act normal," Noran added in a whisper. "Do not look like you are hurrying."

Meliu grinned impishly and grabbed a basket before strutting out into the street. Allenya and Laasinia followed with their own burdens, leaving Noran to pull himself up to the board.

"Get yourself inside, and have something to eat," he called to the boy, who bobbed his head, tied the abada's rope through the yoke and scampered back into the yard.

The nobleman sat looking at the back of the abada, unsure what to do. He glanced around and saw a long switch hanging in a loop of rope on the side of the wagon. He pulled it free and tapped the abada on the shoulder with its tip.

"Move," he said.

The abada did nothing.

Noran tried again with the switch, slapping it against the beast's hindquarters.

"Get on," he said. "Move!"

"Give it a proper crack," he heard Allenya say from the back of the cart. "Use your wrist, man."

"Right, you big, grey bastard," Noran snarled. "You will not ignore me this time."

He brought the switch back over his shoulder and then flicked it down as hard as he could. With a crack, he smacked against the abada's ribs. The beast gave a pained snort and leaned into the yoke, the wagon lurching forward over the cobbles of the road. There were cries of discomfort from behind as the cart's occupants were bumped around and Noran almost fell off the driving board.

He snatched up the yoke ropes in his free hand as the abada settled down into a fast walk. The wheels clattered like thunderclaps in the dawn quiet. Noran winced every time they bounced over a hole or mound in the street. The grand houses of merchants and nobles passed by on each side, peeking over stuccoed walls and ornately carved gates.

They were almost at the end of the street when Noran realised he did not know which way to turn; or for that matter, how to turn. The quickest route would be to the right, along the main thoroughfare that wound down the Hill of Chiefs and to the avenue that led to the city gate. It would also be getting busy with the pre-market traffic; better to turn left and go around by the wall, he decided.

Coming to the junction, he hauled back on the left-hand rope, turning the abada's head. The creature came to a stop, the traces and harness bunching as the front of the wagon rolled into its rear end. Noran tugged to the left again, and applied the switch lightly to the stubborn creature's shoulder. The combination worked as the abada heaved into the yoke again, turning to the left.

A short distance and a more accomplished turn later and the wagon was moving along the muddy road that lined the outer wall of Magilnada. The wall loomed up on the right, various craft shops, tanneries and mills in its lee. Guards patrolled overhead, paying no attention to what was going on within the city.

"That was not so hard," Noran said over his shoulder. "We should be at the gate well before the ring of the next hour."

"Just watch what you are doing," Allenya replied. "Keep an eye on the road."

"Bloody women," he muttered under his breath.

IV

The street was quickly filling with people, visible to Allenya through the opening in the back of the wagon. Most were traders, with baskets on their backs or pulling handcarts laden with their wares or tools. Nobody seemed to be paying attention to them. She sat on the boards of the cart leaning against the side, Laasinia beside her, Meliu opposite. Her sister had a wide-eyed expression of excitement; no doubt imagining this dismal exit from Magilnada as part of some romantic adventure.

Picking at the hem of her rough dress, Allenya cursed herself for being so naive. Ullsaard had warned her against Anglhan's manipulation, but she had allowed herself to be talked into staying; she had all but volunteered to become a hostage. Luia would not have made the same mistake.

She turned her mind to other matters as soon as her thoughts tended towards the strange nature of Noran's recovery. It was best not to think about it too much. Instead, she focussed on her husband, happy to know that he was well. She pictured some of the best times they had shared, imagining their reunion, but try as she might, Allenya kept being drawn back into feelings of shame at the mess she had made of things. She had allowed herself to be manipulated and that had made Ullsaard vulnerable.

He was king now and she was a queen, and that entailed a different approach to life. Allenya and her sisters came from Askhan nobility, and there had always been an undercurrent of domestic politics; her world had changed and only now was she realising just how much.

She heard someone calling Noran's name from the street and tensed. Moving to the front of the cart, she tugged at a knotted rope and pulled a small gap in the covering. Peering through, she saw a man dressed in a fur-collared coat hurrying towards the wagon, a gaggle of servants behind.

"Hey!" he cried out. "Hey Noran!"

"Who is he?" whispered Allenya. "Ignore him"

Noran said nothing, snapping the switch against the abada to keep it moving. The stranger hurried through the puddles on the street and fell in beside the driving board. Allenya pulled back to avoid being seen but could still see the man through the parting in the awning. The man's face seemed familiar, but she could not place from where.

"Noran, it's Haastin, Haastin Kasvha!"

The name meant nothing either.

"You are mistaken," growled Noran.

"No, surely not," said Kasvha, laying a hand on the side of the cart as he walked alongside. "Noran Aaluns, that's you. Everybody thought you were dead."

"Not me," Noran replied.

"Oh, I see, keeping out of the way, are you? All of those stories about you dashing off with Ullsaard and getting yourself killed are just a cover, eh?"

"You are mistaken," said Noran, shifting uncomfortably.

"Look here, don't take me for an idiot," barked Kasvha. "I've had dealings with your father for years. Don't know why you're pretending not to know me, but it isn't flattering to you, let me say."

Allenya heard Noran sigh and his body obscured her view as he leaned over.

"Look, take the hint," snapped the nobleman. "My business is my business!"

"Odd business it is too," replied Kasvha. "Don't you have men to drive carts for you? Fallen on hard times? Or is it something a bit more… clandestine. Come on, you can trust me."

"Please go away," insisted Noran. "Look, people are starting to pay attention. I shall send you a letter, I promise."

"A letter? I should be so favoured. I'm sorry to intrude."

Noran sat up and Allenya saw Kasvha backing away, hands on hips. The cart trundled on for a short way before she heard Noran lean back to whisper.

"There were a couple of men that hared off up into the city as soon as my name was mentioned," he said. "It could be nothing, but I would rather not take chances."

"What do you suggest?" replied Allenya. "Should we leave the wagon?"

"That might be a good idea," said Noran. "I will keep an eye out for a yard to pull into."

A wheel dipped into a pothole, jarring Allenya against the boards. Their passage was getting rockier, a sign that they were on the less maintained roads of the lower city.

"How far?" she asked.

Noran did not reply, but he gave a grunt, presumably pulling back hard on the reins. The wagon creaked to a halt.

"Quarter of a mile, no more," said Noran. "Get out here."

The cart rose a little as Noran jumped from the board. Allenya turned to see Meliu and Laasinia watching her intently.

"It will be all right," said Allenya. "We are almost out of the city."

Noran appeared at the back of the wagon to lower the tailgate. Offering up a hand, he helped Laasinia first. Meliu wrapped her arms around his neck as he lowered her to the ground.

"You are ever so brave," she said.

He gently pushed her aside and gestured for Allenya to follow. The queen did not recognise the street, but she had spent little time in the lower part of Magilnada so that was not a surprise. There were barracks here, supplied by smithies and armourers, and a great many single storey dwellings of the lower classes.

Street vendors were already hawking their wares and trades. It was a matter of moments before Allenya and her companions were amongst the swelling crowd, their clothes the surest form of disguise.

"This way," said Noran, taking the lead of the small group.

Allenya followed without argument, Meliu to her left, Laasinia a little way behind. Noran's urgency was not fuelled by the fear of discovery alone, she realised. He was weak, feet scuffing through the mud every few steps, his face soaked in sweat, eyes bloodshot as he glanced back every now and then. They reached a corner and the nobleman leant against the wall for a moment, catching his breath.

"Are you all right?" Allenya asked quietly, stopping next to Noran.

He looked as though he was about to dismiss any concerns, but sagged when he met her gaze, flickering a worried look towards Meliu.

"My recovery is temporary," he said, pitching his voice so that only Allenya could hear. "I do not know how long it will be before I succumb again. Promise me that you will get back to Ullsaard, whatever happens."

Allenya reached out to help him, but Noran pushed away, taking a deep breath.

"Enough of this," he muttered. "We should keep moving. The gate is just a couple of streets away."

Setting a steady pace, Noran headed on, head turning left and right as he worked out the best route and kept a wary eye for Anglhan's agents. Allenya felt a hand slip into hers and glanced to the side to see Meliu. Her expression was sombre.

"This is not such an adventure is it," she said. She almost bumped into Allenya as she side-stepped a puddle with a look of distaste. "If Anglhan catches us, it is going to be horrible."

"Noran will make sure we do not get caught," said Allenya, giving Meliu's hand a squeeze. "We are almost out of Magilnada."

They crossed another street and turned to the right. The tops of the gatehouses could be seen over the roofs of the buildings, less than two hundred paces away. Noran cut into a narrow alley between a bakery and a low tenement, kicking through the debris on the ground.

"Why do they have to be so filthy?" said Meliu as she picked her way amongst the garbage.

Laasinia hurried past from behind and said something to Noran, who glanced over his shoulder. Allenya looked back out of instinct and saw a handful of soldiers – Anglhan's city militia rather than legionnaires – pushing through the crowd towards the alleyway.

"That cannot be good," said Noran. "Come on, we have to just run for it!"

Breaking into a jog, the group ignored a shout from behind and stumbled out into the square behind the gate. After just a few dozen paces, Allenya was already out of breath and Meliu was panting beside her; their lives had not been a preparation for physical activity.

Ahead the gate was open and a line of abada wagons and abada carts trundled into the city. There were more guards around and about, not paying much attention. The square was busy with traffic and people and Allenya did her best to follow Noran as he wove amongst the throng, but she lost sight of him. She kept a firm grip on Meliu's hand and dragged her sister towards the gate, almost slipping over on the wet cobbles as a turning abada forced her to stop. The driver shouted down at her to be careful.

There was a growing commotion behind but Allenya did not dare look back. She realised it was stupid to focus on the gate as some kind of line to be crossed; their pursuit would not end at the wall. For a moment it seemed ridiculous. There was no chance they would get more than a hundred paces from the city before the guards caught up with them.

Emerging past a queue of customers at a costermonger's stall, Allenya saw the way was open to the gatehouse. Still there was no sign of Noran but she had no time to look for him.

"This way!" called Laasinia, appearing to the left. There was a smaller gate in the tower for foot traffic and the handmaiden veered towards it, half-running and half-walking until the two queens had caught up with her.

"Where's Noran?" Meliu said suddenly, jolting Allenya as she stopped to look around.

"He'll meet us outside," said Laasinia. "He said he'll make some kind of distraction."

"I hope he does not do anything stupidly heroic," said Allenya as she tugged at her sister to get moving again.

They walked quickly into the shadow of the secondary gateway. There were a few other people heading out of the city, though not enough to conceal the group.

"Try not to look so nervous," said Allenya, noticing Meliu's eyes darting around fearfully. "We should talk about something, make things appear normal. Tell me what you plan to do now that Noran is back with us."

"Oh, I had not thought about that," said Meliu, a hand raised to her mouth. "I am just so happy that he has recovered. It is all mixed up in my head at the moment. I know I have been acting silly, nursing him like a lover. We only had sex that one time, and he said nothing about it after. And when Ullsaard suggested we divorce, it was like a knife in my gut."

Allenya allowed Meliu to continue talking, only half-hearing what her sister said while she kept an eye on what the guards were doing. Several were sat on a bench just inside the other end of the gate-tunnel, spears and shields resting on the wall.

With every step, Allenya expected the other soldiers to come charging into the gatehouse to raise the alarm. It took every effort not to look back. As the group came level with the sentries, Allenya smiled and nodded as Meliu prattled on. She felt her sister's grip tighten for a moment and her words faltered.

"I am sure we can get everything sorted out when we are back with our husband," said Allenya. "When every-body is calmer, we shall talk it over with Ullsaard and Noran."

They came out into the daylight again and Laasinia stepped off the road.

"I'll wait for Noran," she said. "Keep going."

Allenya nodded and carried on walking, looking along the road as it stretched straight into the Magilnadan Gap, sloping gently down from the mountains. It was good to be outside the walls, and not just because of the circum-stances. For more than a year, Allenya had not left the city, and for half of that she had barely set foot outside the house.

A year and more of worry, of loneliness, of ignorance had worn down her spirit and it was not until she saw the expanse of pastures and fields that Allenya recognised how insular she had become. She took a deep breath, breathing air free from the taint of the city. She realised how different it could be, not to smell smoke and people and animals, but to catch the scent of grass and flowers, feel a fresh wind on her cheek.

She realised that Meliu was still talking.

"We shall have a banquet!" Allenya declared, cutting across her sister. "When we get back to Askh, we will invite Jutaar and Ullnaar, even Luia and Noran and have the whole family together. Oh, they should bring Neerlima, and little Luissa too! I bet she has grown so much. And all of our old friends as well! The house will be full of people, and we will have songs and wine and children running around."

"And Pretaa, yes?" said Meliu. "It would be lovely to see her in less trying times. She seems such a lovely lady."

"Yes, Pretaa too," said Allenya, smiling at the picture she was painting in her mind. She squeezed Meliu's hand and leant over to kiss her sister on the cheek. "I have been such a misery. I am so sorry for ignoring you lately; it has been as hard for you as it has been for me."

"Do not think it a moment more," said Meliu. "I am glad to see you happy again. It has been torture, to see you so sad and knowing that I could do nothing to help. Do you think Ullsaard has changed at all? I bet he has been winning lots of battles and doing great things."

They talked in this way for some time. Now and then they looked back for a sight of Laasinia or Noran, but saw nothing of them. After a mile or so, Allenya grew worried about this.

"Should we stop and wait for them?" she suggested.

"Laasinia said to keep moving," replied Meliu. "She seems a sensible person, we should listen to her."

"A short break would be all right, I think," said Allenya. "Just a little while to give them the chance to catch up."

There were tracks winding away from the road, leading to farms and villages. Copses of blossoming trees and dark-leaved bushes broke the grasslands around and it was to one small stand that Allenya now walked. The sky was filled with clouds and the sun was not strong, but after the effort of walking, it was nice to slip into the shade for a moment. The pair found a spot on the edge of the copse free from undergrowth and sat on the grass.

"We should have brought some food," said Meliu. "We have not had breakfast yet."

Allenya did not reply. Her attention had been attracted by a group of men a little further up the road. They sat around a small fire, and were constantly watching the carts and people. Now and then one or other would stand up and pace a little way from the camp, looking towards the city. They had two abada carts with them. It struck Allenya as strange that such a group would make camp so close to the city. It was well into morning now and any person with normal business would be moving towards or away from Magilnada, not simply staying by the side of the road.

"Do you think they are Anglhan's men?" said Meliu, leaning across Allenya to see what had distracted her. "Or are they Ullsaard's? How do we tell?"

"They could be anyone," said Allenya, but she felt uncomfortable. "You are right. I think they are looking for us."

"I did not see any soldiers passing us on the road," said Meliu. "Do you think word will have been sent from the city so quickly?"

The men on the other side of the road seemed to have spotted the two women and were paying close attention. Allenya did not know how to react. If they did harbour ill intent, the worst thing to do would be to attract more attention.

"We should get going again," said Allenya, standing up. "Two servants dawdling under the trees might look odd."

"Wait!" said Meliu as she clambered to her feet. She pointed back towards Magilnada. "Is that them?"

Allenya looked and about half a mile away she saw a man and a woman, walking at some speed. They certainly looked like Laasinia and Noran. Allenya's dilemma deepened and she glanced over at the watchers. Three of the men had walked down to the road and were heading towards them.

"What should we do?" said Meliu, moving close to Allenya. "We cannot outrun them."

Allenya had no answer for her sister. There was nothing they could do but wait. The three men crossed the road about fifty paces away and came straight towards the trees. One held up a hand in greeting. The small group wore shirts and kilts rather than trousers, marking them out from the Salphors, but Allenya took no reassurance from this. She stole a glance back up the road and was sure it was Laasinia and Noran that she had seen. They were still some distance away.

"Can we help you?" she called out.

The men stopped about a dozen paces away and eyed the two women. They held a whispered conversation before the one who had waved stepped closer, arms held out from his sides.

"I'm sorry," he said. "We didn't mean to frighten you. I am Second Captain Luurha, and these are my men. The king sent us to find you."

Tears of relief welled up in Allenya's eyes and she saw Meliu sway for a moment. Her sister then dashed forwards and threw her arms around the surprised captain's neck. He laughed and looked to Allenya for help.

"Leave him alone, sister," Allenya said with a smile.

Meliu took a few faltering steps back. "Tell us captain, how far away is our husband?"

Luurha smirked, turned to raise a fist to the rest of his men along the road and gestured for the two women to follow him. One of the other men set off along the road at a jog, heading away from the city.

"A lot closer than Anglhan thinks," he said as they walked towards the road. "Does anybody know that you have left the city?"

"We have to wait for our friends," said Meliu. She pointed up the road again. "There they are."

"Is that Noran Aluuns?" asked Luurha. "Okay, we'll wait."

"We do not know if anyone saw us leave," said Allenya. "We thought perhaps we were being followed, but we have seen no chase."

They waited in silence until Noran and Laasinia had caught up. The nobleman was looking very tired, his face drawn, and the sallow hue had returned to his skin. He waved away Meliu's attentions and squared up to Luurha.

"Who is this?" he asked warily.

"I was sent by the king," Luurha answered. "You must be Noran. Thank you for getting the queens out of Magilnada, the king will be very pleased."

"I am sure he will," said Noran. He laid a hand on the captain's shoulder and seemed on the verge of collapse. "Have you any water?"

"Yes, of course," said Luurhan. He pulled a skin from his belt and offered it to Noran, who drank sparingly, eyes closed. "Are we safe from pursuit?"

"For the moment," said the nobleman. He turned to Allenya and laughed nervously. "The guards did not know who we were. They were after us for leaving the cart blocking a passageway. They thought I had stolen it."

"What did you do?" asked Meliu, slipping an arm across Noran's back to help him stand.

"You owe Laasinia a couple of Askharins," said Noran. "A lie and some coin eased their concerns."

"We should move away from the city," said Luurhan.

"I think the excitement has got to..." Noran's voice was a croaking whisper.

Allenya turned to see the noble crumpling to the ground, slipping out of Meliu's grasp. Meliu crouched over him, a cheek to his mouth, hand on his chest.

"He is still breathing," she said, looking desperately between Allenya and Laasinia, tears forming. "Is he going to be all right?"

V

Crouched over Noran, Ullsaard thought he saw his friend's eyelids flicker. Lakhyri stood behind him, arms crossed, watching Noran intently, probably more fearful for his own life than the nobleman's. Askhos had drifted away, literally; he had professed a lack of interest and faded from view like fog in a strengthening wind.

There was another twitch in Noran and Ullsaard looked over his shoulder.

"Is that good or bad?" the king asked. Lakhyri gave no response. "You don't know?"

"You should," replied the priest. "Your energies and his are connected. Do you feel nothing?"

Ullsaard concentrated but was unaware of any change in himself or his friend.

"Nothing," he said. "What should I feel?"

"I do not know," admitted Lakhyri. "My only experience is the sensation of gaining power through this world, not relinquishing it. Perhaps it is good that you are unaware of it."

"Perhaps?" Ullsaard stood and rounded on the high priest. Lakhyri backed away a step, one had held up. "You have been guessing all along, haven't you?"

"I knew that what I proposed was possible," said Lakhyri. "I warned you that there were risks."

Ullsaard's next words never reached his lips; Noran gave a ragged exhalation. Ullsaard saw his eyes flutter open and slowly focus. He stooped to help his friend sit up.

"What has happened?" asked the king. Lakhyri crouched and laid a hand upon Noran's forehead. "Allenya, is she all right?"

Noran smiled weakly.

"She is with your man," he said. "They will be with you soon, I am sure."

"What of you? What happened?"

Pulling on Ullsaard's arm, Noran came to his feet and wobbled unsteadily for a moment.

"My body is still very weak," he said. "I held on for as long as I could, to make sure they were safe. I could not fight back any more."

"What does that mean?" Ullsaard said to Lakhyri.

The priest pushed the two men apart a little way and held a hand to the chest of each. He closed his eyes and runes smouldered in his flesh.

"The link is sustained," declared the priest, opening his eyes and folding his arms. "It is only Noran's physical weakness that sends him here."

Ullsaard noticed Lakhyri stopped himself suddenly, as if he was about to say something else.

"What is it?" the king demanded.

Lakhyri's eyes switched back and forth between the two of them as he replied.

"Your energy, Ullsaard, is sustaining the body of Noran. Without it, he will not recover fully."

"What does that mean?" said Noran. "That when this is finished, I will slip back into the deathly sleep?"

Lakhyri nodded.

"I promised that I could help bring your wives and friend to safety," said the priest, addressing himself to Ullsaard with a sombre expression. "Even this small endeavour will have its cost."

"But it could be sustained?" said Ullsaard.

"No!" said Noran, stepping in front of Lakhyri to stop him answering. "I do not understand exactly what is going on, but I get the idea. You have done enough, Ullsaard. Do not concern yourself with me."

"That's for you to decide, is it?" said Ullsaard. He looked past his friend. "Is it possible? Could you make the link permanent? How does it work, will I have to stay close to him?"

"Do not talk about me as if I were not here!" snapped Noran. "This is madness. Stop this now."

Ullsaard ignored his friend's objection and looked at Lakhyri. The priest nodded, as much to himself as the king.

"The link is established, it need not be severed," he said. "With your strength, Noran will be able to recover some semblance of himself. Distance is of no import in this world, I merely brought you closer to Magilnada so that you would be able to act in the physical world as well as here. I cannot tell you the consequences, save one. You will be living two lives, Ullsaard, or as close as to make no difference, given the meagre energies left with Noran's body."

"Enough, enough!" said Noran, pushing the priest away. "No more of this, please! I could not rob you of any more than I have already taken."

"It is not theft if I give it to you," said Ullsaard, grabbing Noran's shoulder. He looked at the priest. "How long?"

"I cannot say for sure," said Lakhyri. "Half as long as you would have had. You have the Blood, and that grants life beyond normal measure. I would say you have forty more years left to you. That would mean you would both have twenty if you draw from the same well."

"You are not going to give me twenty years of your life, you just cannot," said Noran.

"There will be no other physical symptom of your connection," Lakhyri continued. "No loss of strength or wit. The force that gives your existence will simply be used up more quickly. In a sense, we are all inter-connected at a certain level, sustaining and being sustained by each other. The join between you will simply be stronger, and uneven."

There was pleading in Noran's eyes, but Ullsaard's mind was made up.

"I cannot condemn you to a half-life," he said. "For my sake, for Meliu's and for everyone else that cares for you, it is better that I do this. Lakhyri, take us back to the real world."

Noran made fresh protest but already light and sound was becoming faint. The dream subsided, washing away into grey nothingness.

VI

A little after noon, the first signs of Ullsaard's army could be seen; pickets on kolubrids moved down through the foothills. Within a mile, columns of legionnaires were on the road, heading hotwards down the valley. Company after company marched past as the two wagons juddered up the rough trail, Allenya and Meliu in the back of one, next to the comatose Noran. Meliu tended to him with a moistened flannel as she patted affectionately at fever soaked clothes.

"Where do you think they are all going?" Meliu asked, looking at the thousands of legionnaires.

429

"Magilnada," replied Allenya.

While she watched the army marching past, she felt some satisfaction. She had not felt Anglhan's threats in person, but what he had done appalled her in a way she could barely articulate. Above everything, it was the betrayal of Ullsaard that angered her; the governor was ingratitude incarnate. She did not care that he had turned on Askh and its king, but she deeply resented the treachery towards her husband; a man who had given Anglhan every opportunity and considerable power in return for his help. To throw away such gifts was a selfish stupidity that Allenya abhorred, and she hoped that when Anglhan was taken she would be there to see his punishment. Had Anglhan spent the entire time with a knife held at her throat she would have felt less repulsion, but he had not even the courage to openly threaten her family.

She wanted to see Anglhan bloodied and broken, begging for mercy for what he had done.

These thoughts of justice gave way to expectation as the tops of pavilions came into view at the head of the pass. Ullsaard was so close now she could feel him, like a presence in her breast beside her quickening heart. There had been times she had hated him, staring out of her window at the winter skies wondering why he had deserted her. She had spent hours crying in her bed, cursing herself for marrying a soldier, sobbing at the injustice of being kept apart from a man who was the most powerful in an entire empire. She had wondered if he chose to be away, remembering the manner of their parting and his aversion to her.

Not now those dark thoughts. Seasons of longing welled up inside, tightening her chest, a flush of heat coursing through her body. She wanted to see him, touch him with her hands, assure herself that he was real.

Meliu mast have noticed the change, for she reached over Noran and laid her hand upon Allenya's knee.

"It is fine, sister," she said. "He sent Noran for you so that you could be together."

Allenya opened her mouth to reply but instead a sob of happiness engulfed her at the thought. Meliu clambered across the rocking cart and hugged her as the tears came again; tears of joy and relief rather than grief.

It was in each other's arms that the two sisters passed into the camp. Allenya looked up, wondering which was Ullsaard's tent, straining for that first sight of him. Excitement bordered on desperation and she stood up, fighting to keep balance as the wagon bumped over the uneven ground.

Two of the soldiers ran ahead from the group, heading towards the centre of the camp. Allenya wanted to run with them, but Meliu saw what was going to happen and dragged her back to the boards of the wagon by her skirt.

"Come now, sister, and remember yourself," she said. "You wear a servant's dress and your hair is in total disarray. The last thing Ullsaard needs to see on top of that is red eyes and tear streaks."

Allenya allowed Meliu to fuss at her appearance, using her fingers to comb some sense into her hair, and the hem of her skirt to dab the tears from her face. The fluttering acted to calm Allenya, who wiped her nose with the cuff of her dress and took a deep breath, trying to stay calm. Meliu stroked a hand down Allenya's arm and kissed her lightly on the cheek before sitting back.

"See now?" said Meliu with a laugh. "At least you look like a queen in a commoner's dress, and nothing worse."

Allenya smiled and patted Meliu's hand in thanks. Feeling a little more herself, she looked again at the camp, trying to judge its size. It was not quite as big as the one she had been in before, but certainly larger than a single legion. She moved to the front of the wagon to talk to the driver.

"How large is my husband's army?" she asked the man.

"Three legions, queen," he said.

It was then she saw the flag of Askhos flying from the pole of a nearby tent. She was on her feet even as the driver brought the abada to a halt; and over the side without waiting for help. She ran through the mud, dress flapping at her legs, and dashed past the startled sentries at the door to the pavilion.

They lunged after her, but were too slow.

Inside, she saw Ullsaard standing at a map table, two men in the finery of first captains with him. There was a shout from the guards that alerted all three, who turned just as Allenya reached them. The king's eyes widened in shock a moment before Allenya launched at him, throwing her arms around his neck, her lips seeking his as sure as any hunter's arrow.

For a heartbeat, Ullsaard was stunned; hot tears washed down Allenya's face again. Then his arms encircled her and she felt her heart would burst at his embrace. He returned the kiss, beard tickling her face, strong arms pulling her so tight for a moment he might crush her. Her hands gripped his hair, not letting him move a fraction as the taste and smell of him washed over her. Her legs buckled and only then did she relinquish her grip, her cheek falling to his chest, hands clasped behind his neck.

"Hello, wife," he said.

The sound of his voice started Allenya crying again and she could not speak. She dimly sensed the other men moving away, but her every sense was focussed on the two of them, reunited.

432

Suddenly she felt guilty at causing such a scene. She wriggled from his arms, hands stroking the back of his as they parted. Wiping away her tears, she tried to restore some semblance of decency, hands held to her waist.

"It is good to see you again, husband," she managed to say.

Confused by her change, Ullsaard blinked rapidly, his eyes moist.

"And it is good to see you too," he replied uncertainly.

He took a step, hesitated, and then engulfed her again with his arms, kissing her on the neck and through her hair, over and over. All thought of propriety and appearance washed away and Allenya gripped his shirt in her fists, moving her face so that his kisses fell upon her lips.

She had no idea how long they spent in this way, and wished for it to last forever. Her hands and eyes explored every part of his face, and she felt a flutter of fear as they encountered bandages across his chest and shoulder, and saw a fresh scar above his right eye.

"You have been fighting," she said in a scolding tone. His expression of hurt dignity caused her to laugh out loud.

"I may have been in a few battles," Ullsaard said with a smile. The smile faded and he looked away. "I am so sorry for leaving you. I have been such a poor husband too you."

"Never say that!" The thought that Ullsaard blamed himself for what Anglhan had done fired her anger. "Never! I would never wish to be married to another man."

His eyes strayed and widened. Looking around, Allenya saw Meliu poking her head through the door of the tent.

"I would like to greet my husband, if he would welcome me," she said.

Ullsaard looked conflicted, happiness and confusion battling in his eyes. After the passing of two heartbeats he grinned and waved for her to enter.

"Why would I not welcome you?" he said, but Allenya felt the jollity a little forced.

It made no difference to Meliu. She hurried across the rugs and under Ullsaard's arm, wrapping herself about his waist. With his free hand, the king pulled Allenya into the embrace.

After a time, they parted. Recovered from the surge of emotion that had enthralled her, Allenya's mind filled with questions. Her thoughts turned to another whom she had missed dearly.

"What of Jutaar?" she asked. "Is he with your army?"

The look of pain that crossed her husband's face was like nothing she had seen in him before; she immediately knew the answer to her question and emptiness swallowed her from within.

"What has happened?" she said before Ullsaard could speak.

The agony in Ullsaard's face was replaced by the deepest of scowls.

"Killed," he said between gritted teeth. "Killed by that traitor, Anglhan."

Though Ullsaard's reaction had told Allenya everything, hearing the words made the realisation sink into her heart. The emptiness engulfed her, robbing her limbs of all strength. She felt herself sway a moment before she hit the rugs, overwhelmed. She heard Ullsaard and Meliu calling out in concern, felt their hands upon her, but as if from a distance.

The world was unreal, a swirl of movement and colours; herself a vapour on the breeze. It was a dream, Allenya told herself. A nightmare visited upon her out of loneliness and desperation. She was in her bed, in that hollow house in Magilnada, and her dreams taunted her with joy and misery, giving life to the hopes and fears that had plagued her for so long. She could not feel her body, or the bed beneath her. It had to be a dream.

It was a terrible dream and she wanted to wake up.

Something cold and wet touched her lips and she swallowed out of instinct. Revived by the sensation, her eyes cleared and she found herself sat on the rugs, Ullsaard knelt behind her while Meliu held a cup to her mouth.

"Still a dream," she murmured. She looked at her husband and sister, not really recognising either. "Just a bad dream."

Ullsaard shifted and cradled her head in his lap, hands stroking her hair, face grim. Meliu was crying, the hand holding the cup shaking like a branch in a storm, water spilling to the rug.

The thought that this was real emerged from the fog of Allenya's thoughts. The touch of Ullsaard's fingers, the tears dropping on to her leg from Meliu, both were real. And if that was real...

She gave a groan of deep pain as the truth bit into her thoughts. Jutaar, her son, her wonderful son, was dead. The joy she had felt, the light that had filled her from Ullsaard, turned to grief, and to darkness, and she cried again, burying her face in her hands.

VII

"Can I help, governor?"

Anglhan looked over his shoulder at Lenorin and smiled before returning his attention to the canvas map of Magilnada hanging on the wall of the aide's office. He prodded a pudgy finger at the lower coldwards quarter.

"It seems to me that we should clear space for a second marketplace," said Anglhan. "We could diverge the two to better cater for the differing needs of our city; jewellery, gems, clothes, debtors and such in the upper market, food and household goods in the lower. Much of the latter comes from out of the city and in transporting it to the Hill of Chiefs the streets get too busy. Better to steer that trade to this area and allow easier access to and from the city for the highest people of the populace."

"I see that you have been hearing the petitions of Callsuin, Lassean and Elghiad, governor," said the aide. "I have already considered their proposition and while it sounds good I am not sure what the expense of such changes would gain in return."

"The better flow of commerce, Lenorin!" Anglhan exclaimed, turning with arms thrown wide. "We clear these old hovels, build some new houses for the people, and help keep the streets a little clearer for everybody. You cannot simply weigh up such expense with the amount of gold that comes back. The people will be happier, and a happier city is good for trade."

Lenorin looked dubiously at his master's generosity. Anglhan continued, walking around the desk to lay a hand on Lenorin's shoulder.

"Think longer term, my unimaginative follower," said the city ruler. "An Askharin spent today can be worth four in a year. Which brings me to something else I have been considering. We already mint our own coin. Isn't it about time we dispensed with the pretence of Askhan currency? I was thinking something with the gate tower on one side and my face in profile on the other? Anglhins or something like that?"

Lenorin sighed, pinched his nose and levelled a stare at Anglhan that made no attempt to hide his dismay.

"You don't think that would seem egotistical, do you?" said Lenorin, and answered his question before Anglhan had the chance. "No, you don't, governor."

"And that's another thing," said Anglhan, removing his hand to hold up a finger in front of Lenorin's face. "We have to stop this 'governor' talk. Everyone in the city knows what has been going on. It's not really any secret that Ullsaard or any other Askhan commander has not been seen in the city for a year. I think I should announce our true independence and assume a proper title."

Lenorin puffed out his cheeks and blew hard at the suggestion.

"What title would be more fitting? Lord Anglhan? Chieftain Periusis?"

"I was thinking King Anglhan would be fitting," said Magilnada's lord. Lenorin's breath escaped him explosively, pitching him into a coughing fit. "You think king is too strong? Why not, am I not king of these lands now? Ullsaard calls himself king and half his people would gladly see him dead. Aegenuis calls himself king and he commands about as much loyalty and respect as a turd in a bucket. I think that my power, and my responsibilities, are adequately akin to kingship."

"It would be a bold move," Lenorin managed to say, face red, one hand clasped over his mouth as his convulsions continued. "Certainly the chieftains would be amused."

"I've got three legions and the ability to finance at least that number again, so the chieftains can suck my cock and thank me for the privilege," Anglhan snapped. "Any of them that want to argue are quite happy to."

"Which brings me to why I have been looking for you, er, king," said Lenorin. "I received word this morning from the First Magilnadan on the Ersuan border."

"I'm wondering about that name as well," said Anglhan, not at all interested by the interminable messages his commanders had been routinely sending since their patrol of the border had started. "First Magilnadan was a bit of a compromise for the sake of unity with Ullsaard. I much prefer the First Perusiun Legion; it speaks more highly of my role in their creation."

"You can call them Anglhan's Best Boys for all I care," said Lenorin, his patience finally snapping. "Whatever the name, a runner arrived this morning bringing the news that two Askhan legions have crossed from Ersua."

"What?"

"Do I need to repeat myself?"

"Shut up," said Anglhan. He waddled to the window and stared down at the city. "These two legions, did they break the blockade? Is this an attack?"

"There was no battle," explained Lenorin. "They slipped through the foothills of the mountains on the coldwards edge of the gap. It would appear they headed further into the mountains, as they have not been seen since.

"Since? Since when?" Anglhan rounded on his chancellor, jowls wobblingly, spittle flying. "How long ago did they cross?"

"Five days."

"This is intolerable!" Anglhan clasped his hands to his head, astounded by the incompetence of his underlings. "They could have been at the city by now. So much for having good warning!"

"The runner is awaiting your orders," said Lenorin. "Are the legions to move coldwards to protect the city?"

Anglhan thought about this, trying to understand the import of the development. It was unlikely Magilnada was the target; Ullsaard would never order such a thing and if the objective had been the city, they would already be at the walls. Was Ullsaard trying to spook him into making a move? Was this a bluff?

"Why the mountains?" he asked aloud. "It's a terrible place to launch an attack from."

"I would assume that the army hoped to keep their whereabouts unknown, perhaps to await further orders."

"It could be a distraction," Anglhan spoke his thoughts as they came to him. "Ullsaard might have some kind of relief force organised, with supplies to launch a fresh offensive. If I move the legions out of position, the bastard could walk a hundred thousand men through the gap and I wouldn't know about it. No, that has to be the explanation. The legions are to maintain their vigil and allow no column or caravan to pass except to Magilnada."

"Very well, is there anything else?"

"This news disturbs me, Lenorin, disturbs me a lot," Anglhan admitted. "I think the time for being nice is over. Ullsaard is up to something, and I need to remind him of his responsibilities. Have his wives arrested and brought to the palace. We'll keep them at my convenience for the time being. I'm sure Allenya will be only too happy to write to her husband, decrying such treatment."

"I did recommend that you did such a thing from the outset," said Lenorin. "I have no idea why you thought it would be beneficial to let them wander around at will."

"You can be an arsehole, Lenorin," said Anglhan. "I have nothing against Allenya and Meliu; they are lovely ladies whose company I enjoy. They were watched and guarded without bars just as easily as with, so why not allow them what comfort I could? I expect them to be properly accommodated here; I'll not have them thrown into some dank room out of sight. They are queens, Lenorin, and should be treated as such."

"As you wish," Lenorin said with a nod. He left with short, quick steps, shaking his head.

Anglhan walked back to the map and returned to his study of it. There was so much still to be done. Magilnada could barely contain the people living there already, and as the city's power and influence and wealth increased, it would have to find room for more. Anglhan was no architect, but looking at the map he could see where a few simple changes could be made in the short term. In a year, perhaps two, they would have to think on a larger scale.

He had thought about the options for some time. He could extend the city walls to hotwards, perhaps doubling the size of the city. It was the simplest solution and for that reason the least satisfying. His preferred course was the settling of a second city of the Free Country, in the Ersuan Mountains on the hotwards side of the Magilnada Gap. That was a statement of intent that every person could understand. It was the sort of thinking that had created an empire for Askhos.

Caught up by his own idea, he rifled through Lenorin's records until he found a chart of the Free Country. Various tribal lands were marked on it in different coloured paints. Anglhan looked at various possible sites, running through a list of features that would be needed; rivers for water, hills for defence, close to woods and good farmland for supplies and trade. He snatched a rod of charcoal from Lenorin's desk and started marking areas for further investigation.

"Should I keep my seat here, or move it?" he wondered. "I think that if it is to have the best start possible, Anglhanada would need me there. What a way to start a new era, with the founding of a proper, modern city. It will be the envy of Askh."

He engrossed himself in mental preparations for this leap forward in the Free Country's fortunes. He had once discussed the name with Ullsaard, but now he had a different view on the matter. Anglhan considered various options but was broken from his thoughts by the sound of running feet on the wooden stairs.

Wondering who could be in such a hurry at this time of day, he stepped towards the door of the office, to be met by a breathless Lenorin. The chancellor ran into Anglhan and rebounded hard, falling to his backside. He looked up at his master with fear-filled eyes.

"They're gone!" he said, voice breaking.

Anglhan pulled the man to his feet, straightened his shirt and guided him towards his stool.

"Who is gone?" he asked.

"The queens, and even Aluuns!"

Anglhan's grip failed in his moment of shock, leaving Lenorin to fall to the floor again. A cold sweat ran down his back.

"Are you sure?" he said, fighting back panic. "Aren't they just out shopping?"

"Three of your men have been combing the city for them since this morning," confessed Lenorin. "One of the servants has confirmed that Noran Aluuns is no longer in his bed."

"Well, let's not do anything too hasty," said Anglhan, whilst trying to think of something hasty he could do. If Ullsaard found out about this, it was all over. "It's only been a few hours, they cannot have got far."

He looked at Lenorin, who was white as a cloud. He was shaking his head, seemingly in disbelief.

"What is it?" demanded Anglhan, grabbing the man by his shirt to haul him to his feet. "Is there something else?"

Lenorin shuddered from head to foot and looked as if he was going to vomit. It took him several attempts to speak.

"Talk amongst the merchants in the city," he managed. "A legion has been seen on the road."

"What legion?" said Anglhan. "My legions are nowhere near the city.

Lenorin's plaintive eyes were the only answer Anglhan needed.

"Close the gates, call out the guards, you idiot!"

Anglhan hurried to the door, waving for Lenorin to follow.

"Do these rumours say how far away this legion is?" Anglhan asked as he headed along the landing towards his chambers. He stopped and grabbed Lenorin by the shoulders, his next words a desperate shout. "Do I have time to get out of the city?"

VIII

The sky was darkening to dawnwards as the army marched into view of Magilnada. Cloud hung low above the peaks behind the city, the walls a bright white against the grey of the cliff against which it was built.

Ullsaard had considered long and hard how he would conquer this place, spending sleepless nights during the last year working out the best way to counter its defences. Even when he had been plotting and conducting the campaign against the Mekhani, his thoughts had moved to this place and the means to exact his revenge on the man who claimed rulership there.

"Shall we send a deputation to accept surrender?" asked Aalmunis, commander of the Fourth.

Ullsaard resurfaced from his dreams of vengeance to consider the question. He marched alongside Aalmunis and Hemmin, his counterpart in the Eighteenth, at the heart of the column, one legion in front and the other behind. Second captains followed a short way behind with the staff baggage, ready to disseminate the orders of their superiors.

"No," the king replied. "No offer of surrender."

"We are to retake the city by force?" said Hemmin.

"I don't make empty threats," said Ullsaard, remembering words he had spoken to Anglhan on the day of his investiture as governor. "And besides, this place has been a pain in the arse of Askh since it was built. Magilnada is to be destroyed. I want the city razed to the ground."

"And the people?" Hemmin's question was calmly asked, giving no hint of the commander's opinion on the matter.

"Kill them," said Ullsaard. "Any chieftains or persons of note are to be captured if possible. This place does not exist to me. Your legions are free to take what they want, goods and slaves, and then burn everything. Everybody else is to be slain. I want nothing but ash and dust by the time we are finished."

"As you command," chorused the two First Captains, showing no signs of hesitation.

The army continued its advance to within a mile of the city. Company by company the legions peeled away from the road to set up the siege. Wagons carrying the parts of catapults and spear-throwers gathered while crews and legionnaires crowded around to unload the war machines. Sawing and hammering and the swearing of labouring men cut across the evening air as the sun set and the barricades defending the legions' positions were erected.

Ullsaard made his camp directly opposite the gatehouse. A log palisade was thrown up around a dozen pavilions of the senior officers, Ullsaard's tent at the centre. He had sent his family back to Askh under escort. Their grief over the news of Jutaar's death was too fresh and harsh to bear, and he needed clarity not distraction. The tears of his farewell with Allenya haunted his inner thoughts, but his mind was focussed on the task at hand. There was no reason for his wife to witness the destruction and carnage that was going to be wrought in her name; it was enough that she was safe and honour would be satisfied on her account.

Feeling none of the rage he had experienced on hearing of Anglhan's betrayal, the king now viewed the razing of Magilnada as a necessary task to be performed. When he had Anglhan in custody was when he would let his true feelings be known.

Just as the last ray of the sun were dimming, there came news that the gates had opened and a delegation could been seen moving along the road. Ullsaard heard the calls from within his pavilion and hurried out, wondering if Anglhan had shown some uncharacteristic shred of decency and surrendered himself to save the city. He was not shocked to see that Anglhan was absent from the group of four men who were carried up the road on a large covered wagon pulled by two abada. At least twenty armed men accompanied them on foot.

"Let them enter the camp!" Ullsaard directed, heading towards the newly-constructed gate.

It was not long before the wooden gates opened to permit the delegation to enter. The warriors looked nervous, spears in hand, shields raised protectively around their masters. Ullsaard beckoned to a nearby second captain.

"Get me two hundred men with bellows-bows," he said. The officer nodded and set off at a run. Turning his attention to his visitors, Ullsaard strode in front of the wagon and stood with his hands on hips until they had clumsily disembarked over its high sides.

The four chieftains, for their fur cloaks, gold jewellery and enamelled helms marked them as such, took their places in a single line facing the king. Each was armed, but all four were even older than Ullsaard, one of them so frail he looked as if he might expire on the spot. The tallest, a black-haired, wiry man with a patch over one eye, took a step towards Ullsaard, a hand raised in greeting.

"King Ullsaard, I am J–"

"I would fuck a sow before I care for your name," snarled Ullsaard. "Wait there."

He turned his back on the delegation and stalked back to his tent, where he snatched up his spear from its rack and waited at the door. When he saw the bow-armed legionnaires arriving, he walked into view again.

"I'll give you each one chance," Ullsaard called out as he paced quickly towards the cluster of chieftains. He hefted his spear meaningfully. "Kill me man-to-man and save your city, or die like dogs, shot through with arrows."

The king stopped ten paces from the men, swapped his spear to his left hand and drew his sword.

"I'll give you a chance, I won't even use a shield," he told them. "Come on, one of you must be up for it!"

There was laughter from the legionnaires, who had circled around the group and formed a wall of shields behind which others stood with bellows-bows hefted to their shoulders. Out of the corner of his eye, Ullsaard saw some of the officers whispering and coin changing hands.

"It's a rich man that takes a bet against me," he called out.

"We're wagering which of these dogs has the balls to fight you," a third captain shouted back. "My money's on the ancient one."

There was more laughter, much to the fury of the chieftains.

"I have five Askharin that none of them have the guts for it!" Ullsaard glanced to his right and saw Aalmunis shouldering through a knot of his officers.

"Ten! That one of them is stupid enough to try!" Hemmin countered from the left.

It was the one who had spoken that broke first, snatching his sword from his belt.

"I'll cut your fucking head off, you son of a whore," he shouted, taking three quick steps.

Ullsaard judged the man carefully. He was still quick and supple, despite his age, but having one eye could only be a disadvantage. The king took a couple of steps to his right and saw that the man had to turn his head to keep him in view.

"My mother was indeed a whore," Ullsaard called back. He raised his spear high and looked at his warriors. "But my father was a king!"

There were roars of approval and clapping. The legionnaires started a beat, thumping the butts of their spears on the ground and uttering a wordless chant.

The chieftain edged closer by another two steps. Ullsaard held his ground, slightly crouched, spear held to the front, sword held back ready to be swung. He sidestepped again, forcing the other man to turn on his heel.

He looked at his opponent's face, seeing the tension in the tightness around his eyes and the clench of his jaw. Ullsaard stood up straight and looked at his men.

"I can't be bothered with this," he declared sheathing his sword. "These piss-drinking dog-fuckers are not worth a drop of our sweat. Shoot them!"

He turned his back and walked away as the slap of bow strings sounded around him. There were screams from the Salphors mixed with the thud of arrows into wood and flesh. Ullsaard stopped after a dozen paces and looked at Hemmin.

"Save the heads of those four," he said, pointing his spear at the bodies of the chieftains, each pierced by a dozen bolts. Around the cart, the other warriors lay in heaps, some of them still alive, moaning and crawling. "Finish off the rest. Send everything else back to the city."

Confident that his First Captains had matters well in hand, Ullsaard retired to his pavilion.

At first, sleep did not come. He fretted over his decision to send Allenya away so quickly. He had been away from her for years at a time before, but it seemed different now. She was vulnerable, a target for his enemies in a way that she had never been before.

Ullsaard tossed restlessly and wondered if he would have been happier if Aalun had not entangled him in the succession of the Crown; he had never set out to become king. His mother would argue that the Blood had its own demands, and after meeting Lakhyri and the abomination that was now Erlaan, Ullsaard was tempted to think it a curse more than a blessing.

Despite being unsettled by these thoughts, Ullsaard relaxed, realising that there was no point thinking about such things. He was king, he did have the Blood and he was waging a war to become the ruler of all the lands from sea to sea. Most importantly, Allenya was safe. Nothing mattered more. If her security caused him unhappiness, he would willingly pay the price.

Such thoughts focussed his mind on the immediate future. It was a simple plan, when he thought about it. Once Salphoria was conquered, he could return to Askh and leave the problems of the empire to the Brotherhood. He smiled as he fell asleep, wondering what he would do with his time when he no longer had to wield a sword.

When he awoke, Ullsaard was unsurprised to find that preparations for the attack were well underway. Engineers had worked through the night assembling the war engines, constructing revetments to protect them and distributing ladders amongst the companies chosen for the assault. Two huge wheeled rams had been fashioned from felled trees and wagons, pulled by teams of abada.

Armourers were fitting the fuel casks to the lava-throwers and preparing braziers for the war machine crews.

Up before Dawnwatch, Ullsaard wandered from his camp to the lines, a mile or so away. By the time he arrived, some of the legionnaires were already being woken by their third captains and sergeants. Expectant muttering greeted the dawn, and the soldiers joked with each other and their king as he made a round of the temporary fortifications.

His inspection took several hours, during which the army was roused, fed and set to work reinforcing the embankments and clearing the road of any debris so that the rams could move freely. A second line of earth-and-wood walls was rising from the fields a quarter of a mile ahead, from which the war engines would be in range. Unfortunately, this also put them in range of the catapults Anglhan had mounted on the walls of the city.

As he left the safety of the siege line to survey the forward work, he saw bodies strewn along either side of the road. There were several hundred as far as he could tell, some in scattered groups, most in a swathe of corpses about half a mile from the city. Men, women and children lay dead together.

"What's this?" he asked the second captain of a company digging a ditch alongside the road. The captain glanced at the piles of bodies.

"A bunch of 'em tried to flee the city after midnight," said the officer. "Orders was to let nobody escape."

"They'll be rotten within days, we can't just leave them here," said the king.

"That's why we're digging," the captain said with a cruel laugh. "Can't waste fuel on burning 'em, so the First Captain said to bury 'em."

"Very wise," said Ullsaard. "Hope you're getting double beer for your troubles."

"From Captain Hemmin?" The captain laughed again. "Even you'd be parched of thirst before he offered a drop of wine or beer."

"I'll have a word," said Ullsaard with a grin. "We'll see if we can loosen his fingers on the barrel tap."

Whoever was in charge of the city's defenders – Ullsaard doubted even Anglhan was so conceited he would consider himself a keen military man – knew a little about sieges. Magilnada's catapults began bombarding the closer siegeworks as Low Watch began. Rocks rained down from eight machines on the walls, sending up fountains of earth, turning braces and wooden walkways into storms of deadly splinters. The barrage was not quick, but it was steady and accurate.

Teams dashed forwards to drag the dead and wounded back to the main line while fresh companies were sent in to continue the labouring. Ullsaard knew this would be a tough time for the men, dying at the hands of the enemy before they could strike back. Most of them already knew where their duties in the assault would put them; those carrying ammunition or manning the machines knowing they took their chances early on while those in the attack companies would face even greater danger when they stormed the walls.

Ullsaard walked slowly back to his camp. Sieges were drawn-out affairs, even if an early assault was planned. It was one thing to smash into a wooden-walled Salphorian village or fort; it was an entirely different prospect to storm a city like Magilnada. Ullsaard contented himself with the thought that it was all good practice for when they reached Carantathi, which if rumour and legend were to be believed would present even more of an obstacle than Magilnada. It was claimed the capital of Salphoria, though not large, sat atop a mountain and could only be reached by a single causeway. Rather than dreading such a task, Ullsaard was looking forward to overcoming the challenge.

On arriving at his tent, the king summoned his First Captains, reviewed their orders and the dispositions of the legions and then dismissed them to concentrate on other matters. Ullsaard had avoided some of the more onerous duties of his position whilst chasing the Mekhani, but his responsibilities had caught up with him in Ersua and there was a chest full of documents, letters and petitions to read through.

He applied himself to the task as he would any other campaign, dividing the work by type. Trade proposals went in one pile, with reports from the governors in another. Marriage, death and birth announcements he set aside for the time being. Invitations to galas, openings, fairs, ship launches, feasts and celebrations were tossed on to a growing heap under the map table.

With everything ordered as he wished, Ullsaard drank a little wine, ate some lunch and took a nap. At the ring of High Watch, he woke up, realising that he had slept longer than he had planned. He looked at the piles of documents and wax tablets and sighed. Filling another goblet of watered wine, he left the pavilion in search of some distraction.

Just as he stepped out into the camp, a great cheer was raised to his left. The gate towers were crowded with legionnaires, some of them pointing at Magilnada. Ullsaard hurried across the camp and pulled himself up the ladder of the right tower. Pushing to the front, there were a few grumbles from the soldiers until they realised their king had joined them. One hand on the parapet, the other raising the goblet to his lips, Ullsaard saw what provided so much entertainment.

The battery of catapults had been moved into range and commenced their bombardment. This initial barrage consisted of bronze globes filled with lava. As one, the engines launched their ammunition, the fire bombs arcing over the walls to explode onto the buildings within. Smoke was rising from several fires already; towards the dawnwards wall the flames of a growing inferno flickered above the curtain wall.

"When do we get to go in, king?" asked a leather-faced sergeant to Ullsaard's left.

"Three days," he replied, "unless something comes up sooner."

"Three days of this and there'll be nobody left to fight," the sergeant said with a hint of complaint.

"That's the idea," replied Ullsaard. "But I wouldn't be so sure about that."

He pointed to the city wall, where distant figures could be seen gathering opposite the engine battery. On the towers, trebuchets continued their counter-bombardment, launching rocks into the midst of the Askhan machines. The shattered bodies of men were hurled through the air by a direct hit, the catapult flying apart into a shower of timbers and rope. The soldiers in the gate tower groaned at the setback.

A horn sounded somewhere to the left, the warning note taken up by other musicians in the legion. Ullsaard's eyes immediately went to the gates, which were opening to release a stream of men. The Magilnadan warriors advanced towards the closest engines, their intent obvious.

Guard companies from the legion mobilised quickly, departing their camp to intercept the raiders. Such was the speed of the Magilnadan attack, they were upon the closest catapult while the Askhan reinforcements were still several hundred paces away. Fighting erupted along the revetment and the Magilnadans broke through in places, hacking at the ropes of the war machine and smashing canisters of oil. As the legionnaires closed in on them, the raiders set a fire in the fortification and scrambled away. They dashed back towards the gate, the more heavily armoured Askhans unable to catch them.

With the Magilnadans no more than a hundred paces from safety, a squadron of kolubrids closed quickly, unleashing a storm of bellows bolts. The running men were defenceless against the torrent and several dozen fell before a cloud of shafts lifted up from the walls and descended upon the Askhan cavalry. Driven back, the kolubrids turned away and the raiders escaped into the city.

"We should have some companies watching the gate," said a legionnaire behind Ullsaard. "They've got too much time for this sort of thing."

"Do you want to stand out there in range of their engines, just waiting for them to come out?" another replied. "Not me, for sure."

There were murmurs of agreement and muted laughs.

"When there're enough fires burning, we'll sort out the towers and the catapults," Ullsaard told his men. "It's just a matter of being patient. Unless you want to have a go now?"

Nervous denials greeted the offer and Ullsaard grinned.

"What if I said I was going to be first in?" the king suggested. "Would you follow me?"

This time the legionnaires were more enthusiastic, though there were several who did not seem to relish the prospect of the forthcoming assault. Ullsaard smiled, patted a few shoulders in encouragement and clambered down from the tower.

A second captain awaited the king when he reached the ground.

"First Captain Aalmunis requests that you see him in his pavilion, king," said the officer. "Scouts have arrived from hotwards."

"Thank you," Ullsaard said with a nod.

He followed the captain through the camp to Aalmunis's tent. The guard outside stood to attention and presented their spears at his approach. With a nod to return the salute, Ullsaard stepped inside.

Aalmunis had several maps spread out on the rugs. Three men in leathers stood with him, one of them pointing at something on a map of the border between Ersua and Free Country. All looked up as Ullsaard entered.

"News?" said the king.

"The Magilnadan legions have left their stations on the border," said Aalmunis. He crouched and drew a finger along a serpentine line of blue paint. "They're moving along the Neegha River."

Ullsaard studied the map. The traitors' route took them to duskwards, at least fifty miles behind the siege lines. If they meant to lift the siege, there were much easier roads to take.

"They're trying to get away," said Ullsaard.

"That was my conclusion," said Aalmunis. "We can't spare enough men to block their retreat, unless you want to forego an assault and starve out the Magilnadans."

Scratching at his beard, Ullsaard sifted through the maps until he found one on which were marked the camps of the legions further to duskwards. He made a quick assessment of the situation and who was best positioned to act.

"Send messages to the Eleventh, Fourteenth and Nineteenth," he said. Aalmunis took up a wax slate and stylus from a table and started making notations. "They'll have to move quickly. Have them break camp and march to

Eaghrus and Lennina. They should be able to catch the Magilnadans as they try to cross the bridges."

"What if they turn further coldwards, through these forests here?" asked one of the scouts, pointing to a huge swathe of green that spread into the foothills of the Ersuan Mountains.

"We'll have to let them get away," Ullsaard replied with a sigh. "If that end of the line is moved further coldwards, the legions will be too isolated and vulnerable to a Salphor attack."

"I'll have orders written up by the next bells," Aalmunis told the scouts. "Get yourselves something to eat and fresh mounts, you'll be leaving as soon as possible."

The scouts acknowledged their orders with quick bows and left. Ullsaard fixed Aalmunis with a stare.

"I want those Magilnadan scum slaughtered to a man," said the king. "Those legions killed my son, a prince of the Blood. Do you understand?"

"Yes, king," said Aalmunis. "We'll make sure those treacherous bastards wish they'd never crawled out of the bitches that spawned them."

IX

Smoke hung over the city in a thick pall, coating every surface with soot. Blackened bodies lay sprawled in fuming ruins, and the streets were choked with the crushed and bloodied. At first the people had tried to move the bodies into the lower city, but now there were just too many and everybody was too tired.

Groups of people wandered the streets with vacant looks, some of them clutching children whose grimy faces were streaked with lines of tears. Others sat in the rubble and wept, or simply stood unmoving at street corners while the desperate and the traumatised shuffled past.

The gate towers had fallen shortly after the bombardment had recommenced at dawn. The parapet of the wall was like a row of broken teeth, and in places the wall itself was crumbling, slopes of stone tumbled into the streets behind.

Anglhan picked his way through the destruction, swathed in a hooded cloak, a handcart dragged behind carrying a small chest of coins and gems. His head throbbed from lack of sleep; for the whole of the previous night the Askhans had beaten drums, a slow, terrifying tempo that presaged the assault to come. For just three days they had battered Magilnada, but in three days they had brought Anglhan's city to ruins.

He was numb, in mind and body. He saw the remains of a mother and two children buried under a pile of bricks, their bodies crushed by the collapsed building, and it meant nothing to the lord of Magilnada. Blood stained the flagstones underfoot and he stumbled through ruddy-tinged puddles. Dust filled the air, coating his clothes, choking eyes, ears and mouth.

The handcart jarred against something, bringing Anglhan to a stop. He looked back dumbly and saw that a severed arm had become trapped in the spokes of a wheel. Disgust, despair, anger had all run their course, and now Anglhan bent down, tossed aside the offending object and carried on without a second thought.

A boulder smashed through the roof of a house ahead, sending up shards of tiles and a cloud of plaster dust. Anglhan did not flinch. He barely heard the shriek of a man who came stumbling out of the damaged building, a splinter the size of a sword jutting from his shoulder. He made a grab for Anglhan, eyes pleading, but the ruler of the devastated city swiped away the man's hand and pushed him back.

He had to get out.

The city was surrounded. As far as Anglhan knew, no-body had escaped the ring of Askhans. Until that morning, he had harboured the hope that he would be able to slip away in the confusion and carnage of the final assault. That hope had been dashed the moment he realised the Askhans planned to kill everyone in the city. It would not matter if he could disguise himself in a flood of refugees, he would be cut down all the same.

So it was that he followed the last-ditch plan he had concocted more than a year ago, when he had first considered crowning himself ruler of the Free Country. He did not do so with hope of expectation, or even desperation. He walked through the city simply because the alternative was to wait in the palace to die. He was not a fighter, and he was sure that Ullsaard would give orders to ensure he was captured alive. Anglhan bore no illusions about the fate being taken prisoner would bring. Torture and an agonising death would be his only future.

He came upon Spring Road, where the wells that served the city were found, fed by underground rivers from the Altes Hills. There was a large crowd of people, scrabbling with one another to get fresh water. People wanted to drink; none gave thought to the dozens of fires that still burned in the city.

Anglhan was not interested in the fresh springs. It was pointless to stave off death by thirst just to wait for a legionnaire's spear. He moved around the crowd, avoiding the gazes of the desperate citizens, and made his way over a shallow pile of debris into a half-ruined wooden hall.

Inside stank of shit and piss, for this was the waste-house of the upper city. Separate from the river and pools that brought the city drinking water, another foaming rivulet cascaded down into the plains, accessed by three deep brick-lined holes. In normal times, the nightmen and pissboys would collect the waste of the nobles and flush it away down the open sewer; the common folk brought their own filth to dispose. Nobody knew where the stream went – Shit River as it was known – and until now nobody had cared.

Anglhan pulled a scarf from his belt and wrapped it over his mouth and nose; it did little to ward away the stench, but at least he would not get sprays of effluent in his mouth. He lifted the small chest from the cart and set it onto the lip of the closest sewer well. From the cart he brought forth a length of rope and tied it about his chest in the manner of a topman on his old landship. A memory flickered through his dulled mind, of teaching the same knot to a rebel chieftain.

Searching for something secure to tie the other end of the rope to, he spied a fallen beam from the broken roof. Tying the rope with nimble hands, he tested the knot and shuffled back to his chest. He passed the rope through a metal ring on one end and secured the chest to his belt. It weighed heavily at the moment, but it was only half-full, the rest of the space taken up by an inflated bladder that would keep the chest afloat once he was in the waterway.

Without any hesitation, no thoughts of what he had lost or the misery he had brought upon the thousands of people he had ruled, Anglhan flicked the rope over the wall of the well and heaved himself up to the lip. Inside, the bricks were coated with an uneven layer of dried waste, looking much like brown and black ice. The smell hit him with renewed strength as he swung his legs into the opening and dangled at the edge.

Working the rope through the special knot at his waist, Anglhan lowered himself towards the foaming water far below. In small drops, feet braced against the wall, the former lord of Magilnada left his city, face red with effort, the scarf across his face wet with his panting breath and sweat.

His foot slipped and for a moment he swung from side to side, toes scraping at the accreted shit for purchase. He eventually came to a stop and started down again. His feet were almost in the torrent when he noticed something different. He listened and could not place what he heard; then realised that it was quiet.

The Askhan drums had stopped. The assault was about to begin.

With a last effort, he slipped the knot free and dropped into the water. Foam bubbled around him as the current grabbed his legs and swept him away. His sodden clothes dragged at him and he clawed at the surface of the river. He snatched away the scarf and arched his neck to gasp for air, the small chest of money bobbing along beside him.

Only now did he feel something. Freedom. He laughed and spluttered, imagining Ullsaard's rage when he discovered Anglhan had escaped.

"Fuck Ullsaard!" Anglhan shouted, barely hearing his own voice over the rush of the river.

A moment later he was dashed against an outcrop of rock, his head cracking against stone, knocking him out.

X

Ullsaard had razed farms, villages, even towns, but he had never destroyed a whole city. A bank of oily smoke obscured the peaks behind Magilnada, blotting out everything around the city. Most of the flames were pyres, upon which the thousands of dead were burned. It had taken four days to take Magilnada; already five days had been spent collecting and disposing of the bodies. It was a grim task made all the more laborious because of Ullsaard's instructions to check every corpse to identify Anglhan's body. So far he had not been found, and Ullsaard was depressed at the realisation that in all likelihood the former governor had somehow eluded him.

Those companies not detailed on the corpse-burning were at work with the engineers, levelling every building, pulling down the great curtain wall, shattering bricks and breaking up stone blocks. The sound of their labour rang far across the Magilnadan gap, and it would continue for many more days to come.

Ullsaard sat in his pavilion and worked out what to do next. There was so much debris to search through, it could take dozens of days before Anglhan's remains might be found, if they existed at all. Practicality had to triumph over vengeance for the moment; supplies were already moving dawnwards to the Askhan legions and the offensive needed to start again. There was nothing Ullsaard could do to hasten the discovery of Anglhan or help with the utter destruction of Magilnada. His duty was to rejoin his army after long absence and lead the attack on Carantathi.

"Happy with your handiwork?"

Looking up, Ullsaard saw Noran stepping into the cloth-walled chamber. Some of the colour had returned to his face, but he still looked weak.

"You should be resting," said the king, standing up to direct his friend to a chair.

Noran sagged into the canvas seat with a long exhalation. He took a moment to regain his breath.

"You have not answered my question," said Noran. "Are you happy now that Magilnada is destroyed?"

"Happy? No," said Ullsaard, sitting down again. "You know that I do not enjoy senseless slaughter. Satisfied, perhaps, but not happy. I'll be happy when I see Anglhan's mutilated remains hanging from a pole."

"A whole city killed for revenge against one man? That seems excessive, even by our standards."

"This wasn't just about Anglhan, though he was the reason it began," said the king. "I've destroyed Magilnada. When word of that spreads, who will dare to oppose my legions? I will send a message that any who choose to fight me will suffer the same consequences. I was too soft in my last approach. Not this time. We will do this the true Askhan way. Any that submit will be helped; any that resist will be slain. Even Aegenuis cannot ignore that message."

"Are you so sure that Aegenuis will receive the message?" said Noran. "Nobody is left alive to take it to him."

"He will get the message," Ullsaard assured his friend with a wry smile. "If not from the living, then from the dead. But enough of that, why are you here? You really should not be out of bed; your recovery is just starting."

"I am leaving," Noran said, meeting Ullsaard's gaze. "I cannot stay here."

"Is that wise?" said the king. "You don't look fit to travel yet."

"Yet travel I will," said Noran. "I will leave camp today. I would appreciate it if you could provide me with a small guard; I gather Askhans might not be too popular in these parts at the moment."

"Of course," said Ullsaard. "I can provide an escort back to Askh without any trouble. Twenty men should suffice."

At this, Noran looked away.

"I am not going to Askh," he said.

"Why not? Your family is there. So is Meliu, if you are still interested in her. Where else will you go?"

"To the villa in Geria. I cannot think to see my family at the moment, and though she is wonderful, I can do without Meliu's fussing too."

"Why leave at all? I know the campaign road is not comfortable, but I would be glad of your company on it."

At this Noran's face was creased by a pained expression. Ullsaard was out of his chair in a moment, crossing to his friend's side. He placed a hand on Noran's shoulder but it was shrugged away. Noran pushed himself up and stepped towards the door.

"I cannot stay," said the nobleman. "Not here. Not with you."

"Why not?" said Ullsaard, following after him. "Have I done something wrong?"

"Being near you is not good for me, Ullsaard!" Noran confessed, the words uttered through gritted teeth. "I love you like a brother, I suppose, but these last years, you have brought me pain and misery and little else."

"I am sorry," said Ullsaard, flushed with regret. "I thought that perhaps I had restored the balance, by giving you the means to live again."

"And that is the worst of all!" snapped Noran. "What do you think I see when I look at you? A friend? A king? No, I see the man whose own life diminishes by an hour for every hour that I live. I would end it now, if I was not such a coward, and if it would not make a mockery of the sacrifice you have made already. So, I have to leave. Seeing you is a torture to me. Thinking about what you have done, it torments me, more even than the death of Neerita and my son. Death follows you Ullsaard, and mine should have been counted amongst the toll, but you could not even allow me that."

"I had no idea." Ullsaard sought for the right words, for an argument, for something that would give Noran comfort. His mind was too tumultuous for any such thing.

"I do not know if I will ever be able to look at you again, as we both get older, knowing that I live only at your expense when I sought to save your life," said Noran. There were tears in his eyes as he reached the door and looked back, almost flinching at what he saw. "I do not blame you, Ullsaard. I do not hate you, though some would say I have reason to. You did not do this to me out of malice, but you ignored my wishes and we both have to live with the consequences."

Then he slipped outside, leaving Ullsaard alone. The king was stunned. He had never contemplated such a thing happening. Immediately his thoughts went to Allenya, and he wished again that he had not sent her away. He sat down in his chair, hands on knees, and tried to make sense of what had just happened.

APARTIS, SALPHORIA
Summer, 212th year of Askh

The water jug was empty. Aegenuis placed it back on the table and sighed. He questioned again the counsel that had brought him here, to the most arid part of Salphoria, at the height of summer. It had seemed a wise decision at the time, to scatter the tribes ahead of the renewed Askhan advance, hiding in the mountains and forests; the Askhans would be mad to send any force of size into the scrub of Apartis. If the Askhans could not find their foes, they could not defeat them, or so had been the wisdom of his advisors. So it was that he was sat in a dead chieftain's ramshackle hall in a half-ruined town, seven thousand of his men drinking the meagre wells dry.

The Askhans' tenacity infuriated the Salphorian king. Half starved, assailed for three seasons by their foes, the Askhans had simply sat tight in their camps and waited. It was unnatural, the king had concluded. The Brotherhood must put something in their rations to make them so obedient. Thinking of the Brotherhood led Aegenuis's thoughts to Leraates, the Brother who had promised so much. Nothing had been seen of him since he had returned to the empire last winter. With the Askhan legions advancing dawnwards more quickly than last time, Aegenuis knew when he had lost an ally.

In fact, his list of allies was rapidly dwindling to none. It was obvious that Anglhan had failed in his bid to cut off the Askhan legions. Of the three dozen tribal leaders who had sworn new oaths of allegiance last summer, perhaps twenty were still alive and loyal; the others had thrown in their lot with the Askhans or simply vanished. Even those who still professed to follow Aegenuis, he could number on one hand those that he actually trusted.

He tipped jug to cup again, forgetting that there was no water. Frustrated, he hurled the ewer at the wall. Hearing the commotion, two servants hurried into the hall from the kitchens.

"More water!" Aegenuis bellowed at them.

"There is no more," one said while the other shrugged apologetically.

"Find some!"

The servants scurried away, darting anxious looks at their ruler before vanishing into the kitchens. Aegenuis's fists thumped onto the table as he leaned forward, bowing his head to his chest. Sweat dripped from his nose and brow, and matted his long hair and beard. He licked dry lips, trying to put aside his thirst so that he could think properly.

The main doors creaked open. Sunlight streamed into the hall to overwhelm the guttering light of the candles in the windowless hall. Several men entered, the first of them Aegenuis's son, Medorian. The other four, chieftains from the tribes of Apartis, followed Medorian into the hall, two of them dragging sacks behind them.

"What do you want?" said Aegenuis, lowering his head again, trying to ignore the ache inside it. "Close the door, it's too bright."

"These were found in an abandoned cart on the road to Alassan," said Medorian.

The two laden chieftains came forward with their burdens and placed the sacks before the empty fire pit. Another closed the doors, plunging the hall into gloom.

Aegenuis roused himself from the chair and went to the sacks.

"Look inside," said Medorian.

Pulling the cord tie on the closest sack, Aegenuis heaved up the bag to spill the contents onto the dusty floor. Heads bounced and rolled over the flags, causing the king to drop the sack and take two steps back. He leaned closer and saw that each had been branded on the forehead with the face of Askhos. In the dim light, he recognised some of the rotting faces.

"That's Serbicuis," he said, shocked by the sight. He looked at his son, who was nodding with a sour expression. "And Lassiun, and Ulghan. How many?"

"Eighteen chieftains," said Medorian. "Seven from Magilnada, the others from Free Country and the Altes Hills. Executed by the Askhans."

"I can see that!" snapped Aegenuis. "Do you know what this means?"

"That the Askhans are a bunch of sword-happy arseholes?" suggested Medorian.

"That Magilnada has fallen," replied the king. Medorian's smirk faded. "The new Askhan invasion, it's possible because they've taken Magilnada. Probably worse, judging by these poor bastards."

"Why did they leave them on the road?" asked Aghali, one of the tribal leaders. The short, scrawny man prodded the unopened sack with his foot. "Seems an odd thing to drop off the back of a cart."

"They were left for us to find, you idiot," said Medorian. "They're trying to intimidate us."

"They're not trying, they're succeeding," said Aegenuis, sitting himself on the bench alongside the main table. "It's not just chance that they left them here. They know where I am."

"Then why haven't they attacked?" This was from another chieftain, called Lastabruis. "These were found not more than a morning's walk away."

"Why do they have to attack?" said Aegenuis. "The whole point of being in this shithole is so that the Askhans do not know where we are. I wonder how many of the other armies have been discovered. Fuck, for all I know, everybody else is dead. There's no reason to attack, they don't think us a threat."

"That's where we prove them wrong," said Medorian, putting a foot up on the bench beside his father and leaning over him. "I've sent riders out to Caraghlin, Tanna, Gathluis, and a few others. With our warriors, that's nearly fifty thousand. They're going to meet us at the Hadric Mounds in twenty days."

"Well, that's nice," said Aegenuis, pushing his son's foot from the bench. "At least we'll spare the Askhans the trouble of finding us before they kill us. The Hadrics are at the heart of their advance."

"That's my plan!" said Medorian. "They won't expect us to be there. We'll hide in the wooded hills and wait for them to march on Carantathi and then attack from the rear."

Aegenuis laughed, and once he had started it took a supreme effort to stop. Medorian looked at him with a frown while he recovered from the fit.

"You think Ullsaard and his men are just going to walk past?" said the king. "They have scouts you know. Hiding fifty thousand warriors isn't like putting a coin in the bottom of your shoe. They tend to get noticed."

"Which is why we'll give the Askhans something else to look at," said Medorian, crossing his arms and looking like he had already won the victory. "The Casabha and Kighans are going to lure the Askhans on, make it look like part of a larger force falling back towards the city. Ullsaard won't be able to resist it. He'll set off after them, thinking he has us on the run and wanting to catch us before we reach the safety of our walls. He'll be looking ahead to that, not worrying what's behind."

Aegenuis tried hard to consider the plan on its merits, but it seemed pointless. It didn't make any difference. All of the tricks and ploys would not defeat the combined might of Askh. Even with Anglhan's duplicity and constant attacks from the tribes, the Askhans had not given a pace backwards. It was not a question of whether the Askhans would win, it was a question of when, and how many would die to delay that inevitable victory.

"No," said the king. He stood up and paced in front of his son and the chieftains. "I have a better plan, one that will not throw away the lives of thousands. Son, I have failed you, and for that I am sorry. I will be the last king of Salphoria. You must put aside your pride and come to terms with what I have been forced to accept. The Askhans will win."

"You cannot surrender," said Medorian. "Would you be remembered as a coward?"

"The memory of my rule has already been determined," said the king. "Some Askhan chronicler will note that the line of the Salphorian kings ended, and the rule of Askhos's descendants began. Whether I fight, or seek peace, that cannot be changed."

"So you must at least fight," insisted Medorian. "Do your lands, your people mean so little to you?"

"Does being king mean so much to you?" countered Aegenuis. He pointed to his war-helm, left at the end of the table. It was made of precious iron, rimmed with gold, its mask decorated with a silver wolf's face, a ruby set at its brow. "Take it, wear it, if you want to be king, for all the good it will do you."

"I will," said Medorian. He took a step towards the table, arm outstretched. "Our people deserve a leader that does not abandon them!"

Aegenuis grabbed Medorian's wrist and twisted, kicking at his ankle to send him tumbling to the ground. The young man struggled against his father, swinging and missing with a fist. Aegenuis twisted again, turning Medorian to his belly, and placed a knee in the small of his back.

"You do not deserve it!" hissed the king. "I suffered the same vanity as you. I killed my father, as you want to kill me right now. I thought I was great, a leader worthy of these lands. I have been proven wrong. I look to dawnwards and I see an empire that will crush us or swallow us, it cares not which. That empire was founded by another king, and his will has won over ours. We have fought for rulership, and built nothing. We spilled the blood of our own while Askhos's followers raised cities and armies that we cannot match."

Releasing his hold, the king stepped back.

"It is no great mystery," he continued, as Medorian rolled over and sat up. "The spirits have abandoned us. We are at the mercy of the Askhans and all we can choose now is to preserve those lives the spirits have entrusted to us with their passing. I'll not be responsible for the deaths of women and children born under my rule. Future generations may not remember me, but if they do, they will thank me for putting their prosperity above my pride."

Medorian snarled and sprang up, snatching a knife from his belt. Aegenuis easily slapped his son's arm aside and drove his forehead into Medorian's face, crushing his nose. The prince stumbled back, blood pouring onto his shirt.

"Take him!" Aegenuis called to the chieftains. For a moment they hesitated, but Aghali seized Medorian, ripping the dagger from his hand, and the others followed his lead, grabbing the king's son by the arms and neck. "I could have you slain on the spot for drawing a blade on me. However, I would not see my last act as king be the execution of my son. I killed my father and to this day I have not regretted it. You shall live, and reap the benefits of my mercy."

He waved the chieftains away, but then called for Aghali to stay when the group reached the door. When the others had gone, Aegenuis motioned for Aghali to sit beside him on the bench.

"Spread the word to any chieftain that will listen," said the king. "They are to offer no resistance to the Askhans. They are not to provoke them in any way. I will send word to Ullsaard himself and invite him to Carantathi. There I will hand him my crown, bow my knee to the Askhan king and offer him my throne. Do you understand?"

The old chieftain's eyes glimmered with tears. He grasped the king's shoulder and squeezed tight.

"I never had no love for you, nor your father," Aghali admitted. "Your son has the same failings. But if it means anything, I am happy to call you king now. There are those as won't like it at all, and the Askhans will deal with them in their way. But you are right, we can't fight no more. Let's not spill the blood of our children for land they will never own. The past is past. We need to bury it with our dead."

The two of them stood and gripped each other's arms in parting. Aegenuis walked with Aghali to the doors and stepped onto the street outside. The sun was bright overhead, the air dry on his skin. He felt as parched as the land, and had no tears to offer.

A group of warriors stood guard a short distance away, sheltering under a ragged awning. As Aghali walked away, the king turned to the men and called out.

"Send out the word to the camp. Find me someone that can write the words of the Askhans."

They signalled their compliance and Aegenuis returned to the hall to compose his letter to King Ullsaard of Greater Askhor, soon-to-be ruler of Salphoria.

SALPHORIA
Midsummer, 213th year of Askh

I

The mountains ahead were wreathed with clouds, though the sky above was clear and the sun scorching hot. To cold-wards, on the edge of sight, more hills rose up, dark with trees. The tramp of thousands of feet brought up a great swathe of dust that swirled in light wind and settled on the armour of the legionnaires. At the front of the Askhan column, ahead of the worst of the cloud, Blackfang panted heavily as she padded alongside Ullsaard on her rein. He patted her flank out of reflex, pleased to be reunited. She was, he considered, more loyal than many he had once considered friend or ally.

The ground underfoot was baked hard, the sparse grass withered and brown. There were no roads and no rivers to follow, so the army marched straight to duskwards. Ahead, somewhere in the mountains, lay Carantathi, the seat of the Salphorian king, soon to be Ullsaard's second city.

Twenty days ago he had received Aegenuis's offer of peace. He had marched the next morning, and for twenty days not a single tribe had offered resistance to his advance. Companies were despatched as garrisons to the settlements they passed, while two of the eight legions that had set out had been sent to hotwards to deal with any chieftains that objected to the new state of affairs.

Ullsaard had been met by elders and war chiefs, and each had accepted him as their new king. In the last twenty days he had taken more ground than in the previous two years. There had been times when he had doubted he would achieve his goal; when he had been slipping into Ersua fearful of discovery; when Erlaan had led the Mekhani horde into Greater Askhor.

The king harboured no illusions that the future would be simple, but he could dream as such. He could enjoy the peace for a few years, at least. He had not had time to commemorate Jutaar's life properly, and there were many rifts with his family to seal. The taking of Carantathi would be symbolic, but there would be many Salphors who would continue to resist. The Brotherhood would have to extend their reach into these untamed lands and instil the ethos of Askh into the hearts and minds of the barbarians. The Mekhani were ever an issue to be dealt with, and in a few years he would bring them under the sway of his empire too.

Despite these things, perhaps even because of the challenges he still faced, Ullsaard was in a good mood. He had an army thirty thousand strong at his back and a land to conquer. After so many tribulations, he was pleased to be up against the simple obstacles of war. He had left behind the distractions of kinghood, the worries of family and the politics of home. Here he faced the trials of logistics and discipline, strategy and disposition; obstacles he greeted with the contentment of familiarity. The reassurance of routine coupled with the hundred details of each day served to steady Ullsaard. It was this life, not the blood and glory of battle, which held his heart, though he would never shirk from bloodshed.

It was an odd feeling, to be marching to victory knowing that no enemy army awaited him. It was a vindication of everything he had done, a bloodless end to his ambitions in Salphoria. He had some respect for Aegenuis. The Salphorian king had fought hard to keep his place, and Ullsaard would expect nothing less. He had also shown sense and humility to accept Ullsaard's inevitable triumph, and as much as his canny strategy, it was this that earned Aegenuis the Askhan ruler's good opinion.

There was no need to be vindictive about the war. Even Aegenuis's alliance with Anglhan was excusable; had not Ullsaard himself raised up the treacherous dog? Salphoria was too large to be governed by one man, but Ullsaard had decided that should Aegenuis wish it, he could stay on as ruler of a province in Carantathi. That would bring some problems, the king was sure, but it solved many others. Ullsaard was determined not to let the example of Anglhan poison his thoughts against the idea of the local chieftains retaining positions of power.

Salphoria was almost a second empire in itself, and so it was from Askhos's original plan that Ullsaard took his vision for these new lands. He would accept and legitimise those warlords who accepted him, and give them dominion over those tribes that resisted. Their fate would be inextricably linked to the fate of the empire, just as in those early years.

He heard footfalls hurrying up from behind and looked back to see Anasind marching briskly to join him. He slowed for a moment to allow the general to catch up. Anasind's expression showed urgency, excited not apprehensive.

"Some fresh news to break the monotony of the march?" said Ullsaard when Anasind came alongside.

"True enough," replied the general. "Our scouts report sighting a Salphorian force a few miles ahead. Five or six thousand, at least. They did not appear ready to lay down their weapons peacefully."

"What do you want to do about it?" said Ullsaard.

"I thought it might be nice to kill them," Anasind said with a grin. "A peaceful occupation is all well and good, but I would rather my men earned their pay with their spears now and then."

Ullsaard clapped a hand to his companion's shoulder and laughed.

"Give a man an army and he wants to fight everything he can," said the king. He saw disappointment in the general's eyes and laughed again. "I agree, but I'm coming with you. We'll split the column. The Thirteenth, Fifth and Seventh will come with us, the rest will press on to find and secure Carantathi. We'll chase down these Salphors and rejoin the main army in a few days' time."

"I shall prepare the orders immediately," said Anasind, filled with energy. "With your leave?"

Ullsaard waved him away with a smile. As Anasind hurried back towards the army, Ullsaard was pleased with his choice of general. He would probably need to appoint two or three more fairly soon, to keep the Salphors in order while the Brotherhood set about bringing them into the imperial way of life.

The prospect of battle quickened the king's heart. Chasing off a few defiant tribesmen might not be the height of glory, but it was a timely distraction from the long march. It would be good to fight with the Thirteenth again.

II

The moon had set and the army marched by starlight and lamplight. The barren stretch of land had given way to more fertile soil as it rose higher towards the hills. For two days and nights, Ullsaard's legions had pursued the

Salphors, who had demonstrated their violent intent with several attacks, skirmishing with the kolubrid companies.

The air was warm and a stiff breeze rustled the long grass as Gelthius and his company followed the lantern carried at the head of the group. The uneven ground made it impossible to walk in step, and two days of forced march with no break had left the legionnaires tired, so that each stumbled and pressed on at his own pace.

Gelthius looked up at the spray of stars. He had never been this far dawnwards before, though he had heard tales of tribes living in the wooded hills. He had told the king what he knew of these lands, of the few scattered people living in the area. Ullsaard had thanked him for the information and sent him back to the company. There had been no change, and the army had continued after the enemy without pause.

"Fuck me, my feet are sore," said Loordin. "Feels like I've been marching my whole bloody life."

"If you don't keep up the pace, we'll never catch the bastards, and then you'll have even more marching to do," replied Muuril.

They walked on in silence for a few hundred paces. The still was broken by murmuring from the companies in front, growing in volume as news spread back along the column. Second Captain Naasta emerged from the darkness.

"Campfire sighted, about two miles ahead," he said. "Looks like a river crossing."

The captain moved on, his voice dwindling as he passed on this information to the other officers.

"Reckon we'll wait 'til dawn," said Muuril. "If them Salphors are on the other side of a river, it'll be a nightmare crossing and attacking in the dark."

The sergeant's prediction was borne out. Orders came along the line to make rough camp in half a mile. Double guards would be set and the legions were to muster an hour before Dawnwatch. The soldiers plodded on.

"What time is it now?" asked Loordin.

"Just past Gravewatch, didn't you hear the call?" replied Gelthius.

"Three hours kip," said Loordin. "Better than nothing, I suppose. I hope we don't spook the Salphors and set them off again; the king will want to press on if they do."

The army spread out as it reached the staging area. Abada carts rumbled up from the rear, bringing the legionnaires their blankets, while fires were set and rations and water distributed.

"No beer before battle," said Muuril as the company hunkered down around their fires. "That's an odd regulation, ain't it? If ever there was a time for a cup of beer, it's the night before a fight."

Gelthius nodded in agreement and tore a chunk of salted pork with his teeth. He chewed the tough meat rigorously, washing down the mouthful with a swig of water from his skin. Hunger staved off, he took off his helmet and bunched his blanket into a pillow. He lay down on one side, head propped on his hand, and looked into the fire.

"All the Salphors will be Askhans soon enough," he said to nobody in particular. "I suppose I should've seen that coming ages ago."

"Nobody gives up without a fight," said Muuril. "It's the way, isn't it? Don't matter how sensible something might be, nobody likes things to change."

"Except them Maasrite cowards," said Loordin. "They didn't put up no fight, did they?"

"They were clever, not cowardly," said a deep voice from the darkness

The legionnaires looked up and saw King Ullsaard

walking into the light of the fire. He waved them to stay where they were as they moved to stand. Muuril offered his blanket for the king to sit, but Ullsaard waved it away and settled into the grass, adjusting his scabbard as he leaned back on one arm. The king looked at Gelthius, who felt uncomfortable under that gaze, the firelight flickering in Ullsaard's eyes.

"You can't ever guess what's going to happen," said the king. "I bet you cursed the day you were taken as a debtor, right?"

"Right enough," said Gelthius, surprised the king remembered such a thing. "Worst day of my life that was."

"Taken from your family, enslaved to another man," said Ullsaard, nodding. "But if you think about it, that might have been the luckiest day of your life."

"How do you figure that, king?" said the Salphor.

"The joy of unforeseen consequences," replied Ullsaard. "If you hadn't been on Anglhan's landship, you would have never become part of Aroisius's rebels. If you hadn't been a rebel, you'd have never joined the Thirteenth. And if you hadn't been in the Thirteenth, you and your family would have been killed with the rest of your tribe."

"Never thought about it like that," admitted Gelthius. He thought of his wife and children, amongst the camp followers that were with the main force. "Don't suppose I'd ever see Carantathi as a farmer, neither. I like being in the Thirteenth, don't get me wrong, but I can't say as this is the life I would have chosen."

There came a sigh from the king, almost wistful. He picked up a branch from the flames and prodded at the fire.

"How much of our lives do we get to choose?" Ullsaard said. "Who we kill? Who we fall in love with? Who falls in love with us? Maybe life is just about getting on with the best that gets handed to us."

"Easier said by the man who's just been handed another crown," said Loordin with a laugh.

There was a moment of tense silence as the soldiers waited to see if Loordin had overstepped the mark. Ullsaard tossed the brand into the flames and stood. He looked down at Loordin.

"What's your name, legionnaire?" the king asked.

"Loordin, king," the soldier replied, getting to his feet. "Apologies, if my joke offended."

"No offence taken, but your point is mistaken," said Ullsaard. "Aegenuis may hand his crown to me, but he gives it to all of Greater Askhor. The victory is everybody's. You think he'd surrender to me if I did not have you villains to back me up? The victory is Askh's, where even a bastard son of a court whore can become king. There's hope for all of you yet!"

The king nodded and smiled, and walked away to the next fire. Loordin sat down again and the legionnaires sat in silence, contemplating Ullsaard's words.

"Nice of him to say that," said Muuril.

"Yeah," said Loordin. "I bet he still wouldn't give me that crown if I asked for it though."

"Right enough," said Gelthius, settling onto the ground.

He swiftly fell asleep, glad that he was not in one of the watch companies for that night. He was woken by Muuril shaking him, the ring of the watch bells still sounding through the army. Stiff and still tired, he hauled himself to his feet and poked the fire into more life while the sergeant roused the others.

"The Salphors ain't moved," said Muuril, returning to Gelthius's side. He raised his voice. "Looks like we're going to have a fight today, after all. The king wants the Thirteenth at the front, so move your arses."

Gelthius scratched his balls, yawned and stooped to pick up his helmet.

"Stupid bastards," he muttered. He grabbed his spear and shield from the pile. "Let's not keep 'em waiting, eh?"

III

Glittering in the dawn light, the river meandered down from the forested hills and curved gently to dawnwards. It foamed over rocks, the banks lined with bushes and reeds. It was at least half a mile across at the ford, which stretched over a quarter of a mile, the vegetation trampled flat from the passing of the Salphors.

The lead companies edged cautiously into the swirl, using their spear butts to test the depth and footing. Reining in Blackfang, Ullsaard dismounted and walked her down to the bank as the first companies waded through the water. He stopped at the river's edge, water lapping at his boots, and peered through the gloom to the far bank.

Dozens of glimmers from the Salphorian fires danced in the darkness, perhaps no more than a mile from the crossing. Under the urging of their captains, the Thirteenth legion forged across as quickly as possible, the first companies now forming up on dry land to guard those still in the water.

As Ullsaard took his first steps into the water, Blackfang skittish beside him, warning trumpets sounded from behind. The clatter of spears and shields sounded deafening in the early morning calm as thousands of legionnaires responded; those on the far bank halted their advance, those in the water pushing on as fast as possible to reach safer ground.

The signal blasts could mean only one thing: attack.

Ullsaard dragged his ailur back and threw himself into the saddle. With a flick of the reins and a shout, he urged Blackfang into a run, heading back up the column. Company by company, the legions were falling into position, the phalanxes arranging themselves back-to-back, unsure in which direction danger lay.

Riding hard, Ullsaard came upon Donar and his staff half a mile along the column. The king pulled Blackfang to a halt beside the First Captain of the Fifth.

"Report," snapped Ullsaard.

"Scouts report Salphors coming down from the forests," said Donar, pointing to the wooded hills silhouetted against the rising sun.

"You think the ones we are chasing have double-backed, perhaps across another part of the river?" asked the king.

"I don't know," admitted Donar. "Where's Anasind?"

"On the far bank, at the head of the army," said Ullsaard. "Don't worry about him, he can handle himself. Get your line in order, and send out more scouts, we need to know how many there are."

Donar nodded and turned to his subordinates, rattling off orders. One-by-one the captains rode off on kolubrids, taking their orders to the companies spread along the line of advance.

"Hold here," Ullsaard said, turning back towards the river. Blackfang broke into a run at his command, rushing across the ground with head low.

Back at the river, the Thirteenth were divided. Those in the water had finished crossing, leaving two thirds of the companies on the far side and a third on the closest. As he rode passed, Ullsaard called to the captains to form a perimeter around the ford and to hold their ground until they received fresh orders.

Running down to the river, Blackfang slowed as she reached the water.

"Get in there!" shouted Ullsaard, slapping the reins against her shoulder.

The ailur tensed and then sprang forwards, splashing up to her belly. Ears flat, tail twitching, she pushed further across the river, until the water was up to Ullsaard's knees. She baulked as she met a swirl around a cluster of rocks, but moved on at Ullsaard's command. He guided her around the worst obstacles, and set the reins to her again as the river ahead cleared. Feeling the water growing shallower, Blackfang broke into a run, erupting from the water in spume. Anasind was waiting a few dozen paces from the river as Ullsaard rode up the gentle slope. The king jumped to the ground, one hand keeping a firm grip of Blackfang's reins as she shook water from her fur.

"What's the situation here?" asked the king.

"Our friends are getting brave," said the general. "Seems they were waiting for us to cross. The camp was a decoy; they were waiting downstream in the vegetation. No more than half a mile away and coming straight for us. At least four thousand."

Ullsaard made a quick assessment of the land. There was not enough time to get the companies back across the river before the Salphors arrived. He pointed to a rise in the ground about a quarter of a mile from the water.

"Set up your line on those hills," he said, speaking quickly but calmly. "Keep five companies here to guard the ford, you'll have their flank protected, and send for the other companies to cross over and reinforce."

"What's happening back there?" asked Anasind, looking across the river.

"Not really sure yet," said Ullsaard, following the general's gaze. "More Salphors. No idea how many. I think two legions should be enough to hold them off."

"You think this was their intent all along?" said Anasind. "Is this some trick of Aegenuis?"

"Looks like it," said Ullsaard, tugging at Blackfang's reins to pull her closer. "No point worrying about that for now. You sort out things here; I'll lead the rest of the legion up to the hills."

The king mounted again as Anasind signalled for his captains to gather. Ullsaard shouted out to the companies that were to follow and turned Blackfang duskwards. In the growing light, he could see the Salphors in the distance, approaching quickly. He reined in his ailur.

"Anasind!" The general looked back at his king. "Forget that plan, we don't have time. Form up here and get those other companies across!"

Anasind raised a fist in acknowledgement. Within moments, the spear companies were gathering in line, eight men deep, widening their frontage to counter the enemy's greater number. Ullsaard sought out the legion icon with the first company and rode up beside them.

"I hope these lying dog-fuckers have had breakfast," he called out to the legionnaires. "They're not going to survive to have lunch!"

Laughs and cheers came back in reply. Ullsaard bellowed for an orderly and dismounted.

"Think I'll fight with you lot today," he told the men of the first company. He pulled his spear and shield from the ailur's back. "I think you need the help."

This statement was met with good-natured jeers as a youth took the reins from the king and led Blackfang away. Ullsaard took up his place in the front rank, next to the icon. He glanced at the captain holding the standard.

"What's your name, captain?" said Ullsaard. "What happened to Venuid?"

"I'm Kassil, king," said the man. "Promoted from seventh company. Venuid got shot in the eye by a Salphor."

"That's a shame," said the king.

"Yes, bad luck for him," said Kassil.

"Good luck for you," said Ullsaard.

"Dead man's sandals, isn't it? It's the legion way."

"Works for kings too," said Ullsaard, bringing up his shield.

In the glow of the rising sun, the Salphors were only a couple of hundred paces away. Several hundred moved ahead of the mass, bows in hand. The warning was shouted along the line and the phalanx shifted, raising their shields for the coming volleys. Ullsaard peered through a gap and saw the first cloud of arrows lifting into the air. The king ducked back his head. A few tense heartbeats passed and then the arrows fell, bronze heads rattling against shields like heavy hail. Here and there came a cry of pain, but the line held firm.

IV

There were a lot more than a few thousand Salphors pouring out of the woods into the early morning light. Donar sent a messenger running for First Captain Naathin of the Seventh, while he continued to watch the dark patch of men spreading from the forest.

The Salphors advanced with purpose though not precision. Their tribal groups were gathered about cloth standards in clumps of warriors rather than proper lines. With them came small chariots pulled by large wolf-like beasts with spiked bronze collars and coats of mail armour, two warriors in the back of each waving spears and javelins as they trundled past their foot-bound comrades.

They kept coming, horn blares signalling the arrival of three more tribes from duskwards. Donar guessed there were at least fifteen thousand of the barbarians, almost twice his own command. The general glanced toward the river, but was unable to see much at all past the glitter of the dawn light on the water. He could hear shouts and see clouds of arrows, but had not yet heard the clash of spear or sword on shield. The battle there was only just beginning.

He could not expect help from the king any time soon. "What's the plan?"

Donar turned at Naathin's voice. The Seventh's commander was of a similar age to Donar, his skin less weatherworn, thin strands of blonde hair trailing from under his helmet. Naathin was a stocky man with a bit of a gut, but his arms were as thick as many men's legs and his chest bulged under his breastplate. Donar was surprised to see that he was smiling.

"What are you so happy about?" demanded Donar, jabbing a finger toward the Salphorian army. "Do you like unexpected visitors first thing?"

"Better to fight in the morning, it's going to get hot later," replied the First Captain. Naathin's expression turned solemn as he saw the extent of the enemy force. "Oh. I wasn't expecting that many guests."

"Let's thin out their numbers, perhaps then they'll think twice about spoiling our breakfast arrangements." Donar swept his hand from one end of the Salphaorian army to the other. "Form crescent line, left flank anchored to the river, right flank over by that bluff to dawnwards."

"Do you want the river or the bluff?" asked Naathin.

"Not fussed," replied Donar. "We'll combine our engines between the two legions and form a screen in front with a few companies. That'll stop the Salphors trying to press into the divide."

The jingling of armour and shouts of the second captains increased in volume as the legionnaires were brought to line around the two First Captains. A gaggle of messengers was gathering behind the pair, waiting for orders. Donar acknowledged them with a raised hand and looked at his companion.

"I'll take the bluff, if it's all the same to you," said Naathin. He looked down toward the river and patted his armoured belly. "Less of a walk, you see?"

Donar couldn't stop a laugh.

"If you're worried about getting out of breath, perhaps you should retire with the baggage? I think we're both going to get plenty of exercise today."

"Like I said, morning fights are better. Means I'm not tired before we start. General orders to hold?"

"Yes, just keep the line strong, let the spear throwers and catapults goad them onto our spears. Put four companies in reserve behind your front, ready to plug any gaps."

"And you should put your veterans next to mine at the centre to protect the machines," said Naathin, looking around as he examined the ground. "I think we should fall back about a hundred and fifty paces though, the ground levels out more."

"Good point," said Donar with a glance over his shoulder. He shrugged. "Anything we haven't thought of?"

"Probably," replied Naathin. "Let's just make sure we hold them off until the king is done with that bunch over there."

"Pass the word!" Donar called out to the waiting captains. "No retreat! Fight to the last man!"

It was an indication of the legionnaires' mood, and general humour, that this announcement was greeted by a resounding cheer all around the two First Captains.

The air was still chill when the Salphors first sallied forth. They had evidently decided the war machines were the easiest foe to overcome and bunched together at the centre, coming on quickly with shouts and waving axes and spears.

Four salvoes of devastating spears and boulders was enough to dissuade them of this notion before they had crossed half the distance. The defiant shouts were soon quieted and the Salphor chieftains urged their men to withdraw, all swagger gone. Donar saw a huddle of garishly dressed nobles in gilded armour gather about the largest banner for some time. They evidently decided that a full attack would be too costly. Instead, the tribes broke apart, bringing out their bows and arrows.

Naathis and Donar called out the order to prepare for the archery attack. With only their machines to hide behind, the engine crews were vulnerable. The central companies were tasked with closing about the machines, forming solid ranks in front while they reloaded, parting to enable them to loose their deadly fire.

Undaunted by this manoeuvre, the Salphors continued to target the engines with their arrows, and from amongst the gaggles of warriors came forward their next ploy.

The Salphor chariots raced back and forth along the line, the riders casting dozens of javelins into the Askhan companies while the warriors laughed and jeered from further away. With remarkable bravery and dexterity, the two-man teams would take it in turns to climb upon the yoke of the moving chariots to throw their weapons while the other steered. Though the additional height was not great, this tactic meant the showers of javelins came in from a steeper angle than usual, forcing the Akshans to form up into their shield walls. The lupus snarled and yowled, eager to hunt, but the Salphor charioteers were too clever to allow themselves to be drawn into a fight with the closed ranks of their foes.

The slap and thud of the war engines was near constant, a barrage of spears and rocks hurtling into the

Salphor tribes. At first they tried to hit the harassing chariots, but their targets were too small and nimble to hit at the close range, so Donar passed the order to concentrate on thinning out the enemy numbers.

The Salphors had responded by breaking apart, widening the gaps between their men to present fewer opportunies. Despite this, several hundred of them had fallen to the war machine onslaught.

Donar fidgeted with a loose scrap of leather from his sword's binding, but refused to look toward the river. The loose formation of the enemy was ripe for counter-attack, but he knew that the Salphors could gather again quickly and press their numerical advantage. If the Askhans chanced their hand too soon, they would lose the benefit of a cohesive line and allow themselves to be drawn into a brawl in which their discipline and manoeuvring would be for nothing.

There was more movement from the enemy after a little more than a half an hour. The lupus chariots drew together as one group and headed toward the flank of the Seventh. Meanwhile, the infantry gathered again under their standards and gonfalons and advanced to the call of hunting horns.

"Seems they want to have another go," Donar said to the men around him, but he knew his bravado would seem thin compared to the bone-deep confidence of a man like Ullsaard. With a snarl of annoyance, he ripped the stray piece of leather from his sword hilt and settled his grip.

The enemy split, some following the chariots to keep the Seventh occupied, the rest advancing toward the river. Donar wiped his mouth with the back of his hand and swallowed hard.

There were a lot of Salphorians bearing down on his legion.

V

Ullsaard saw another volley already in the air, the rest of the Salphors breaking into a run under the cover of their archers. It was a good tactic. The all-encompassing shield wall was a poor formation to receive a charge; with shields lifted overhead to protect against falling arrows the legionnaires were unable to direct their spears towards the enemy. If they lowered their shields too soon, the bowmen would take a heavy toll; too late and the phalanx would not be able to fight back against their onrushing foes.

"Stand ready!" bellowed Ullsaard as more arrows descended in a deafening clatter. He took another peak at the approaching Salphors. They were fifty paces away, more arrows streaming over them. "One more volley!"

His shield shook in his grasp under the impact of several shafts, but none pierced the bronze-plated wood. Ullsaard wriggled his fingers on the haft of his spear, getting a better grip.

"Break shields! Present spears!" he roared, pulling down his shield and lifting his weapon into position.

His eye was immediately drawn to a Salphor directly ahead, an axe in both hands as he sprinted at the Askhan line. You're mine, thought the king, sliding back his right foot and bracing his shield against the man next to him.

"For Askhor!"

The cry drowned out the shouts and curses of the Salphors as the enemy hit the line with an earth-trembling crash. Ullsaard thrust his spear at the throat of the axeman, catching him below the jaw as he swung back his weapon. Twisting and wrenching, he pulled the spear free as the man's body tumbled into the dirt.

Something smashed against his shield, but Ullsaard did not break his attention from the front; whatever happened to his left was someone else's problem. Kassil's shield, protecting Ullsaard, shuddered under an impact. The king jabbed his spear, feeling the tip hit something, gouging into flesh.

Then the press of the Salphors was brought to bear, the bearded, wild-eyed warriors slashing, stabbing, dragging at shields. Ullsaard's right arm was like a piece of an engine, moving back, slamming forward, moving back for the next blow. He barely heard the snarled insults, the cries of the wounded, the racket of clashing shields and snapping wood.

Jaw clenched, he adjusted his footing as something heavy fell against him. Glancing down, he saw a Salphor's face, a ragged gash from cheek to brow. He stomped on the man's throat to be sure.

After some time, both sides battering away at each other, the Salphor pressure began to give. With no word given, the first company began to push forwards, taking the fight to the enemy, stepping over the dead. There was movement all around Ullsaard as the ranks redressed, men from the back filling in where legionnaires had fallen.

As more and more of the Thirteenth arrived from the river, the Salphors' advantage of numbers dwindled. With natural momentum, the line of battle swung away from the river as freshly arrived companies ploughed into the fight from the ford, hurling back the Salphors on the right.

Ullsaard reckoned that more than an hour had passed since the first charge. The battle was breaking up into smaller combats as some of the tribesmen broke away, leaving companies free to flank and surround those that remained fighting. Sensing a pause in the immediate fighting, Ullsaard broke from the first company, heading back through the ranks to clear ground.

The Askhans had advanced more than three hundred paces from their original position, their progress marked by hundreds of bodies from both sides. The wounded lay mangled and groaning, the dead sprawled where they had been cut down. A short distance away stood Anasind, messengers running back and forth as he continued to direct the battle. Ullsaard strode between the piles of casualties and raised his spear to attract the general's attention.

Anasind broke off from what he was doing and met his king halfway.

"Any word from the other side?" asked Ullsaard.

"Not yet, but it does not look good," said Anasind.

Ullsaard turned his gaze across the river. In the full morning light, the situation was revealed. The undulating ground sloping down to the river was filled with battle, stretching for almost a mile in a curving line to dawnwards. The hills were awash with Salphors, many thousands of them, a swaying mass that charged, fell back and charged again at the thin line of Askhans holding them back.

"We have to finish here quickly and get back across," said Ullsaard.

"Yes, but how?" said Anasind. He pointed at the battle between the Thirteenth and their foes. "We're only just getting the upper hand. I suppose I could pull back a few companies at a time as they become free, send them over as soon as I can."

"That won't help," said Ullsaard, shaking his head. "They'll just get fed into the melee piecemeal. We need to do something decisive to turn the battle."

Anasind looked lost for ideas, brow knotted as he watched the ongoing fighting.

"Sound the withdrawal," said Ullsaard.

VI

It was almost impossible not to give ground under the relentless attack of the Salphors. Naathin was red in the face, his breath coming in gasps as he swung his sword at the next enemy, the blow cleaving into the bearded man's forehead. The First Captain wrenched the blade free, showering himself with blood. Spitting the fluid from his mouth, he brought up his shield to catch the spear of another Salphor.

There was no retreating, as had been decided. Despite that, his Seventh were slowly being pushed back. The Salphors were ill disciplined, but were fighting ferociously, defending their lands with their blood and lives. Every time his soldiers paused for a breath or faltered, the Salphors pressed on, taking a step forward for every backward pace by his men.

The Ersuan had to credit them for at least trying, even as he wished they had all surrendered peacefully and let him return to his wives and daughter. Another blow shuddered his shield. He thrust without looking, feeling the tip of his sword push into flesh, the blow eliciting a yelp of pain from the man in front of him.

"Move to the right!" he bellowed, realising that the companies on the flank were in danger of being pushed away from the rocky bluff that prevented them being flanked.

Javelins were still being hurled over the heads of the Salphors from the roving chariots, which loitered menacingly, waiting for the smallest break in the line to dash forward with a deadly charge. If they were allowed the get behind the companies, havoc would break out and the line would crumble; orders to fight to the last notwithstanding.

"Push them back! Regain the crest!" he roared, smashing his shield into the chest of his opponent.

"We're bloody trying!" the legionnaire to his left snarled through gritted teeth.

"Well bloody try harder!" the First Captain shouted in reply.

VII

"What? Withdraw?" Anasind was horrified by the idea. "But we're winning. The Salphors will hound us back to the river if we let them."

"Which is why when they come after us you'll sound the counter-charge," said the king.

Anasind looked uncertain.

"Pulling back from engagement is not easy," he said. "We'll lose a lot of men if we time this wrong."

"We'll lose a fucking lot more if that line breaks," snapped Ullsaard, jabbing his spear towards the battle on the other side of the river. "You have your orders."

"Yes, king," said Anasind, bowing his head. He signalled for the handful of trumpeters to approach.

Ullsaard turned away and stared over the water, willing Donar and the others to keep fighting. The arc of the legions was contracting slowly, each fresh Salphorian attack pushing back part of the line as other companies retreated to keep the formation coherent. From this distance it was clear to see that the Salphors were concentrating their attack to dawnwards, at the end of the line not guarded by the river. Like a rod slowly bending under a smith's hammer blows, the legions were being forced into an ever tighter space, the far end of the line curling back towards the river.

Trumpet blasts split the air as the retreat was sounded. The signal was repeated three times, until all of the Thirteenth were falling back, still facing their enemies. For a while, the Salphors were taken aback by the move and a gap of a hundred paces or more opened between the lines. Faster and faster, the legion contracted, stepping back over the bodies of their own dead. Ragged volleys of arrows followed them, cutting holes in the tight ranks. Messengers and captains hurried to meet the retreating companies, bearing news of the plan to counter-attack.

"They'll be shot to pieces," said Anasind. "I'll have to sound the attack now."

"Wait!" said Ullsaard as the general lifted his arm to the musicians. "Just a little longer."

Anasind lowered his arm slowly and returned to his king's side. The shouts and yells of both sides could be heard, carried by the strengthening wind. Ullsaard glanced across the river. The Askhan line was still holding, though it was perilously close to breaking in places.

The noise of the Salphors recommencing their attack rumbled over the other sounds. Anasind again moved to raise his arm, but Ullsaard grabbed his wrist.

"Not yet," he said quietly. "We need to make sure the Salphors are fully committed."

"A legion doesn't change direction in a heartbeat," replied Anasind. "Too late, and they'll be caught anyway. We need to..." His objection trailed away as Ullsaard fixed him with a stare.

"In a moment," said the king. "This has one chance to work, let's not waste it."

Anasind fidgeted, arm still gripped by Ullsaard. In his head, the king was picturing the scene, obscured by the line of the legion. The Salphors had been no more than a hundred and fifty paces away. Allowing for the speed of their attack and the pace of the retreat, subtracting a little for the order to be enacted...

"Now," he said, letting go of Anasind.

"Sound the attack!" the general bellowed, raising and dropping his arm quickly.

The trumpets blared out. The Askhan companies came to a hesitant stop. As the signal rang again, they surged forward, meeting the Salphors head-on with a wall of bronze, a throaty roar drifting down to the river.

The line broke as some companies surged into the enemy while others met stiffer resistance. The soldiers closest to the river, where the freshest companies were found, swung inwards, sweeping away the Salphors in front of them. On the far right, the line was at a virtual standstill, while the centre advanced in determined fashion, the ring of weapons mingling with more screams and cries.

It seemed to take an age to Ullsaard, though in reality perhaps less than a quarter of an hour passed as the Askhan attack gained momentum. Having thought they were on the brink of victory, the courage of the Salphors crumbled quickly under the renewed assault, and they streamed away from the river in their dozens, leaving those fighting to their fate.

With open country behind and determined foes in front, the Salphor retreat spread into a rout. Here and there knots of Salphors fought on, their chieftains too brave, too stupid, or too trapped to run away. Some of the Askhans were pressing after the fleeing foe, and there was a danger of an ill-disciplined chase.

"Sound the recall," Anasind shouted to the musicians, just as the order was reaching Ullsaard's lips.

On the third sounding of the order, the pursuit was halted. Company by company, the Thirteenth came back in line and marched back to the river. A few companies detached as a rear guard, covering the withdrawal against a possible – though unlikely – resurgence from the fleeing Salphors.

Ullsaard looked at the legion, noticing that many of the companies had suffered heavy casualties. Those that had been fighting from the onset were at half strength or worse. It was with weary eyes and tired limbs that the legionnaires reformed on the general and king.

VIII

Ullsaard called for Blackfang and mounted. Spear in hand, he rode along the line.

"Congratulations on winning the warm-up!" he shouted to his men. He pointed over the river with his spear. "The real battle's over there. You're tired. Many of you are hurt. It would be easy to stop now. I can't let you do that. You're the Thirteenth. You're *my* Thirteenth, and that means you don't stand around while others do the fighting."

Ullsaard turned Blackfang around and rode back in the other direction.

"The Fifth and the Seventh are over there, trying to make a good show of things," he continued. "Looks like they're outnumbered by two-to-one at least. They're Askhans, so they're going to win anyway. But people will wonder what the Thirteenth were doing while the Fifth and Seventh earned such glory. Do the Thirteenth want to be known as the legion that were spectators at Askh's great victory?"

"No!" The shouted reply was a bit ragged. Taking a breath, Ullsaard pitched his voice even louder.

"Are the Thirteenth going to be remembered as the legion that won two battles in a single day?"

"Yes!" came the cry, stronger than before.

"Which legion is going to kill these annoying Salphorian bitchfuckers for me and march me to Carantathi?

"Thirteen!" The cheer was accompanied by the crashing of spears on shields and the stamping of feet.

With a shout, Ullsaard urged Blackfang into a run and headed like an arrow for the river. Excited by the blood and mayhem, she plunged into the water without hesitation as the Thirteenth quickly filed after at a trot, forming column company by company.

Ullsaard did not look back as Blackfang splashed over the ford. His eyes were fixed on the battle ahead. It would be easy to join the line where it was closest to the river, but the companies fighting there seemed to be doing well against relatively light opposition. The real danger lay at the far flank, where the Salphors were threatening to overlap or break through at any time. All of the reserves from the Fifth and Seventh had been committed, and still the Salphors were pushing them back.

Angling Blackfang for the further extent of the Askhan line, Ullsaard slowed her to a fast walk. Behind him, the Thirteenth followed at a swift march, hidden from the enemy by the fighting. Looking over his shoulder, Ullsaard checked the far side of the river and was reassured to see that the Salphors had all but disappeared. That problem had been solved for good.

When he was a few hundred yards from the fighting, he urged Blackfang on again. He waved his spear forwards and grinned as behind him the trumpets of the Thirteenth signalled the attack. It had been a long while since he had fought from Blackfang's back, but he felt he owed it to the ailur after neglecting her for so long.

A gap opened up between two companies ahead and, reins in his shield hand, Ullsaard directed her into the opening, spear at the ready.

"Get ready, my beauty," he said to Blackfang, bracing himself as they hurtled towards a group of Salphors.

Just a dozen paces from the enemy, Ullsaard used the rim of his shield to knock loose the catch on the ailur's blinker-chamfron. The spring-loaded plates over her eyes snapped open, and Blackfang looked upon her prey for the first time in years.

The Salphors looked around in shock as a piercing snarl split the air. They turned to see a golden-speared warrior charging at them, upon the back of a spitting mass of claws and fangs with red flames for eyes.

Before the tribesmen realised their peril, Ullsaard and Blackfang were upon them, spear flashing, teeth and claws rending and tearing. Ullsaard clung to reins and saddle horn with an iron grip as the ailur pounced and ripped. With his spear held overhand, the king lanced its point into any foe he could reach, plunging his weapon into chests and backs, splitting faces and piercing limbs. He snarled and roared with his mount, spittle flying from his mouth as blood sprayed from Blackfang's jaws.

Just as they were recovering from the shock of Ullsaard's charge, the Salphors were confronted by the first company of the Thirteenth. Golden face of Askhos held aloft, the legionnaires plunged into the fray, chanting the name of their king.

This fresh assault smashed into the Salphor line, company after company poured into the fray, driving deep into the tribesmen whilst behind them the men of the Seventh surged forwards with renewed strength.

Ullsaard's heart hammered in his chest and the Blood rushed through his body, lending its strength to every blow he landed. He kicked aside the shield of a Salphorian warrior and drove his spear into the man's gut. Blackfang leapt, crushing the helm of another with a swipe of a paw.

Something approached at speed from Ullsaard's right. Blackfang reacted quicker than the king, turning with a strangely disturbing shriek to leap directly at the lupus chariot. Ullsaard gripped tightly to the reins as feline and lupine collided, the ailur spitting, slashing with her claws, the lupus lunging at her throat with jaws wide. The king's eyes met with those of a charioteer, both of them slightly startled by the encounter.

The Salphor recovered and lifted up his arm, a javelin in hand. Ullsaard swayed to his right as the missile left the man's grip, the sharp tip passing just a hand's breadth over the king's shoulder. A feral roar from Blackfang warned Ullsaard to centre himself. He swung back into position just as the ailur leapt across the lupus's back, one paw raking its shoulder, her jaw latching on to the back of the other beast's neck.

Traces parted and the yoke snapped under the lunging attack, pitching the chariot into the muddied earth. Ullsaard jabbed out with his spear, catching the javelin-thrower in the shoulder, pitching him from the side of the light chariot. The driver had been half-pulled over the front and floundered to throw down the reins and regain his balance. Ullsaard's spear tip caught him full in the side of the face, punching through jaw and cheek.

With a plaintive howl, the lupus died, Blackfang's dagger-like teeth clamped into its spine. The enemy close at hand were running away, many dropping shields and weapons as too cumbersome. Through his battle-fever, Ullsaard remembered to close Blackfang's war-mask; almost immediately she calmed, contenting herself with mauling and chewing on the dead lupus.

Through a haze of excitement, Ullsaard tried to see what was happening. The Salphors had been thrown back by the arrival of the Thirteenth, but were by no means broken by it. Already, the fleeing warriors were mustering around their chieftains and returning to the battle.

"For victory!" bellowed the king, waving his legions forward with his shield. "For Askhor!"

CARANTATHI
Autumn, 213th year of Askh

I

The road was wide, but treacherous, in places the rock split by wide cracks and crumbling where the mountainside dropped down to a sheer cliff on the right. The base of the cliff was hidden in the white murk of a thick mist. The upper towers of the Salphorian capital could be seen ahead over the shoulder of the mountain, grey tiled roofs shining with rain. The downpour sent rivulets across the roadway and rattled on the armour of the legionnaires.

Rounding a sharp outcrop, Ullsaard found himself almost bumping into the back of a group of legionnaires. The road was packed with soldiers, who pressed against the rock away from the edge, fearful of the drop.

"What's the delay?" he demanded. "The Salphors?"

"Can't move forward," answered someone from the tightly packed men. "Everyone ahead has stopped."

Ullsaard turned around and shouted to the captain of the following company.

"Call the halt! Pass on the order! Call the halt!" He returned his attention to the throng of men in front. "Make way for your king."

The legionnaires did the best they could, opening a gap just about wide enough for Ullsaard to squeeze through sideways. The situation got no better the further he went, several hundred men all cramped together. He spied the crest of a captain and pushed his way to the officer.

"What is holding everybody up?" said the king. "Is it the Salphors?"

"Don't think so, king," said the third captain. "I heard someone shout that the road ended."

"Road ended?" Ullsaard frowned and shoved his way onwards, pushing men aside to find out what was going on.

After some time, he finally reached the front of the halted column. Men stepped aside at his approach and he immediately saw the problem.

A few paces ahead, the road did indeed end. With an edge as clean as a cut, the mountainside dropped away sharply, at least ten times the height of a man, down to a swift river and jagged rocks. Seventy or eighty paces ahead, the road resumed. A mass of ropes and timbers hung to one side; a bridge of some kind the king assumed. On the opposite side of the gorge stood a small knot of men.

"You must be Ullsaard," one of them called out, hands cupped to his mouth. He wore heavy plates of bronze armour and a shining warhelm decorated with a gem at its brow. His beard was thick and braided and his hair hung past his shoulders.

"You must be Aegenuis!" Ullsaard shouted back.

The man raised a hand in acknowledgement.

"You should know that I did not send those tribes to attack you," said the Salphorian king. "That was my son. I thought I had him under control, but some of my chieftains helped him escape. I have not broken my word."

Ullsaard considered this but was not sure whether he believed the man or not.

"Your Askhan is very good," he said.

"I thought it wise to practise more, considering the future."

Ullsaard could not help but smile. The Salphorian king seemed to be the sort of man he could deal with.

"Now you have to keep your word," yelled Aegenuis. "If I give you the city and my crown, you must swear there will be no looting, no rape, no burning."

"And if I don't?" Ullsaard replied.

"Enjoy finding another way in," said Aegenuis. Laughter echoed from the walls of the canyon.

"This?" said Ullsaard, waving a hand at the ravine. "I'll be across that in ten days at the most."

"I think not! We have engines and archers above you. It would be bloody work."

"All right, twenty days. My engineers will dam the river and build a new bridge. I have men from Ersua and Anrair; men that grew up in the mountains. They'll take care of your engines and archers easily enough."

"And then? This is but the first of many obstacles. Carantathi has strong defences."

"So did Magilnada and I took that city in four days!"

This silenced Aegenuis for a while and he conferred with the chieftains around him. Eventually he stepped out from the group.

"It seems like a waste of time and blood to not have to give your word," declared the Salphorian leader. "Why not promise me what I want, and I'll walk you through the gate myself. You'll have me as hostage, and I you."

Looking back at the soldiers clustered behind him, Ullsaard saw shadowed eyes and haggard faces. They had marched and fought for nearly two thousand miles. Soon the rain would become snow, and the road treacherous with ice. He certainly couldn't starve out the Salphors over the winter.

"You have my word," he called out. "With the brave men of the Thirteenth as my witnesses, I swear that there will be no violence unless provoked by you."

Again the Salphors huddled together in discussion. Evidently they agreed to the terms. More men hurried to the bridge contraption. They heaved on ropes and laboured at wheels, swinging the mass of wood around to the gap in the road. Rain drummed on timbers as the bridge extended, heavily hinged sections straightening across the gorge. Ullsaard and the foremost legionnaires were forced to retreat a short distance as the bridge thumped down.

"Wait here," he told his soldiers. "If these bastards kill me, slaughter the lot of them."

There were savage growls of assent from those close by.

Aegenuis walked to the middle of the bridge and waited. Taking a breath, Ullsaard set out. He was taking a considerable risk, he realised. The Salphors could probably raise the bridge before two dozen men had got onto the span. He stopped a few paces onto the thick boards, wondering whether it might not be better to dismiss any deal and take the city by force. He scrutinised Aegenuis as best he could, but could see little of the man's face behind the silver visage of a wolf.

"Fuck it," the king muttered. "If you're dead, you're not going to care what happens next."

He strode across the bridge with more confidence, stopping just in front of Aegenuis. The other king was a little shorter, and nowhere near as broad. The scabbard at his hip was empty and Ullsaard saw no knife in his belt.

"I am unarmed," said the Salphor.

"Nice hat," said Ullsaard, nodding towards Aegenuis's helm.

"It will be yours soon," said the Salphorian king.

Ullsaard shook his head and extended his hand.

"I think not," said the Askhan. "I have enough troubles with the crown I've already got."

Ullsaard bit back a laugh as he saw bemusement in the eyes of the other man. Aegenuis grabbed Ullsaard's forearm and squeezed tight, the king of Greater Askhor returning the gesture. They parted and Ullsaard turned around and raised his fist, eliciting a cheer from the legionnaires that could see him. The Salphors were understandably less jubilant.

"I think I still have some of your wine somewhere," said Aegenuis, putting his hand on Ullsaard's shoulder as the king turned back from his soldiers. "We should share it."

"How did you get my wine?"

Aegenuis laughed and slapped Ullsaard on the back.

"I'll tell you on the way to Carantathi," he replied.

II

With a smile, Ullsaard drained the last of the wine from the cup and placed it on the table beside the bed. He stripped off his armour and flopped on the woollen bed covers in kilt and jerkin and boots, exhausted. He listened to the clink and pad of the legionnaires on the other side of the chamber door and closed his eyes.

He had deigned to allow Aegenuis to stay in the king's hall; some unfortunate chieftain had been turfed from his house to make way for Ullsaard and his officers. Billets had been found for the Thirteenth in the city, which was half-empty. Aegenuis had bluffed well; less than two thousand warriors protected Carantathi, nowhere near enough to defend against Ullsaard's army. The rest of the Askhan army was returning to camp at the base of the mountain.

He did not begrudge Aegenuis the peaceful resolution he had wanted. Over the course of a somewhat frugal banquet, Ullsaard had come to the conclusion that he liked the Salphorian king, though not enough to let him stay king, he had pointed out.

Tomorrow Aegenuis would formally hand over power to Ullsaard. It was not the end of the Salphorian campaign, the king knew, but it was the start of the next stage of conquest. Ullsaard thought he would feel triumphant at this moment, but from the swirl of emotions going through him, it was relief that felt strongest. Once again his vision had been vindicated. Perhaps even more than when he had wrested the Crown from Lutaar, he had many times wondered whether he would be victorious.

Feeling sleep tugging at his eyelids, he divested himself of his boots and kilt, flinging them to the bare wooden floor. Certainly Carantathi could benefit from a few Askhan improvements, such as carpets and baths. All of that would come in time.

He listened to the rain drumming on the roof and walls and rolled to his side. Allenya was in Askh, three thousand miles away or more. He wondered what she was doing. Probably sleeping as well. He would have to spend the winter in Salphoria, establishing his rule, sizing up which chieftains could stay and which would have to be killed. Come the spring, he would return to Askh, leaving Salphoria to Aegenuis, Anasind and others.

It was a pleasing thought that carried him to the cusp of sleep.

Ullsaard sat up sharply, hand clasped to his temples as agony flared through his mind. A howl of pain was wrenched from him as he twisted and fell to the floor, daggers piercing his thoughts. He did not see or hear the door slamming open as a pair of legionnaires rushed in. He felt nothing but burning, a flame that consumed his brain, seared his eyes and scorched through his Blood.

While his body writhed in torment, in his mind he was

carried up, up through the roof, into the clouds and beyond, spreading out beneath the stars. Like a rushing of a gale within him, he felt himself being torn apart, scattering through the air.

A thunderous clamour deafened him as he speared across the sky, the sun rising ahead, its first rays touching upon the walls and domes of Askh. His being funnelled down, swirling like a tornado, rushing faster and faster, drawn towards the palace on the Hill of Kings.

For a moment he saw a flash of a person and fell into the man's eyes, sharing his body for an instant, feeling something that froze his heart, even as his mind exploded again.

With another feral shriek, he surfaced from the fit, panting and wild-eyed. A legionnaire bent over Ullsaard, eyes fearful,

"King, what is wrong?" asked the soldier.

Ullsaard replied without thought, telling the man what he had seen in his vision, even as the throbbing pain in his head pounded.

"Urikh... Urikh has put on the Crown of the Blood."

About the Author

Gav Thorpe works from Nottingham, England, and has written more than a dozen novels and even more short stories. Growing up in a tedious town just north of London, he originally intended to be an illustrator but after acknowledging an inability to draw or paint he turned his hand to writing.

Gav spent 14 years as a developer for Games Workshop on the worlds of Warhammer and Warhammer 40,000 before going freelance in 2008. It is claimed (albeit solely by our Gav, frankly) that he is merely a puppet of a mechanical hamster called Dennis that intends to take over the world via the global communications network. When not writing, Gav enjoys playing games, cooking, pro-wrestling and smiling wryly.

mechanicalhamster.wordpress.com

A GUIDE TO SALPHORIA,
ITS PEOPLES & ENEMIES

The lands known collectively as Salphoria have been home to many peoples and cultures from before the founding of the Askhan empire. It is a large area with a widely dispersed population, bound together only by ancient ancestry and the common foe of Askh. In this appendix, we look at some of the traditions and organisation of the Salphors and their loose nation.

People

The Salphors are not a single people, but comprise many different tribes and tribal conglomerates that have mingled over the centuries. The majority of Salphorian settlements are located along its long rivers, on the outskirts of its dense forests and amongst the foothills of the mountain ranges. Most tribes are located within a single town or village, though some have spread further and may be found living in neighbouring settlements; a few are widespread, having been dispersed across Salphoria by migrations in times past due to famine, drought or war.

The tribe is the basic block of society, an extended family drawing descent from shared ancestors that can number several thousand folk. Each tribe has its unique traditions, and often its own dialect and folklore. Inter-marriage between tribes is quite common, as is the kidnapping of womenfolk from rival tribes, so the exact familial boundaries between tribes is often indistinct.

Several tribes make up each of the Salphorian peoples. The peoples are spread over a much larger geographic area and share common language, coinage and beliefs. Many started out as alliances in the distant past but the cultural identity of a people has grown out of the disparate customs of the founders, creating an identifiable society. A Salphor thinks of himself as one of a people first, his tribe being a subdivision of their identity.

There is a linked but separate group of Salphors known collectively as Hillmen, living for the most part in the Ersuan Hills. They live apart from the rest of Salphorian society, surviving on brigandage for the most part. Considered savage and backwards by any self-respecting Salphor, the Hillmen are not counted as a people in their own right, but simply a ragtag mass of renegades and descendants of barbarians.

Politics

Each tribe is ruled over by a chieftain and his family. The position is traditionally hereditary through the male line, but such is the nature of tribal life a chieftain or would-be heir that does not have the support of the tribespeople will find it very difficult to maintain control.

The chieftain oversees all matters of local law and presides over weddings, funerals and other ceremonies. He is the war-leader of the tribe, and will often be the most accomplished fighter. His chosen band will have the best equipment and be made up of the most able warriors, acting as militia to enforce the chieftain's rule. Sons and brothers typically form the council of the chieftain, along with any other elders who have proven themselves sufficiently wise or favoured. Patronage is the general rule, as the chieftain is ultimately responsible for settling land claims, marriage or inheritance disputes and other disagreements. It is a brave Salphor who risks the displeasure of his chieftain, and those who do not earn his favour will be shunned until they make appropriate gifts or leave in self-exile.

Amongst the chieftains of a people, rank is determined by a fluid hierarchy of personal ability, old debts and the power of his tribe. The chieftain's council of each people meets irregularly to discuss important issues and resolve inter-tribal disputes, but it is a temporary organisation. In times of war or hardship, a chieftain may call upon his fellow council members for warriors or aid, and the council will decide whether the people will act or not. As with tribal politics, there is little loyalty between the chieftains despite oaths sworn and gifts exchanged. Just as a tribesperson that angers a chieftain is isolated, a chieftain that continually acts against the council's wishes or does not support the council's decisions will find his tribe treated as pariahs.

The most senior and well-respected chieftains of a people, usually no more than a half-dozen, form an inner circle to act as representatives to the king. In this role they represent the people as whole – in theory, at least.

The Salphors are ruled over by their king. For many decades, he has been the chieftain of Carantathi, by far the largest settlement in Salphoria; though the city has been conquered several times and the line of kings changed. It is a precarious position to be king, imparting great power to call on the peoples of Salphoria but always responsible to the chieftain councils. More than one king has found his support taken away, to be usurped by a more favoured chieftain.

The king is responsible for the most important decisions of tradition in law, presiding over disagreements between peoples, mustering armies from many tribes and responding to unexpected disaster such as pestilence or invasion. As is typical of the contrary nature of the Salphors, a king may be roundly despised by all of his subjects and yet remain in power if he deals suitably with the demands of the chieftain councils.

Salphorian Debt

One of the biggest causes of inter-tribe strife used to be the matter of unpaid debts, blood money owed from violent clashes and the under-payment of dowries. So great did the problem become, a new Salphoria-wide law was passed to govern the making and settling of debts.

A Salphor who reneges on a debt becomes a marked man (and in this case a debt may be not just monetary, but also a lack of service to his chieftain, refusing to take up arms when needed, or even failure to make proper contributions to the local shrines). His debt is recorded on a tin debt token and until it is paid off, he is less than a person, considered the property of whoever owns the debt token.

The emergence of debt tokens led to the rise in debt guardians; merchants who traded solely in debt to gather bodies of men to work their mines, fields, orchards and caravans. Debt guardians despise the term "slave" for their debtors as it implies that their charges work for free. On the contrary, a debtor accrues wages throughout his service, until he has paid off the amount owed to have his debt token melted down. As with other commodities, debt tokens have a face value but quite often their true worth may be more or less than this amount, depending on how many debtors are in a region or other circumstance.

Amongst some merchants, debt tokens are treated as a second tier of coinage, and ownership of a debtor might change hand several times before he is actually able to start to work of what he owes.

There are strict laws governing the treatment of debtors and the sanctions against debt guardians who keep men beyond their term, pay less than expected against the debt or mistreat their debtors are severe. Debt guardians are seen as an undesirable but necessary part of modern Salphorian society by most, though there are those chieftains who still prefer to settle such matters in the old-fashioned way with swords and shields.

The Spirits

Whereas the ancient beliefs in supernatural beings has been quashed throughout Great Askhor, in Salphoria the belief in and worship of "spirits" still survives. The exact nature of the ceremonies and shrines varies from region to region and even from tribe to tribe, but the intermingling of old customs has led to a more or less coherent pantheon.

Spirits are known by many names across Salphoria, and their exact appearance, deeds and moods may change, but all are embodiments of nature and the world. The spirits bring rain and sun, cause plants to grow, raise up mountains and sweep the lands with plague. They can be entreated for favour or appeased with offerings, but their relationship to the peoples of Salphoria is inconsistent – just as likely to deliver pestilence as a bountiful crop.

Some tribes have priesthoods dedicated to the spirits, though usually this role is taken on by the chieftain as being their most favoured individual. Priests do not act as intermediaries to the spirits, but they are responsible for creation and upkeep of shrines dedicated to a particular deity. There are many ceremonies and festivals attended by Salphors throughout the year, particularly in spring and autumn when crops are sown and harvests made. On these occasions, the people sing the praises of benevolent spirits and build great fires and raise a great clamour to drive away those that are hostile.

GLOSSARY

People

Adral – Governor of Nalanor.

Aegenuis – King of Salphoria, father of Medorian.

Aghali – Salphor chieftain.

Aleoin – Daughter of Aegenuis.

Allenya – Eldest of Ullsaard's queens and mother of Jutaar.

Allon – Governor of Enair.

Anasind – First Captain of the Thirteenth Legion, later Askhan general.

Anglhan Periusis – Governor of Magilnada.

Aranathi – Daughter of Gelthius.

Ariid – Chief servant of Ullsaard's household.

Asirkhyr – Hierophant of the Temple.

Askhan – Collective term for both the native people from the tribes of Askhor and those peoples brought into the empire of Greater Askhor.

Askhos – First King of the Askhans, founder of the empire and sire of the Blood.

Asuhas – Governor of Ersua.

Bariilin – Second Captain of the First Magilnadan Legion.

Brotherhood, The – A widespread administrative sect

responsible for many of the functions of the empire, including criminal law, taxation, trade, infrastructural organisation and the suppression of pre-empire superstitious beliefs. Proselytisers of the Book of Askhos.

Canaasin – First Captain of the XIV legion.

Daariun – Second Captain of the First Magilnadan Legion.

Donar – First Captain of the Fifth Legion.

Eriekh – Hierophant of the Temple.

Erlaan – Prince of the Blood, son of Prince Kalmud, grandson of King Lutaar..

Eroduus – Askhan noble, admiral and fleet owner.

Etor Astaan – Merchant and noble of Askh, father of Noran.

Faeghun – Son-in-law of Gelthius.

Furlthia Miadnas – Former first mate of Anglhan's landship, chief member of anti-Askhan conspirators.

Gannuis – Eldest son of Gelthius.

Gebriun – Legionnaire of the XIII legion.

Gelthius – A former fisherman, farmer and bandit of the Linghan people in Salphoria, Gelthius has served as a debtor on Anglhan's landship, joined Salphorian rebels, been involved in the fall of Magilnada to the Askhans, was drafted into the Thirteenth Legion and fought in the overthrow of King Lutaar. He longs for a return to a quiet life.

Haeksin – Legionnaire of the XIII legion.

Harrakil – First Captain of the XVII Legion.

Huuril – Third Captain in the Thirteenth Legion.

Huurit – Wrestler, lover of Queen Luia.

Juruun – Legionnaire of the XIII.

Jutaar – Son of Allenya, second eldest of Ullsaard. First Captain of the First Magilnadan legion.

Jutiil – First Captain of the XII Legion.

Kaasin – Icon bearer of the First Magilnadan Legion.

Kalmud – Prince of the Blood, eldest son of King Lutaar, father of Erlaan. Infected by a devastating lung disease whilst campaigning along the Greenwater River.

Kalsaghan – Warrior of the Linghar, son of Naraghlin.

Kasod – Second Captain of the First Magilnadan Legion.

Kubridias – Salphor chieftain.

Kulrua – Governor of Maasra.

Laadir Irrin – Askhan noble.

Laasinia – Chief handmaiden of Queen Allenya.

Leerunin – Court chamberlain of King Ullsaard, treasurer of Askh.

Lenorin – Chancellor of Magilnada, aide to Anglhan, with anti-Askhan sympathies.

Lerissa – Widow of governor Nemtun, noblewoman of Geria.

Liirat – Dockmaster of Geria.

Liitum – Merchant of Geria.

Linghal – Chieftain of the Hadril.

Liradin – Chieftain of the Cannin.

Loordin – Legionnaire of the XIII.

Luamid – First Captain of the Sixteenth Legion.

Luia – Second eldest of Ullsaard's queens and mother of Urikh.

Luisaa – An infant, daughter of Urikh, grand-daughter of Ullsaard.

Lukha – Noble of Askh, private legion commander.

Luuarit – Second Captain and surgeon in the Thirteenth Legion.

Luusin – Second Captain of the First Magilnadan Legion.

Maalus – Noble of Askh, private legion commander.

Manamosalai – Mekhani shaman-chief.

Mannuis – Warrior of the Linghar, son of Naraghlin.

Maredin – Wife of Gelthius.

Medorian – Son of King Aegenuis.

Meesiu – First Captain of the III legion.

Meliu – Youngest queen of Ullsaard and mother to Ullnaar.

Minglhan – Youngest son of Gelthius.

Murian – Governor of Anrair.

Muuril – Sergeant of the XIII legion.

Naadlin – First Captain of the II legion.

Naathin – First Captain of the VII legion.

Naraghlin – Chieftain of the Linghar.

Neerlima – Wife of Prince Urikh.

Nemasolai – Shaman-chief of the Allako.

Nemurians – Non-human species that live on a chain of volcanic isles lying off the coast of Maasra. Standing
more than twice as tall as a man, and of broad girth,
Nemurians are heavily muscled, covered with thick
scales and possessing prehensile tail. Extremely se-
cretive, the only Nemurians known to the people of
Greater Askhor are those who hire out their much
sought after services as mercenaries. Nemurians are
also well known for the skill in metalworking and
the quantity of iron in their weapons and armour;
an element still rare in the empire.

Noran Astaan – A noble of Askhor, sole heir of the Astaan
family and royal herald in service to Prince Aalun.
A long time friend and ally of Ullsaard, rendered
comatose whilst protecting Ullsaard against assas-
sins.

Pretaa – Mother of Ullsaard, former courtesan in Askh
and lover of Cosuas.

Rondin – First Captain of the X Legion.

Serbicus – Salphor chieftain, co-conspirator of Furlthia.

Thasalin – Chief brother of Geria.

Ullnaar – Son of Meliu, youngest of Ullsaard. Clever and
cultured, Ullnaar is studying civic law at the col-

leges in Askh, under the tutelage of Meemis.

Ullsaard – King of Greater Askhor. Married to Allenya, Luia and Meliu. Father to Urikh, Jutaar and Ullnaar. Pretender to the Crown of the Blood.

Urikh – Son of Luia, eldest of Ullsaard, Governor of Okhar. As heir of the family, Urikh has spent considerable time expanding his personal assets and influence across the empire.

Named Salphorian peoples and tribes: Pretari, Caelentha, Deaghra, Hadril, Hannaghian, Laeghoi, Linghar, Menaeni, Orsinnin, Vatarti, Vestil.

Places

Altes Hills – Low mountain range stretching coldwards from the Magilnadan Gap to the coast of Enair. This range forms the duskwards boundary of coldwards Ersua and all of Anrair. Sometimes referred to simply as the Altes.

Arondunda – Salphorian settlement, home of Kubridias.

Askh – Founding city of the empire, capital of Askhor, birthplace of Askhos. The largest and most advanced city of the empire, boasting the Grand Precinct of the Brotherhood, the Royal Palaces, the Maarmes arena and circuit and many other wonders of the world.

Askhan Gap – The widest, and only easily navigable, pass in the Askhor mountains. Protected by the Askhan Wall and dominated by the harbour at Narun.

Askhor – The homeland of the Askhan empire, situated in the dawnwards region of the empire, bordered by the Askhor mountains and the dawnwards coast.

Askhor Wall – A defensive edifice stretching the entire width of the Askhor Gap, built in the earliest years of the empire to defend against attack from the neighbouring tribes. The Askhor Wall has never been attacked.

Carantathi – Current capital of Salphoria and seat of King Aegenuis's court. Lying far to duskwards of the Greater Askhor border, its precise location is unknown to the empire.

Cosuan – New settlement at the mouth of the Greenwater.

Daasia – Settlement on the Greenwater, hotwards of Geria.

Enair – Most coldward province of the empire, brought into the empire during the reign of King Lutaar's predecessor. A land of strong winds, frequent rain, large marshlands and heavy forest. Enair has no major cities and relies on timber trade and sea fishing for its low income. Birthplace of Ullsaard.

Ersua – Most recent province of the empire, situated dawnwards of Nalanor and separated from Salphoria by the Free Country. Consisting mostly of the foothills of the Altes Hills, Ersua is now Greater Askhor's main source of ore for bronze.

Ersuan Highlands – A range of mountains that separates Ersua from Nalanor, curving several hundred miles to duskwards between Ersua and Anrair.

Geria – Harbour town on the Greenwater, capital of Nalanor, whose quays are owned by the Astaan noble family.

Grand Precincts of the Brotherhood – An imposing black stone ziggurat situated on the Royal Hill in Askh, predating the founding of the city. The centre of the Brotherhood's organisation, it is here that ailurs are bred, the fuel known as lava is created and the great library of the empire - the Archive of

Ages - is found, and adjoining the precinct are the highest law courts of Greater Askhor. No-one other than a Brother or the king have ever set foot within.

Greenwater River – More than seventeen hundred miles long, this is the greatest river of the empire and main route of trade and expansion.

Labroghia – Salphorian region situated on the duskward slopes of the Lidea mountains, infamous for its mines run by debtor labour.

Landesi – Village in Salphoria, populated by a tribe of the Linghan peoples. Birthplace of Gelthius.

Lidean Mountains – range of mountains separating Ersua and Near-Mekha from Salphoria, marking the coldwards edge of the Magilnada Gap and extending more than a thousand miles coldwards to the sea.

Maarmes – Area of Askh, dominated by the sporting circuits and arena of the same name, where ailur chariots are raced and wrestling tournaments take place. Maarmes is also home to the bloodfields of Askh, where nobles can resolve disputes in mortal combat. All duels on the bloodfields are to the death. Commonly, such duels are over marital disputes; if a marriage proposal is opposed, a noble that kills the head of a noble family undertakes to marry the daughters of that family.

Maasra – Province of the empire situated hotwards of Askhor, with a temperate climate and long coastline. The chiefs of the Maasrite tribes acceded to the empire without battle, though they initiated the Oath of Service by cutting out their tongues so that they could raise no opposition to the conquest. Its people are known across the empire for their placid disposition and its wine is considered the best in the empire. Nemuria lies just off the coast of Maasra.

Magilnada – A city founded by Baruun at the coldwards extent of the Altes Hills, in opposition to the rise of Askh. Magilnada has changed hands through many Salphorian chieftains since its founding, until its status as a free and protected city was guaranteed by agreement between King Aegenuis and King Lutaar. Though fallen into much disrepair, Magilnada remains a formidable fortification on the border between Greater Askhor and Salphoria, and the presence of its garrison protects the vital trade routes between the two.

Mekha – An arid land hotwards of Nalanor and Ersua, divided into the semi-scrub of Near-Mekha and the deserts of Deep (or Far) Mekha. Home to the Mekhani tribes.

Naakus River – A river in Near-Mekha, considered the border between Greater Askhor and Mekha. Site of Ullsaard's camp during his Mekha campaign and proposed location of a new Askhan settlement in the region.

Nalanor – Province of the empire lying to duskwards of the Askhor Gap and first to be conquered by King Askhos. Consisting of rich farmlands, Nalanor was once the centre of trade of the empire, but as Greater Askhor has grown, the province faces stern competition from Salphorian importers and growing farmlands in Okhar. Despite this, Nalanor is considered the gateway of the empire, as it is linked by the Greenwater to other parts of Greater Askhor and sits next to the only secure route into Askhor. Its capital is situated at Parmia.

Narun – Largest harbour on the Greenwater, situated on the border of Nalanor and Askhor. Known as the Harbour of a Thousand Fires due to its many light towers that allow safe navigation even at night. Many decades of construction have made Narun a huge artificial laketown boasting dozens of docks and quays. Almost all trade along the Greenwater passes through Narun at some point on its journey and most of the empire's shipbuilding is centred in Narun. The jewels in the crown of Narun are the stone built docks at the King's Wharf.

Nemuria – A chain of smoke-shrouded islands situated to dawnwards of the Maasra coast. Home to the in-human Nemurians, little is known of this realm other than its volcanic nature and richness of iron. Nemuria is protected by arrangement with the empire so that no ship may approach within a mile of its shores.

Nemurian Strait – A narrow stretch of water separating the shores of Maasra from the isles of Nemuria.

Okhar – Province of the empire flanking the Greenwater River coldwards of Askhor and bordered to dawn-wards by Maasra, duskwards by Ersua and hotwards by Mekha; of rich farmlands, vineyards, forested uplands and numerous harbour towns. After Askhor, the richest province of the empire, due in large part to its much-prized marble and linen. Governed by Prince Nemtun from the capital at Geria.

River Ladmun – River that runs along the border of Anrair and Enair from the Altes Hills.

Royal Way – The broad thoroughfare running from the main gate of Askh up to the palaces on the Royal Hill.

Salphoria – Lands situated to duskwards of Greater Askhor, separated from Ersua by the Free Country, of unknown size and population. Populated by disparate peoples and tribes, nominally ruled over by King Aegenuis from the capital at Carantathi.

Ualnian Mountains – Range in Salphoria, site of Carantathi.

Creatures

Abada – Large herbivorous creature with prominent nose horn, used as a beast of burden throughout Greater Askhor.

Ailur – Large species of cat bred by the Brotherhood as beasts of war and status symbols for Askhan nobility. Possessed of savage temper, only female ailurs are ridden to war, and do so hooded by armoured bronze masks. Known to attack in a berserk frenzy when unmasked.

Behemodon – Large reptilian creature native to the deserts of Mekha. Employed as beasts of burden and war mounts by the Mekhani tribes.

Blackfang – Ailur owned by Ullsaard.

Kolubrid – Large, snakelike beast native to Maasra, employed by Askhans as mounts for messengers and skirmishing cavalry.

Lacertil – Giant reptile used by the Mekhani as mounts.

Lupus – Large, wolf-like beast used by Salphorians to draw war-chariots.

Storm – Ailur owned by Ullsaard.

your Robot overlords.

Twitter @angryrobotbooks

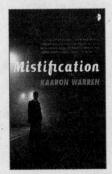

ANGRY
ROBOT

CALL YOURSELF A FAN, MEAT THING?
Collect the whole Angry Robot catalog!

angryrobotbooks.com